It was the sort that had brush rollers, the car being pulled along on a cogged affair beneath. "This is odd," Napoleon murmured. "Why didn't he—"

Two men stepped out of the shadows and jerked the front doors open. For a brief moment, Napoleon stared into a lean, hard, Roman face.

"Apologies, sir," the fellow said. "Strip to the waist and put these on."

"Strip to the what?" Wellington had gotten out of the car, and even in the semi-darkness, his face was decidedly red.

"Shut up." Napoleon handed his work shirt to the waiting Roman and slipped into one that had been tie-dyed, drawing a fringed leather vest over it. "Hurry."

Wellington's muttering was lost in the rushing water. The Roman handed Napoleon three last items: several strings of love beads, a frizzy wig that looked like it had been left plugged into a light socket all night, and a pair of dark glasses.

"Dammit, Caesar," Napoleon growled under his breath. "Friendship can only go so far."

ANGELS IN HELL
JANET MORRIS

ANGELS IN HELL

This is a work of fiction. All the characters and events portrayed in this book are fictional, and any resemblance to real people or incidents is purely coincidental.

A Baen Books Original

Baen Publishing Enterprises
260 Fifth Avenue
New York, N.Y. 10001

First printing, October 1987

ISBN: 0-671-65360-1

Cover art by David Mattingly

Printed in the United States of America

Distributed by
SIMON & SCHUSTER
1230 Avenue of the Americas
New York, N.Y. 10020

CONTENTS

HANDMAIDS IN HELL

Chris Morris

When you have died, there will be nothing.
No memory of you will remain,
not a trace
to linger after:
you do not share
the rose of the Muses with us,
and will wander unseen
in the hall of the dead,
a fitful shade among the blinded ghosts.

—Sappho

"The thing to remember is," said the Devil's private secretary to the new girl, "that Satan doesn't just want it done right, he wants it done yesterday."

"Yesterday, Marilyn?" asked the new girl, mystified. Her name was Helen and she had just been jerked, without warning, from the battlements of

1

Troy, beyond whose slanted walls the 365th refighting of the Trojan War was well under way. "How can something be ordered done before the order is given?"

Everything about New Hell was as strange as the woman whose hips swayed before her in the badly lit penthouse of the Hall of Injustice. "Ooh, honey, don't ask," cooed Marilyn, the hint of a frown shadowing her creamy brow as she looked reproachfully at Helen over her shoulder. "Or I'll send you to the Observatory to help Zeno, and you wouldn't like that. No, you wouldn't. Being one of the Devil's handmaids—on staff, child—is the best a woman can do here."

"*Hand*maid?" echoed Helen, her spine stiffening. She slowed. She stopped in the crooked-walled hallway and edged away from a glassless window through which a wild wind wheezed. "I'm no one's handmaid. I'm Helen, daughter of Zeus and Leda—a faded goddess, but a goddess, nonetheless."

"Honey, I was the sex goddess of the Western World, and a lot of good it did me." Marilyn turned, put her hands on her tiny waist, and thrust out her breasts. "You just quiet down, settle in, and then you can come over to my flat tonight and tell me all about being abducted by Theseus." Marilyn's red lips formed a perfect O. "Ooh," she breathed in kittenish delight. "That must really have been something."

"Legends," Helen began, searched for words in English, then shook her head miserably and waved Marilyn on. There was no expressing her tender, aristocratic sentiments in this crude and horrid tongue, more suited to architects than noble queens. Helen wanted to protest that there must be some mistake, but of course, there had been—this was Hell, wasn't it? There were always mistakes.

At least these mistakes would be different from those Paris made, over and over; and those Priam made; and those made by the Atreides on the beach. As Marilyn led her around a corner, into a narrow hallway where the doors were scrawled with palimpsest graffiti, Helen told herself that there was nothing here to be frightened of.

This was the Hell of which the New Dead who had come to her land had spoken: this was where Authority lay. And Helen, wife of Menelaus, knew exactly how to get along with Authority. You lay down beside it.

The painted whore switching her white-skirted hips in Helen's face didn't know it yet, but she was in for a run for her money . . . and for other things.

The Face that Launched a Thousand Ships, the body the had lured Theseus into peril, and the brains that had remade an empire weren't Helen's for nothing.

As Marilyn stooped to fit a key into the lock of one of the obscenely decorated doors, Helen of Troy told herself that she didn't care what the Devil was like, only what he could do for her.

If Satan had scaly black wings and claws the size of her fingers, if his skin was red and tough and warty, if his teeth were long and snaggly, if his member was like that of a horse, still she would seduce him and take from him all power thereby.

But she didn't really believe he'd be all that scary, or all that ugly, or all that well-endowed.

Which was exactly why, of course, the Devil came to her later that evening in the primal shape of her most primitive imaginings. Helen had learned many things in the deeper Hells of antiquity, but she hadn't learned this week's Satanic Rule: sinners get what they expect.

*   *   *

Sappho was lying on her couch, surrounded by women and girls, when Marilyn came bursting through the curtained doorway.

Mata Hari raised a tear-stained face from Sappho's lap, sniffed, "See, I told you so, Sappho. Even the Marble Maiden is on the verge of tears. What hope is there for me, a mere harlot among the Devil's Children?" She strangled a sob and scurried away, clutching a lace shawl to her maimed breast.

Marilyn hesitated in the doorway. Sappho's house bordered on the golf course, and errant balls had long ago broken every pane of glass. Through the latticework of spidery cracks, across the greens, beyond the Country Club, the Hall of Injustice towered, with its swollen pinnacle and its lighted domes silhouetted against the restless, rufous sky.

"Damn Him," Marilyn muttered unnecessarily, and took mincing steps into the classical domain of Sappho, careful not to trip, in five-inch stiletto heels, over the cushions or the lengths of gauze and bowls and pitchers strewn over the marble floor.

Sappho watched Marilyn come with a glow like a wolf's in her eyes. Reclining upon her couch, she was the central piece in a Phidian alabaster frieze, with all the young girls at her feet. She held out a hand in welcome. "Come and tell us what's wrong, sister. And we'll help you find a balm for your pain."

And the young girls chorused, "Yes, come. Tell us, tell us."

But Marilyn ignored the chorus: "Sappho, I've got to speak to you alone." Never had Marilyn dared this deed, no matter how bad things had gotten with Satan. No matter what slut he picked out of Hell's innumerable gutters, no matter what ridiculous demands he made, no matter how difficult the Devil was to get along with, Marilyn had always made do.

After all, you couldn't do any better than Nick, not in Hell. And she wasn't just another bimbo, she was The Boss's private secretary. She had power, position, a salary, and free dry cleaning. She had the finest perfumes and cosmetics. She had . . . clout.

Clout, however, didn't keep her warm at night. It didn't make the slights any easier to handle; and it caused complications. Drugs were one way to ease the pain Marilyn was feeling, but Satan had ordered a drug crackdown, and New Hell was as dry as the proverbial bone, even if you had clout.

He'd also ordered her to stay away from the new floozie, Helen, and had the temerity to send Michael, his small-winged, small-clawed, small-toothed, and small-everything-else familiar to keep Marilyn company—to keep her from seeking more human company while the Devil was Too Busy.

He was Too Busy with the Dissidents and the narco-terrorism that supported them, he said. He was Too Busy with treacherous factions inside the very Pentagram, he'd confided. He was Too Busy because time itself, in Hell, was experiencing a recession. He was Too Busy, he'd complained yesterday in the office when Marilyn had noticed he'd come to work with unmatched socks, with Roman troubles and Alexandrian troubles and movie-making troubles and troubles within the Devil's Children even to *think* about such trivial matters as his personal gratification—or anyone else's.

Hers, he meant.

But Marilyn knew better. Nick was Too Busy with Helen of Troy even to find the right socks, let alone time for her.

And Marilyn's psyche couldn't handle rejection.

She had only two choices: drugs, or another lover. Quick. And damn the consequences, if consequences could be any more damning than they were already.

She blinked and focused on Sappho, still smiling, still with an outstretched, inviting hand. Taking a female lover would get Satan's attention, but it wasn't what Marilyn had in mind. So she said to Sappho: "I'll tell you, as soon as we're alone," and gave Sappho a look that said, *This is government business; I'm an agent of Authority; get those twats out of my sight.*

Sappho read the look, shooed the girls away, and sat up in her now-empty chamber. "Sit, then, Madame Secretary, and let us discuss your problem."

Marilyn minced the rest of the way across the treacherous floor, sat primly on Sappho's couch, and puffed out her cheeks before she said, "It's these damned heels. Can't walk in them." And she grinned her Norma-Jean grin, disarming as all get-out.

Sappho simply watched Marilyn through half-lowered lids, but in that gaze, and the body supporting it, and the personality inhabiting it, was everything Marilyn had never dared to be, or even dared hope to be.

The actress looked at the poet and murmured, " 'There are those who say that an array of horsemen, and others that marching men, and others that ships, is the most beautiful thing on the dark earth. But I say it is whatever one loves,' " quoting a poem of Sappho's.

And the poet replied with a laugh, "I've rewritten that last line since then. Now it reads, 'But I say it is freedom.' "

Every hair on Marilyn's most beautiful body stood on end. She had done it! She had found the Dissidents! Right here in New Hell! Under Nick's very nose! Revenge, as the Devil's Children say, is the best revenge.

"Ooh," Marilyn replied carefully, "that's lovely. And it's just what I'm looking for."

"And why is that?" asked the poet, so much smarter than she, stretching rosy arms as if she could touch the sky. Then Sappho sighed and brought those arms down, hugging herself. "You have everything Hell has to offer. You've slept your way to the top. What seek you now? Meaning? I assure you, for one of your sort, there is none."

Marilyn blushed. She couldn't help it. The flush became one of anger once the first hurt had past. Such women always assumed she was an empty-headed receptacle for male desire. And since that was the root of her problem, she hung her head and said, "Satan has taken a new lover. A handmaid named Helen. Oh, he won't admit it, of course, but I just know he's being unfaithful to me."

"Of course he is, you silly twit! He's the *Devil!*" Sappho's voice was sharp. "Male, after all. What do you expect?"

"I expect to find a way to be unfaithful in return, to teach him a lesson. He can't do this to me—maybe to the rest of those . . . those . . . broads, but not to *me!*"

"Ah," said Sappho with a nod. "Now I see. And you think I can help you? Why should I? You are no member of the Sisterhood. You care only for your-self, and for what men as you can manipulate."

"And you don't?" Marilyn looked up from her ankle, where she was trying with no success to un-buckle the thin strap that secured the stiletto heel of her red patent-leather sandal. "Come on, honey, you didn't get all this—" Marilyn's free hand extended, gesturing to the beauty all around—to the Grecian building style in all its elegant simplicity, to the fine textiles, the chargers, the rhytons, the video-cassette machines, and the giant TV screens. "—from your women friends or from selling subsidiary rights to your poetry."

"I did get *all this*, most exactly, from my women friends. You forget your history. I am, after all, a famed courtesan and a keeper of courtesans."

Marilyn hadn't known Sappho was a hooker; she'd thought the woman was gay. "Look, can you help me, or not?"

"I can," Sappho replied. "In many ways. It remains to be seen whether I will, in any way."

"Any way but working the street, okay; let's get that clear." Marilyn had a hard voice, too, and she could use it when she needed it. "I want revenge, I told you. I want to sign on with the Dissi—"

"*Ssh! Ssh!* The walls may have ears." Sappho crouched down on the couch and drew her knees up toward her chest, encircling them with her hands.

"Don't be a fool. I checked with Records before I came over here. The place is clean—no bugs."

"Yes, the girls keep it immaculate. But—"

"Idiot, don't play innocent with me. You know what kind of bugs I mean. Now are you going to help me or not? If not, I'll be on my way and you won't tell anyone I was here, or you'll find yourself hooking out of a garbage can on—"

"I will put you in touch with one who can help you, if your heart is true." Sappho unwound from the couch and stood up. "His name is Just Al. He's—"

Marilyn's throat closed up. She hardly heard the rest of what Sappho said. It was too late to turn back now. She'd really done it—found the Dissidents, an active cell. She was in too deep for the panic that overswept her. She almost broke and ran, ran back to the Hall of Injustice and her awful bed where only Michael waited.

But she didn't. She was too angry with Nick. He might be the Devil, Satan himself, but he had no right to shame her with some antiquated slut named Helen.

So she waited for the appearance of Just Al, hoping that the angel would remember the time Marilyn had felt pity for him when he'd fallen into the Devil's clutches. Waited for the single angel in Hell who was on permanent assignment, an angel named Altos, a beacon of hope unto the Dissidents and other fools who didn't realize that damnation is forever.

There were in Hell many kinds of people; under the roiling red skies that masked paradise from the damned, sinners abounded.

There were those here for sins of commission, and for sins of omission—those who had actively violated the letter or spirit of God's laws by doing evil in thought or deed upon their fellows, and those who had merely done nothing good.

The waste of a life's opportunities for goodness was a sin that left a peculiar mark upon a man. Such men were among the hardest to convince that they were in Hell for good reason, since it was their selfishness and arrogance, coupled with a deadly indolence, that had gotten them here to begin with.

And a man must be convinced that he has sinned before he can repent. The only type harder to reach than the wastrels of goodness were the sociopaths—those who truly could not recognize the evil they had done for what it was; those whose egocentricity, or whose self-deceiving misplaced faith, allowed them to justify all means in pursuit of their ends.

The ends of such men, inevitably, were in the

Mortuary, on the Undertaker's table, where ressurrection prepared them for new tortures. There was no death, no rest, for the wicked.

In the Mortuary today, among the multitude of slabs, Altos was searching for a particular victim of the Devil's Children: a primitive, hairy man called Enkidu, who had been recently murdered.

The Devil's Children, His Satanic Majesty's Secret Service, was pushing the Dissidents hard lately, very hard. So hard that Altos, the Lord's single full-time representative stationed in the Underworld, was finding it necessary to push back. Helping the Dissidents had once been optional, so far as Altos was concerned.

Since the firebombing of their base camp and the subsequent ouster of Che Guevara in favor of Alexander of Macedon, aiding the rebels had become an imperative.

This had never happened in all the eons Altos had served among the damned, and he was aware that on this path lay danger. It might be that the Devil had laid a trap to ensnare him, using the Dissidents— that the exceptional torture of these Dissident souls had been devised purely to lead the angel into darkness.

For Altos had come to love the Dissidents. He'd come to believe in their cause—in rebellion. Other angels had fallen from grace from like sentiments— even Satan himself. On this path might lie Altos's damnation, for on it lay emotion, commitment, the temptation to let the ends justify the means.

Thus the angel was very worried as he looked for Enkidu, gliding among the white-sheeted slabs out of which stuck dirty and purple and bloody and black-and-blue toes with tags tied to them.

Enkidu was a native of civilization's dawn, a creature in whom man's original sins and original glories were clear and unmuddied. Altos needed to sit and talk with Enkidu and refresh himself as to what Mankind was all about.

But he couldn't find the hairy man among the newly dead, or the recidivists, and when Sappho's girl came whispering his name, the angel fluttered down to the floor with a flick of his wing tips and bent his head to listen.

And as he listened, his wings drooped, folded in against his back, and dissolved. Sometimes, when the cares of these mortals weighed most heavily on him, when his own faith was shaken, when he was saddened beyond bearing, his wings dissolved right into his back and he was flightless, like a maimed bird.

When Altos followed the lesbian out of the Mortuary and down to the freight elevator where Marilyn waited, there was not a pinion, not a feather to be seen upon his broad back. He looked like a big blond fellow with rents in his white robe, nothing more.

But Marilyn had seen Altos before—with wings and without—and when she gazed upon him, her eyes glittered with unshed tears.

She fell to her knees, breathlessly petitioning for forgiveness.

Altos put a hand on her platinum hair, stiff as straw, and said, "Of course, my child, the mercy of You Know Who extends even here. Now, get up and tell me your problem, quickly."

Quickly because the freight elevator took the newly reconstituted upstairs, to Reassignments. Altos had no intention of being caught in the nerve center of New Hell by Hell's Angels in jackboots, or junior Morticians looking for quick advancement, or by members of Authority's numerous police organizations or—

Heaven forfend—by one of the Devil's Children coming back from assignment via the Undertaker's Table.

Marilyn scrambled to her feet, shooed the lesbian with an impatient hand, and leaned close, whispering, "Sappho sent me."

"Yes? So?" Marilyn was the Devil's very private secretary; Altos wasn't to be fooled this easily. Sappho's connection to the Dissidents was one of the best-kept secrets in Hell. Or had been.

"Ooh, don't tease me," breathed Marilyn with a frown. "I'm in terrible danger, even being here."

"You're not the only one," murmured the angel. And then, louder: "What can I do for you, Marilyn? Speak plainly. I haven't much time."

"You're treating me this way because of that time you were captured, right? Listen, Catherine the Great—it's not my fault she'll never become a woman. That was *your* boss's decree, after all. She's corrupt enough as a kid. It's not my fault . . ."

The angel shook his head, and the quivering lower lip of Marilyn bucked up. "I know. I'm not vengeful. I never blame anyone for anything: I'm not . . . capable . . . of it. Just tell me what aid and comfort you require."

"Great, terrific." Marilyn crossed her arms over her fabled breasts.

The angel closed his eyes. When he opened them, the breathy, childlike voice was explaining: ". . . so you see, I want to join the Dissidents. Teach that bastard a lesson. Screwing around with a handmaid! Revenge is the only thing Satan understands." Her eyes were gleaming.

A deep and abiding sadness came over the angel like a shroud. It was as if he'd stepped into the cloud left by a frightened skunk, or a mosquito-infested marsh at midnight. He barely managed to elucidate his bottomless despair to the unrepentant creature of evil standing before him:

"I cannot help you with revenge, Marilyn. Nor with spite, or hatred, or prurient desire; not with adultery or greed or any other evildoing. I am an *angel*. You must understand."

Marilyn's lip quivered, and this time it extended into a pout. "Under*stand?* Understand what? That I'm not *good* enough for you? Not *good* enough for your precious Dissidents?" Her voice had a hard and horrid edge that made the angel's ears ache.

"That is most exactly what I'm saying," he replied as gently as he could, already retreating, his finger reaching out of its own accord to push the "up" button as he backed over the threshold of the elevator and into the hall. "You are not *good* enough. Not good enough by far." And, as the elevator doors started to slide shut between them, he added: "Not yet," because he was here to offer hope, to urge reformation and repentance upon the evil ones by giving them a good example to follow.

But Marilyn may not have heard him, because as the elevator doors began to close she was ranting, ". . . go back to Nick and solve this without any help from you and your limp-wristed followers, buddy. And don't think he won't hear about you and yours from me! The Dissidents, my ass! They're going to be the Dismemberments, when I get—"

The doors smacked shut, mercifully shutting out her tirade. Exhausted by this confrontation with unremitting evil, Altos slumped against the cinderblock of the basement wall.

Marilyn was *not* good enough, not yet. Not by a long shot. When the pall of vengeance faded, Altos's wings manifested once more and he glided down the hall, back into the Mortuary to resume his search for

Enkidu, the ancient hairy man in whom he hoped to find new hope for a hopeless race.

Sometimes there was night in New Hell—when the Devil wanted manifest darkness. There was night now. The very absence of ruddy, garish light galled Marilyn as she left the Administration complex and headed over to the Hall of Injustice in her chauffeured pink Caddy.

She knew damn well why Satan had decreed an evening: he was a romantic fool. And that evening would last until he was played out, sore in the appropriate places, and ready for one of his infernal trysting breakfasts.

Marilyn ought to know. She'd been there. She'd also been to the Hall of Records, pulling strings and calling in favors, and even up into Reassignments itself since the angel had snubbed her.

Altos was a fool, and there were plenty of those in Hell. Marilyn was still fuming from this latest rejection, but she'd realized she was not without resources.

Now that she was ready to use them. In her pocketbook, a giant human-skin satchel with little holes here and there, custom made for her by Madame Lafarge, was the key to Satan's penthouse, and a solution for the problem called Helen of Troy.

A solution that, when applied directly to the person in question and coupled with the preparations Marilyn had made with fellow conspirators in Reassignments and Records, would get Helen of Troy out of Marilyn's hair for the better part of forever.

The Caddy pulled up to the Hall of Injustice and Marilyn dismissed car and driver, saying, "That's all for today, Ford." The auto manufacturer didn't answer. He couldn't. His tongue never manifested with his body—not in Hell, which was oversupplied with Better Ideas.

She could have walked, but she hadn't. She could have climbed the stairs, but she didn't. She used her key card to take the executive elevator.

In it, as arranged, was a man sent to her by Niccolo Machiavelli, a slight Semite named Zaki, who had a crushed seed cap in one hand and a small pouch in the other.

"Miss Marilyn," said the short dark man with the big nose and a Mediterranean lilt to his English, "I am honored." His liquid brown eyes were fixed on her, his pupils wide.

"Gee, thanks, but you're doing me the favor." She smiled her most dazzling smile. He was frightened, Marilyn realized, her attention taken by the seed cap he kept fingering nervously, then by the pouch he held out to her.

"No one must know of this," he said, eyeing the floor indicator, which had two stops lit. "You realize that."

"For my sake as well as yours," she said complacently. Now that she was embarked upon her revenge, everything seemed to be happening to someone else, some other Marilyn, as if she'd stepped into a play where she was both player and audience. "That's it, the Water of Forgetfulness?" She reached out to take the pouch.

The Semite let the pouch fall into her open hand. "The Lethe water, yes. We don't have any more, that's the lot," he lied.

She smiled. Helen of Troy was going to forget who she was, and so was the Hall of Records. When Reassignments got hold of Helen, she was going to be a Jane Doe. It had cost Marilyn a number of favors owed and favors sold to secure this manipulation of the system, but it was the only way.

Without changes in the Records and Reassignments computers, this Jane Doe would pop right back to the beach at Ilion, from which Satan could then recall her with the flick of a claw. This way, she would be a Disappeared, a Misplaced Person, and she'd be Misplaced a long, long time where she was going.

"Thank you, Za—"

"I gotta go," said the diminutive Semite when the door opened onto one of the Procurement floors. As he was leaving, he jammed his seed cap down onto his head, over his black curls. The legend on it in white block letters read, *Eat More Pussy*.

Marilyn watched him go. She'd thought only the Chinese ate cats. Marilyn liked cats. If anything went wrong, this Zaki person was going to be the first name on her list of conspirators.

She'd intended to ask to be remembered to Machiavelli, but Zaki was gone and the elevator lurched upward again.

Oh well, it wasn't as if this was Machiavelli's idea. It wasn't as if Niccolo even understood what she was doing: she'd merely made a phone call, a demand to be acceded to, no questions asked, and followed his instructions concerning the car and the executive elevator.

The other thing she'd needed, she'd found under the white leather seat of the pink Caddy. She hoped she could follow the directions she'd been given.

She was still thinking about following those instructions when she shouldered her human-skin satchel, put her key in the lock of Nick's penthouse, and slipped inside.

Once she'd closed the door in the darkened apartment, she had no more qualms, no doubts. She leaned against the closed door, breathing shallowly, listening to the ugly, obscene sounds of passion coming from the bedroom.

Then she stuck her hand in her satchel, let the satchel fall away, and took the Beretta machine pistol off safe.

Finally, ready, she tiptoed as quietly as she could across the carpeted anteroom, toward the bedroom, trying to remember whether she'd ever acted in a movie where the jilted lover went to such extremes.

She darted across the doorway, a shadow with a deadly weapon, and peeked around it, flattened there like she'd seen a hundred men do in movies, her weapon raised. She could smell the gun oil and, mixing with it, the stench of passion from the other room.

Carefully, so carefully, she peeked around the doorjamb. The trick was to get Helen without hitting the Devil.

She'd have to wait, she knew, until Helen was on top.

The tangle of legs and arms on the giant, red, five-pointed bed writhed and rolled, and the longer she waited, the angrier Marilyn became.

Finally, Satan groaned and rolled one more time and up popped the honey-haired head of Helen of Troy.

Marilyn leaped from cover, teetering on her high heels, braced herself, legs spread wide, and fired, stiff-armed.

The racket was horrendous. The recoil of the Beretta, spitting out its entire clip because Marilyn's finger was clamped spasmodically on the trigger, was so severe it sent her staggering backward. The gun's muzzle jerked wildly. Bullet holes appeared everywhere: on the ceiling, the bed's headboard, in the bedclothes, in Helen of Troy.

Just as suddenly as it had begun, the deafening noise ceased: the machine pistol was empty.

Helen of Troy lay, bullet-riddled, sprawled in her own blood, across the bed, already beginning to smoke as the Undertaker's Table called to her.

Out from under her slipped the Devil, metamorphosing into his most frightful, black-winged, yellow-eyed form.

And in that guise he crossed the floor to where Marilyn leaned bonelessly on the wall against which the machine pistol had pushed her.

He took the empty pistol from her unresisting fingers, then wiped the tears of horror and remorse from her cheeks with one long, black claw.

Then the Devil said, through a gaping, fanged mouth whose breath was gaggingly foul, "M'dear, I didn't know how much you cared. I'm touched."

And Satan drew her unerringly to the bed, where the corpse still dripped and smoked and made awful little noises from its relaxing bowels, and pushed her down upon the dead body, saying, "I think we ought to videotape the rest of this, don't you?"

It took all Marilyn's presence of mind to remember to sprinkle Lethe water surreptitiously over the lips of the corpse.

THE FASCINATION OF THE ABOMINATION

Robert Silverberg

Or think of a decent young citizen in a toga— perhaps too much dice, you know— coming out here in the train of some prefect, or tax-gatherer, or trader even, to mend his fortunes. Land in a swamp, march through the woods, and in some inland post feel the savagery, the utter savagery, had closed around him—all that mysterious life of the wilderness that stirs in the forest, in the jungles, in the hearts of wild men. There's no initiation either into such mysteries. He has to live in the midst of the incomprehensible, which is also detestable. And it has a fascination, too, that goes to work upon him. The fascination of the abomination—you know, imagine the growing regrets, the longing to escape, the powerless disgust, the surrender, the hate. . . .

—Conrad: *Heart of Darkness*

There was fire everywhere: red fire in the sky, blue fire in the water, green fire dancing along the rim of the shore that receded behind the swiftly moving boat. The air had the stink of sulphur about it, and worse things. The clouds here were thick and heavy, with fat gray bellies that scraped against the nearby mountains. And the mountains themselves were demons in stone: a dozen angry volcanoes that were spewing fumes and flame up and down the coastal plain as far as Gilgamesh could see. Out here on the western edge of Hell, beyond the bleak plains of the Outback, it seemed to the Sumerian that the whole world must be burning, down to its deepest roots.

The dolphin-prowed ship with the scarlet sail plunged on and on through the reef-strewn phosphorescent sea toward the island of Pompeii. The boat was the royal yacht of the dictator Sulla, who was somewhere belowdecks, far gone in wine.

Come with me back to Pompeii, Publius Sulla had said to Gilgamesh. Let us talk of finding the treasures of long-lost Uruk, you and I. Well, why not? Gilgamesh wondered. If it was true that the city of his life had been founded anew in Hell, and these Pompeiians had heard some tale that could help him learn where it might be situated, why not strike a deal with Sulla? What was life, in this interminable life after death, if not one long unending *Why Not?*

The towering, dark-haired Sumerian stared toward Pompeii. Off in the distance the magical city glimmered in the half-darkness with a strange light of its own.

"Been here before?" a voice said.

Gilgamesh looked to his left and down, a long way down. "Are you talking to me?"

"To my shadow," the man standing beside him at

the rail said. He was short and sharp-nosed, with thick, curly hair and dark, greasy skin. "I was trying to make conversation. It's an old shipboard custom. Do you mind?"

Gilgamesh glanced balefully at the little man. There was a soft, sleek, pampered look about him. He dressed well—a Roman-style toga and glossy Italian leather shoes, and some sort of little brocaded skullcap perched jauntily at the back of his head. A shrewd face. Bright, beady eyes with undeniable intelligence in them. But there was something fundamentally unlikable about him. And pushy. Surely, he ought to be able to see at a glance that Gilgamesh wasn't the sort who cared to be approached by strangers.

The big brindle dog Ajax, sleeping by Gilgamesh's side, awoke, peered, growled. Ajax didn't much care for the little man either, it would seem.

Gilgamesh scowled. "I don't know you."

"Who knows anybody in this Godforsaken place? My name's Herod. Herod Agrippa, actually. What I asked you was whether you'd been to Pompeii before."

"Probably," said Gilgamesh, shrugging.

"Probably? You aren't sure?"

Gilgamesh considered tossing the tiresome little pest over the side.

"Maybe I have, maybe I haven't. You wander back and forth across the face of Hell long enough and all places begin to look the same to you."

"Not to me," Herod said. "And I've done my share of wandering. More than my share. A regular wandering Jew, that's me. Anyway, Pompeii's different. I know, I know, memory's sometimes a problem here in Hell, but if you'd been to Pompeii before, you'd remember it. It's unforgettable. Trust me."

"A wandering Jew?" said Gilgamesh vaguely. "I've heard that story, I think."

"Who hasn't? But I'm not *the* Wandering Jew, you understand. That's Ahasuerus. He's still cruising around Upside, the way the original curse requires. Roaming Earth until the end of the world comes, which apparently hasn't quite happened yet. I'm simply a wandering Jew. A different one. Herod."

"So you told me." Pushy little bastard, yes, Gilgamesh thought. From the pushiness alone, it would seem that the little man was one of the New Dead, that irritating horde of scrambling, noisy, incomprehensible, aggressive folk who had come swarming into Hell in the last few thousand years, pretty well ruining the character of the place. But yet there was some sort of Old Dead emanation about this man, too. A borderline type, maybe. From that period when what the New Dead called B.C. was shading into their A.D. time. Gilgamesh rummaged through his thousands of years of memories. "I met a Herod once. Some sort of minor desert prince, he was."

"King of Judaea, in fact."

"If you say so."

"Plump-faced man, bald in back, bloodshot eyes?"

"He might have been. He had a rotten look about him, that much I recall. Like fruit left out in the rain too long."

"Herod the Great, that's who you mean. My grandfather. A very nasty man, that one. A very bad piece of business indeed. Ten wives—that alone should show you how unstable he was. And other character deficiencies. A total paranoid, in fact. Though all that ugly nonsense about Salome and John the Baptist, the seven veils, the silver platter—that wasn't him, you know. That was his son, Herod Antipas, just as crazy. And it didn't actually happen anything like that. The silver platter stuff was only a fable. And as for Salome—"

"I don't have any idea what you're talking about."

"On the other hand," Herod went on, as though Gilgamesh had not spoken, "my grandfather *did* order the slaying of the firstborn. Including his own. The man was a lunatic. I'm not surprised you didn't care for him. He cut a soft deal for himself with Augustus, though. Augustus was always willing to do business with lunatics if he saw political benefits in it for himself. Which is the only reasonable explanation of how my grandfather managed to hold his throne under the Romans for so long. But I understand Augustus won't have anything to do with him now. That's Kleopatra's doing, because Kleopatra still hates him. Old Herod turned her down when she propositioned him—didn't like the shape of her nose, or something like that—but imagine carrying a silly grudge for God knows how many centuries—"

"You buzz like a wasp," Gilgamesh muttered. "Don't you ever stop talking?"

"I like to talk, yes. You don't, I assume. The strong, silent type. A difference of style—nothing to get upset about. Oh, I say, look there—there goes Vesuvius again!"

"Vesuvius?"

Herod gestured toward the island-city. "Our volcano. Smack in the middle of downtown, it is. You ever see anything so gorgeous?"

Gilgamesh looked off across the channel toward distant Pompeii. There was new fire in the sky—a single, startling point of brilliant scarlet cutting through the murky smoke-fouled atmosphere like a torch, fifty times as bright as the flames coming from the mainland volcanos. As though driven by a giant pump the blaze rose higher and higher, climbing toward the roof of the cosmos. Under its blinding glare the towers and battlements of the city took on a dazzling, mirror-bright sheen.

"And the city?" Gilgamesh asked. "Will it be destroyed?"

Herod laughed. "There's an eruption just like this every week. Sometimes more often than that. The Pompeiians wouldn't have it any other way. But it never does any harm. All light and no heat, that's the deal in the contract. And never any particulate matter. After the way they got trashed in 79, it's hardly surprising that they don't want an encore. That's 79 A.D., you know. If you count your years New Dead style. If you count your years at all. At any rate, it was after my time, probably after yours. You talk to someone who was there, he'll tell you that it was a total nightmare, but he'll also say that he can't get to sleep at night if there isn't a decent volcano rumbling away nearby. Amazing the way some people not only adapt to danger but actually come to depend on living in the constant presence of—"

Gilgamesh was barely paying attention. He was staring at the volcano-riven night sky. In that sudden fiery illumination, a host of airborne monsters and demons stood revealed. Things that were all mouth and no body, things that were all wing and no head, things that were mere claws, things that were nothing but giant, red-streaked, yellow eyes borne up by jets of green gas, all of them whirling and screeching high above the sea. Ajax, barking and snarling, capered up and down the deck, leaping wildly as if to challenge the monstrosities that thronged the sky.

Herod laughed. "Publius Sulla's pets. I told you, once you see Pompeii, you never forget it. Demons everywhere you look. And wizards. Sorcerers, mages, thaumaturges. Sulla collects them, you know. You

can't walk nine paces without someone trying to turn
you inside out with one of his tricks."

"Let them try," Gilgamesh said.

He drew an imaginary bow and sent an imaginary
shaft soaring through the gullet of one of the foulest
of the monsters overhead.

"Oh, they'd leave *you* alone, I think. Man your
size, who'd fool around with you? And you look like
you might have a little magic yourself. Publius Sulla
hire you for his bodyguard, did he?"

"I am not a mercenary," said Gilgamesh stiffly.

"You look like you were a fighting man."

"A warrior, yes. But never for hire, except once,
when I was a boy in exile. I was a king."

"Ah. A king! We have something in common, then.
I was a king, too, you know."

"Were you?" said Gilgamesh without interest.

"For four or five years, anyway, after Caligula
finally banished my miserable uncle Antipas from
Judaea and gave the place to me. Very popular with
my subjects, I was, if you don't mind my saying it. I
think I did quite a decent job, and if I had lived a
little longer, I might actually have been able to wipe
out Christianity before it really got started, thereby
saving the whole world six bushels of trouble, but—"
Herod paused. "You aren't a Christian by any chance,
are you? No, no, you don't look the type. But you
say you were a king. Where was that, may I ask?
Somewhere out toward Armenia, maybe? Cilicia?"

This was becoming infuriating.

Gilgamesh drew himself up to his full, looming
height and intoned, "Be it known to you that I am
Gilgamesh of Uruk, great king, king of Uruk, king of
kings, lord of the Land of the Two Rivers."

"King of kings?" Herod repeated. "Lord of the
Land of the Two Rivers?" He nodded as though might-

ily impressed. "Ah. Indeed. And what rivers would those be?"

"You don't know?"

"You must forgive me, my friend. I am a mere provincial, a Judaean, even though it was my good fortune to be educated at the court in Rome. Although I was probably taught something about those Two Rivers of yours, they seem to have slipped through one of the many damnable holes in my memory, and therefore—"

Gilgamesh had heard such speeches many times before. Hell was full of Johnny-come-latelies.

Coolly, he said, "You Romans knew my country by the name of Mesopotamia."

"Oh, *those* rivers!" Herod cried. "Why didn't you say so? King of Mesopotamia! A Parthian, then, is that what you are? Some relative of Mithridates?"

I *will* throw him overboard, Gilgamesh thought in fury.

With great control he said, "Not a Parthian, no. A Sumerian. We are before the Parthians. Before the Babylonians and Akkadians. Before the Romans as well. *Long* before the Romans."

"A thousand pardons," Herod said.

Gilgamesh glowered and turned away. He peered bleakly into the fire-riven night. The eruption over Pompeii was dying down, now. He wondered how much longer it would be before they reached the island. None too soon, if he had to listen to this Herod's maddening jabber all the way across from the mainland.

After a while Herod said, "Do you intend to be king again?"

"What? Why should I?"

"Most kings who come here do."

"Are *you* a king again?" Gilgamesh asked, without turning.

"I prefer not to be. I never found being a king all that fascinating, to tell you the truth. And I like living in Pompeii too much. It's the first place that's felt like home to me since I died. But Pompeii is Publius Sulla the Dictator's town, and I don't have the urge to try to take it away from him, not that I'd be able to. If he and his namesakes enjoy being bosses here, let them do it, is what I say."

"I understand," said Gilgamesh. "You are beyond these ambitions."

"Well, you know the old line about how it's better to reign in Hell than to serve in Heaven. That might be true, though I don't really know much about Heaven. Assuming there is any such place. But so far as I'm concerned, it feels better to let someone else reign in Hell. My notion is neither to reign nor serve, but just to do my own thing. I suppose that doesn't make much sense to you, does it? If you're like all the rest of the big *goyishe* sword-swingers I've known here, you're itching to get yourself up on a throne again—some throne, any throne—"

"No," Gilgamesh said.

"No?"

"What was that line you used? 'Just to do my own thing?' I like that. *My own thing*. Which was for me, as for you, to be a king; but that was a long time ago, in another life. Here I have no interest in it. What is there to rule, here? This land of trickery and sorcery, where places come and go as though in dreams, and time itself flows fast or slow according to some demon's whim?" Gilgamesh spat. "No, Herod, you mistake me if you think I would be king again! Let me rove freely, let me hunt where I will. And let me find again my one beloved companion, whom I have lost in this land of Hell as I lost him once in the land of the living. Let me be reunited with Enkidu, my true brother, the friend of my heart, who is the only one I have ever loved, and that is all I require. Let others be the kings here. While the likes of you and me do our own thing." Gilgamesh grinned and slapped Herod broadly on the back, knocking the little man up hard against the rail. "Eh, Herod? I think we have more in common, you and I, than it seemed at first. Is that not so, King Herod? Is that not so?"

2.

The mainland and the lowering fury of all its roaring, sputtering volcanos dropped away aft and the royal yacht slipped gracefully through the gleaming water toward Pompeii. The city stood large before them now. Green ghost-fires danced on its many-towered walls.

Here on the verge of arriving at a place unknown to him, Gilgamesh felt a faint flicker of excitement. It was the merest shadow of his ancient curiosity, that world-devouring hunger for knowledge and adventure that had sent him roving everywhere within the confines of the Land and far beyond it. Once the bards of Sumer and Akkad had sung of him as the man to whom all things had been made known—the secret things, the truths of life and death. They hadn't been so far from wrong, those long-ago singers. He had wanted to know everything, to see everything, to taste everything, to do everything.

Most of that was gone from him now, burned out of his soul in the thousands of years he had spent roving this immense and incomprehensible place af-

ter death that was known as Hell. He lived quietly
now, seeking little, asking scarcely anything for himself. But some fragment of the old vanished Gilgamesh
must yet remain alive within him, or else why did he
stare so intently at the bizarre island-city that rose
glittering before him out of the phosphorescent sea?

"Make ready for landing!" someone shouted. "All
hands make ready!"

Herod disappeared below-decks. Crewmen sprang
from nowhere—half a dozen little oily-looking Levan-
tine types who ran around doing busy things with
lines and capstans. Surprisingly, a Hairy Man emerged
from the depths of the boat: squat, thick-bodied,
heavy-jawed, with hardly any chin and great jutting
brows. He was wearing Roman costume. You found
them in the most unlikely places, those harsh-voiced
beings out of the dawn of time, from that lost and
forgotten world before the Flood. This one appeared
to be in the service of Sulla, judging by his dress and
the decorations he was wearing.

Publius Sulla came out next, leaning on Herod's
arm: a balding, portly, fleshy-faced man, his face
mottled with red blotches, his eyes red-rimmed from
too much wine and too little sleep. The dictator of
Pompeii was known to be a man much given to the
excesses of the body, and yet you could see the
power of his spirit within the flab and behind the
blotches, the iron strength of soul, the unwavering
hunger for power. That hunger had survived Sulla's
own life. It was a pity, Gilgamesh thought, that a
man of Publius Sulla's caliber wasn't able to tran-
scend his own lustful appetites. Gilgamesh knew something about appetite himself, and about lust and
excess, but he had never allowed it to show on the
surface the way this man did. His body was his

temple, and throughout his life he had kept it holy. And throughout his long death-life, too.

"Ah," Sulla said. "The king of Uruk. Well, there's Pompeii, just a few hundred yards off our bow. Your first glimpse of my little city. What do you think of it, Gilgamesh?"

"It is not without merit," said Gilgamesh.

"Not without merit? Is that the best you can say of it, King of Uruk?" Sulla's red blotches deepened to angry scarlet. Then, in a softer, more diplomatic tone, he said, "But of course my Pompeii is as nothing beside your great capital. I understand that."

"Your city is most splendid," Gilgamesh said.

In truth, he had almost begun to forget the look of Uruk in all this time. The details of construction and design were going from him. About all he remembered were general outlines, low brick buildings with flat roofs, narrow streets, a temple high upon a platform of whitewashed brick. Which was the way Hell's own cities too had looked, or some of them, at any rate, when first he had come here. But that was all so long ago, and everything was changed now. This Pompeii was a place of narrow spires set with bands of precious stones, parapets that went curving off at improbable angles, boulevards that wound in eye-baffling zigs and zags up the slopes of the lava-rimmed mountain that dominated the island. A gaudy place indeed, no doubt much transformed over time from the simple old Roman town after which it had been originally modeled. Nothing stayed the same in Hell for very long—not even the mountains and rivers.

Sulla said, "My prime minister, the Jew Herod."

"We have met," said Gilgamesh.

So Herod, for all his pious disclaimer of interest in power, nevertheless was prime minister here? Well, perhaps that was his way of—what was the phrase he had used?—doing his own thing. Let others be the kings here, he had said, but nevertheless, he had managed to worm his way into a high enough position among these Romans. Gilgamesh was reminded of that Mongol, Kublai Khan, whom he had encountered while he was wandering the kingdoms of the Outback. The tale was that Kublai, in his time on Earth, had been one of the grandest of emperors, but here he claimed to have no imperial ambitions and avowed himself quite content to serve as minister of war for Mao Tse-tung's Celestial People's Republic. Which was easier than being an emperor, no doubt: but it was still a position of power.

It seemed that your life on Earth determined the way you lived here. Perhaps it was so. The mountains and rivers might be in constant flux and transition here, but human souls, so it seemed, never really changed. Look at all those Achaean Greeks, off there somewhere still fighting and refighting their absurd little Trojan War. Or that little man Che Guevara, feverishly launching plot and crazy counterplot in his endless pointless insurrection against the invisible and probably nonexistent demonic rulers of Hell. And all the kings and emperors trying to replicate their ancient realms in this other world—Caesar and Mao and Elizabeth and Prester John and the rest. This soldierly Sulla, reconstructing his Pompeii right down to the volcano that once destroyed it. Even those like Herod and Kublai, who claimed to have renounced the lust for power, tended to turn up somehow among those who gave the orders rather than among those who took them.

No, Gilgamesh thought, no one ever truly changes in Hell.

Except me. Except me. I was the king of all the

Land, and gloried in my mastery, and made all men bow to me. I conquered cities; I erected temples; I built walls and canals. Here I have done nothing for untold thousands of years but hunt and roam, roam and hunt, and it has been sufficient for me. Whether they will believe it or no, it has been sufficient.

"And this," said Publius Sulla, "is my grand mage and high wizard, whose name, of course, I am unable to tell you."

He indicated the Hairy Man.

"Peace and gladness, King of Uruk," said the Hairy Man. Or so Gilgamesh thought. He never had an easy time understanding the speech of those peculiar folk. Like everyone else here now they spoke English, and before that they had spoken Greek when Greek was the main language of Hell. But whatever language they spoke, they spoke it in a deep, gruff, furry, all but incomprehensible way, as though speaking through a thick stack of oxhides, and as though their tongues were attached the wrong way on. Perhaps they spoke their own language that way, too.

The Hairy Men were mysteries to Gilgamesh. They had no names, or at least none that they would tell to anyone not of their own kind. They worshipped gods without names, too. They looked almost like beasts, covered as they were with dense, coarse, shaggy pelts of brown—or, more usually, reddish—fur. Enkidu was famed among men for his rough, thick-haired body, but even he, shaggy as he was, seemed nearly as hairless as a woman beside a Hairy Man. Bestial though they looked and sounded, however, they conducted themselves as men among men, and when you spent a little time with them, you quickly came to see that they were shrewd and wise, with deep cunning and a mastery of many arcane skills.

The tale was that they came from the beginning of

time, in those early days before the Flood, when the kingship of men first descended from heaven. Maybe so. But once when Gilgamesh had questioned one about those days, asking him what he knew of Alulim, the first king who had reigned at holy Eridu, or Alalgar his successor, or En-men-lu-Anna, who had been king after him with his capital at the city of Bad-tibira, the Hairy Man had simply shaken his head.

"These are only names," the Hairy Man had said. "Names are nothing."

"They are kings! Alulim was king for 28,800 years! Alalgar for 36,000! In Bad-tibira En-men-lu-Anna ruled for 43,200 years! Every boy learns of them in school. And you who lived before the Flood, you who come from deepest antiquity—how could you not know the names of the kings?"

"They were not kings to me," the Hairy Man had replied indifferently. "They were never. They were nothing." Or so he seemed to be saying, in his thick-tongue, indistinct way. And when Gilgamesh had asked other Hairy Men about the same matters, the answers that he got from them were always the same.

Well, perhaps they had forgotten. It was such a long time, after all. Before the Flood! Or could it be that the Hairy Men were not men at all, but demons native to this other world? Nowhere in the books that Gilgamesh had studied when he was king in Uruk had he ever seen it said that in the days before the Flood men had looked like beasts. A mystery, yes. Maybe while he was in Pompeii he would attempt to learn more on these matters from this mage of Sulla's.

Looking shoreward, Gilgamesh beheld slaves bustling around at the pier, some waving flags to guide the royal yacht into its slip, others unrolling an astonishingly long magenta carpet for Sulla. A trio of gunners detonated bright smoke-bombs, perhaps as a salute to the returning monarch, and perhaps just to scare off the evil-looking winged creatures with scaly yellow necks and long glistening fangs that flew in wild circles, flapping and screaming over the harbor.

Publius Sulla said, "A few days to rest and enjoy the baths, yes, King of Uruk? A feast, a theatrical show, a circus in your honor with a hundred gladiators. And then we must get down to business, and discuss the expedition to find the kingdom that by rights is yours."

Gilgamesh frowned. "But I covet no—"

Herod nudged him quickly to silence.

"What's that you say, great king?" Sulla asked.

He needed no further warnings from Herod. "I said, How good it will be to enjoy your baths, Sulla. The feasting, the theatricals, the gladiators."

"And then to search for your city of Uruk, eh?"

Gilgamesh made no reply. Serenely, the royal yacht glided into its slip. Swarms of slaves and sycophants rushed forward to greet Sulla.

To search for Uruk, Gilgamesh thought. *What* Uruk? Where? Uruk was lost in the swirling mists of time. There would never be another Uruk. What he wanted was Enkidu, who had been carried off or perhaps even slain by that scuttling bunch of gun-wielding drug-running New Dead who had followed them here, even to the end of the Outback and beyond. He would accept Sulla's help in finding Enkidu, yes. But Uruk? Uruk?

"You will enjoy our circus," said Herod at his side. "In your honor we will send the hundred mightiest gladiators of Pompeii to the Undertaker."

Gilgamesh gave him a sour look. "That matters little to me. Why should a hundred heroes die for my amusement? You Romans and your bloody games—"

"Please," said Herod. "You keep calling me a Roman, but actually, I prefer to think of myself as a Jew, you know. Although technically, I suppose I could be thought of as a Roman—Julius Caesar did make my great-grandfather Antipater a Roman citizen, after all—but we Jews have a far more ancient lineage than the Romans, after all, and—"

"Do you ever stop running off at the mouth?" Gilgamesh burst out.

"Have I given offense, great king?"

"This chatter of Jews and Romans, Romans and Jews. Who gives a demon's fart about you or your lineage? I was a king when your land was nothing but a swamp!"

Herod smiled. "Ah, Gilgamesh, Gilgamesh, forgive me! Of course, your nation is far older than Rome, or even Judaea. But then again, there are others here to whom even grand and glorious Sumer is but a recent event." He looked slyly toward the Hairy Man. "Under the specter of Eternity, Gilgamesh, most of us have been in Hell only an hour or two. Next to *him*, that is. But forgive me. Forgive me. I do speak too much. Nevertheless, I urge you to attend the contests in our coliseum. And I bid you welcome to my adopted city of Pompeii, King Gilgamesh. Both as Roman and as Jew do I bid you be welcome here."

3.

In Pompeii, Gilgamesh took up residence in Publius Sulla's palace, a huge, rambling building laid out around a courtyard and set in an enormous walled garden. His suite had a bath in the Roman style, a vast, circular bed that somehow seemed to float in midair, and its own staff of valets, butlers, courtesans, and sycophants to meet his every need. Just at the moment he felt very few needs, a general austerity having been his mode for more years than he could remember. But it was good to know those comforts were there, he supposed.

Herod came to him in early evening, when the murky glow of Paradise was beginning to tint the garden with the deep purples of twilight. He perched casually on a windowsill and said, "Tell me about this Uruk of yours."

"What can I tell? It was a city long ago, where I was born and lived and was king and—died. The River Buranunu ran along its flank. Enlil was the god of the city and Inanna its goddess, and—"

"No. I mean the new Uruk, that is here in Hell."

"I know nothing of any such city," said Gilgamesh.

Herod studied him closely. "Publius Sulla thinks you do."

"He does? Whatever I know of the new Uruk, which is very little, I've learned from Sulla."

"Ah. I begin to see."

"The first I heard of it," Gilgamesh said, "was when I encountered Sulla across the bay in the land of the flaming mountains. There is a city called Uruk in Hell, he told me. He told me that this Uruk is a city much like the city of my life, and there are people of my kin there. This Uruk, he said, is a city of fabulous wealth and enormous treasure."

"Yes. The true picture does come into focus now," said Herod.

"He asked if I would join him in an expedition to

Uruk. His soldiers, he said, are bored and seek adventure."

"And also he seeks treasure."

"The treasure of Uruk?"

"Any treasure," Herod said. "Have you looked at the walls and towers of this palace? He's encrusted it with emeralds and rubies and sapphires and diamonds. And gems the names of which no one knows, which were never seen on Earth, but are found only in Hell. His appetite for such decoration is enormous. Five wizards conjure more stones into existence for him all day long and all the night, but of course, those stones last only a short while. He craves the genuine article. If Uruk has great treasure, Sulla hungers for it."

"I took him for a wiser man."

"There is much wisdom in him. But this is Hell, Gilgamesh, where the decay of time turns wise men to folly. He loves bright stones."

"There were no stones at all in Uruk," Gilgamesh pointed out. "We built our city from bricks made of mud. We had neither emeralds nor rubies."

"That was your Uruk. Publius Sulla means to find Hell's Uruk. He thinks you know the way."

"I told him that I did not."

"He thinks you lie," said Herod amiably.

"Then he's an even greater fool. I've been in Hell twice as long as your Sulla, or even longer. Doesn't he think that in all that time I'd have heard of it, if my countrymen had built a new Uruk for themselves here?"

Herod rocked slowly back and forth on the windowsill, smiling to himself. "You two have really screwed each other over, haven't you?"

"What do you mean?"

"The valiant Gilgamesh and the shrewd Publius

Sulla have led each other ass-deep into confusion. He believes you can find Uruk for him. You believe he can find it for you. Each of you thinks the other one holds the secret of Uruk's location. But in fact, neither of you knows anything at all about the place."

"I certainly don't, at any rate."

"Neither does Publius Sulla. I assure you."

"Then how—"

"Some wandering swindler came to him a little while ago. One Hanno, a Carthaginian, claiming to be a maker of maps. You know how reliable maps are in Hell, Gilgamesh? But this Hanno began telling tales of the treasures of Uruk, and Sulla's eyes lit up like the jewels he covets so hungrily. Where can I find this Uruk, Sulla asked. And Hanno sold him a map. Then he disappeared. When Romans start buying maps from Carthaginians, no good can come of it, I say. The day after Hanno left Pompeii, Sulla proudly brought me the map and told me the story. Let us plan an expedition of conquest, he said. And unrolled the map. And its lines ran crazily in every direction, so that it would make your eyes ache to follow them, and even as we stared, they flowed and twisted about. And then in five minutes the map was blank— just an empty piece of demon-hide. I thought Sulla would have a stroke. Uruk! Uruk! That was all he could say, over and over, grunting like that Hairy Man wizard of his. Then off we went to the mainland, where some caravan had arrived from the Outback—scoundrels and villains of some sort, dealers in drugs. Sulla had business with them. He's mixed up in all sorts of garbage of that kind. I don't have to pay any attention to it. And what do we hear but that there are two gigantic hulking Sumerians traveling with the caravan, and one of them is Gilgamesh, the king of Uruk! Uruk again! Do you see, Gilgamesh? He means for you to lead him to Uruk!"

"Sooner would I be able to lead him to Paradise. There is no Uruk here in Hell, Herod."

"Are you certain of that?"

"Who can be certain of anything here? But why haven't I ever heard of it, if it truly exists?"

"Hell is very large, Gilgamesh. It may hold everyone who has ever lived, and yet it is not at all crowded and there are enormous open reaches. I've traveled in it for twice a thousand years and I haven't even seen a tenth of it, I suspect. And you, much older even than I—even you, I wager, are a stranger to much of Hell. You told me yourself that you had never been in Pompeii before."

"Agreed. But Uruk—a city built by Sumerians, inhabited by Sumerians—no. Impossible that it could exist without my knowing of it."

"Unless you knew of it once, and have forgotten that you did."

"Also impossible."

"Is it?"

"There is no Uruk in Hell," said Gilgamesh sullenly. "Accept the truth of that or not as you like, King Herod. But *I* know where the truth lies in this matter."

"Merely a fable, then?"

"Absolutely. A phantom of this Hanno's imagination."

"Why would he name his phantom Uruk, which time itself has forgotten?"

"Who knows? Perhaps he met me once, and the name stuck in his mind. I am well known in Hell, Herod."

"So in truth you are."

"There is no Uruk. Sulla deceives himself. If he

thinks I know how to lead him there, he deceives himself doubly."

Herod was silent a long moment.

At length he said, "Then answer me this, Gilgamesh. If this place really doesn't exist, why have you agreed to join Sulla in an expedition to find a nonexistent place?"

"Because," said Gilgamesh carefully, "the thought came to me that it might just exist after all."

Herod's eyes widened in amazement. "What? You told me yourself two minutes ago that there was no way for it to exist without your knowing about it!"

"This is Hell," said Gilgamesh. "Nothing is ever as we expect it to be here. There was Publius Sulla, telling me that he has heard wondrous tales of Uruk. It sounded crazy to me, that there should be any such place, but what if I was wrong about that? As you said, Hell is large beyond anyone's comprehension. For all I know, Uruk does perhaps exist somewhere far off in this incomprehensible place, and through some fluke, I had never heard of it. Now the powerful dictator Sulla is offering me a chance to go searching for it. Why should I refuse? What do I have to lose?"

"The only information that Sulla had about Uruk was absolute nonsense. He was gambling that you could fill in the blanks on his map for him."

"I wasn't aware of that."

"He meant to use you. He'd let you take him to Uruk, where he could get his hands on all those strongboxes full of precious gems that Hanno said were there. And in return, he'd set you up as Uruk's king."

"As you know, I have no wish to be king of any city. Particularly one that doesn't exist."

"But Sulla didn't know that. He thought you'd jump at the chance."

"I told you. I want only Enkidu."

"Your missing friend, you mean?"

"My friend. My hunting companion. My true brother. Closer to me than any brother could be."

"And where might he be?"

"Gone. A mystery. He was with me on the mainland—and then he was gone. The others in our camp were all dead, horribly butchered, no one left alive at all, only this dog Ajax. But of Enkidu's body there was no trace. Vanished into the sky, it would seem, or into the bowels of the earth. He would never have fled a battleground, so he must have been carried off."

"By whom?"

"I have no idea. But I mean to search for him."

"Even though you have about as much chance of finding him as you do of finding Uruk?"

"At least I know that Enkidu exists."

"But he could be anywhere. A million miles away. Ten million. He could be dead. Who knows? You could look for a thousand years and never find him again."

Shrugging, Gilgamesh said, "I have lost him before, and eventually found him. I'll find him again, and if it takes me a thousand years, Herod, so be it. What's a thousand years to me? What's ten thousand?"

"And meanwhile?"

"Meanwhile what?"

"Uruk," Herod said. "What do you plan to do about that, now that you know Sulla's been bluffing you? Will you go along with him anyway on this lunatic expedition? With him hoping that you really do know the way—or at least can figure it out somehow—and you absolutely sure that there's no such place, but praying that somehow you'll get to it anyway?"

Herod's waspish buzzing was beginning to bother Gilgamesh again. The little man was constantly probing, pushing, maneuvering. For what purpose?

Gilgamesh walked to the window and loomed over him.

"Why are you so concerned about the Uruk journey, Herod?"

"Because it means nothing but trouble for me."

"Trouble for you? Why for you?"

"If Sulla takes off on a crusade to God knows where with you, he's going to leave his kinsman Lucius in charge. And you know he won't do crap, which means I'm going to be stuck here running the shop until Publius Sulla gets back. Which could be centuries, and me trying to preside over this madhouse all the while. Do you think I'm looking forward to that? Pompeii is stacked to the rafters with crazy heroes, most of them oversize and mentally underfurnished, who'd like nothing better than to kill me, or you, or each other. And if they aren't enough trouble, there are all these sorcerers, too, turning the air blue with their incantations, a great many of which unfortunately, are quite potent. I'd go out of my mind without Publius Sulla here to keep a lid on everything."

"If being regent of Pompeii would be such a burden for you, King Herod, you could always come with us to Uruk."

"Fine! Much better! March day and night for a hundred years through the demon wilderness looking for some place that isn't even there!"

"And if it is there?"

"And if it isn't?"

Gilgamesh felt himself losing the last of his patience. "Well, then move somewhere else! You don't have to stay in Pompeii. Get yourself a villa in New Hell, or have one of the Outback princes take you in. You could settle with the Israelis, for that matter. They're Jews like you, aren't they?"

"Jews, yes," said Herod dourly. "But not like me. I don't understand them at all. No, Gilgamesh, I don't want to do any of those things. I like it here. Pompeii is my home. I've got a sweet little niche here. I have no desire whatever to live anywhere else. But if Sulla—"

The ground rumbled suddenly as if monsters were rising beneath the tiled mosaic floor of Sulla's palace.

"What's that?" Gilgamesh asked.

"Vesuvius!" cried Herod. He turned toward the window and stared out into the dusk. The ground shook a second time, more fiercely than before, and there was a tremendous roar. Gilgamesh plucked the little man aside and leaned out the window. An eye-dazzling spear of red flame split the darkness. Another roar, another, another: like the angry growls of some great beast struggling to break free. From the crest of the mighty volcano in the center of the city came cascades of bubbling lava, showers of pumice, choking clouds of dense black smoke, and throughout it all, that single fiery scarlet lance kept rising and rising. Fearless though he was, Gilgamesh had to throttle back a reflexive impulse to run and hide.

Hide? Where? Here on the slopes of that dread volcano there was no safety anywhere to be found.

"Let me see!" Herod said, tugging at Gilgamesh's arm. He was panting. His face was streaked with sweat. He forced his way past Gilgamesh's elbow and thrust his head forth to have a better view. There came another world-shaking convulsion underground.

"Fantastic!" Herod whispered. "Incredible! This is the best one ever!" There was awe in his voice, and reverence. Slowly it was dawning on Gilgamesh that this eruption was arousing extraordinary delight in Herod. He looked transfigured. His eyes were aglow, shining, and there seemed to be an almost sexual excitement throbbing in him. He seemed almost crazed with ecstasy. "Twice in two nights! Fantastic! Fantastic! Do you see why I could never leave this place, Gilgamesh? You've got to talk Publius Sulla out of going off looking for Uruk. You've got to. I beg you!"

4.

Under the cloud-shrouded red light of Paradise, Gilgamesh made his way through the daytime streets of Pompeii. By Enlil, had there ever been a city like this in all the world? There was witchcraft and deviltry everywhere.

Streets that wound in on themselves in tight spirals, like the spoor of a drunken snail. Narrow, high-vaulted buildings that looked like snails themselves, ready to pick up and move away. Black-leaved trees with weeping boughs, from which came curious sighs when you got close to them. And everywhere the dry, powdery smell of last night's eruption, motes of dark dust dancing in the air, and little sparkling bits of flaming matter that stung ever so lightly as they settled on your skin.

Hands plucked at him as he walked briskly along. Hooded eyes stared from passageways. Once someone called him by name, but he could see no one. Ajax, trotting along at his heels, paused again and again to howl and glare, and even to raise the fur along his back and spit as though he were a cat rather than a dog, but the enemies that Ajax perceived were all invisible to Gilgamesh.

Now and again flying fiery-eyed demons swooped through the city at rooftop height. No one paid any attention to them. Frequently they came to rest and perched, preening themselves like living gargoyles, beating their powerful wings against the air and sending down dank, fetid breezes over the passersby below. Gilgamesh saw one of the winged things suddenly sway and fall, as though overcome by a spell. Little glossy, scuttling creatures emerged from crevices in the gutter and pounced upon it. They devoured it before Gilgamesh had reached the end of the street, leaving nothing but scraps of leathery cartilage behind.

When he looked off in the distance it seemed to him that there was some sort of translucent wall in the sky beyond the city, cutting Pompeii off from the rest of Hell. Its blue-white sheen glimmered with cold ferocity, and it seemed to him that there were monstrous creatures outside—not the usual hell-creatures, but some other kind of even greater loathsomeness, all crimson beaks and coiling, snaky necks and vast wings that flailed in fury against the wall that kept them out. But when he blinked and looked again he saw nothing unusual at all, only the heavy clouds and the dark glimmer of the light of Paradise struggling to break through them.

Then he heard a sound that might have been the sound of a tolling bell. But the bell seemed to be tolling backward. First came the dying fall, and then the rising swell of sound, and then the initial percussive boom; and then silence, and then the dying fall again, climbing toward the clangor of the striking clapper:

mmmmmmoooMMMMNGB! mmmmmmoooMM-
MMNGB! mmmmmmoooMMMMNGB!

The impact of the sound was stunning. Gilgamesh
stood still, feeling the immense weight of time drop
away, centuries peeling from him with each heavy
reverberation. As though on a screen before him in
the air he saw his entire life in Hell running in
reverse, the thousands of years of aimless wandering
becoming a mad flight at fantastic speed, everything
rushed and blurred and jumbled together as if it had
happened in a single day—Gilgamesh here, Gilgamesh
there, brandishing his sword, drawing his bow, slaying
this devil-beast and that, climbing impossible mountains, swimming lakes of shimmering color, trekking
across fields of blazing sand, entering cities that were
twisted and distorted like the cities one enters in
dreams, penetrating the far regions of this place even
to the strangest region of all, in the north, where the
great drifting ivory block-shaped creatures known as
the Hoar Gods moved about on their mysterious
tasks. Now he was wrestling joyously with Enkidu;
now he watched the brawling swarms of New Dead
come flooding in and filling the place with their noisy
incomprehensible machines and their guns and their
foul-smelling vehicles; now he was in the villa of
Augustus in New Hell among Augustus's whole unsa-
vory crew of cold-eyed conspirators and malevolent
bitchy queens; and now he sat roistering in the
feasting-hall of the Ice-Hunter king Vy-otin, with
Enkidu laughing and joking by his side, and Agamem-
non, too, and Amenhotep and Cretan Minos, and
Varuna the king of Meluhha, his great companions in
those early days in Hell. How long ago that was! And
now—

"Great king!" a woman cried, dashing up to him

and clutching at his wrist. "Save us from doom, great king!"

Gilgamesh stared at her, amazed. Not a woman but a girl. And he knew her. Had known her, once. Had loved her, even. In another life, far away, long ago, on the other side of the great barrier of life and death. For her face was the face of the girl-priestess Inanna, she whom he had embraced so rashly and with such passion in old Uruk, in the life he had led before this life! During his long years in Hell he had thought more than once about encountering Inanna again, had even once or twice considered seeking her out, but he had never acted on the thought. And now, to blunder into her like this, here in Pompeii—

Or was he still in Pompeii? Was this Hell at all?

Everything was swirling about him. A thick mist was gathering. The earth was giving up its moisture. It seemed to him that he saw the walls of Uruk rising at the end of the street—the huge white platform of the temples, the awesome statues of the gods. He heard the clamor of his name on a thousand thousand tongues. *Gilgamesh! Gilgamesh!* And in the sky, instead of the dull red, glaring light that people here called Paradise, was the yellow sun of the land that he had not beheld in so unimaginably long a time, blazing with all its midsummer power.

What was this? Had that tolling bell lifted him altogether out of this world and cast him back into the other—the world of his birth and death? Or was this only a waking dream?

"Inanna?" he said in wonder. How slender she was! How young! Strings of blue beads about her waist, amulets of pink shell tied to the ends of her hair. Her body bare, painted along its side and front with the pattern of the serpent. And her dark-tipped breasts—the sharp, stinging scent of her perfume—

She spoke again, this time calling him by his name of names, the private name that no one had called him in thousands of years, since that day when he was still half a boy and he had put on the mantle of kingship and had for the first time heard his king-name roaring like a flooding river in his ears— *Gilgamesh, Gilgamesh, Gilgamesh*. He himself had forgotten that other name, that birthname, but as she spoke it, the dam of recollection burst in his soul. What wizardry was this, that he should be standing before the girl Inanna again?

"I am Ninpa, the Lady of the Scepter," she murmured. "I am Ninmenna, the Lady of the Crown."

She reached her hand toward his. As he touched her she changed: she was older now, fuller of body, her dark eyes gleaming with wanton knowledge, her deep-hued skin bright with oil. "Come," she whispered. "I am Inanna. You must come with me. You are the only one who can save us."

A dark tunnel was before him—a buzzing in his ears, as of a thousand wasps about his head—a brilliant purple light glowing before his eyes—a mighty roaring, as though Enlil of the Storms had loosed all his winds upon Hell—

And then a fiery pain at his ankle. Ajax, sinking his fangs deep! Gilgamesh stared down at the dog, astonished.

"Careful, Gilgamesh!" Ajax barked. "This is enchantment!"

"What? What?"

The woman held him by the hand. Heat came from her, and it was overwhelming, a furnace heat. And she was changing, again and again. Now she had his mother's face, and now she was the round-breasted temple-woman Abisimti, who had first taught him the arts of love; and then she was the child-Inanna again, and then the woman. And then she was a thing with a hundred heads and a thousand eyes, pulling him down into the nether pits of Hell, into the yawning blackness that lay beneath the smoldering heart of the Vesuvius volcano.

"I am Ereshkigal of Hell," she whispered, "and I will be your bride."

Down—down—descending a ladder of lights— blinding whiteness around, and a bright red mantle of copper fluttering in the breeze out of the pit, and demons dancing below. On all sides, lions. From high overhead, golden wine fell from two inverted wine-cups. The wine was thick and fiery, and burned him where it touched him.

He heard the furious howling of the dog. He felt the terrible pull of the black depths.

"It is enchantment, Gilgamesh," said Ajax again. "Stay—fight—I will get help—"

The dog ran off, uttering terrible wolf-cries as he went.

Gilgamesh stood his ground, baffled, shaking his head slowly from side to side like a wounded bull. If only Enkidu were here! Enkidu would pull him back from the abyss, just as Gilgamesh once long ago had tried to bring Enkidu out of that tunnel of old dry bones that led to the land of the dead. He had failed, then, and Enkidu had perished, but they were older now, they were wiser, they knew how to deal with the demons that surrounded them on all sides—

Enkidu! Enkidu!

"You should not have come to this street alone," a new voice said. "There are many dangers here."

Enkidu, yes! At last! The dog Ajax had returned, and he had brought Enkidu with him to Gilgamesh's side. Gilgamesh felt his soul soaring. Saved! Saved!

Through blurred eyes he saw the powerful figure

of his friend: the great muscles, the thick pelt of dark hair, the burning, gleaming eyes. Enkidu was struggling with Ereshkigal-Inanna, now—shoving the hell-demon goddess back toward her pit, wresting her cold hands free of Gilgamesh's wrist. Gilgamesh trembled. He was helpless to act on his own behalf. In all his years in Hell he had never known such peril, had never fallen so deeply into the power of the dark beings of the invisible world. But Enkidu was here— Enkidu would save him—

Enkidu was freeing him. Yes. Yes. The frightful chill of the abyss which had enfolded him was relenting. The blinding lights had receded. The temples and streets and sun of Uruk no longer could be seen. Gilgamesh stepped back, blinking, shivering. His heart was pounding in dull, heavy thuds, almost like the tolling of that backwards bell. Tears were streaming down his face. He looked about for his friend.

"Enkidu?"

Through blurring eyes he saw the shaggy figure. Enkidu? Enkidu? No. The heavy pelt was like a beast's. A reddish color, and coarse and dense, letting none of the skin show through. And the face— that underslung chin, those fierce, brooding ridges above the eyes—why, this was not Enkidu at all, but rather the Hairy Man who was Sulla's wizard. Or perhaps not, perhaps another of that tribe altogether— it was so difficult telling one Hairy Man from the next—

The very ugliness of the Hairy Man was comforting. The squat bulk of him, the solidity. This creature who had lived when the gods themselves were young, who had walked the earth in the days before the Flood, who had lived fifty thousand or a hundred thousand or a hundred hundred thousand years in

Hell before Gilgamesh of Uruk first had come here. Ancient wisdom flowed deep in him. Next to him, Gilgamesh felt almost like a child again.

"Come with me," said the Hairy Man, thick-tongued, husky-voiced. "In here. You will be safe. You will be protected here."

5.

It might have been some sort of warehouse. A huge, dark, long room, walls of white plaster, curved wooden ceiling far overhead. A single piercing beam of light cutting through from above, illuminating the intricacies of the rafters and slicing downward to show the sawdust-strewn floor, the rows of bare wooden tables, the hunched and somber figures sitting on backless benches behind them. They were staring straight forward and exclaiming aloud, each in the midst of uttering some private recitation, each ploughing stubbornly onward over the voices of all the others.

"I am Wulfgeat. For chronic disorder of the head or of the ears or of the teeth through foulness or through mucus, extract that which aileth there, seethe chervil in water, give it to drink, then that draweth out the evil humors either through mouth or through nose."

"I am Aethelbald. Seek in the maw of young swallows for some little stones, and mind that they touch neither earth, nor water, nor other stones; look out three of them; put them on the man, on whom thou wilt, him who hath the need, and he will soon be well."

"I am Eadfrith. Here we have rue, hyssop, fennel, mustard, elelcampane, southernwood, celandine, radish, cumin, onion, lupin, chervil, flower de luce, flax, rosemary, savory, lovage, parsley, olusatrum, savine."

In wonder and bewilderment Gilgamesh said, "Why, who are these people, and what's all this that they're babbling?"

"—again, thou shalt remove the evil, misplaced humors by spittle and breaking. Mingle pepper with mastic, give it to the patient to chew, and work him a gargle to swill his jowl—"

"—they are good for headache, and for eye-wark, and for the fiend's temptations, and for night-goblin visitors, and for the nightmare, and for knot, and for fascination, and for evil enchantments by song. It must be big nestlings on which thou shalt find them. If a man ache in half his head, pound rue thoroughly, put it into strong vinegar—"

The Hairy Man said, "These are dealers in remedies and spells, and this is the market where such things are sold in Pompeii."

"—and also mastic, pepper, galbanum, scamony, gutta ammoniaca, cinnamon, vermilion, aloes, pumice, quicksilver, brimstone, myrrh, frankincense, petroleum, ginger—"

"—that he by that may comfortably break out the ill phlegm. Work thus a swilling or lotion for cleansing of the head, take again a portion of mustard seed and of navew seed and of cress seed, and twenty peppercorns, gather them all with vinegar and honey—"

"—and smear therewith the head, right on top. Delve up waybroad without iron, ere the rising of the sun, bind the roots about the head with crosswort, by a red fillet—"

Gilgamesh shivered. "I think this place is no better than being in the street. A marketplace of wizards? A hundred mages bellowing spells?"

"No harm can befall you here," the Hairy Man said. "There is such a constant crying-forth of magics in here that each cancels the other out, so there is no peril."

"—the seed of this wort administered in wine is of much benefit against any sort of snake, and against sting of scorpions, to that degree that if it be laid upon the scorpions, it bringeth upon them unmightiness or impotence and infirmity—"

"—for ache of loins and sore of the thighs, take this same wort pulegium, seethe it in vinegar—"

"I am Aethelbald."

"I am Eadfrith."

"I am Wulfgeat."

"—this wort, which is named priapiscus, and by another name vinca pervinca, is of good advantage for many purposes; that is to say, first against devil sicknesses, or demoniacal possessions, and against snakes, and against wild beasts, and against poisons—"

"Good sir! Good sir!" It was the one who said he was Aethelbald, waving wildly at Gilgamesh.

"What does he want with me?"

"To sell you something, no doubt," the Hairy Man replied. "Why were you wandering in these streets by yourself?"

"My head was aching when I awoke. From the noise of the eruptions all night long, and, I think, from some prattle of the Jew Herod last evening. So I went out to walk. To clear my head, to see the city. I saw no harm in it."

"—and for various wishes," shouted the one called Eadfrith, "and for envy, and for terror, and that thou may have grace, and if thou hast this sort with thee, thou shalt be prosperous, and ever acceptable—"

"Good sir! Here, good sir, here, if you please!"

"No harm? No harm?" The Hairy Man guffawed, showing huge chopper-like teeth. "No harm playing tag with a mastodon, either, eh, my friend? If you're big enough, I suppose. Walk right up to it, tweak it by the trunk, pull its ears? Eh?"

"A mastodon?" Gilgamesh said blandly. A strange word: he wondered if he had heard it right.

"Never mind. You wouldn't know, would you? Before your time. Never mind. But I tell you, this is no city to be strolling around in unprotected. Nobody warned you of that?"

"Herod said something about wizards and mages, but—"

"Good sir! Good sir!"

"But you ignored him. Herod! That clown!" The small deep-set eyes of the Hairy Man were bright with contempt. "Sometimes even Herod will tell you something useful. You should have heeded his warning. Pompeii's a place of many perils."

"I have no fear of dying," said Gilgamesh.

"Dying is the least terrible thing that could happen to you here." The Hairy Man placed a wrinkle-skinned, leathery-looking hand on Gilgamesh's arm. "Come. Here. Walk about with me a little, up and down."

"Do you have a name?"

"Names are nothing," said the Hairy Man. "It was a fright for you, what happened outside, eh?"

Gilgamesh shrugged.

The Hairy Man leaned close. There was an odd, sweetish flavor about his furry body. "There are places in the streets here where the other worlds break through. That is always a danger, that the fabric will not hold, that other worlds will break through. Do you understand what I'm saying?"

"Yes," Gilgamesh told the Hairy Man. "There was such a place in Uruk. A passageway that ran down from our world into this one. Inanna the goddess descended through it, when she went to Hell to visit her sister Ereshkigal. And during the rite of the Closing of the Gate I dropped my drum and my drumstick into that passageway when a girl startled me by crying out the name of a god." He had not thought of these things in centuries. Recollection, flooding back now, swept him with uncontrollable emotion. "The sacred drum, it was, which Ur-nangar the craftsman made for me from the wood of the huluppu-tree, by which I entered my trances and saw the things that mortal eyes are unable to see. That was how I lost my friend Enkidu, the first time, when I dropped my drum and my drumstick into that dark and terrible hole of cinders and ashes, and he entered the nether world to bring them back."

"Then you know," the Hairy Man said. "You have to learn where these places are, and stay away from them."

Gilgamesh was trembling. Old memories were surging with new life within him.

Enkidu! Enkidu!

Once again he saw Enkidu, gray with dust and snarled in masses of tangled cobwebs, coming forth from that pit in Uruk that led down to the world of the dead. And Enkidu as he came forth was a dead man himself, shorn of all life-strength, who within twelve days would be carried off forever to the House of Dust and Darkness. How great had been the mourning of Gilgamesh! How he had cursed the gods of death for taking Enkidu from him! And then, after Gilgamesh's own time had run its course and he had joined Enkidu in Hell, losing him again—what pain it was, to be reunited with him and then to lose him that second time, when Enkidu had stepped between quarrrelsome Spaniards and Englishmen and caught a bullet meant for someone else—

"And once more he is lost to me," Gilgamesh said aloud. "As though the curse of Inanna follows us even to Hell, and we must find each other and be parted again, and find each other once more, and part once more, over and over and over—"

"What is this you say?" asked the Hairy Man.

"We were on that far shore, Enkidu and I, among those strangers—those sleazy, conniving New Dead—because Enkidu craved the new kinds of weapons those people had, and I think also he desired one of their women. And while I was gone from the camp, while I was down at the water's edge speaking with Sulla and his minions, there was an attack on the camp, and when I returned I found all of them dead except this brindle dog Ajax. But of Enkidu there was no sign. Demons must have swept him off, to torment me by separating us once again. But I will find him, if I must seek until the gods grow old!"

"In Hell there is no finding anyone," the Hairy Man said, "except by accident, or the whim of those who rule this place. You surely must know that."

"I will find him."

"And if he is dead?"

"Then he'll come back again, as all the dead here do sooner or later. I tell you I will find him."

"Come, now," said the Hairy Man. "Come and walk with me, until your head is clear."

"Wait," Gilgamesh said. He brushed the Hairy Man's hand aside. "Do you think that these doctors here could give me a spell that would help me trace him?"

"They will tell you they can. But in Hell there is no finding anyone, Gilgamesh."

"We'll see about that."

Gilgamesh went toward the rows of wooden tables and benches.

"Good sir, I am Aethelbald," said one of the merchants of spells eagerly.

"I am Eadfrith," said the one beside him, beckoning.

"I am Wulfgeat. I have here a drink that is good for giddiness and fever of the brain, for flowing gall and the yellow disease, for singing in the ears, and defective hearing—"

Gilgamesh impatiently waved them to silence. "Who are you people?"

"We are Angles here," said Wulfgeat, "except for this Saxon beside me, and masters of wortcunning and leechdom are we, and starcraft. Our work is substantial! Our skills are boundless!"

"Wortcunning?" Gilgamesh said. "Starcraft?"

"Aye, and may it be that we have a spell for you! What is your need, good sir? What is your need?"

"There is a man for whom I search," said Gilgamesh after a moment. "A friend whom I have lost."

"A lost friend? A lost friend?" The spell-mongers began to murmur and confer among themselves. "Viper's bugloss?" suggested one. "The ash of dead bees, and linseed oil?" Another said, "Cammock and thung, wenwort and elder root, steeped in strong mead or clear ale." But the third shook his head violently and said, "It must be done by dreaming. The tokens must needs be induced. To see a well opened beside one's house, or a hen with chickens, or to be shod with a new pair of shoes—aye, those are the tokens, and we must give him the potion that brings on such visions as will be useful, and then the next night—"

"What is this?" a sudden familiar, buzzing voice cut in. "What's going on here?"

Herod, pushing and shoving his way through the throng, appeared abruptly at Gilgamesh's side. The Hairy Man scowled and muttered something unintelligible beneath his breath. The merchants of spells looked alarmed, and turned away, gesticulating toward the opposite side of the building and loudly crying out the merits of their wares to those gathered over there.

"Where have you been?" Herod demanded. "Sulla's had people looking all over the place for you."

"I thought I would walk through the town."

"And came *here?* Ah. Ah, I know why. Shopping for a spell that'll lead you to Uruk, are you? Is that what you're up to? Despite everything I told you last night?"

From afar came the sound of a mighty voice crying, "The Book of the Fifty Names! Who will buy the Book of the Fifty Names?"

"The Hairy Man brought me in here," Gilgamesh said. "I was simply wandering from one street to another when something strange happened to me, a fit, perhaps—in the days when I lived on Earth I was subject to fits, you know, though I thought I was exempt from that in Hell—and I grew dizzy—I saw faces—I saw ancient streets—" Angrily, he shook his head. "No, I'm not trying to buy a spell for finding Uruk. Enkidu is what I seek. And if these wizards—"

"Marduk! Murukka! Marutukku!" roared the mighty voice.

"These wizards are fishmongers and rabble," Herod said scornfully, making the sign of the horns at Aethelbald and Eadfrith and Wulfgeat. They shrank back from him. "Peasants is what they are. Shopkeepers, at the very best." He drew the six-pointed star in the air before them and they turned from him, pale and shaken. "You see? You see, Gilgamesh?

What can they do? Cure an ague for you, maybe? Stop up a sniveling nose? These are foolish men here. They will not find your Enkidu for you."

"Can you be sure of that, Herod?"

A crafty look came into Herod's eyes as he peered up at Gilgamesh.

"King of Uruk, if I show you a true wizard who will give you the answer you seek, will you abandon the idea of taking Sulla off on this insane expedition?"

The Hairy Man's yellow-rimmed eyes widened in surprise. "You speak of Calandola?" he asked in his thickest, harshest tone.

"Calandola, yes," said Herod.

The Hairy Man scowled, twisting up his ape-like jaw and lowering his brows until he seemed almost to be winking, and emitted a rumbling sound from deep within his cavernous chest. "This is unwise," he said, after a time. "This is most unwise."

Herod glared at him. "Let Gilgamesh be the judge of that!"

"Asaraludu!" boomed the caller of the Fifty Names. "Namtillaku! Narilugaldimmerankia!"

"And who is this great wizard you offer me?" Gilgamesh asked.

"Imbe Calandola is his name," said Herod. "A Moor, he is—no, a Nubian, or something of each, perhaps. Black as night, terrible to behold. He maintains a temple in the dark tunnels far below the streets of Pompeii, and there he presides over the giving of visions. There are those who think he is the Lord of Darkness himself—the Prince of Hell, the Great Adversary, the vast Lucifer of the Abyss: Satan Mephistopheles Beelzebub, the Archfiend, the King of Evil. Perhaps he is, but I think he is in truth only a great savage, who knows the wisdoms of the jungle. In either case, he will tell you what you wish to know. The Hairy Men, I understand, consult him frequently."

Gilgamesh looked toward the ancient one.

"Is this true?"

The Hairy Man scowled again, screwing up his face even more bizarrely than before.

"He sees into the other worlds, yes, this Calandola. And he can make others see what he sees."

"Then I mean to go to him," said Gilgamesh.

"There are dangers," the Hairy Man warned.

"So you frequently tell me. But what need I fear? Death? You know that death is a joke to one who has already met it once!"

"Have I not said already that death is the least terrible thing to be feared in Pompeii?"

"You have said that, yes. But what you say means nothing to me."

"Then go to Calandola."

"I will do that," Gilgamesh said. He turned to Herod. "How soon can you bring me before him?"

"Do we have a deal? I take you to Calandola, you persuade Sulla to abandon the idea of going off in search of Uruk?"

It was maddening to be haggled with this way, as though he and Herod were tradesmen striking a bargain in the marketplace. With difficulty Gilgamesh resisted the urge to pick the little Judaean up and hurl him across the vast room.

"Let there be no talk of favors for favors," said Gilgamesh icily. "I am a man of honor. That's all that should concern you. Take me to this wizard of yours."

6.

Downward then they went—down into the depths,

down into demon country, down into the tunnels of
the devils, where the light of Paradise never was
seen, where this black and monstrous Imbe Calandola
had his dwelling place.

When he was still a boy in Uruk, a slave wearing
the badge of the goddess Inanna had come to
Gilgamesh one day as he practiced the throwing of
the javelin, and had said to him, "You will come now
to the temple of the goddess." And the slave had
conducted him to the temple that his grandfather
Enmerkar had built on the platform of white brick,
and down through winding passageways he had never
seen before, into mysterious tunnels that descended
beneath the white platform toward the depths of the
earth. Past hallways where distant lamps glowed in
the subterranean dark, and places where magicians
did their work by candleglow, and cross-passages
that afforded him glimpses of shaggy, goat-hooved
demons silently going about their tasks, until at last
he had come to the secret room of Inanna herself, far
below the sun-baked streets of Uruk.

That had been long ago, in the days of his life. It
had been his first glimpse of the worlds that lie
beneath the world, where invisible wings flutter and
the sound of scratchy laughter echoes in dusty corri-
dors. That day the young Gilgamesh had learned that
there was more to the world than its familiar surface:
that layer upon layer of mystery existed, far from the
sight of ordinary mortals. Again and again he had
entered that lower world in the course of his kingship. And Enkidu too had gone into it once, to his
cost; for it was the breaching of the hidden mysteries
that had deprived him of his life, that time he had
gone down into the pit of darkness to fetch Gilgamesh
his drum and drumstick.

Now here in Hell, where nothing ever was familiar

and mystery was everywhere, Gilgamesh found himself descending once more into a world beneath the world.

He had discovered long ago that Hell had its own subterranean region—a Hell beneath Hell—a land of tunnels and passageways of unfathomable dimensions and incomprehensible complexity. In the early years of the days of his death he had prowled those tunnels, for then he was still in the grip of the insatiable curiosity that once had driven him to the ends of the earth. But he had quickly lost interest in such explorations, as the aimlessness and passivity of his Hell-life had settled upon him, and this was his first descent into the tunnels in an eon and a half, or more.

There were those who believed that a way out of Hell lay through those tunnels. Gilgamesh doubted that. To him it was meaningless to speak of a way out of Hell; to those who had come to dwell in it, Hell was forever, Hell was eternal. Some, he knew, had gone down into the tunnels and had never emerged. But to Gilgamesh, that did not mean they had found a way out, only that they were lost in some doubly nether Hell—perhaps the House of Dust and Darkness itself, that terrible place of which the priests in Uruk had told, where the dead were clad like birds and sadly trailed their feathers in the dust. Gilgamesh had no yearning to go down into that forlorn land of unending night.

But now, for the sake of finding out where Enkidu had gone this time—

Down. Down. Herod's torch flickered and sputtered. The air was thick and oppressive here. There was the taste of fire in it. In the dimness Gilgamesh saw hideous scenes carved on the tunnel walls, that made his eyes throb and pound. It was all he could do to tear his gaze away from those dreadful pictures.

The tunnels curved and twisted, now plunging almost straight down, now rising in steep ramps. They crossed one another and seemed to blend and meld, and then to split apart again, so that it was all but impossible to remember which path they had originally been bound upon. Herod seemed to know the way, but even he was baffled now and again, and turned to the Hairy Man, who would gesture brusquely with one finger, jabbing the long dagger of his fingernail in the right direction: this way, this, this. No one spoke. They encountered few others in the tunnels. Occasionally demon-sounds reverberated in the distance: cacklings, screechings, hissings, moanings.

And then music: a dreadful barbaric drumming, with the jabbing shriek of flutes or fifes rising above it.

"The house of Calandola lies just beyond," said Herod.

"What must I do as we enter?" asked Gilgamesh.

"Stand upright. Show no fear. Meet him eye to eye."

Gilgamesh laughed. "That will be no great task."

"Wait," Herod said. "Tell me that five minutes from now."

The tunnel swung abruptly to the left, and Gilgamesh found himself staring into a secondary tunnel, long and narrow and lit only by the faintest of star-gleams. The only way to enter it seemed to be through an opening hardly suitable for a dwarf. "In here," Herod said, clambering through. Gilgamesh, crouching, had to shuffle in on his knees, crawling at an angle, first this shoulder, then that. The Hairy Man followed.

Beyond the one narrow point of light that illuminated the opening, the darkness within was like a night within night: blackness upon blackness, so stark and deep that it struck the eyes like the hammering of fists. Gilgamesh was stunned by the depth of that darkness. He understood now for the first time what it must be like to be blind.

"This way," Herod said confidently. "Follow me!"

And what if a fathomless pit yawned before them on the path, with boiling oil or colossal serpents waiting at the bottom? What if swinging scythes were to reach forth from the sides of the tunnel to disembowel any comers who passed close by? What if swords on tripwires hung overhead, ready to descend and cleave? He could see nothing. He must surrender himself totally to faith.

And yet, and yet, being blind in this fashion, other senses came into play—

He could hear Herod's Roman robe rustling on the heavy air. He felt the tread of Herod's sandal-shod feet pattering against the ground. The skin of his cheeks and forehead told him of the breeze that Herod's movements created. Like a hunter tracking his prey in the night, Gilgamesh read all these signs, and more, and followed along without fear or hesitation.

The tunnel narrowed until it pressed like a clammy fist on all sides. The tunnel widened until it became a vast, echoing cavern. The tunnel narrowed again. It dipped; it rose; it twisted about and about. And abruptly it delivered them into an immense deep-shadowed room irregularly lit by smoldering torches set in brazen sconces—a room of angles, where ceiling met walls in a manner that oppressed and bewildered the eye. And toward the center of the room there sat enthroned a man of immense presence and authority who could only have been the great sorcerer Imbe Calandola, of whom it was rumored in Hell that he was the Archfiend, the King of Evil, the true Lucifer, the Lord of Darkness.

Gilgamesh saw at once that this was not so. He

knew with one glance that this Calandola was neither god nor demon nor devil, but a man of human flesh and blood, such as he was himself, or had been when he had lived. But having perceived that, Gilgamesh perceived also in that same moment that the man before whom he stood was one who was extraordinary in the extreme. Who, mortal though he might have been, might well have the blood of gods in him.

As did Gilgamesh, who had known from childhood that he was two parts god and one part mortal, which was the source of his great stature and the depth of his wisdom. Though none of that had spared him from dying and coming to make his home these long years in Hell.

"Stand and give obedience," a deep rumbling voice commanded out of the shadows behind Calandola's throne. "Yield yourselves, strangers, for you are in the presence of the great Jaqqa, Imbe Calandola."

Gilgamesh stared, and felt an emotion as close to awe as anything he could remember feeling in five thousand years.

The blackness of Calandola was like the blackness of Calandola's tunnel: a blackness upon blackness, the blackness of a void without suns, a blackness so intense that it seemed to suck light from all that was around it. Black-skinned men had not been unknown to Gilgamesh in his life before Hell. In his wanderings in distant places he had seen the flat-nosed, thick-lipped, woolly-haired sailors of the kingdom of Punt, who came from a land in the south where the air was like fire and darkened the skins of those who lived there. From far-off Meluhha had come other black ones with thin noses and lips, and long straight hair so dark it was nearly blue. And in Hell itself he had encountered many who were black in one of these fashions or another, from lands whose names meant nothing to him—Nigeria, Ethiopia, Nubia, Mali, Quiloa, India, Socotra, Zanzibar, and many more. Perhaps there were blacks in every part of the world, as also there were yellows and reds and browns, and, for all Gilgamesh knew, blue and green and piebald ones, each kept in a Hell of their own. But he had never seen anyone like Calandola.

His skin had the blackness of the people of Punt, but his nose was straight and his lips were narrow and harsh, something like the features of the men of Meluhha and India, though they were small men and this Calandola was huge, a giant verging on the great size of Gilgamesh himself. His hair was thick and long and curling and there were seashells woven into it, and around his neck was a collar of large shells of a different kind, that stood out like twisted turrets. A strip of glittering copper as long as a man's small finger was thrust through his nose, and two more such strips dangled from his ears. His loins were clothed in a swath of brilliant scarlet cloth, but the rest of his massive body was bare. Red and white designs had been painted down his sides, and where he was not painted, his skin had been cut and carved and otherwise tormented into astonishing raised welts—some sort of monstrous decoration, that had the form of flowers and knots and lines. His skin also was oiled to a high gloss, so that reflections of the torchlight gleamed on him.

And his eyes—!

Gods! Enlil and Enki and Inanna, what eyes!

They were black and bright and deep—pools of utter darkness set in fields of dazzling white. Gilgamesh knew them at once for the eyes of a true king. They were eyes that could seize and hold, eyes that could beat and oppress. Eyes that could charm if they had to, eyes that could kill.

Gilgamesh felt no fear, for fear was a thing he had never been taught to know. But he felt a deep awe and a strange admiration. He knew that he was in the presence of one who was his equal in strength and force; and that was not an experience he had often had, either in Hell or out of it.

Who was this man? Where had he reigned in life? Why did he dwell now in this cavern beneath Pompeii in the depths of Hell?

Calandola rose, stepped down from his throne, and took a few slow steps toward Gilgamesh. There was a curious dark odor about him, a sour reek, which Gilgamesh suspected came from the oil that made his body shine. He moved with extreme deliberation, calm and measured and sure. It became apparent now that Calandola was not as tall as Gilgamesh by half a head, but then, few men were. His look of great size he owed to the massiveness of his neck, the mighty breadth of his shoulders, and the power of his upper arms, which were as thick as thighs.

He nodded in a sniffing way at the Hairy Man, and shrugged at the trembling, fawning Herod. To Gilgamesh, he said in a voice that seemed to rise from some tunnel beneath even this tunnel, "Why have you come to me?"

"I have questions, and they say that you have answers."

"I know where answers may be found, yes. Give me your hand."

And he put forth his own, extending it palm upward. It was dark below and pink in the palm, and its span was enormous—enough to have allowed him to take a man's head in his grasp and squeeze it to a ruin. Gilgamesh, after a moment, placed his hand outspread atop Calandola's, and waited. The outermost two of Calandola's thick black fingers closed in on the sides of Gilgamesh's hand and dug deep, and deeper still, until Gilgamesh could feel a faint stirring of pain, and the bones beginning to move around. A test of endurance? Very well. It was childish, but Gilgamesh would accept it. He withstood the terrible clamping pressure of those two fingers as though he were being stroked with feathers, and when the pain became too intense, he sent the pain from him as one might banish an annoying fly.

A vein stood out now on Calandola's gleaming forehead. The strange ornamentation of raised scars that had been carved upon his skin appeared to rise still higher, and to throb and pulse. The two fingers pressed inward even more fiercely. Unflinching, Gilgamesh looked down with indifference at his hand and Calandola's beneath it. And then, without a word, he slid two fingers of his own along the sides of Calandola's wrist, and returned the pressure with one of his own that was just as powerful.

Calandola seemed not to react. It was as though he felt no pain, or else that he knew how, as Gilgamesh did, to treat pain as unworthy of his notice and dismiss it from awareness.

As they stood locked this way, hand in hand, fingers digging deep, Calandola said, "You are too big to be a Portuguese and too dark to be an Angleez. But not dark enough, I think, for an African."

"No. I'm not any of those."

"Then what are you?"

Gilgamesh stepped up the pressure. Still Calandola showed no sign of discomfort. They were unable to hurt one another, it seemed.

"When I lived on the other shore," Gilgamesh said, "my land was known as the Land of the Two Rivers. Or we called it Sumer."

"In Africa?"

"Not in Africa, no." Now and then Gilgamesh had
seen maps. He put little faith in them, but other
men seemed to live by them, and on the maps,
Africa was the name they gave that great hump-
shouldered land far to the south of his own, where
the sky was like fire. "Some called my land Mesopotamia."

"I don't know of that place."

"Very few do, in these times. But once it was the
center of the world."

"No doubt it was," said Calandola, sounding unimpressed. He released Gilgamesh's hand, casually letting go, not in any admission of defeat but merely,
it would seem, because whatever test he had imposed had brought him whatever answer he sought.
"These Two Rivers of yours: which two were those?"

"The nearer was the Euphrates, as some call it.
The other was the Tigris. We said the Buranunu,
and the Idigna."

Calandola nodded remotely. Plainly those great
names were nothing but noises to him. He seemed
lost in private calculations.

"Bring wine," he called suddenly, gesturing to
someone in the rear of the cavern.

Gilgamesh saw that a considerable entourage lurked
in the darkness behind Calandola: half a dozen black
men nearly as huge as their master and perhaps
eleven women of the same sort, all of them clad in
little more than beads and shells, and their dark
skins glossy with oil. One came forward now with a
wooden bowl full of some thick, sweet-smelling wine.
Calandola dipped his fingertips into it, and shook
wine out over Gilgamesh's head as if anointing him,
and then slowly rubbed the wine deep into his scalp,
while murmuring in an unknown language. Gilgamesh
submitted to the rite unprotestingly. Then the black

giant offered the bowl to Gilgamesh. For an instant the Sumerian wondered if he was supposed to anoint Calandola in return. But no, apparently all he was meant to do was take a drink. He sipped, and found it heavy and almost nauseatingly sweet. Calandola watched him carefully. After a moment's hesitation Gilgamesh reached for the bowl again and took a second draught, draining deep.

Calandola threw back his head and laughed. His mouth was enormous—a great, world-gulping hole set about with white teeth of formidable size. Four of the teeth were gone—two above and two below—so symmetrical in their absence that it seemed likely to Gilgamesh that they had been removed deliberately, perhaps for beauty's sake, or in some witch-rite. And when Calandola's laughter set the men and women of his tribe laughing with him, Gilgamesh saw that they too were missing two upper and two lower teeth, in the same pattern.

"You drink like a king," Calandola said. "Do you have a name?"

"I am Gilgamesh the Sumerian, who was king of Uruk."

"Ah. I am Calandola the Jaqqa, who was king of the world." He clapped his hands. "Oil for King Gilgamesh!" he roared.

Two of the black women came forward, struggling with a huge wooden tub that held some sort of dark grease. Dipping his immense hands in it, Calandola scooped up a great gobbet of the stuff and clapped it to Gilgamesh's bare chest. And then, with a surprisingly tender touch, he rubbed it in, chest and back and shoulders and the column of the neck, until the Sumerian gleamed as brightly as any of the Jaqqa folk. The same sharp and sour odor came from the oil that emanated from Calandola himself. Gilgamesh felt it permeating his skin, sinking in deep.

When he was done, Calandola held Gilgamesh a moment in a tight embrace. Gilgamesh sensed the bull-like force of the man, the mountainous mass of him.

Then Calandola let go of him and stepped back. "When you return, King Gilgamesh, perhaps we will seek the answers to these questions of yours."

Calandola flashed his eyes and grinned his gap-toothed grin, and then he turned in clear dismissal and stalked away into the shadows, and his entourage closed in behind him so that Gilgamesh no longer had sight of him.

For a long moment Gilgamesh stood staring, feeling the weight of the sweet wine within his gut and the slippery slickness of the grease with which Calandola had besmeared him. Then he looked about to see what had become of his companions. The Hairy Man leaned against the wall, arms folded across his deep shaggy chest, thin lips clamped in a look of glowering disapproval. As for Herod, he was kneeling in a sweaty heap, eyes fixed in the distance, arms hanging slackly. He looked dazed. It was something of the same look that he had had when he was staring out the window of Gilgamesh's room at the furious outpouring of flame from the erupting Vesuvius.

Gilgamesh poked him with his toe.

"Come," he said. "Get up. I think we have to go now."

Numbly Herod nodded. His eyes were wide. "He gave you the wine!" he murmured. "He gave you the oil! Extraordinary! Astonishing! On the first visit, the wine, the oil!"

"Is that so unusual?" Gilgamesh asked.

Herod was shivering with excitement. "The power

of the man! The sheer awesomeness of him! I can't believe he gave you the wine the first time. And the oil. It was as though he looked at you and sized you up in a single glance, and said to himself, Yes, this man and I, we are of the same spirit. My god, how I envy you! To be taken right into Calandola's arms—" He swung around toward Gilgamesh, and the Sumerian saw the look of sickening devotion on Herod's face.

In some strange way, Gilgamesh felt undeniably impressed by Calandola himself. But not like this. Not like this.

From the shadowy corner the Hairy Man snorted contemptuously. "So much for half a million years of evolution. You lie down with savages and before long you turn into one yourself."

"And what are you?" Herod flared, whirling around in sudden fury. "You animal! You ape! You half-human thing! You wrap yourself in a toga and you think you're a Roman. But I know what you really are!"

"Come," Gilgamesh said.

"Before Adam ever was," Herod said fiercely to the Hairy Man, "you ran naked in the forests, and lived in holes in the ground, and knew no gods or language or civilization, and ate worms and grubs and leaves. Talk about savages! We know what your kind was. Savage is too polite a word. Let me tell you something: You people are just here on a technicality. Hell is for humans. If we have a few of you grunting ape-men here, too, well, that's just somebody twisting the rules a little. Maybe certain starry-eyed New Dead types have fooled themselves into thinking that you're our ancestors, but we both know that that can't be possible. And when you start putting on airs and pretending that you actually are human beings—"

"Enough of this, Herod," Gilgamesh said, more sternly. "Up. Out. Lead me back to the upper city." To the Hairy Man, he said apologetically, "He's just overwrought. The air down here, I suppose—"

"He wants to sell his soul," said the Hairy Man. "The trouble is, he doesn't know where to find it. But I take no offense. I'm as accustomed to being called an ape as you are to explaining where your land used to be. If he needs to think of himself as the crown of Creation, what's that to me? He knows nothing of the life we lived when the gods had not so much as imagined any of you." The Hairy Man laughed and scratched his furry chest. "Ask him, later, what that grease was that the black wizard rubbed into your skin. Not now. Ask him later."

7.

"—human fat?" Gilgamesh said, incredulous.

Herod moved his head in a quick affirmative. They were in Sulla's palace again, by the courtyard fountain.

"But where does he get it?"

"There are plenty of bodies available. Life isn't simply cheap in Hell, you know. It's free for the taking, and who's to say no?"

Gilgamesh knew that well enough. No gods governed this world, and law and order, or the lack of it, was a matter of purely local whim. There were marauding armies everywhere, and freelance bandits, and swaggering bullies, and mere casual random killers. Death was a daily commonplace. But Death here was only an irritating annoyance, a bothersome but brief interruption of the endless ongoingness of your stay in Hell. There were those who had died three times the same week and came bounding back from it each time, apparently unchanged. Somewhere behind the scenes they reconstructed your body from whatever bits and pieces could be found, stuffed your soul back into it, and turned you loose to live again. Not that he had experienced it himself: so far as he could recall, he had died only once in all his thousands of years, and that at the expected time, when his span on Earth had come to its appointed end. But keeping himself from being killed in Hell was only a matter of pride for him. Enkidu had said that of him once, hurling the accusation at him in anger the one time they had quarreled: "Too proud to die. Too proud to accept the decree of the gods—" And Gilgamesh had had to admit to himself that it was true. Because he had been who he had been, he took care to guard himself constantly against attack here, and when he was attacked, he saw to it that his strength or his cunning always would prevail. He would have no man able to boast that he had slain the mighty Gilgamesh. Yet if by some mischance he did someday die again, he was aware that it would not be for long.

Still and all, to be slaughtering people or hauling in the corpses of those slain by others, and oiling one's skin with the grease of them—!

"Does it disgust you?" Herod asked.

Gilgamesh shook his head. "A little. I don't know. It seems displeasing. Who is this Calandola? He said he was a king in Africa. But that means little to me."

"And to me. The Africa we Romans knew was a land of light-skinned folk, just across the water from Rome. He's from deeper down—the dark part of the continent. And of a much later time, they say. He lived by the river Zaire, in the land called Kongo, in the days when the Spaniards and the English and the Portuguese were building empires across the seas."

"Just the day before yesterday, that is to say."

"Yes. His people were known as Jaqqas. Nomads, they were—warriors who would destroy everything that lay in their path, for the sheer love of destruction. There was something almost religious about their fondness for smashing things. Purifying the earth is what they called it."

"And when his army was finished purifying, he'd shine himself up with the fat of the conquered, is that it? A cheerful custom which he takes pleasure in continuing to practice in Hell?"

"Oh, he does worse things than that."

Gilgamesh raised an eyebrow. "Does he?"

"Far worse."

"Such as?"

"Don't ask me to tell you. You'll have to discover the rest for yourself. I'm pledged to reveal nothing. If I break my oath, he'll know right away and cast me out."

"Out of what?"

Herod seemed surprised. "His presence! His fellowship! His—his light!"

Light was an odd term to use, Gilgamesh thought, for one who reigned in darkness and who seemed himself to be the very embodiment of darkness. He stared at Herod in distaste. "You worship him, don't you?"

"That's a bit of an overstatement, I'd say."

"As you wish."

"I'd say that I'm fascinated by him, is all."

"Merely in the way of scholarship?"

"It's more than scholarly," Herod said. "I won't deny that I'm in awe of him. Fascinated to the point of awe, yes. Yes. But so are you. Admit it, Gilgamesh! I was watching you. He's practically as big as you are, and maybe just as strong as you are, and there's something about him—something mysterious and powerful—that draws you in, just as he's drawn in everyone else who ever came near him. Admit it! Admit it, Gilgamesh!"

Herod's high-pitched voice had taken on that buzzing intensity again, and for a moment Gilgamesh had to struggle to keep from swatting him. There were, Gilgamesh had heard, certain poor souls in Hell who had been given the forms of strange insects when they were reborn here, instead of bodies of their own. Well, Herod's body certainly seemed human enough, but it was as if there was something of the insect about him as well. A wasp, a fly, a gnat. He was certainly infuriating.

And this fascination that Herod claimed to feel for Calandola. This awe. There was something sick about it—weak, submissive, ugly. Clearly the black man emanated some magical force that Herod had allowed completely to seize possession of him. Gilgamesh understood now why he had taken so quick a dislike to Herod. The man was looking for some power greater than himself to which he could surrender everything: his identity, his soul, his entire self. If not Sulla, then the volcano. If not the volcano, then Calandola. Gilgamesh had never been able to understand the value of surrender of any sort, and certainly he had never held much regard for those who went about searching for it.

"He may be able to see through the mists," Gilgamesh said, "and tell me where Enkidu has gone. That's where my interest in your Lord Calandola begins and ends."

"Not true! Not true! But you won't own up to it."

"You tax my patience, Herod."

"You don't find him—attractive?"

"Attractive? Not in the least. 'Repellent' is the word I'd use."

"I wish I could believe that."

"Do you tell me that I'm lying?" asked Gilgamesh ominously.

"I tell you that you may be hiding things even from yourself," said Herod. "Oh, perhaps not! Perhaps not!" he added quickly, as Gilgamesh glared.

"Oiled in the fat of the dead! I never heard of such a thing in any land, not even the most barbarous. It is a monstrous thing to do, Herod."

"All right, so he's a monster. But won't you at least agree that he's a glorious monster? Larger than life, a monster of monsters. Oh, how my grandfather Herod would have loved him! So big, so dark. Those diabolical eyes. The way his skin is all carved up and covered with bumps and welts. And those four teeth knocked out to make him look prettier—the way he shines in the darkness, that gleam that he has—"

That gleam, Gilgamesh thought somberly. Yes.

"A monster, no question of that. I'm not so sure about glorious. The Hairy Man speaks the truth: your Calandola's a savage."

"Of course he is," Herod said at once. "That's what's so wonderful about him! A marvelous, overwhelming, hideous, ghastly, frightful savage! But he's a seer, too. You mustn't overlook the reality of his powers. You'll find out. He can open the darkness for you. He'll do the rite of the Knowing with you. And whatever questions you have will be answered."

"Ah, and will they be?"

"Have no doubt of that, Gilgamesh. None at all. All that is secret will be laid bare."

Gilgamesh pondered that. Opening the darkness? The rite of the Knowing? A half-naked savage with a piece of copper thrust through his nose, laying bare

all that is secret? Well, maybe. Maybe. The only
thing that was certain in Hell was the absolute strangeness of it. What had been invisible on Earth, or
nearly so, was made manifest here. On Earth one
sometimes caught glimpses of demons out of the
corner of one's eye; here, they sat down and played
at dice with you, or sprawled by the fireside in a
tavern, singing curious songs. Witchcraft was everywhere. Gilgamesh had no reason to doubt this
Calandola's powers of divination. And if covering
one's skin with loathsome grease was the price of
finding the path to Enkidu, well, that was not too
high a price to pay. No price would be too high for
that.

At the far side of the courtyard, Sulla and his
Hairy Man appeared. The dictator beckoned.

"Gilgamesh! Where have you been?"

The Sumerian answered only with a shrug.

"Will you be at the party tonight?" Sulla called.

"Party?"

"After the games! Women, Gilgamesh! Wine! Rivers of wine! Don't forget!"

"Yes," Gilgamesh said, without enthusiasm. "Of
course." Rivers of wine? Wine meant nothing to him
now. The image of the Jaqqa Imbe Calandola rose up
in his mind, soaring like a colossus above him, and
then he had a sudden, startling view of himself swimming desperately against a terrible current, in a river
not of wine but of blood.

8.

"Take," Calandola said. "Drink."

For a second time Gilgamesh, led by a tense and
apprehensive Herod Agrippa, had gone down into

the tunnels below Pompeii. For a second time they had penetrated the torchlit chamber that was the lair of Imbe Calandola and his Jaqqa minions. And for a second time the black wizard-king had offered Gilgamesh the sweet wine and had rubbed his body with the oil of dread origin.

Now some further, deeper rite was about to commence. The room was more crowded than it had been the other time. There seemed to be even more Jaqqas than before—a great, shadowy crew of them, thirty or forty or even more—stalking like long-legged goblins through the dim, smoky recesses of the cavern performing tasks that not even Gilgamesh's keen vision could clearly perceive. But also there were eight or ten or a dozen other figures in white Pompeiian garb, men and women, kneeling in the center of the room like acolytes, initiates. Some of them were masked with strips of black cloth and others had their faces bared. Like Herod, they seemed uneasy: their pale faces were glistening with perspiration and their eyes flickered constantly from side to side. Often during the rite of the wine and the oil they stared at Gilgamesh with great intensity, and sometimes with a strange expression that might have been loathing and fear, or perhaps pity and sorrow: he could not tell. It might even have been envy. Envy? For what? He felt like one who was about to be sacrificed to an unknown god.

From the depths of the room came music. The Jaqqas were playing fifes that made an ear-piercing, shrieking sound, beating on drums fashioned from the scaly hides of demon-beasts, and tapping their fingers against thin boards mounted on wooden stakes. Four of the women came dancing across the room in wild, cavorting, prancing leaps, their oiled breasts bobbling, their gap-toothed mouths wide open in frozen grimaces. Calandola himself, shining and immense, sat astride a small, three-legged stool intricately carved with the faces of demons and rocked back and forth, bellowing in pleasure.

Then he rose and signalled, and two of the Pompeiian acolytes sprang to their feet—a man and woman. Out of the darkness of the cavern's strange-angled corners the man brought a crook-necked flask and the woman fetched a tasseled red pillow on which there rested a cup of strange design, wide and shallow.

The music rose to a feverish, frantic pitch. To Gilgamesh, all music was irritating noise, save only the delicate flute-music and the light and lively drumming of Sumer, which he had not had the joy of hearing in five thousand years. But this Jaqqa stuff was a noise beyond noise: it was a thunder that thrust itself inside you and occupied all the space that there was within you, so that it threatened to evict your own soul from its housing.

"This is the royal wine," said Calandola in a voice like the dark rumbling of a bear. "It will make the first Opening for you—the Opening that comes before the Knowing. Are you prepared, King Gilgamesh?"

"Give me your wine."

"First your dog, and then you."

"The dog?"

"First the dog," Calandola said again.

"Very well," said Gilgamesh. This was all madness to him, but he saw none of it as any madder than any other part. The dog? Why not the dog? "If the dog is willing, give the dog the royal wine."

Calandola made a brusque signal with three fingers of his left hand. The woman holding the pillowed cup knelt; the man poured the royal wine from the crook-necked flask.

When the cup was full she turned toward Ajax.

The dog uttered a growling sound, but not, so it seemed, in any angry way. He looked up at Gilgamesh, and there was an unmistakable questioning in his eyes.

Gilgamesh shrugged. "You are to go first," he said. "That is what I have been told. Drink, Ajax. If you will."

The room grew hushed. The dog drank, lapping quickly at the bowl, wagging his tail, making little snuffling sounds: the royal wine appeared to please him. Gilgamesh had never known a dog to drink wine. But Ajax was a dog of Hell. There was no reason why the dogs of Hell could not drink wine, or fly through the air, or do any number of other unnatural things. Hell was not a natural place.

At length Calandola signalled again, and the woman withdrew the cup from Ajax. The dog remained motionless. His eyes seemed strange: unmoving and, so it appeared, glowing.

Gilgamesh reached now for the cup.

"No," Calandola said. "Not yet. Your other dog first."

"I have but one dog."

"This one," said the Jaqqa, and pointed with his foot at Herod.

The Judaean prince looked astounded. He had been kneeling beside the other acolytes. Now he rose, shaking his head in disbelief, tapping his breast as though to say, "Me? *Me?*" Calandola pointed a second time, making a contemptuous hooking gesture with his outstretched foot to draw Herod forward. Gilgamesh thought the little man would topple over before he had managed to take five steps. But somehow he stayed upright long enough to approach the cup-bearer. She proffered the pillow. He took the cup from it, resting it in both his hands and putting his face down and forward, practically into the cup. In long sighing gulps he drank it dry. Then he swayed and shook. The cup-bearer seized the cup before he could drop it. Herod backed away, wearing now the same glazed look in his eyes that the dog Ajax did, and took up his kneeling position once more.

This time Gilgamesh waited to see whether there were any more dogs in the room. But no: at last it was his turn to taste the royal wine.

The man with the crook-necked flask poured. The woman who held the pillow carried the cup to the Sumerian.

"Take," said Calandola. "Drink."

Gilgamesh lifted the bowl as Herod had done, in both his hands. It was cool and smooth, like fine ivory, but irregular of shape beneath. As he stared down into it he ran his fingers over its undersurface and came to realize what sort of thing it was that he held in his hands: beyond any question a human skullcap, with the parts below the eyesockets cut away. Very well, he thought. We drink here from a polished skullcap. Why not? He was beginning to understand Lord Calandola's style of doing things. A skullcap is well suited to be a cup. Why not? Why not?

The wine was dark—not honey-colored like the other stuff, but tinged with red. He took a sip. There was an overpowering sweetness to it: a sweetness like that of the sweetest nectar, or perhaps even more intense. It lay strangely on his tongue, a heavy, thick-textured wine. He swallowed it and took another, and suddenly he knew what it was that gave the wine its sweetness, and what tinged it with red. This royal wine of Imbe Calandola's was a wine made of blood. Knowing that, he thought his stomach might rebel at it, and hurl it back. But no. No, it slipped down smoothly enough. He had some more.

He drank until the cup was empty, looked up, smiled, and handed it back to its bearer.

And waited.

The Opening, this was. That comes before the Knowing.

Well? Why was nothing happening? Why had his eyes not gone glassy, as had the dog's, as had Herod's? Why was he not swaying? Why not dizzy? Was he immune to Calandola's monstrous wine? Was he so lost within the walls of his own self that there could be no Opening for him?

He looked toward Calandola. "There is no effect," he said. "Perhaps another draught of your wine, Lord Calandola—"

Calandola laughed—a strangely drawn-out laugh that sounded thin and far away, and came cascading down over Gilgamesh like the tumbling of a waterfall. He made no other reply.

Then came a weird droning voice from somewhere to his left, saying, "Alas, alas, you fall in error, world-striding Gilgamesh! No further wine do you need! The walls are down! The Opening is at hand!"

"What? What?"

"See me revealed! My previous self is what you behold."

The Sumerian gasped. Ajax had disappeared, and in his place a bizarre creature fluttered midway between the floor and the level of Gilgamesh's shoulders. It was something like a wasp, but larger than any insect Gilgamesh had ever seen, and covered with a shining blue incrustation almost like some precious stone. From its rear jutted a cruel-looking green stinger, and its tiny face was the face of a human woman. It buzzed and beat its wings as it hovered beside him.

"You see?" the wasp-woman cried. "In the Opening, much is shown! In my last life I was this, who am come back into Hell now as Ajax the dog."

"Your—last life—"

"As insect, yes. though even before that did I have human flesh, the same as you. Yet I gave self up to sin, and down I was forced to slip. For my penance was I made insect and greatly did I suffer. But then in later times, for loyal service, was I granted dog. You see, it is down the ladder and then sometimes up again. I still aspire, beyond dog. I rise again, and be better than dog. Though dog is good. When one has known insect, dog seems good."

Ah. That was it. Gilgamesh understood. His dog Ajax, then, was one of those unfortunates whose fate it was to drift from body to body, from form to form, during their eternal stay in Hell. So it seemed Calandola's wine was doing some work, if he was able to see such things as this. Yes, he was sure now: an Opening of some sort had been achieved, and he was perceiving things beyond the ordinary realm of perception.

"Indeed, dog is good," the wasp-woman was saying. "To have King Gilgamesh as my master is good. I follow the mighty Gilgamesh and he will take mercy on me some day and put me into a woman-body again. Or even a man-body. What does it matter, man or woman, if only human? Human I would be again, as who would not?"

Gilgamesh smiled. "If I can, I will," he said.

Instantly the wasp was a dog again, and Ajax lay flattened by his feet, nuzzling close.

Gilgamesh bent and stroked the beast fondly. Then he rose and turned toward Herod.

"And what of you?" asked Gilgamesh. "You, wasp in human form, what shape do you present now?"

But no outward change had come over Herod under the influence of Calandola's drink. Herod was still Herod—a small, bushy-haired, quick-eyed man wearing a rumpled white toga, slumped in a kneeling position halfway across the chamber. Yet something was different now. The Herod whom Gilgamesh had come to know in these few days in Pompeii was a man of tricks and chatter, fast and flashy of mind, forever swiftly weaving a web of words about himself to keep bigger and more stupid foes at bay. It was a defense that must have served him well in his centuries in Hell, but now it seemed that the royal wine of the Jaqqa king had stripped all that away from him.

Herod was wide open, defenseless: a sad, frightened, dependent man who was spending the years of his death as he had spent the years of his life, searching for a master. Once it had been the Roman Emperor Caligula, who had turned him briefly into a king. Later—much later, here in Hell—it had been Sulla. Now it was this monstrous, overbearing creature of darkness, Calandola. It could just as well be Gilgamesh next. Or Che Guevara, or Mao Tse-tung, or Prester John, or any of the million million other emperors and princes and demigods and warlords who had set themselves up to rule some little corner of this vast and unknowable realm that was called Hell. Herod needed a master. He would probably be happier as a dog: if only he and Ajax could trade bodies somehow! Look at him, sitting there half slumped—wishing he had a tail to wag, wishing he had soft, brown, worshipful eyes that he could turn lovingly upon his master, instead of those beady, clever ones of his.

Gilgamesh felt a surge of scorn for Herod, that pitiful and most unkingly king.

But the scorn was short-lived. It melted at once and gave way to a deep sense of compassion that swept through Gilgamesh with unexpected force and left him shaken and weak. How could he feel kindness for the dog who had been a wasp and yearned to be a human again, and not for this human whose soul was the soul of a dog? To despise Herod because he was no hero was itself a despicable thing. There was no shortage of heroes in Hell. By the thousands and tens of thousands they swaggered about, replaying in death the dramas they had chosen in life. And if Herod—poor, miserable little Herod—could manage nothing better than to find the joy of his life in the shattering outbursts of a volcano and in the barbaric blood-feasts of a nightmare savage, why, it was because he was who he was. He had no choice. No one had any choice. The gods decreed everything.

You, Gilgamesh: you will be a hero of heroes, a man like a god, a king among kings. And it will be your doom to die nevertheless, and to live forever in Hell.

You, Enkidu: you will be a bold hunter and warrior, friend to the great king. And it will be your doom to die again and again, while the king your friend seeks you through all the halls of eternity.

You, Herod: you will be clever and cautious, a mouse in a world of lions. And you will have wit enough to deceive them all and keep your throne and your life, no matter how terrifying the risks of power may be to you.

We are who we are, all of us. The gods determine. We play the parts assigned. Why, then, feel contempt for those who play parts unlike our own? Herod, Publius Sulla, Calandola, the Hairy Man, the little scheming quarrelsome New Dead folk, and all the rest—each was playing his proper part, each was fulfilling the decree of the gods. And each was in his own way the hero of his own drama, doing as it seemed fit for him to do. How could anyone be condemned for that?

Gilgamesh went to Herod's side and bent down to take him by the arm.

"Up," he said gently. "No more crouching, here. You are a man. Stand up like a man."

"Gilgamesh—"

"There's nothing to fear. I am your friend. I will protect you against whatever it is that you fear."

But even as he spoke the words, Gilgamesh realized that the spell was breaking, became aware that the power of the wine was slipping from him. The warmth and tenderness he felt for Herod fell away. The irritation and scorn returned. This sad, weak man: why offer to protect him? What was Herod to him? Let him fend off his demons for himself. Let him grovel before Calandola. Let him dance on the rim of the crater of Vesuvius and throw himself into the volcano's boiling heart, if that was where he thought the true home of joy was to be found. Gilgamesh looked down at Herod and shook his head, released his hold on Herod's arm, and turned away.

"Well, then, it seems to be over," said Calandola, his voice coming as though from a great distance.

Gilgamesh stood blinking and baffled like one who has stepped from midnight darkness into the full noonday blaze of the sun.

"That was it?" he asked. "The Opening?"

"When other souls stand bare before you, yes, that is the Opening, King Gilgamesh."

"And what now? Now the Knowing?"

"No," said Calandola. "Another time. You resisted

the wine; you achieved only a partial Opening. Your soul is a stubborn one. It will not yield to forces from outside. Come back another time, King Gilgamesh, and then we will see if you are strong enough to accomplish the Knowing."

9.

"What did I do wrong?" Gilgamesh asked. "Where did I fail?"

"You held back," said Herod. "You were nearly there, and then, at the last moment, you held back. When the Opening begins, it's necessary to surrender completely to it. You were fighting it."

"Fighting is in my nature. Surrender isn't."

"Do you want the Knowing or don't you?"

"I thought I was yielding to the wine," Gilgamesh said. "I entered the soul of the dog. I saw what he had been in his last life. A wasp-creature, do you know that? With a woman's face and the body of some hideous insect. And then I turned to you—I saw your soul, Herod. I saw the true self within you. I—"

"All right. I don't need to hear about it."

"I saw nothing that would shame you."

"Thanks all the same, but I'd rather not know."

"It was as if the walls that separate us from each other had broken down. And then—then they were up again. The wine had worn off. Maybe if I had taken more—"

"Maybe," Herod said. "You're so damned big. Maybe Calandola misjudged the quantity. But he's been doing this for centuries. He knows what quantity is right. I think it's you, Gilgamesh. You held back. You kept some part of yourself in reserve. I can understand that. But if you want to learn the answers to your questions—if you hope to discover where Enkidu has gone—"

"Yes. I know."

"Calandola may not allow you to return to him for a week, or even a month. But when he summons you, go. And whatever he asks of you, do it. Or there'll be no Knowing for you. Eh, Gilgamesh?"

"What are you two chattering about?" Sulla asked, appearing suddenly beside them. "Hatching a good conspiracy?" The dictator, grinning, clapped one hand to Gilgamesh's broad back and one to Herod's. "It's useless, you know. I have seers who tell me everything. Past, present, and future lie revealed to them. the slightest hint of subversion here will show up instantly as a blip on their screens."

"No need to fear," Gilgamesh said. "I think Herod prefers being prime minister here to any higher responsibility. And surely you know that to rule in Pompeii is not a thing that I desire either, Sulla."

"I know what you desire, Gilgamesh. Come to me this time two days hence, and we'll study the map of Uruk together. We should be thinking of setting forth soon. What do you say, Gilgamesh? King of Uruk that was, King of Uruk that will be! How does that sound to you?"

"Like music," said Gilgamesh.

Publius Sulla laughed and moved on.

Herod, looking troubled, said when the dictator was out of sight, "Is that true? You do want to be king of Uruk again after all?"

"I said Sulla's words were like music to me."

"So you did."

Gilgamesh chuckled. "But I am no lover of music."

"Ah. Ah."

"And as for the journey to Uruk—well, let's see

what wisdom your great Calandola can offer me,
first. When we do the true Opening. And the Knowing that follows it. And then I'll comprehend whether
I am to make this journey or not. Let's wait and see,
King Herod. Let's wait and see."

10.

The room of angles in the cavern of the tunnels.
The smoldering torches in the brazen sconces. The
drums, the fifes, the masks, the dancers. The long-
legged black men pursuing unknown rituals in the
shadows. The honeyed wine, the shining oil. This
was Gilgamesh's third visit to the dwelling place of
Imbe Calandola. Once more now he would under-
take to make the Opening; once more he would
drink of the second and stronger wine, the thick,
sweet, red beverage. Once more he would see beyond
the barriers that divide soul from soul, and this time,
perhaps, all the veils of mystery would be stripped
away and he would be allowed to know the things he
had come here to learn.

"I think you are ready," Calandola said. "For the
deeper feast. For the full Knowing."

"Bring me the wine, yes," said Gilgamesh.

"It will not only be wine today," replied Calandola.

In the darkness, chanting and drums. Fires flickering behind the Imbe-Jaqqa's throne. Figures moving
about. A sound that might have been that of water
boiling in a great kettle.

A signal from Calandola.

The bearer of the wine came forth, and the bearer
of the cup. Ajax once again drank first, and then
Herod, and then Gilgamesh. But this time Calandola
drank also, and drank deep, again and again calling

for the cup to be filled, until his lips and jowls were smeared with red.

"Belial and Beelzebub," Herod whispered. "Moloch and Lucifer!"

Gilgamesh felt the strangeness of the Opening settling upon him once more. He could recognize its signs now: an eerie hush, a heightened awareness. Invisible beings brushed past him in the air. There was a deep humming sound that seemed to come from the core of the world. He could touch the souls of Ajax the dog and Herod the Jew; and now there was the formidable presence of black Calandola also revealed to him. Revealed and not revealed, for although Gilgamesh saw the inwardness of Calandola, it was like a huge black wall of rock rising before him, impenetrable, unscalable.

"Now will you join our feast," said Calandola. "And the Knowing will descend upon you, King Gilgamesh."

He threw back his head and laughed, and made a gesture with his massive arms like the toppling of two mighty trees. From the musicians came a crashing of sounds—a terrible thunder and a screeching. The throne was drawn aside, and a great metal cauldron stood revealed, bubbling over a raging fire of logs.

Calandola's minions were preparing a rich and robust stew.

Into the cauldron went onions and leeks and peppers, beans and squash, pomegranates and grapes, vegetables and fruits of every sort imaginable. The steaming vessel seemed bottomless. Ears of corn and sacks of figs, huge gnarled tuberous roots of this kind and that, most of them unknown to Gilgamesh. Clusters of garlic, double handfuls of radishes, slabs of whole ginger. A barrel of dark wine, of what sort Gilgamesh dared not think. Spices of fifty kinds. And meat. Massive chunks of pale, raw meat, flung in whole, still on the bone.

A troublesome feeling stirred in Gilgamesh. To Herod he said, "What meat is that, do you think?"

Herod was gazing at the cauldron with unblinking eyes. He laughed in an oddly nervous way and said, "One that is not kosher, I would suspect."

"Kosher? What is that?"

But Herod made no answer. A shiver ran through him that made his whole body ripple like a slender tree beset by the wild autumn gales. His face was aglow with the brightness that Gilgamesh had seen in it that time when the volcano had erupted. Herod had the look of one who was held tight in the grip of some powerful enchantment.

By the virtue of the dark wine they had shared, Gilgamesh looked into Herod's soul. What he saw there made him recoil in amazement and shock.

"*That* meat?"

"They say there is no better one for this purpose, King Gilgamesh."

His stomach twisted and turned.

He had eaten many strange things in many strange lands. But never this. To devour the flesh of his own kind—

No. No. No. No. Not even in Hell.

Gilgamesh had heard tales, now and then, of certain races in remote parts of the world that did such things—not for nourishment's sake, but for magic. To take into themselves the strength or the wisdom or the mystical virtue of others. It had been hard for him to believe that such things were done.

But to be asked to do it himself—

"Unthinkable. Forbidden. Abominable."

"Forbidden by whom?" asked Herod.

"Why—by—"

Gilgamesh faltered and could say no more.

"We are in Hell, King Gilgamesh. Nothing is forbidden here. Have you forgotten that?"

Gilgamesh stared. "And you truly mean to commit this abomination? You want me to commit it with you?"

"I want nothing from you," Herod said. "But you are here in search of knowledge."

"Which is obtained like *this*?"

Herod smiled. "So it is said. It is the gateway, the way of the full Opening that leads to the Knowing."

"And you believe this insanity?"

The Judaean prince turned to face him, and there was a look of terrible conviction in his eyes.

"Do as you please, King Gilgamesh. But if you would have the knowledge, take and eat. Take and eat."

"Take and eat!" came the booming voice of Calandola. "Take and eat!"

The cannibal tribesmen leaped and danced. One who was whitened with chalk from head to toe and wore straw garments that seemed to be the costume of a witch rushed to the cauldron, pulled a joint of meat from the boiling water with his bare hands, held it aloft.

"Ayayya! Ayayya!" the Jaqqas cried. "Ayayya!"

The witch brought the meat to Calandola and held it forth to him for his inspection. From Calandola came a roar of approval. He seized the joint with both his hands, put his jaws to it, and buried his teeth in it.

"Ayayya! Ayayya!" cried the Jaqqas.

Gilgamesh felt the wine of the cannibals flowing through his soul. He swayed in rhythm to the harsh and savage music. Beside him, Herod now seemed wholly transported, lost in an ecstasy, caught up entirely in the fascination of this abomination. As though he had waited all his life and through his life after life as well to make this surrender to Calandola's foul mystery. Or as though he had no choice but to be swept along into it, wherever it might take him.

And I feel myself swept along also, thought Gilgamesh in shock and amazement.

"Take," said Calandola. "Eat."

Joyously he held the great slab of steaming meat out toward Gilgamesh.

Gods! Enlil and Enki and Sky-father An, what is this I am doing?

The gods were very far from this place, though. Gilgamesh stared at the slab of meat.

"This is the way of Knowing," said Calandola.

This?

No. No. No. No.

He shook his head. "There are some things I will not do, even to have the Knowing."

The aroma from the kettle mixed with some strange incense burning in great braziers alongside it, and he felt himself swaying in mounting dizziness. Turning, he took three clumsy, shambling steps toward the entrance. Acolytes and initiates drew back, making way for him as he lumbered past. He heard Calandola's rolling, resonant laughter behind him, mocking him for his cowardice.

Then Herod was in his path, blocking him. The little man was drawn tight as a bow: trembling, quivering.

Huskily he said, "Don't go, Gilgamesh."

"This is no place for me."

"The Knowing—what about the Knowing—"

"No."

"If you try to leave, you'll never find your way out of the tunnels without me."

"I'll take my chances."

"Please," said Herod. "*Please*. Stay. Wait. Take the Sacrament with me."

"The Sacrament? You call this a Sacrament?"

"It is the way of Knowing. Take it with me. For me. Don't spurn it. Don't spurn me. We are already halfway there, Gilgamesh: the wine is in our souls, our spirits are opening to each other. Now comes the Knowing. Please. Please."

He had never seen such an imploring look on another human being's face. Not even in battle, when he raised his axe above a foe to deliver the fatal stroke. Herod reached his hands toward Gilgamesh. The Sumerian hesitated.

"And I ask you, too," came a voice from his left. "Not to depart. Not to abandon loyal friends."

Ajax.

The dog was flickering like the shadows cast by a fire on a wall: now the great brindle hound, now the strange little wasp-woman, and now, for only a moment, a hint of a human shape—a sad-eyed woman smiling timidly, forlornly.

"If you take the meat you can set me free," said the dog. "Reach into soul, separate dog and spirit. You would have the power. Send poor suffering soul on to next sphere, leave dog behind to be dog. I beg you, mighty king."

Gilgamesh stared, wavering. The dog's pleas moved him deeply.

"Your friends, great hero. Forget not your friends in this time of savioring. Long enslavement must end! You alone can give freedom!"

"Is this true?" Gilgamesh asked Herod.

"It could be. The rite releases much power to those who have power within them."

"Forget not your friends," the wasp-woman cried again.

For a moment Gilgamesh closed his eyes, trying to shut out all the frenzied madness about him. And a voice within him said, *Do it. Do it.*

Why not? Why not? Why not?

This is Hell, nor is there any leaving of it.

He crossed the room to Calandola, who still held the meat. The cannibal chieftain grinned ferociously at Gilgamesh, who met his fiery gaze calmly and took the meat from him. Held it a moment. It was warm and tender—a fine cut, a succulent piece. Out of the buried places of his mind came words he had been taught five thousand years before, that time in his youth when he was newly a king and he had knelt before the priests in Uruk on the night of the rite of the Sacred Marriage:

> *What seems good to oneself*
> *is a crime before the god.*
> *What to one's heart seems evil*
> *is good before one's god.*
> *Who can comprehend the minds of gods*
> *in heaven's depths?*

"Take," Herod whispered. "Eat!"

Yes, Gilgamesh thought. This is the way. He lifted the slab of meat to his lips.

"Ayayya! Ayayya! Ayayya!"

He bit down deep, and savored, and swallowed, and from the volcano Vesuvius, somewhere not far away, there came a tremendous roar, and the earth shook. And as he tasted the forbidden flesh, the Knowing entered into him in that moment.

It was like becoming a god. All things lay open to

him, or so it seemed. Nothing was hidden. His soul soared; he looked down on all of space and time.

"Your friends, Gilgamesh," came a whispering voice from high overhead. "Do not forget—your friends—"

No. He would not forget.

He sent forth his soul into the dog that was the wasp-woman that once had been a human sinner. Without difficulty he distinguished the human soul from the dog-soul and the wasp-soul, separated the one from the others, and held it a moment, then released it like a bird that one holds in one's hand and casts into the sky. There was a long sigh of gratitude, and then the wandering soul was gone. Ajax the dog lay curled sleeping at Gilgamesh's feet, and of the wasp-creature there was no sign.

To Herod then he turned. Saw the sadness within the man, the weakness, the hunger. Saw too the quick, agile mind, the warm spirit eager to please. And Gilgamesh touched Herod within, only for an instant, letting something of himself travel across the short distance from soul to soul. A touch of strength; a touch of resilience. *Here,* he thought. *Take this from me, and hold something of myself within you, for those times when being yourself is not enough for you.*

Herod seemed to glow. He smiled, he wept, he bowed his head. And knelt and offered a blessing of thanks.

Gilgamesh could feel the presence of monstrous Calandola looming over him like a titan. Like a god. And yet he seemed no longer malevolent. Distant, dispassionate, aloof: serving only as a focus for this strange rite of the joining of souls.

"Seek your own Knowing now, Gilgamesh," said the Jaqqa. "The time has come."

Yes. Yes. The time has come. Now—Enkidu—?

Where?

Ah: there. There he was, among that contentious pack of fools with whom they had been traveling when they first came into this region of Hell. With an effort Gilgamesh brought their names to mind. There was red-haired Achilles darting here and there; and the woman, the beautiful sorceress, who was called Tanya Burke; and the black-clad man with the gun was Nichols; and the other one, Welch, whose hair was cut as short as stubble. New Dead, all of them except Achilles, who might as well have been one of them himself, since he had adopted all their ways—the guns and the helicopters and the cheap, coarse language and the cheap, coarse way of thinking that those modern people had. Why was Enkidu with them? Why, because he was their prisoner. Yes. Nichols's gun was trained on Enkidu's chest. They were in a gulley somewhere on the mainland—a steep ravine—and the helicopter was damaged. It must have landed badly—it was tipped up on one side and smoke was coming from it. Enkidu? Enkidu? Gilgamesh felt tears crowding into his eyes at the sight of his friend, his brother, held captive by these tawdry people. Enkidu was squatting down, studying them, seemingly held in spell by that golden-haired woman's beauty. Gilgamesh knew how a woman could bind Enkidu that way. But also he knew that that squatting posture of Enkidu's, knew that it was his way of gathering strength and force, that he was waiting, tightening himself like a coiling spring—

Rising suddenly—lunging, darting for freedom—

"Enkidu! No!" Gilgamesh cried.

But it was like crying out within a dream. He could do nothing. He was not a god, and this vision, he knew, was sealed already into the irremediable past. Enkidu, rushing toward the edge of the ravine. Nich-

ols raising the gun, aiming and firing almost in the
same instant. Enkidu lurching, staggering, falling—
Falling—
Then there was only nothingness where Enkidu
had been. His spirit had been swept away to that
mysterious place of reassignment, where he would
wait in limbo until it was his turn to be given flesh
and breath again, and be sent forth into the death-in-
life of Hell.

"Where will I find him?" Gilgamesh asked.

And a voice replied, "You must seek him in Uruk
of the treasures."

Fiercely, Gilgamesh shook his head. "There is no
Uruk!"

"No? No? Are you sure, King Gilgamesh? Is that
what the Knowing tells you?"

"Why—"

He looked. And saw. And the veils of memory
dropped away.

Uruk!

It lay glittering upon the breast of a broad, dark
plain—a white city bright as a jewel. There was the
platform of the temples. There were the sacred buildings. There were the ceremonial streets. Uruk. Not
the Uruk where he had been born and been king and
died, but that other Uruk—New Uruk, the Uruk of
Hell. That great Uruk which he—

—had founded—

—had ruled for a hundred years, or was it a
thousand—

—he—he—a king in Hell—

The Knowing came upon him like a torrent. Why
had he thought he was an exception to the rule that
the heroes in Hell must recapitulate the struggles of
their lifetimes? How had he deceived himself into
thinking that he and Enkidu had spent all their thou-

sands of years in Hell merely wandering, and hunting, and wandering again, shunning the ambitions
that raged like fire in the rest? Of course he had
sought to reign in Hell. Of course he had brought
followers together here once upon a time, and built a
city, and made it magnificent, and defended it against
all attack. How could he not have done such a thing?
For was he not Gilgamesh the king?

And then—then—

Then to forget—

He understood now. Memory was tricky in Hell.
Whole centuries might collapse into a single moment, and be forgotten. Whole empires might rise
and fall and go unremembered. There was no history
here. There was really no past—only a stew of
events that did not form a pattern. And there was no
future, and scarcely any present, either.

In Hell everything is flux and change, though beneath the flux nothing ever changes. He had truly
thought the lust for power had been burned out of
him by time. Perhaps it had. But there was no
longer any denying the things he had so long been
able to hide even from himself. He knew now why
all those little men engaged in conspiracies and revo-
lutions and the other trips of power here in Hell.
Without striving, what is there to keep one from
going mad in this eternity? He had put striving behind him, or so he thought. Perhaps. Perhaps. But
perhaps he was not entirely done with it yet.

He stood stunned and gaping in the midst of
Calandola's terrible feast. Within him blazed the
forbidden food that had opened his eyes.

Enkidu dead. Uruk real. Himself not yet entirely
immune to the craving for power.

Now I have had the Knowing, Gilgamesh thought.
Enkidu is gone from me once more. And I have

been a king in Hell. He dropped to his knees, covered his face with his hands, and let great sobs of mourning rip through his body. But whether it was for Enkidu that he mourned, or for himself, he could not say.

11.

"So soon?" Sulla asked. "What's your hurry? We need time to plan things properly."

"I mean to set out for Uruk in five days or less," said Gilgamesh. "You may come with me or not, as you please. I have my bow. I have my dog. I am well accustomed to traveling by myself through the wilderness."

Sulla looked mystified. "Just a day or two ago I had my doubts that you wanted to go to Uruk at all. You didn't even seem to believe the place was there. And now—now you can't wait to get started. What happened that turned you around so fast?"

"Does it matter?" Gilgamesh asked.

"It's your friend Enkidu, isn't it? Some wizard here has told you that he's waiting for you in Uruk. Am I right?"

"Enkidu is dead," said Gilgamesh.

"But he'll be reassigned to Uruk. By the time you get there, he'll be waiting. Right?"

"It could be."

"Then there's no hurry. He'll be there when you get there. Whenever that is. Relax, Gilgamesh. Let's organize this thing the right way. Picked men, decent equipment, give the Land Rovers a good tuneup—"

"You do those things. I don't plan to wait around."

Sulla sighed. "Rush, hurry, go off half-cocked, never

stop to think anything through! It's not my style. I didn't think it was yours. I thought you were different from all the other dumb heroes."

"So did I," said Gilgamesh.

"Ten days?" Sulla said.

"Five."

"Be merciful, Gilgamesh. Eight days is the soonest. I have responsibilities here. I have to draw up a schedule for my viceroy. And there are decrees to sign, material to requisition—"

"Eight days, then," said Gilgamesh. "Not nine."

"Eight days," said Sulla.

Gilgamesh nodded and went out. Herod was waiting in the hall, cowering by the door, probably eavesdropping. Almost certainly eavesdropping. He looked up, his eyes not quite meeting those of Gilgamesh. Since the last visit to the cavern of Calandola, Herod had been remote, furtive, withdrawn, as though unable to face the recollection of the terrible rite he had led Gilgamesh into.

"You heard?" Gilgamesh asked.

"Heard what?"

"We leave for Uruk, Sulla and I. In eight days."

"Yes," Herod said. "I know."

"You'll have to be in charge here, I think. I'm sorry about that."

"Don't be."

"You didn't want this to happen."

"I didn't want to be in charge, no. But I won't be. So there's no problem."

"If you aren't going to do the work, who will?"

Herod shrugged. "I don't have any idea. Sulla's Luck, for all I care, or Calandola." He reached out uncertainly toward Gilgamesh, not quite touching his arm. "Take me with you," he said suddenly.

"What?"

"To Uruk. I can't stay here any longer. I'll go with you. Anywhere."

"Are you serious?"

"As serious as I've ever been."

Gilgamesh gave the little man a close, long look. Yes, he did indeed seem to mean it. Leave the comforts and tame terrors of Pompeii, take his chances roaming in the hinterlands of Hell? Yes. Yes, that was what he appeared to want. Maybe the experience in the cavern beneath the city had transformed Herod. It was hard to imagine going through something like that and not coming out transformed. Or perhaps it was simply that sad little Herod had formed one more attachment that he felt unable to break.

"Take me with you," said Herod again.

"The journey will be a harsh one. You've grown accustomed to ease here, Herod."

"I can grow unaccustomed to it. Let me come with you."

"I don't think so."

"You need me, Gilgamesh."

It was all Gilgamesh could do to keep from laughing at that.

"I do?"

"You'll be a king again when you reach Uruk, won't you? Won't you? Yes. You can't hide that from me, Gilgamesh. I was there when you had the Knowing. I had the Knowing, too."

"And if I am?"

"You'll need a fool," Herod said. "Every king needs a fool. Even I had one, when I was a king. But I think somehow I'd do the other job better. Take me along. I don't want to stay in Pompeii. I don't want to visit Calandola's cavern again. I might want another dinner there. Or I might *become* dinner there. Will you take me along with you, Gilgamesh?"

Gilgamesh hesitated, frowned, said nothing.

"Why not?" Herod demanded. "Why not?"

"Yes," Gilgamesh said. "Why not?" His own favorite phrase floating back at him. The great unending *Why Not?* that was Hell.

"Well?" asked Herod.

"Yes," said Gilgamesh again. There was some charm in the idea, he thought. Herod was intelligent, and shrewd besides: a good combination, not overly common. He could be a lively companion, when he wasn't buzzing and chattering. A better companion, very likely, than old wine-guzzling Sulla. And possibly Herod wouldn't buzz and chatter quite so much, while they were on the march, out among the rigors of the back country. It might almost make sense. Yes. Yes. Gilgamesh nodded. He smiled. Yes. "Why not, Herod? Why not?"

THE PRICE OF AN EGG

Alexandra Sokolov

*The widespread impression among the lite-
rati that it's enough to die for your name
to shine on forever has not been confirmed
by practice. Here hundreds of centuries
have elapsed since anyone has peeked into
a library. Alas! you scribblers, the pace of
history is pale and irreversible.*

Palisander Dahlberg, *Memoirs of Old Age*
(published posthumously in 2757 by Crystal
Kremlin)

NIHILIS
Chapter 1
Satan's Work of Annihilation

"In the end Satan destroyed the heaven and the
earth . . .

And Satan said, Let there be darkness, and there was darkness . . .

And Satan called the darkness Day, and the darkness he called Night . . ."

Mikhail Alexandrovich Sholokhov shuddered, put the freshly typed manuscript down, and buzzed for his secretary, Innessa Armand, Lenin's mistress. Sholokhov was still new at this, having been kicked upstairs after he had triumphantly confessed at the Centennial Conference of the Rewriters' Union that he indeed did rewrite *And Quiet Flows the Don* and that his only truly authentic work was *Virgin Soil Upturned*. The initial moment of impressed silence was then followed by a ten-minute standing ovation, after which the Head of the Rewriters' Union, Maxim Gorky, presented Sholokhov with this century's Golden Award for Insurpassable Corruption, Fraud, and Deceit and informed him that the Rewriters were honored to appoint him as Principal Editor of Hellizdat Publications.

"Yes, Comrade Sholokhov?" Innessa's voice spoke to him out of the intercom box.

"What department is this supposed to be in anyway, Fiction or History?"

"I don't know. Let me check. What's the title on that?"

"Well, there's no cover page, and the first thing that looks like a title is Nihilis."

"Hm, well who did it—who's the rewriter?"

Sholokhov shuffled through the first pages, then looked under the manuscript and saw a manila envelope. On it the name Joseph Stalin was written in red. Sholokhov inadvertently jumped back in his chair and swore.

"Jesus Christ, Innessa, it's Stalin! What the Hell is he doing rewriting classics? He's not even an official rewriter!"

"I know, I know, but Gorky lets him do it under his own name. You know he has a soft spot for him, and besides, we all feel sorry for him."

"Sorry?"

"Yeah, even Reassignments won't have anything to do with him. They keep sending him back to us."

"So this is to go under Gorky's name?"

"Yes."

"Well, would you kindly find out what it's called?"

"Yes, Comrade Sholokhov."

Sholokhov turned off the intercom and reached into his briefcase. He pulled out a silver flask and poured himself a shot of brandy. His hands were shaking. He was beginning to find that there was too much responsibility involved in this job, and he longed for the good old days back in the U.S.S.R. when he was a member of the Writers' Union and all he had to do all day was write. After a few shots, Sholokhov buzzed Innessa on the intercom again.

"Yes, Comrade Sholokhov?"

"When's the meeting?" he asked gloomily. He didn't look forward to these daily meetings with the rewriters, each of whom was working on revising, expurgating, and, if necessary, translating a book for the New Hell World Classics Series. There were two departments, History and Fiction, and most of the meeting time was usually spent in arguing over whether or not a given book belonged in Fiction or History.

"At two o'clock, Standard Time," she replied, slightly preoccupied, as if she were in the process of doing her nails or putting on lipstick.

"What's the Local Time?"

"I'm not sure. It hasn't been announced yet."

Standard Time was set, roughly, once a year, whenever New Hell proclaimed it to be New Year. Local

Time was set according to the whims of the latest
Guardian of the Clock of Hell who played Time once
a day, like the lottery, and whatever combination he
rolled out with his die, that was the official Local
New Hell Time of the day. Most bureaucratic institutions were allowed to go by Standard Time; however, most public institutions—bars, cafes, libraries,
and massage parlors—went by Local Time.

Sholokhov buzzed Innessa off and settled back in
his chair for another couple of shots of brandy. He
knew better than to drink on an empty stomach, but
he couldn't stand going to the luncheonette next
door; besides, it was almost always closed by the
time it occurred to him to go there. His direct line
rang, loudly and insistently.

"Hellizdat!" Sholokhov announced in his booming
voice.

There was no sound coming from the other end,
then he heard a shrieking voice say: "What?"

"Hellizdat!" he repeated, patiently.

"What the Hell is that?" the voice on the other
end of the line exclaimed and then broke into a
mocking peal of laughter. Then the anonymous caller
hung up.

"Another goddamned crank call," Sholokhov said
to no one in particular. "Probably that damn Poe
again." He got ready to pour himself another shot,
but then thought better of it. He was already on the
verge of another intestinal attack. The direct line
rang again.

"Look, you crazy coke addict, I've had enough . . ."

"Misha, Mishenka, eto ya," cooed a woman's husky
voice in Russian. It was his wife Masha calling to
inform him that she was on her way to the Black
Market and that she would probably be running late.
"Okay, okay," he said, rubbing the sweat off his face,
"just be careful."

Innessa buzzed him as soon as his wife had hung up: "It's Sartre—says it's urgent."

"Send him in."

Sartre was one of the go-betweens between the rewriters and the actual writers of the classics—those who were in Hell, that is. Rasputin was the other go-between, though he was more formal about it, and called himself a literary agent. The two were arch-enemies and were always making a mess of things, but they were well-paying volunteers and therefore necessary.

The Rewriters' Union and Hellizdat consisted of all those who in real life had ever been at any time members of the Writers' Union of the U.S.S.R. (even if they later denounced it and emigrated West to become members of the more important academies). And both the Rewriters' Union and its publishing house, Hellizdat, had the only permanent positions in Hell. Once a Writers' Union member died, he automatically went to Hell, where he was automatically sent to Rewriters or Hellizdat, and could only be reassigned internally and within that system. Of course, he could die over and over again and go to the Undertaker's Table, but he would always come back to the same place. Their unreassignability was the only advantage the rewriters had over the other damned. The disadvantages were a well-guarded secret, and most of the rewriters were quite adept at parading their punishments as rewards. Their salaries, for example, were fixed for all eternity, going by the maxims of Marxism-Leninism, "to all according to their need." And, as everyone knows, the needs in Hell are quite minimal. Also, the rewriters were doomed to spend the rest of their days in the company of their spouses—wives, that is, being that 99 percent of the rewriters were men. And these

wives were, are, and always will be, as Communist
Party wives are prone to be, the greediest, most
manipulative, venomous, and class-conscious women
of the modern world. So much so that they could put
the old Harpies out of business.

Yet, although the spouses were sent to Hell as
punishments, it was often they who suffered the
most. They could not bear the minimal, fixed salaries
and the fact that in Hell, the rewriters, for all the
airs they put on, were actually in the lower echelons
of the caste system of New Hell—somewhere between blue- and white-collar workers. And so it would
happen that a wife would often consider leaving her
husband, the rewriter, or in any case would threaten
to do so to get what she wanted. For if she did leave
him, he would automatically go to the Undertaker's
Table, where he would undergo innumerable tortures, after which he would be exiled, indefinitely,
to the Land of Nod.

But the rewriters and their wives were so successful
at keeping up pretenses that they were actually be-
sieged constantly by a slew of volunteers who even
paid to work for them (as, for example, Sartre, Rasputin, and Innessa). Others who frequented Hellizdat
were the Founding Fathers themselves—Marx and
Engels, Lenin, Stalin, Brecht, Simone Weil, and a
whole entourage of angry lesbians, homosexuals, fem-
inists, and Gay Rights' Activists who had recently
died of AIDS. In fact, there were so many volunteers
that the rewriters had to depend on the most constant ones to keep track of the growing waiting list
and to make sure that any new volunteer allowed on
the premises had passed the appropriate clearance tests.

There was a knock on the door and a short, ugly
man in a starched Soviet military uniform came in
and saluted.

"Comrade Jean-Paul Sartre, official go-between for Hellizdat, reporting to world renowned and celebrated Satanist-Realist, Rewriter and Principal Editor, Comrade Mikhail Alexandrovich Sholokhov!"

"At ease, Sartre. Now get on with the show. I don't have much time to spare."

Sartre grabbed the nearest chair and settled himself comfortably, letting his legs dangle over the arm of the chair and his manner ease along with his body.

"It's Dante, sir. He won't leave me alone. He wants to know whether or not anyone has started on his *Divine Comedy*."

Sholokhov sighed and began wringing his hands. He reached into his briefcase again for the flask and poured himself another shot. He offered Sartre a drink with a nod of his head, but the latter declined.

"Look, Sartre, I don't know. All I have so far is some unknown manuscript rewritten by a ghost-rewriter. That's all I've seen. No Dante. All the other works are still in progress and you know more than I do where the rewriters stand on them."

Sartre's eyebrows arched slightly at the words 'unknown manuscript' and 'ghost-rewriter.' "Where's this manuscript?" he asked.

Sholokhov put down his shot glass and rummaged through his desk. He dropped the manuscript onto Sartre's lap. After glancing at the first few sentences, Sartre handed it back to Sholokhov. "You mean, you don't know what this is?"

"Should I?" Sholokhov asked, surprised.

"Well, I guess maybe not. It's the Bible. Who's doing it?"

Sholokhov let out a nervous laugh, then picked up his pipe absentmindedly, filled it with tobacco, and lit up. Exhaling, he loosened his tie and looked point-blank at Sartre, and then said conspiratorially:

"So that's why our tyrant, the ex-future-priest, chose it."

"Stalin?!"

"Who else?"

Sartre shrugged and looked out the window. He had the knack for quickly changing the subject. "Okay, I know you don't have all day, so tell me, what am I to do with that damned Dante?"

"Damn you, Sartre, you chose this part, this role . . ."

"I know, sir, but he hounds me day and . . ."

"All right, all right, what's it about?"

"Well, it's an epic poem, and it's divided into three parts: Inferno, Purgatory, and Paradise . . ."

"Easy, just reverse the order: substitute Hell for Heaven, Satan for God, demons for angels. Easy as pie, just as it was done in this here book." Lifting up the manuscript, he continued, "The Bible, as you call it." For the first time that day, Sholokhov smiled.

"All right, I'll tell him, but I don't think he'll . . ."

"Tough shit, Sartre. Tell him he better be grateful his books will see Hell at all."

Sartre got up and then saluted again on his way out the door. As he stepped out of the office, Innessa giggled and said in a whisper:

"You know what I heard?"

"?"

"She's threatened to leave him."

"Who?"

"Who, who! Who do you think? Masha, of course."

Sartre shrugged and said: "All the better for him, I guess."

"You idiot, have you forgotten what that means? Don't you know who'll replace him? Makarenko!"

"So?"

"So, so, are you always so dense? He's a Ukranian!

He'll get rid of us all and hire his own, all-Ukranian volunteers!"

"Look, Innessa, I don't have time for idle chatter. When's your lunch hour?"

"Right now, if I want it to be," she said flirtatiously. She's had the hots for Sartre for ages now, ever since Lenin started hanging around Rasputin and playing chess with him all the time.

"Okay," he said, helping her up from her chair, "let's go."

"Where to?"

"My place, it's nearby. Simone's out giving a lecture somewhere."

Innessa grabbed her handbag and raincoat, and looked at him curiously. "But I thought, you, you know, could do it only . . ."

"No, that was in my youth. You mean only with old women?"

"Yeah."

"Here it doesn't matter anymore. I do it whenever I think I can."

On the way out, Innessa continued babbling about Sholokhov and his wife until Sartre grew impatient and asked: "How do you know all this, anyway?"

"Well, you know, don't you, Rasputin comes over every night to play chess, and he tells Lenin everything."

Sartre pretended to be bored and yawned. As he led Innessa out of the building, he playfully patted her behind, which served to animate her to no end. And, in that tone of intimacy so readily acquired in anticipation of coitus, she continued to ramble on.

Meanwhile, back in Pompeii, it was the month the sun died, the day of either vernal equinox or midsummer, autumn equinox or winter solstice, or the day the rivers overflow and the Dog Star rises. It was the 365th day, and it was meant to stay. Forever.

The most pious Augusta of the previously Byzantine Empire, now not only dethroned but reassigned as well, though still in regal purple, sat weaving on a loom by the window as she had done eons of ages ago on that infamous and sultry night when she, then a mere Bear Keeper's daughter, had caught the fair Justinian's eye. Tonight, however, she wasn't looking for Justinian, for she had, as many an ambitious woman, turned her back on love.

Theodora's status in Hell was relatively stable. In all her centuries there, she had not once gone to the Undertaker's Table, and she had managed, until just recently, to keep one and the same job, which placed her in the upper ranks of the eternally shifting caste system of Hell. What surprised her the most wasn't that she had been reassigned as by whose instrument. It was her lifelong enemy, the great Byzantine chronicler and historian, Procopius, who had been insistent on making her life Hell and was now just as insistent on making her Hell an even greater Hell. Since he was now Chief Advisor of the Devil's Personnel Agency, all he needed to do was to say, once again, that there was no city in Asia where Theodora had not sold her body for pay, for the Devil to request that she be reassigned immediately to Pompeii where she was to run the new whorehouse. Which was exactly what he did.

Nevertheless, Theodora was perfect for the job: having once charmed, both as whore and as queen, all of sloe-eyed Asia, she also still spoke Greek and Etruscan, as well as the ancient tongue of Pompeii. But, as she made it clear to all and sundry, this wasn't going to be easy: she had to put all the local vermin whores out of business and select every single girl for the job herself, all of which took a while.

The final result, though, was so impressive that Hell's Personnel presented her with the title of "Grand Madam of Hell." Despite the insult of being forced to return to her previous profession, albeit in a more glorified manner, and being given a corresponding title to boot, the Despoina showed no trace of irritation or humiliation, and named the house after her own grand quarters in Constantinople, the House of Harmisdas, on which the whorehouse had been modelled.

And so she sat that day, furiously weaving in her window while the house shook with shrieking laughter and wailing cries. To be in the same den of iniquity with the bitchiest women in history was quite unsettling, though Theodora was learning how to placate them. She had not lost her gifts of prophecy and divination, and she still could, by looking into someone's eyes, divine the secret urges of every man or woman, dead or alive. Basically, she felt at home at the House of Harmisdas and preferred her new position to her previous job, but she knew Procopius too well not to realize what his true motives were: to put her in her place once and for all. She had suffered more than enough from him in the heyday of Empire, and now she meant to show the full extent of her gratitude to him for having immortalized her in his book. The only thing she did not know was how.

When she finally put down her weaving, it was already past daybreak, or what can be called daybreak, since day never really formally broke in Hell. Just as Theodora had to learn that the earth was actually round, she also had to accept that the sun never really did rise or set, not even in life. After coming to terms with this, she found it easier to accept that there was no time of day in Hell—it was all just one big lack of time or season. It was just plain Hell. As she leaned back in her chair and scanned the putrid horizon outside her window, she went into a trance and had a vision of the statue of Mercury floating face-down in the Baths of the Forum. The ancient Baths had been recently reconstructed and now adjoined the House of Harmisdas. Theodora came to just as suddenly as she had gone off and found herself standing in front of the House Clock.

It was early, going by Standard Time. Theodora decided to breakfast and then to make her way to the Baths to check on Mercury and to generally make her rounds of the Forum. On the way back to her chambers she paused on the balcony overlooking the square, where her retinue of hetaerae were in the midst of their morning two-hour session of Kama-Sutrobics. The House had a double function. On the one hand, it was a kind of boot camp for those who had been recruited to join the Supreme Commander's Legions; on the other hand, it was a private club for the nomenclature—the privileged class of hell. For partners, the girls were allotted a certain quantity of fresh recruits daily, and usually had to share one among three. And it was during the sessions of Kama-Sutrobics that the recruits were most reminded of the fact that they were indeed in the boot camp of Hell. The nomenclatura, though, were entertained in a slightly different fashion, and usually at night.

Theodora clapped and called to her personal sycophants, Flora and Fauna, to set up breakfast on the balcony. She enjoyed watching the girls give the poor bastards a workout—it even gave her an appetite. In the twinkling of an eye, Flora was by her side with a large plate of crystallized violets, for that was all Theodora could eat, and a glass of sea water, while Fauna set up a marble table for her and seated her in a purple love-seat. She settled for breakfast with Flora feeding her one petal at a time, and Fauna handing her a large spoonful to wash each petal down with. The only flowers that could grow in Pompeii were asphodel, so Theodora had her violets purchased once a month at the Black Market.

The Baths of the Forum adjoined the House of Harmisdas and likewise was closed to the general public; i.e., the old Pompeiians and the war heroes. Consequently, Theodora had to keep guards posted day and night all around the House and the Baths. She would have preferred to hire Janissaries, but the Devil had never heard of them, which most likely meant that they had not gone to Hell, but were in that other valley that some New Dead call Heaven. Unfortunately, these guards were all Aryans. The Devil had insisted on them, and though he called them the Gestapo, they were all barbarians to her.

Theodora passed through the gates, removed her gown, and handed it to one of the guards. She was dressed now only in Hippolyta's girdle, which she had acquired, much to Kleopatra's dismay, when she was still working for the Office of Confiscation and Revocation (OCR) back in New Hell. There was no such thing as absolute ownership in Hell, for everything was the sole property of the state—the state of Hell. Hence, the OCR was given monthly orders to raid random or select citizens' houses and confiscate either particular objects of value or whatever caught the confiscators' eyes. Nor were there any rights of possession: one could very well come home to find that one's diamonds, vintage Jaguar, or villa had been repossessed and the rights to own or rent such things had been temporarily revoked, which meant that you were thrown back to the end of the waiting list, usually incalculably long, unless you could bribe the petty clerks in charge of your file.

To work for the OCR meant that you were privy to who owned what and where it was, since every object purchased or rented had to be, under penalty of law, licensed by the appropriate department of the district where one was registered to live, after which the file was sent for safekeeping to the OCR in the Hall of Records. And so it would occasionally happen that someone would wait for eons to finally process his or her claim for, say, the Shield of Achilles, Hippolyta's girdle, or Pandora's Box, only to find out that it no longer existed. It had been deleted from the files and was either in the possession of an OCR employee or had been sold on the Black Market in New Hell. This was the reason for the random raids—to collect anything that no longer had a file on it and repossess it.

Theodora now removed the above-mentioned girdle and, going by the rules of modern etiquette, stepped into the baths fully unclothed. She put her treasured relic away into a jewelled sack and laid it by the pool. It was too early for the nomenclatura to be bathing, for they usually kept late hours—according to Standard Time, anyway. But there were a couple of new guests here who did not look like members of the nomenclatura at all. The latter were usually petty demons, privileged simply because they posed no threat to the Devilish powers-that-be—grey, indistinguishable, ratlike creatures with no expression in their eyes who took on human form only to have sex. These bathers were different. The woman was blonde, with a regal bearing that Theodora could recognize a mile away. She wore a bathing suit old-fashioned not by Theodora's standards but by those of the upwardly mobile New Dead, and stood on the edge of the baths, squeamishly testing the waters with her toes. In the cool, green water, a lanky, long-haired man in what looked like a monk's gown was doing the dead man's float. The statue of Mercury hovered like God above the triptych that these three made.

Theodora made her way to the other side of the baths and scrutinized the blonde. Here was a woman who had enjoyed being ravished by lackeys, but so what, hell could never fit all the women who did! Besides, once an Augusta, always an Augusta, and there definitely was something of an Augusta in this big-boned blonde. The two women, eyes locked, exchanged a fierce look of rivalry, that of royalty. Past royalty, that is—royalty without property. The eye-locking contest caused Theodora to miss the re-emergence of the monk, whom she noticed only when the blonde turned away and leaned down toward him, cooing and mumbling something in a foreign tongue.

Barbarians! Theodora thought to herself. I should have known. Probably some deposed Visigothian queen who still puts on great airs. But he, who is he? As if summoned, he turned and fixed his grey, nay blue, or white—could they be white eyes? Silver eyes. Justinian's had been grey; but these, they were absolutely mercurian.

The monk waded toward Theodora through the sulphurous waters and, kneeling before her and kissing her hand, said to her in perfect Attic Greek: "My name is Grigory. I am at your service, most pious Augusta."

"Who are you?" she asked, holding on to his hand and searching his eyes. "Are you a god?"

"Nay, Augusta. I am a mere mortal, though I have

served the good Lord, but alas . . ." he raised his eyes upward, mockingly, "I appear to have failed him somehow."

"And the lady, who may she be?" enquired Theodora with a nod toward the blonde.

"This is the Honorable Tsarevna Alexandra, the last queen of the Russian Empire," he said, turning to his lady and then back to Theodora.

Theodora smiled at the queen and said: "I am greatly honored, my lady."

Alexandra looked down, as if she had not understood, and said something brusquely to the monk in that same barbarian tongue. Russian, was it? As Theodora recalled, they were nothing but fruit- and berry-gathering nomads in her time. Even now their ploys and manners were still so barbarian.

"So how are you enjoying the luxuries of Hell?" Theodora asked the monk, spreading her hands with a wide sweep to encompass the Baths.

"Oh, we are indeed. This is our first time here," he replied.

"Are you with the Nihilists' Club?"

"No, we aren't as privileged as that. We're Molotov's guests. Do you know him?"

"Ah, yes, wasn't he one of the first non-petty demon members of the nomenclatura?"

"I wouldn't really know. He's a friend of Lenin's who is a good friend of mine."

"I see."

Alexandra spoke unintelligibly to the monk again, this time imploringly. I don't like this woman, Theodora decided. She'll have to get some sense knocked into her soon. One just doesn't walk around Hell, especially in its privileged circles, and especially in Pompeii, speaking any bloody barbarian tongue one pleases. After all, who was it that said, when in

Rome, do as Rome does? Theodora sighed. She looked up at the monk and wondered what the dickens his name was. She never could remember most barbarian names.

"St. Ambrose," the monk said, as if in reply to someone's question.

"Is that who you are?" Theodora asked, somewhat guiltily.

"No," he replied, "it was St. Ambrose who said: 'When I am at Milan, I do as they do at Milan; but when I go to Rome, I do as Rome does!'"

Theodora was startled, but didn't let on. Ignoring his clairvoyant provocations, she asked: "So how does one do in Hell?"

"One doesn't do in Hell," he replied rather gloomily. His silver mercurian eyes turned charcoal.

"Grisha, Grisha!" The queen shrieked annoyingly, like a little girl.

The monk rushed to her immediately and soothed her. A typical spoiled blue-blood, Theodora thought to herself, and then quickly caught herself in her habitual and caustic internalized dialogue. She knew that this man, whoever he was, could not only read but anticipate every one of her thoughts, and she must not let on, must not open up her old wounds. She would not think of her origins, her ancestors, the past, her daughter, Justinian, and that damned Procopius, defaming them all posthumously. No. Theodora stood up quickly, cursing this stupid New Dead etiquette that insisted on nakedness in the public baths. She felt naked as it was, with her thoughts laid bare to this man's eyes. She called to a guard who brought her her purple, as she called it (not purple gown, robe, or cloak, but just plain *purple*, whatever garment it was) and covered herself with color. Then, picking up her sack with Hippolyta's girdle, she made ready to go.

"Wait," said the monk, "don't leave yet. I have something for you."

He searched frantically through his wet frock and handed her a plastic card:

> GRIGORY RASPUTIN
> At Your Service:
> Professional Healer
> Advisor, and Literary Agent
> Moyka Canal Offices, NEW HELL
> Etruscan Square, POMPEII

Theodora hid the card in her cleavage and turned around brusquely, with her purple swaying behind her. "I will call," she said, dramatically looking over her shoulder.

Theodora, the Gift of God, made her regal way back to the House as if it were the court of Empire. No other woman had ever been both prostitute and queen of an Empire. This combination proved to be advantageous, even in Hell, where regal purple was still a "fair winding sheet." Theodora entered the House and admired the columns of porphyry that framed its entrance; she walked down the corridor and gazed lovingly at the green, blood-red, and white marble walls. She traced her hands along the walls in the foyer, covered with miniature tiles, then moved upstairs to her chambers of carved jade and colored marble, set in mosaic patterns. Solemnly, Theodora walked out onto the terrace, expecting to see her beloved Marmora Sea, but instead she saw putrid smoke, a field of burnt asphodel, cadavers hanging from trees, and something that was supposed to be a sea but smelled and looked more like a cesspool. She turned away and went back downstairs. It was three o'clock in the afternoon. The girls were taking a siesta, and the only sound in the house was that of water dripping onto stone. So much condensation built up in the house throughout the day that it sweated like a cavern.

The Black Market was located near the River Styx, where it intersects the Acheron, another river that flows in the infernal regions. At the point where the two rivers met, the water, though brown and serpentine, reflected whatever one wanted. Masha always saw the Kremlin there, spilling over the water and filling the river with radiant arrows and golden splashes. She stood for a few moments engrossed in this reflection of her favorite palace, then went up the overgrown path that led to the lot where the Black Marketeers would be setting up their stands.

The lot looked as if a nuclear plant had blown up and left nothing but its charred remains, the ground it was built on, and the twenty miles or so which previously surrounded it, now reduced to a congealed, uneven mass that formed a crest. As usual, Masha was the first one there. The rewriters were good friends with old Molotov, who would tip them off ahead of time as to when the Black Market would be in progress and what the hottest items on the market were. The Black Marketeers were, for the most part, petty demons, though there were also some daring employees from the OCR, but they often wore demon disguises.

The atmosphere at the Black Market lately had been pretty gruesome. There was none of that usual excitement and hustle and bustle; instead, everyone, including the demons themselves, was cautious and reserved. And the reason for this had been the recent raid at the Market by some Old Dead who were on a mission to wipe out the narco-terrorists and put a stop to the increasing flow of drugs into New Hell.

Some of the hottest selling items at the Market were flowers, being that they didn't grow in Hell. They were some of the more expensive items: a single rose, for example, could cost anywhere from $100 to $500. Masha had a total of $200 to spend today. She was depressed and desperate. Although she knew that there wasn't much to be expected from life in Hell, she also saw that there were some for whom life in Hell was much better than for her. For example, that rotten little nymphet, Catherine, out of whose hands the Devil was practically eating. Apparently, she had even earned a Hellovision series all of her own, while here Masha and Misha had to scrimp and save to get a few basic luxuries. Unfair. Masha waded through the crowd of murmuring marketeers, repeating their items in the form of incantation. Pink rose, pink rose, pink rose; carnation, damnation, carnation, incarnation; violets, violets, ultra-violets; oranges from Jaffa, Kijafa, oranges from Jaffa; coriander, palisander, coriander.

"Excuse me," she addressed one of the petty demons. "Is that the spice or the perfume?"

"Coriander, palisander, Coriandre, the perfume," replied the demon. "$200 an ounce! Coriandre, Coriandre."

"$200?" Masha's jaw dropped in feigned surprise. She was an old pro at bargaining. "That's more than what the spice costs. You can't charge more for perfume! Even Joy sells for less than roses!" But Masha stopped as suddenly as she had started. From somewhere in the middle of the market, she distinctly heard someone incanting: "Ikona, ikona, ikona . . ."

She rushed to the center of the lot and stood without breathing, listening to the murmurs all around her. Again she heard someone, as if hiccoughing, yell out: "Ikona, ikona, ikona!" Then, somewhere off to the left from the center, she heard: "Fabérgé, Fabérgé!" She rushed off toward the left and looked around her. An Asiatic-looking woman in what appeared to be a belly-dancing outfit had just purchased something and was looking very pleased. She too was rushing about, trying to match a voice with a demon. The marketeer from whom she had just purchased something began to incant again in a low voice: "Fabérgé!" Masha went up to him to find out what his wares were; all he had was a jewelry box designed by Fabérgé. "What did that woman buy?" she asked him, pointing toward the center of the lot. "What woman?" he asked. "The one who was just here, in the belly-dancing outfit," she replied. "Oh, her," he grinned. "Well, I can't really say, but it was a damn good price she gave me."

Masha was beginning to feel like she wouldn't be able to find anything worthwhile after all. She hurried off toward the last possibility, to the center of the lot from where she had heard someone advertising his icon. But there was that woman again, and she had just made another successful purchase— probably the icon. This just wasn't her day, Masha decided. Maybe she should just give up coming here, being that it just frayed her nerves. She went back to the flowers and spices section and listened again for the man selling coriander, Coriandre. When she found him, she went up to him again and asked: "Is that the spice or the perfume?" "The spice only, perfume all sold out," he replied.

Rasputin's office was located in the old Etruscan

district of Pompeii. He commuted here once a week from New Hell by shuttle. Pompeii was still off limits for most New Hell citizens—only the natives and those who had offices set up here were allowed.

Theodora rang the doorbell three times. She wasn't sure why she had decided to come here, but she knew there must have been a good reason for it, and she decided that she would let Rasputin run the show, being that he seemed to know more about why she was here than she did herself. Rasputin finally opened the door and led her into the drawing room. He then called for his sycophants to set up tea. It was served Russian style: a samovar was placed in the middle of the table with a small porcelain tea kettle on top of it. The tea itself was poured into tall glasses framed by golden glass holders. Theodora was impressed by such decorum on the part of barbarians.

"Sugar? Lemon? Milk?"

"Oh, only salt, please."

"Salt?" Rasputin screwed up his face and wondered mockingly which one of them was the true barbarian.

"I can't drink anything unless it's salted," Theodora explained. "I get dehydrated and my skin starts peeling."

"I see." Rasputin settled himself into a chair, took a few sips of steaming tea, and looked at her meaningfully. Then, taking on the manner of a psychoanalyst addressing a hesitant patient, he said, "I heard that you used to work for the OCR?"

"For centuries," she replied. "I would have been promoted to Chief Confiscator had I not been reassigned."

Rasputin leaned forward, picked up a sugar cube from the crystal sugar bowl, and dropped it into his tea. Then he settled back into his chair, deep in thought and mechanically stirring his tea with a tarnished silver spoon. He sat this way, jiggling his spoon against the tea glass, for what seemed like minutes. The sound got on Theodora's nerves and she began to wonder why she had bothered to come here at all. Finally, he quit stirring his tea and acknowledged her presence. He then asked her to tell him about how she had been reassigned.

After he had heard her out, he asked whether or not she still had friends or connections at the OCR. Theodora smiled and said: "Yes, there's that blond man from the Danube, Balisarius. I imagine he has probably replaced me by now."

"You're on good terms . . ."

"Oh yes, we're allies, actually; he was defamed by Procopius, too," she replied animatedly.

"All the better." Rasputin took her hand in his. "Theodora, you and I can be of great help to each other."

"How?"

"Well, what would you prefer, having Procopius killed and reassigned—or out of print?"

Initially, of course, Theodora thought she would rather have him killed, by all means, but then she remembered that they were all dead already anyway, and dying once again was no solution. A more appropriate solution had been offered.

"You mean blacklisted, like Mao and Qadaffi?"

"It can be arranged," he said, his eyes sparkling silver. "His *Secret Histories* can join the ranks of Mao's *Red Book*, Qadaffi's *Green Book*, and the works of Socrates and Che Guevara—all for the price of an egg."

"An egg?"

"I won't go into the details now. Besides, the less you know, the better. You'll have to get a confiscation form for me. I'll fill in the details, then you'll take it to Balisarius, and the rest is history."

"You mean, we're going to bribe someone?"

Rasputin made a clucking noise. "Come, come, Theodora, you disappoint me! This is, after all, Hell. And when in Hell, do as . . ."

"Yes, I know, do as Hell does, but whom are we bribing?"

"Ah, that's for me to know and for you not to find out. It's best that way. So what do you say?"

"I'll think about it."

"But what's there to think about? Don't you want Procopius blacklisted?"

"Well, yes, but I don't want to get tangled up in any shady deals."

"But you won't, I promise!"

"All right," she said, standing up, "I'll talk to Balisarius."

"You won't regret it," Rasputin beamed at her as he escorted her out the door. "Call me when you're ready."

According to Palisander Dahlberg—grandson of Rasputin, and unofficial chronicler and historian of the Soviet Republic, who had been present at every single significant occurrence in the U.S.S.R. from the Revolution in 1917 to the Chernobyl blast 69 years later, and who never was or would be a member of the Soviet Writers' Union, though he managed to survive the purges, the thaw, and the changing of all the guards and seasons throughout the present day—Leonid Brezhnev, who was sitting at his desk one fine autumn day, looking out the window at the falling Norwegian maple leaves and thinking longingly of the massage given him the day before by that gorgeous hotshot whom he called Ninotchka, was startled to death by the sudden ringing of his emergency line, and did not live to pick up the phone and find out that his daughter had just delivered his first grandchild.

And so it was that although Brezhnev was fairly well settled, as well as one could be, in Hell—his favorite buddy, Gagarin, lived near by and his lover, Zulfia, the dark Alma-Ata princess, was by his side, while his wife and all their relatives were far away in that other valley that most atheists call Nonhell—he was still trying to find out what his first grandchild was, a boy or a girl, and, consequently, he had volunteered his services to be the official welcoming committee to all the New Dead from the U.S.S.R., whom he promised to entertain at his own expense at his splendid villa in New Hell.

Just on such an evening, when Brezhnev was about to pop the question regarding the sex of his grandchild to his New Dead guest, Ustinov, the doorbell rang and the scene was suddenly transposed as if into everyone present's past, so familiar it was in its dynamic alternation between violence and surprise.

Ustinov, still fresh from life and hence a bit wet behind the ears, shot up and yelled, "Terrorists!" While Zulfia, always calm in such situations, hushed him and made him sit down, explaining that it was only the Office of Confiscation and Revocation out on its monthly raid, and if they just sat there and pretended that nothing was going on, the masked men wouldn't blast them back to the Undertaker's Table, where, as one always must remember, it's much more dreadful than one can imagine.

The masked man in charge of the raid was tall and had the bearing of a Viking. He knew what he was after, but not where it was kept, and so, with an Old Dead formality, he addressed Zulfia in Attic Greek.

"We have orders to confiscate all your national artifacts of historical and cultural value."

Zulfia nodded and lit a cigarette. "Please proceed, gentlemen," she said calmly. This was their first raid, but she thought she knew how to handle it.

The Viking dropped his Old World formality in exasperation and rounded up his men.

"Okay, lady," he said in English, "either you tell us where the artifacts are, or we loot the place," and, spreading his hands with the look of a doctor offering his patient the alternative of giving up one major organ or dying, he said, "It's up to you."

Zulfia was rather fond of her recent acquisition and was not going to give in so easily. She would even risk dying again for it. And as she headed up toward the stairway, she suddenly blacked out and fell backwards into the arms of the Viking.

"Damn it," he swore, lifting her long, barely clad body and trying to make her stand up. "God damn it, if she doesn't come to," he said, turning to the three men sitting on the couch, "it's curtains for you guys." But Zulfia was a good actress. She began to simulate another fall, at which point one of the OCR raiders fired a shot at the crystal chandelier. Ustinov screamed and jumped up. Zulfia, caught unawares, was startled back into participation and attempted to bolt upstairs.

What happened next, no one really knew for sure. The Viking, alias General Balisarius, a Dalmatian who had once led campaigns against Rome, Naples, Carthage, and a score of Barbarian lands, preferred tactics to modern weapons, and was prone to losing control when he had a machine gun in his hands. He did not particularly like to go on these raids anymore. He was dissatisfied with his position as Chief "Looter" for the OCR, he was a general at heart, and

these raids only frustrated his desire for a real battle.
But he owed Theodora a favor, and besides, he was
doing this to clear up his own record in the history
books. Maybe then he would finally be acknowledged as the superb tactician that he was and get
reassigned to where he knew he really belonged—
the Supreme Commander's Legions.

But he had gotten carried away because of this
difficult, sloe-eyed woman who, although of Asian
appearance, was actually a woman of the modern
world. And so, for some reason unknown to him, he
had blasted one of the guys, evidently a newcomer,
back from whence he had just come, and then he
had his retinue bind and gag the other three, including the woman. Afterwards, they had proceeded to
loot and demolish the place, with gusto, until they
found what he was looking for, then marched out of
the villa heroically.

Still bound and gagged, Zulfia, Brezhnev, and Gagarin looked on passively with a shocked silence at
these marauders who had made them suffer so acutely
the same humiliation that millions of other Russians
had been subjected to throughout the 20th century,
and in their silence they were ashamed—for themselves, for their people, for the general hypocrisy
that apparently rules both in life and in death.

It was late when Rasputin finally got to the Nihilists' Club, a favorite hangout of the Hellizdat volunteers and rewriters. Half the tables in the room were
set up with chessboards, and tonight each chessboard was in active use. Rasputin made his way
between the tables toward Lenin and Trotsky, who
were in the midst of a game. He leaned over them and
said, solemnly, as if for the first time, "I'll play the
winner."

Lenin chuckled in consent and Trotsky eagerly accepted the challenge, even though he inevitably lost every set he had ever played with Lenin. By the time Rasputin finally joined Lenin for a game, there weren't many players left in the club, so they chose the table near the window, far enough away not to be overheard. As Lenin adroitly set up the men on the board, flicking his wrist, he gestured with anticipation.

"So, how did it go?"

Rasputin swallowed his drink, settled back in the chair, then picked up a rook and said, "It's been a dreadfully long day."

Lenin squirmed restlessly in his chair. "I know all about long days," he said. "So tell me, did you succeed?" Rasputin's eyes were violet now from the reflection of the neon lights overhead and sparkled with glee. He enjoyed tantalizing Lenin and making him squirm, so he decided to prolong this as much as possible. After all, he needed some fun to eclipse the nerve-wracking episodes of the day.

"It's your move; succeed in what?"

"God damn it, quit playing ignorant, Grisha. I want to know if you succeeded keeping the Ukes at bay and out of our hair!"

"The Ukes," Rasputin said, stretching out the "u". "Shame on you, Vladimir Illich. I didn't know you held the Ukrainians, the founding fathers of our race, in such contempt!"

"Cut out the crap, you crazy, defrocked priest!" A sudden look of surprise crossed his face, just as he was about to make his move.

"Well, well," he smiled at Rasputin, and at someone behind him. "I guess you have succeeded."

"Why, what do you mean?" Rasputin asked, arching a bit to see who it was who had just come in.

"Oh, why, of course." He lifted his hand up to salute Sholokhov, who looked as if he had just purchased a new lease on life, and who was helping his wife, Masha, off with her coat. The pair waved to the two chess players and settled cozily in a booth, oblivious to their surroundings and happy as newlyweds.

"Your move," Lenin said. "I'll go get us some drinks."

When he came back with the "kaiff", a potent drink made out of brewed tea, he again addressed Rasputin with exasperation. "Now tell me, will you, how did you do it?"

"All right, all right," Rasputin replied, "pull up a chair. It proved to be quite easy. Makarenko, the Uke, will have to wait another century or so, because, as you see," he gestured toward the Sholokhovs, "he's not about to get exiled or nodded out. He's got her under his thumb now. See how she's practically eating out of his hands?" Rasputin paused, made a move, and captured one of Lenin's rooks. "Thanks. Getting a bit careless are you? Forgot that I'm not Trotsky? So anyway, this is what I did for the sake of mother Russia. I arranged to have a couple of Byzantine clerks confiscate a certain object of value which consequently was put in the protection of our honorable rewriter and publisher, thus saving my neck and his."

"For what? What did you get in return?"

"Oh, I just asked Sholokhov to blacklist someone."

"Whom?"

"The common enemy of the Byzantine aparchikis— the chronicler and historian, Procopius. Besides, no one can ever question this motion because no one can even read him except for the aparchikis and Procopius himself."

"You know who he is, though, don't you?"

It was Rasputin's turn to be surprised, "Who?" he asked.

"He's Chief Advisor of the Devil's Personnel Agency."

"Shit!"

"And he's already called Sartre to ask him to take him on. That's what Innessa told me."

"Well, I anticipated he would, and so I asked Sholokhov to give me History and let Sartre deal only with Fiction, so he really can't take on Procopius."

Lenin was having a good time now. His usually severe face took on the look of a prankster who had just gotten away with something, "So," he asked, "I want to know one more thing. What was this object of value that so appeased Madame Sholokhov that she has promised not to leave him?"

"I'll give you a hint. It's something that the Ukes are especially fond of."

"Something religious?"

"Yes, something oval."

"Eggs?"

Rasputin nodded. "An egg, an egg." A smile suddenly broke across Lenin's face. Then a shadow crossed it, furled his brow, and made him take on the appearance of a madman laughing at his own jokes.

Rasputin responded by echoing the laugh, thinking that Lenin was still marvelling at the idea of an egg being his bargaining power. Then Lenin leaned over the board toward Rasputin conspiratorially and said, "You know, Brezhnev called me tonight, just as I was on my way here."

"Yes?" Rasputin asked, pulling his head sideways, out of the glare of the neon light. "You see," Lenin continued, "he'd been raided, and he was devastated. It was during one of his welcoming committee receptions, and this time some Politburo guy named

Ustinov was about to enlighten him, but got kicked off instead. Needless to say, Len'ka was really pissed." Lenin paused. This time he was in a position to keep Rasputin on his toes a bit and squirming in his chair. "I believe it's your move," he said, capturing Rasputin's last pawn.

"And? Go on," Rasputin said.

"Well, Gagarin was there, as usual, but he came out unscathed. And Zulfia—Zulfia is threatening to leave Brezhnev for Gagarin, though Gagarin doesn't know it yet!"

"How come?"

"She says it's all his fault that they got raided and were forced to give up her prize possession."

"Which was?"

"A Faberge egg."

"Bull's eye."

"Bull's eye and checkmate!"

"Shit! Oh well, so what did you say to Comrade Brezhnev?"

"I told him it *was* his fault. I reminded him how, back in the 1970s, he had forbidden the possession of any objects which were of national, historic, and cultural value, claiming that they were the property of the state. Well, I said, it became a self-fulfilling prophecy. Now they are the property of the state, too—the state of Hell!"

Both Lenin and Rasputin laughed heartily, lifted their glasses and clinked. Rasputin said, "I drink a toast to our glorious nation and its people, who have so well paved the road to Hell."

"I second that," said Lenin.

While the two players continued to drink and play, oblivious to the fact that they were, that very moment, being cuckolded by their queens, dawn sank all about them with a smoking splendorlessness, and

Hell lay flat as the chessboard on which pawns, rooks, queens, and knaves moved silently in the still of the night.

"You're awake," Masha said, running her index finger along Sholokhov's profile. "Why, you're all wet!"

"I had a bad dream, I guess. I don't remember what about," he said, wiping the sweat off his brow.

"Don't worry," she attempted to calm him. "I won't leave you, I promise. I see now that you really do care about me, and we've been . . ."

"It's not that," he said. "Frankly, I'm worried about the egg."

"The egg? Why!" she asked him, incredulous. She sat up in her pink satin baby doll and faced him.

"Well, I know it sounds silly, but do you remember that fairy tale about the Deathless Koshej (skeletal creature)?" he asked her.

Masha swung her head to and fro in reply. Her bleached hair shone like a halo.

"You will," he said, "I'm sure. It's about the prince who loses his beautiful princess to the Deathless Koshej. Every day Koshej would leave for the whole day, alone, while the prince and princess would try to figure out how to do away with him. Finally, one day, the princess decides to ask him where he keeps his death. After leading her on a few times, saying that his death is in a broom, or in the fence outside, he finally tells her that his death is in an egg, and the egg is in a duck, and the duck is in a barrel, which is at the bottom of the sea. After this, the prince goes in search of the egg, duck, and barrel, and, as is usual in fairy tales, all the animals that he met on the way when he was looking for the princess suddenly show up and help him. There's a fish, an eagle, and some other animal. So he finally manages to get the egg, and he brings it to the place where Koshej is keeping his princess prisoner, and waits for Koshej's return. And of course, as you probably remember . . ."

"Yes, I sort of do. He confronts Koshej, squishes the egg, and kills him, right? But I don't understand. What does it have to do with us?" Masha asked. "Well," he went on, "you see, this fairy tale keeps haunting me. I just can't figure out which one of them is me—the prince, or Koshej—because on the one hand, I managed to find the egg, with the help of my friends, so maybe I'm the prince. But on the other hand, I am more like Koshej, because I too am deathless, and I see now that my death is in this egg. If this egg gets taken away in a raid or if it's broken, then I'm off to the Land of Nod." Sholokhov sighed and got up to pour himself a drink.

"Don't, dear—not now. You know how bad you feel afterwards. Besides, your intestines will probably kill you before you ever make it to the Land of Nod!" she said, smiling. "Everyone thought I was going to leave you, including yourself, but what would I do alone? Who would I be with? I just wanted you to pay more attention to my needs. I need to be pampered here, too—just as I did in real life."

"So, what would happen if we did get raided and the egg got taken away?"

"Nothing," she smiled at him coyly. "I would just hope that you would find something to replace it."

"Damn," he went on. "That's just what I mean. I don't only have to work, but I have to worry about keeping you satisfied; otherwise, it's curtains for me!"

"Yes, well, we've got to make the best of it, don't we, after all, or it's curtains for us both." Masha got up and went to the dresser, picked up her Faberge egg, and brought it back to bed with her. She sat there, stroking it, and cooing all the while. "You must admit, dear, it is lovely, isn't it?"

"Yes, indeed, it is," he said, taking another swig of brandy.

Elsewhere in New Hell, another couple was having a sleepless night. They stood watching dawn foam around the horizon and spread a putrid vapor all throughout Hell. The woman kept laughing and trying to pull her lover back to bed, while he stood solemnly and stoically staring out the window toward the horizon, as if in anticipation of some kind of disaster.

In Pompeii, the Grand Madam of Hell was waking up to the sound of her hetaerae doing their Kama-Sutrobics to rock and roll. Although she should have awakened at peace with herself, having recently done in Procopius, she was troubled. Down the hall there lay a sleeping pair curled up in each other's arms: the blond man from the Danube and the barbarian Russian queen. Theodora knew this meant trouble. She had heard all about the barbarian ways of dealing with the loss of honor. The last thing she wanted was to get caught sheltering lovers. "Ah," she sighed, and stretching, said to herself, "Never a dull moment!"

REACHING FOR PARADISE

Brad Miner

*Fear cannot be without hope
nor hope without fear.*

—Spinoza

1.

Some men, whether they are alive or dead, will always dream of escape.

This the Welcome Woman knew well, so she was not surprised when the man in black interrupted her in mid-sentence just as her orientation lecture had begun

"Excuse me. Did you say 'Hell'? I'm *very* sorry, but there must be some mistake." His tone was excessively sweet. He was red-faced, white-haired, and overweight.

Ah, the woman thought, here's one who'll do well.

"Really?" she exclaimed. "A mistake! Oh, I hope not. Although *we're* certainly not perfect." She looked at the page on her clipboard and read:

"Rev. John Ryan, S.J., of," and here she paused to shudder, "Holy Angels Church, Park Avenue, New York City." She looked up. "You *are* Ryan, aren't you?"

Fr. Ryan was beginning to feel quite sick. The blood was leaving his ruddy whiskey face, and he swallowed hard. (Gagging on his own treacle, the woman thought.)

"Yes," he admitted, "I'm Ryan . . . I am, but you said this is Hell. You've *got* the right man, but I'm in the *wrong* place surely." He leaned forward to get a look at the clipboard. "Are you quite certain *I'm* not destined for Purgatory?"

"Sorry," she said, pressing the clipboard against her chest, "destined for where?"

"Purgatory."

"I wouldn't know anything about that. Anyway, mistakes are what make Hell Hell."

The rhythm of Ryan's heart changed from a trot to a canter. It was his mother's fault. She'd forced him into the priesthood. Now he was in trouble because the standard of judgment was too high. Or maybe it was Vatican II. It was his mother *and* Pope John . . .

Ryan felt his heart in full gallop, and it took all his strength of will to rein in his doubts and begin to calm himself. Don't accept what *she* says, he thought. For God's sake, you're a Jesuit! Argue!

"My dear woman," he said softly, "I know that I am dead, but I received," he explained, using the old words, "Extreme Unction before I died. I made my confession to the Cardinal Archbishop, himself. Surely—"

"Whoa!" the woman cried, her eyes wide with excitement. "What was that you said? 'Extreme unction?' Geezooey, that sounds hot! *Extreme* unc-tion. Oooo . . ." She swayed her hips and bit her tongue. "I'd settle for plain old unc-tion. *Extreme* unction would burn me up. I'm pretty sure it would. Ahhh . . ."

Unlike most people who end up there, Fr. Ryan had actually believed in Hell while he lived. He believed in Hell and Heaven and, especially, Purgatory, that glorious Catholic place of catholic purging and purifying. That's where *I* belong, he thought. I need time to do penance for sins unremitted. I need to suffer. I'm in this awful mess because, hard as my life was, I suffered too little. I'm really embarrassed to admit it, but it's true of the whole bunch of us. We stayed in the rectory after dinner and drank beer and watched television and broke wind. We should have been out more among His people. We were pretty good teachers, but we failed the hard tests. We never fed His lambs or clothed His sheep. Not that I didn't teach the young couples about sin . . . about avoiding it, I mean. We must all go walking through the fire, I told them. We are base ore—lumps of dross that must go into the refining fire so the core of precious metal may be revealed. I *was* eloquent, wasn't I?

He decided to reason with the woman.

"You see, my dear—"

"Oh, I get it," she broke in. "*That's* why you're here."

She showed him the clipboard, and he read the simple printed form attached to it.

> Ryan, Rev. John, S.J.
> Holy Angels Church
> Park Avenue, New York City
> *extremely unctuous*
> DAMNED

As the Welcome Woman showed him around, Ryan was thinking hopefully that it was evidence of an administrative error that he was hopeful that there *had been* an administrative error. How can I be damned, he reasoned, if I am hopeful about that? *Quod erat demonstrandum.* In any case, the evidence of his senses, if you forgot the hideous woman and the slightly sulphurous smell in the air, did *not* suggest Hell. He was in no pain, although his heart was still racing, and what he could see of the city in the valley below looked more like Youngstown, Ohio, than like Hell. People moved about among office buildings and smokestacks and gas wells from which flames burst. Well, maybe not Youngstown, but more as he imagined a Soviet steel town would look. The citizens on these streets were plainly dressed and walked with their heads down. Occasionally there were distant screams that sent a chill right through Ryan's soul.

I must, *must* be imagining all this, he thought. Nothing here is real except me. I'm creating it. It's a trick of my subconscious—a celestial joke.

But this was not burgeoning self-confidence. He continued to press the woman about Purgatory, and his arguments were very good. Argument always excited Ryan. Indeed, he used to imagine how brilliantly he would reason face-to-face with the Devil himself, given the chance. He thought it a shame, in fact, that he was never called upon to perform an exorcism. He never admitted it to the other priests, but *The Exorcist* was his favorite book. Well, actually, he'd only seen the movie. All that green vomit was *the* very purging and purifying. Who knows? Perhaps there is need for an exorcist here—here in Purgatory.

Ryan turned to his guide and said: "I suppose

telling me this is Hell is a way of making me suffer.
All right. So be it. It's no more than I deserve." He
smiled to show her his sincerity.

She looked at him. They had come finally to the
tall building where she would take leave of him. For
a moment she considered tearing off his face—chewing
it up and spitting it on the ground. But that's demon's work. The little pleasure she took in greeting
these Morons came from being the very first to rub
their noses in *IT*.

"What you deserve, priest, is exactly what you are
getting—but not to worry if you can't accept it just
yet. *Most* priests have a hard time at orientation."

2.

The Welcome Woman left Ryan with a carbon of the
page from her clipboard and instructions to enter the
building and report for work. This was the Department of Error and Illusion, and he was assigned to a
small bureau reviewing Form 666/7-11/Z, Claim of
Wrongful Damnation. Ryan saw the irony, but that
didn't stop him from filling in the form himself.

The Welcome Woman had been quite correct: Fr.
Ryan *did* do well. Ryan was right about himself as
well; he *did* suffer. He adjusted more easily than
most to the myriad rules and regulations that govern
Hell, but the work was unbelievably dull, and it was
endless. Everybody, it seemed, filed Form 666/7-11/Z.

Then there were his co-workers. He shared a small
office with a third century Father of the Egyptian
Church named Origen, and with Gestas, the so-
called Bad Thief, the one Jesus did *not* take with
Him to Paradise. Obviously.

Ryan *had* heard of Origen. One of the early popes

had him excommunicated—something like that. Ryan was unable to remember what horrors Origen had taught. He knew it was pointless to feel angry at being stuck in the same office for eternity with a heretic, but he was angry just the same. Still, it was not possible to be angry at the little Egyptian himself. He was such a quiet fellow. He was no more than five feet tall. His skin was dark and translucent, like worn leather. With his large brown eyes and prominent, angular nose, he looked like the mummy of one of the pharaohs. His most distinctive features were his hands. They were large and bony. Ryan was hypnotized by Origen's long fingers as they flipped unceasingly, listlessly through the stack of forms in which the damned petitioned for exit visas that were never granted. At times Origen's eyes would be wide, as if in horror, but at other times, they seemed closed, as if in sleep; except, as Ryan had learned, few men sleep in Hell. Hour after hour, the skeletal fingers turned the pages, sorting them into boxes marked either IMPROPERLY APPLIED/DENIED or PROPERLY APPLIED/DENIED.

The "world-famous Gestas," as he called himself, reminded Ryan of a retired circus performer, privileged to have spent time in the spotlight—under the Big Top, so to speak. In his case, this meant crucifixion, along with his partner in crime, Dysmas, and with the Son of God. The hands of the Bad Thief were also distinctive.

Gestas quite naturally assumed Fr. Ryan, being a Christian fellow, would be thrilled to meet someone who had actually met the Savior face-to-face. Ryan laughed. Oh, sure. He would have been thrilled under different circumstances.

"However, I'm not convinced I won't be leaving the Faith now. Under the circumstances."

Origen had actually looked up and smiled (if you can call a brief and barely perceptible elevation of one corner of the mouth a smile).

Gestas sat at a desk uncluttered except for a dusting of gray ash. He did absolutely nothing all day but talk about the Crucifixion—another irony not lost on the Jesuit. Ryan had always assumed that disappointment at the End would mean oblivion, nothingness. The Faith would turn out to have been a fiction. In such event, he realized—in the black or white of nothingness—there wouldn't actually be awareness, per se, and so no disappointment. What had never occurred to him was the disappointment he felt now. The Faith *was* true, and he had been found wanting.

Listening to Gestas reminisce, Ryan recalled the tour guide who'd conducted a delegation of Jesuit priests through the Alamo. Ryan had been struck then by the matter-of-fact manner of the guide as he recited the Alamo's long and extraordinary history. Ryan had never had much insight into people, but it was obvious that telling the story over and over *was* the Bad Thief's damnation. Gestas was tormented because the story never changed. He was always the one yelling at Christ to save them. Dysmas was always the one who chastised him for it and turned to Jesus and said: "Remember me."

Ryan thought: Remember the Alamo.

As Ryan was studying Form 666/7-11/Z in an effort to find a loophole, a way out of Hell, Origen surprised him by asking:

"Tell me, Fr. Ryan. Did you read my works when you were in the seminary?"

"Well," the flustered Jesuit began, "I don't recall. I suppose we may have. . . . But then, I recall very little of Augustine or St. Thomas. My field was counselling, you see. I was no theologian."

Origen nodded. His eyes went back to the stack of forms.

"*On Prayer*, perhaps? Or *Exhortation and Martyrdom?*"

"Sorry," Ryan said kindly, but he was embarrassed and angry. Why *should* we have studied a heretic in any case. How ridiculous! And then Ryan remembered that in his seminary days, he and his fellows had joked about the Relics in the cornerstone of the altar in the chapel. The "Chapel of St. Origen," they had called it, and instead of the usual bones in the altar . . .

"Now that I think of it," Ryan said, "don't I recall that you castrated yourself?"

At this, Gestas guffawed and slammed his palm on his desk, sending a cloud of ash into the air, causing him to choke and laugh at the same time.

Origen nodded his head.

"That is true. I believed in the Scriptures . . ."

"Which one?" Ryan interrupted. "Was it the one about . . . '*if any part of your body offends God, you should cut it off?*' "

"No!" Origen replied sharply. "I am referring to the nineteenth chapter of Matthew: 'For there are eunuchs who are so from birth, and there are those who are made eunuchs by men, and there are eunuchs who make *themselves* eunuchs for my sake.' "

Ryan was a man not given to thinking much about his privates, but the notion of self-castration, even for the Kingdom, made him wince. And a lot of good it had done Origen. The Jesuit thought of the cherubic choir boys of the Renaissance who were made permanent sopranos through castration. . . . And there are those made eunuchs for the sake of a high C . . .

Gestas was shaking his head mirthfully.

"I *will* never figure you holy fellas. You cut 'em off," he said, pointing to Origen, and then he cocked his thumb at Ryan, "and he never even used 'em. So you're both without the only decent memories a fella can have down here. No sir, I don't get it. Never will." The Bad Thief held up his hands in surrender. The scars in his palms were dark red.

"What in the world's wrong with women?" he asked. "All your patriarchs and prophets had women, and all them are in Paradise now. I oughta know. The day Jesus came and got 'em was the day I arrived."

3.

Ryan was puzzled.

"The day Jesus came where?" he asked.

"Why, right here where we sit, of course. Well, not here at the Department. There was no Department in them days. But here in Hell's what I mean."

"Jesus in Hell!" Ryan laughed. "Don't be ridiculous."

Gestas winked at Origen.

"This fella don't know too damn much, does he, Monsignor?"

Origen narrowed his eyes at Gestas.

"I was not a monsignor," he said. "I was not even a priest. Fr. Ryan is a modern man, Gestas. He's poorly educated and spiritless. Very few of his age know of the Harrowing."

A modern man, Ryan thought. That's true. What *did* he know of such things? What would he know if he lived in the modern world for another thousand years? Not too damned much.

Then he remembered a line in one of the Creeds.

"He descended into Hell," it read. Fr. Ryan had literally never thought about it.

"Well, priest," Gestas said, rubbing his hands together. "I figure it's time you heard the story."

Ryan braced himself for another of the Bad Thief's golden memories.

I was innocent. That's well known. The Legion was grabbing people right off the streets like they always done before Passover. This was to make the streets safe for the rich who pay the most taxes with the money they steal from the poor.

They collared me and Dysmas and said we'd robbed some merchant from Damascus. They robbed him, of course, but it's us gets thrown in the hole. The Romans put a dagger in his ribs and dumped him on a smoldering trash heap near Gehenna. Then they "found" the body, and next thing you know, we're lugging our crosses behind the Preacher from Nazareth along the Via Dolorosa and out to the Place of the Skull. You with me so far, Ryan? Good.

They nailed us up, and the three of us hang there for, oh, three hours easy. The Preacher's the first to croak. Well, before that, I'm mad with the pain and the heat and I screamed at Jesus:

"Hey," I says, "if you're the Son of Jehova, then get us the hell down from here!"

That's when ol' Dysmas, who never went to synagogue since he was bar mitz'd, who never did an honest day's work, and who pulled more devious shenanigans than any malefactor I ever met, calls out:

"Have you no fear of God? The end is near. We deserve to be hanging here for all our skullduggery, but this man is truly innocent."

Well, I'm speechless. Was this the Dysmas who'd

pillaged all over Palestine? I never heard nothing like it. Well, not until he says:

"Lord," he says, "remember me when you get to Heaven."

Well, I wish I'd said it. Of course, I had no idea who this poor fella between us was. I guess Dysmas played a hunch.

I craned my neck to look past Jesus at Dysmas. I was going to call out to him to shut up and die like a proper thief, when I hear Jesus say to him:

"Verily," he says, his voice all hoarse like a whisper, "Verily." He talked like that, very formal. "Verily, I say unto thee, today shalt thou be with me in Paradise."

Then he died.

It got real dark, although it was only a little after three in the afternoon. An eclipse. Don't ask me. I looked over at ol' Dys, but he was dead, too.

Well, by now I felt, well . . . poured out—all my strength spilled like water. My heart was like wax melting into my bowels—

"Stop!" Origen had risen to his feet and now stared angrily at Gestas. "You will not continue to quote Scripture."

Origen sat down but kept his eyes on Gestas.

"You know better. You know the penalties . . . Please, my friend, no psalms and no gospels. Just the Harrowing, for Fr. Ryan's edification. Get to the Harrowing."

Gestas seemed little chastised. He shrugged and continued his story.

Well, I died. And to my eternal shame, I found myself here, although in them days things was different, don't you know. They even had another name for this part of Hell. It was Sheol, they called it, and it wasn't such a terrible place as now. It was more like cold than hot, to tell the truth, and very dark. There was no flames leaping in the air and no screams. There was just a low moaning and whispering. It seemed like a funeral was going on, but that was no surprise to me.

There was no one greeted me, Ryan. I didn't see no Welcome Woman. So I went stumbling about in the dark all by my lonesome.

But that didn't last long, 'cause I see a campfire in the distance. It takes me a long time to limp on over to it. The rocks were sharp under my feet . . . Well, you can imagine. I'd just been crucified, after all.

When I get close, I see figures seated around the fire. One fellow is standing and talking to the rest, preaching like a rabbi. And what do you know? It's the Naz's cousin I see when the light hits his face. The Baptizer, John. You've heard of him, right? Good.

Well, I'm glad to see a fellow Jew down here—and from my own country, at that, even if he is a fanatic. So I call to him:

"Say, Baptizer. As I know you're from around Jerusalem, I wonder if you've come across my ol' bud Dysmas down here. Him who was so recently and unjustly put to death with me and your cousin, the Preacher from Nazareth?"

All the heads turn to me.

The Baptizer was a big, hairy fella, a beast more than he's a man, and he strides over to me and puts his paw on my shoulder and turns to the others and says:

"This common thief," he says, and I coulda hit him in the eye; 'common,' he says. "This common thief was crucified with another, whom our Lord has gathered up to Paradise this day."

Well, that's the first I get the hint that Dysmas and I won't be spending eternity together.

"Soon," the Baptizer goes on, "the Lord Jesus will descend on this place and likewise gather up you, his chosen."

By the way, Ryan, I should correct something. I heard later that Dys was gathered up all right, but not to Paradise. Not directly. The Savior must have been in a hurry. Dys got left in the clouds or something, and he was weeks finding his way to the Pearly Gates. When he finally got there, he had a Hell of a time convincing people he belonged—even with the holes in his hands and feet.

Anyway, I wasn't really sure what the Baptizer's talking about, but the others are whispering and arguing and generally being excited about the promise of a visit from Jesus.

'Course, some people still talk about getting out of here (I won't mention any names), and I don't hold with associating with dissidents, but then it was my first day, and I was happy just to see some friendly faces.

So I walk up just as bold as you please and begin to add my two cents about the prospects of an exodus to Paradise, and these people are very interested in my thoughts on account of my recent association with Jesus.

Now, had I but known who these people was, I would have been struck dumb for sure. For these was none other than the prophets and the patriarchs themselves. Right from Adam on up to Daniel. And there am I standing among them discussing a jailbreak.

So you can see what I mean about Sheol. Where else could a thief from Bethany strike up a conversation with the Father of Mankind?

And I should have recognized Adam. He was the handsomest fellow you ever saw. He was talking with *the Baptizer and with Seth, his and Eve's youngest boy.*

I get the drift that the breakout is making a lot of the others pretty nervous. I guess they thought God had forgotten them, so the idea that a carpenter's son was going to free them was a little hard to swallow.

But Adam believed. The Baptizer convinced him. Adam pushes Seth into the center of the people by the campfire and says, "Go on, tell 'em. Tell 'em."

So Seth, he says, "Lookie. When my daddy was sick and ready to die, he sent me to the Pearly Gates to borrow some oil so I could anoint him and he'd recover. But the angels told me the oil comes from a tree that grows only in Sheol. I'm sick at heart, but then one angel takes me aside and says, 'Hey, don't sweat it, Seth. One day the Son of God will descend into Hell and get the oil from the Tree and wash your father in it and wash all his descendants in it and bring the whole bunch of you right on up here.'"

When everybody heard this, we all started cheering. I don't know why I got so excited, but I did. I guess I figured to escape, too.

Now meanwhile, Satan's right-hand man, another fallen angel called Hades, you've probably heard of him, too, he gets wind of the breakout and finks to the Boss.

Look, Ryan, don't tell 'im I said this, but Satan was out of touch in them days. I don't know—he thought he was running a seminary or something. He started this place, or God gave him the job, I don't know, but he figured he had it made. All the best people. Abraham, Isaac, and Jacob. Isaiah and Jeremiah and all of them. I don't think it ever occurred to him that the best talent would up and leave one fine day, which, not to get ahead of myself, is exactly what happened.

Anyway, Hades says to Satan, "Talk is this Jesus fellow is gonna come down here with an army and liberate your Jews."

Satan laughs at this because, of course, he'd been up to watch us all get crucified.

"Don't worry," he says. "Jesus is dead and buried like everybody else who ever lived. He comes here, he stays like everybody else."

And Satan was serious—can you believe it? He didn't believe in messiahs any more than anybody else. Hell, he'd even tried to recruit Jesus at one point. He never paid no attention to the demons who came back here after Jesus cast 'em out. He didn't listen to nobody. He was so sure of himself.

But then Hades asks him about Lazarus.

"What about 'im?"

"A short time ago, I swallowed him up, and then a few days later, this Jesus snatches him back right out of my guts."

Well, Satan couldn't explain that. Maybe Lazarus wasn't really dead. Hah! That's a laugh.

"And another thing," says Hades. "The natives are getting restless. All of them, not just your precious faculty. So, I'm telling you. Keep the Preacher out of here!"

But Satan, he wasn't worried. He figured, what the hell kinda mischief can one dead rabbi get into?

Well, Ryan, you can guess it was a lot.

I'm standing around the campfire trying to get a word in edgewise (which ain't easy with your prophets), when all of a sudden I feel something blow up. I'm knocked to the ground, but I don't hear a "Boom!" I look around and all them fellas is on their knees looking up. So I look up, but I don't see nothing.

It's real quiet. I notice the moaning has stopped. And that's when I hear the singing. Oh, it was beau-

tiful music. Not the kinda tune you could hum, but it was beautiful. Right away you knew it was the Heavenly Host.

I stood up, and as soon as I did, I'm knocked on my ass again by another of them explosions.

Now I see a great spotlight has blasted into this place and the Host is galloping down it just like it was a highway.

Jesus wasn't with the first bunch. First comes a recon squad that gathers all around where the light strikes the ground. The light is so bright you can hardly bear to look at it, but you can't turn away from it either. I could see the angels moving in and out of the light and the shadow. In the shadow they glowed, sort of, and the light glinted off their swords.

Then there was trumpet blasts and people all over Sheol start screaming and cheering and here comes Jesus walking down the spotlight just as nice as you please. He's waving to the crowd and folks are shouting and the angels are singing and I'm jumping up and down, in spite of the fact it's killing my feet, and I'm waving my hands in the air and yelling:

"Hey, Preacher. It's me; remember me?"

Then I look around and I'm all by myself by the fire. Everybody else has high-tailed it over to the angels.

I start limping toward the light, but it's tough going, and I walk and walk, but I don't seem to get closer.

I see Jesus disappear into the waiting crowd and I see legions of angels running down the light after him. And all around there is shouting and screaming and sobbing and cheering.

I never saw no fighting. It was all over in a flash. Adam, I hear later, is anointed by Jesus with balm from a tree the Preacher cracks open with a lightning

*bolt. Then Adam and all the rest of them notables go
dancing up the light, clapping and singing. It was the
last anybody ever saw of 'em.*

*Now, finally, I stagger over to where there's a big
crowd of angry folks crowded around the perimeter
of the light, and I push my way toward the center,
and what do I see? There is ol' Satan, flat on his
back. Jesus is standing over him, and three angels
who look like Swedish javelin throwers have lances
pressed against the Devil's throat. Hades is there,
too. He's down on one knee, shaking in front of the
Preacher, who tells him:*

*"Take Satan and bind 'im. Keep 'im in the lock-up
until I come back."*

*So Hades and a couple of his henchmen drag Satan
away. Satan is cursing a blue streak, and I hear Hades
saying:*

*"So, what did I tell you? I told you we needed
new locks on the gates. I told you the Preacher
would make trouble. I told you . . ."*

*And he goes on and on about all the stuff he's told
Satan to do and not to do.*

And Satan just gets more and more pissed.

*Meanwhile, I turned to ask the Lord for a favor,
but just as I do, I get a last look at the beam of light
before, click, the light goes out, and I'm standing in
the dark.*

*So, I'm thinking: Great, they're gone and I'm still
here. And—*

4.

Suddenly the office door was kicked open and in
strode three men. Two entered first, obviously body-
guards. They surveyed the room with expressionless
black eyes. Ryan was not sure they were really human.

But the third man was definitely a person. He was tall, handsome, and elegantly dressed. He swept in behind his bodyguards and stood in the middle of the room with his hands on his hips.

Gestas leapt to his feet and Origen stood up slowly. Ryan remained seated. I don't know who this stranger is, he thought—probably some sort of policeman— but I've done nothing wrong. The worst thing is to *seem* guilty.

"Now Fr. Ryan," the stranger said, "when the Devil comes calling it is customary to stand in greeting."

Ryan froze. The bodyguards made a move toward him, but Satan held up a hand to stop them. Trembling, Ryan struggled to his feet.

"Why, look," Satan said happily, "he's shaking just like a little bunny rabbit. *Isn't* that nice. Good priest. That makes up for not recognizing me. Now sit, all of you."

They sat.

Satan walked to Origen's desk and stood there, staring sadly at the hundreds of forms the Egyptian had been sorting. He took up a handful and began to read. Frightening as it was to look upon the face of Satan, Ryan could not turn away from the Evil One's deep blue eyes as they examined the hopeless protests of Hell's malcontents.

Then the Devil threw the papers to the floor. He leaned back and roared. It was the sound of one hundred martyrs being devoured by one hundred lions. Ryan wished he were dead, then remembered he was and wished he were simply invisible.

The Devil looked at Ryan and said softly:

"Why do they long to leave us?"

The Jesuit shook his head. He was red as a beet and dumb as a rock.

"That's all right, priest. I know what you think. I know everything about you. I know you've filled in a form yourself."

Ryan knew by now that the pounding of his heart was phantasmal. All is illusion now, he thought; this body is just imagination. It is my soul that suffers. I retain a sense of my earthly form in the way an amputee imagines still possessing a severed arm, but there is no form, only tormented spirit.

Ryan concentrated, but could not control his terror.

"You know, J.J.," the Devil began, using the nickname Ryan's mother had favored, "I think your decision to leave the Church makes good sense. The Dope in Rome fooled you, and if you're a man, you'll knock the dust from your shoes and say good riddance. You'll settle in here where you belong.

"Now, I know you were never much of a reader, but I'll wager one thing you *did* read, once upon a time, was the *Inferno*. Yes? I knew it. Well, you remember the sign Dante hung, poetically speaking, over the gates of Hell? Of course you do. Now, you know there's no such sign here, but did you know I have a paperweight on my desk that's inscribed with the legend? Well, I do.

"I want *you* to give up hope, Ryan. I want *you* to be free of these poisonous dreams of escape. That's why I assigned you to this job, to work with these men. I know you'll come to see the futility of the so-called Underground, but I want *you* to understand the true freedom of *my* friendship.

"Remember, I'm an angel. You cannot know yet how rewarding an angel's friendship can be, but you will in time. I like Jesuits, myself. They know how to think. Remember when *you* knew how to think, Ryan? Before you grew so bored. Well, now you can recapture that lost ability. You've all the time there

is. Don't waste it on thoughts of escape, as your
friends here do.

"You're still shaking. You think I'm speaking blasphemy, right? Well, I am. Fluently. Freedom, which
I practically discovered alone, has always been
blasphemous.

"Gestas here says it was cold and dark before the
Harrowing. (You see, I told you I know everything
about you.) Gestas is right. Think back, J.J., to when
you were a boy. You swam in the lake on your
grandfather's farm. Good old Eamon. You would dive
off the float in the center of the lake, and the deeper
you swam, the colder and the darker it became. This
is how it is when *we* contemplate freedom.

"The freer you are, the more you realize that what the
world calls freedom is really slavery. Well, this is the
paradox upon which my kingdom was founded, Ryan.
The deeper you go, the colder, the darker it grows.

"God made me free. In rebellion, I fulfill God's
design. To be free of God is to be truly free. The
farther from God, the freer. The freer, the more in
God's image."

Satan paused to give Ryan a moment to think. He
knew the Jesuit would need time, but the Devil was
sure the priest would respond to the logic.

5.

Origen could see that Ryan was in danger of being
deceived. He knew that Satan would use the priest's
doubt and confusion like silken threads to weave a
web of damnation. And to save Ryan, Origen knew,
he must once again risk torment. It hounded him in
Hell as it had on Earth.

To be pure for the Kingdom, he had undergone

the torment of self-castration, an act of prodigal fervor that had cost him ordination to the priesthood, as well as his testicles. The elderly bishop of Alexandria could neither comprehend nor control, could only censor the gifted young teacher, and so Origen, in torment, exiled himself to Palestine. There he founded a school that outshone the one he'd built in Egypt, that had made Alexandria the center of learning in the Christian world. In reward, the bishop of Jerusalem decided to ordain Origen at long last, and so his dream might have been fulfilled, had not the vindictive bishop in Alexandria intervened. Origen was deposed and banished to Tyre. There he was pilloried, tortured, and there he died, tormented

Satan seemed to long for Origen's allegiance as he longed for no other. The Devil had used all his charm and wisdom to win Origen's heart. To own his soul was not enough. Yet nothing Satan did or said could move the Egyptian from the stubborn embrace of hope. Origen's resistance aroused Satan's melancholy, a state in Hell like thunder and flood, and, occasionally, his rage, more like earthquake and fire. Satan had tested Origen, had tortured and tormented him in every way he knew (and those ways are many), but Origen gave reverence to God alone.

Origen was certain that Ryan would quickly lose hope if he did not once again lock horns with the Devil. So to speak. Wearied by centuries of torment and terrified of the agony to come, he nonetheless determined to keep alive the ghost of a chance of the Jesuit's salvation.

With his eyes on the papers before him, he spoke to Satan in his quiet way, his voice almost a sigh:

"Perhaps you could explain to Fr. Ryan why he or any of us have come to be here where we do not wish to be."

Satan smiled as he thought, So, we begin again.

"Surely, Origines Adamantius, you don't want theological instruction from me."

Ryan screwed up his courage to speak.

"Why *am* I here?" he whispered.

Satan shook his head. He looked at Origen with rising anger. Then he smiled and said to Ryan:

"You're asking me, J.J.? I wouldn't know why you've come. I can tell you how long you'll stay. Would that put your mind at ease? Probably not. In any case, our Egyptian friend would disagree. But don't ask me *why* you're here. It may be because you are a hypocrite. Because you're a solipsist. Or because you marched in the St. Patrick's Day parade every year. Just for *that* you belong here. But I'm only the warden, my friend. I'm not the judge. Or do *you* forget your theology?"

"He's not a theologian," Origen said.

Satan could feel anger knotting his stomach. Frustration was his least favorite feeling.

"Origen, you old schismatic. Still hoping against hope, are you? Ryan," he said, turning back to the American, "you probably wouldn't remember, since you're not a theologian, but did you learn about apocatastasis when you were a baby priest?"

Ryan, Satan could see, had never even heard the word.

"'Apō-ca-tás-tasis,' Ryan. The universal restoration. You, the thief, our theologian here, and, yes, Ryan, even I will one day find our way . . . Home. Think of it! Everybody makes it to Heaven, including thee and me. I call it science fiction. Your Church called it heresy. Maybe that will change if the Dope in Rome decides to get eclectic with the Buddhists. What do you think, Gestas? Isn't Origen, here, a Buddhist?"

Gestas snapped to attention.

"Yessir!"

Satan chuckled, walked over and patted Gestas on the head. The thief sat down, grinning.

"Yes, indeed, Gestas. A Buddhist. A pre-existing soul achieves union with God after cycles of trial. What's that sound like to you, J.J.? Not like Jesusism."

"No."

"Hear that, Origen. One of Loyola's own has an opinion and his opinion agrees with mine. Satan 1, Origen 0."

Gestas laughed rather too hard at this. Once again he brought his hand down on the empty desk and up came another burst of ash. Satan, smiling as Gestas laughed, stood behind him, fanning away the dust.

Then he put both hands on the thief's shoulders and Gestas stopped laughing fast.

"But tell me, Origen, old sport . . . where do you suppose our thieving friend, here, learned to recite from the Psalms?"

Origen said nothing.

"You don't suppose the old Samizdat network is back in business, do you? That's hard to believe when you consider what we put the ringleaders through the last time. You must have painful memories of those days yourself.

"As I recall, you were forced to watch the Bible smugglers be fed to the fishes in the Lake of Tears. You know, Ryan, we never found their torchbearer, but whoever he is, he must suffer when he remembers the ones whom his lies condemned to eternity as fish shit at the bottom of a lake. Living with that must be, well, Hell."

Gestas was sweating and darting glances at Origen, who was looking back at him, hoping his eyes would comfort the thief, hoping Gestas would not despair.

Ryan remembered a summer afternoon on Eamon's farm when dark clouds gathered over the lake, and his grandfather had called him in from the float and together they had run to the house to hide in the basement until a tornado passed by. Now there was nowhere to hide.

6.

"Ryan," the Devil warned, "you must give up hope of escape. You may never know why things are as they are, but you *can* accept that things *are* as they must be."

Ryan looked at Origen and was surprised to see that the Egyptian was nodding.

"You agree?" the Jesuit asked.

"Escape is not possible, Fr. Ryan," Origen replied. "There are rebels in Hell who struggle to reach the border, to then cross the Lake of Purgatory, and to travel on, they suppose, to Heaven itself. You must not be a part of their movement."

Satan was stunned.

"What am I hearing? The original liberation theologian recants! I must be dreaming. But I don't dream, do I? Origen, old friend, can it be that you've finally seen the Dark?"

"No," Origen said simply. He turned to Ryan and said, "You must hold to the Faith and await the Last Judgment."

Satan growled and dug his long fingers and neatly manicured nails deep into the Bad Thief's shoulders. They literally disappeared up to the second knuckles. The pain was so great that Gestas was unable to cry out. His trembling lips failed to form the word

Origen had taught him to call out when despair wracked his soul: *mercy*.

Satan's voice was low and menacing.

"I cannot allow your Sunday school to continue, Origen. You and your cabal are poisoning too many souls with hope. Now I must destroy you, put you forever in flames. What a waste."

"You cannot set fire to God's word."

"I'll fry your soul and feed it to the hounds."

"The Gospel will be proclaimed to the People of God dispersed in this place. He is coming again!"

Ryan was sure Satan would crush Origen for saying that, but the Devil laughed instead.

"No, no, no, no. What madness. He has abandoned you—all of you. Listen up, Ryan. *I'll* tell you about the Harrowing—the one and *only* Harrowing of Hell. You've heard from the heretic and his disciple; now hear the truth.

"I've fixed the locks, Ryan. I've turned up the heat since that day . . ."

Satan walked to the center of the room and stared at the ceiling as he spoke, remembering.

"They came like locusts, my old friends. A swarm of them beating their wings and buzzing. Such pretty music! And I could have sung along, you know. I was a choirboy in the throne room aeons ago, but can you imagine a choir without soloists? And have you ever realized how bourgeois harmony really is?

"My kingdom was a citadel of liberty. Then the locusts and God, Jr., in his rage at our independence, kidnapped my best and brightest and took them to an eternity of orthodoxy. And they say *my* people are damned!

"Since then, my fury has been wanton. We are at war. The army of God, Jr., champions virtue, so I and my legions are the heralds of vice. They teach mercy. I urge revenge. They love. I hate. And so it will always be. Forever. There will be no sequel to the Harrowing. I have made our freedom inviolate."

Satan stood before Origen. He placed his hands on the desk and leaned forward so that his mouth was next to the Egyptian's ear. He whispered:

"You *are* forsaken."

Origen turned to look straight into the Devil's eyes.

" 'I saw an angel come down from Paradise with keys to the gates of Hell in one hand and a chain and manacles in the other. And the angel took hold of the old snake and bound him for a thousand years.' You will surely have a long time to meditate upon repentance."

Satan stared right back at Origen.

"Tell me, little man. Do you believe everything you read?"

" 'And I saw the dead, the famous, and the forgotten, standing before the Judge. Books were opened and the pages read . . .' "

Satan whispered:

"More torment, little man. It'll be a show trial, nothing but a star chamber."

" 'And the Lake of Tears gave up its dead and Hades delivered those whom he held . . .' "

Satan whispered:

"Yes, yes. A second death for you. So it is written in the Book and on your soul, little man, like a brand."

" 'And the Lord will wipe away *every* tear . . .' "

Then Satan shouted:

"There'll be tears enough to drown the Earth. The Gates are secure. They will not swing open again. I will not be bound—not for a thousand years nor for a single second!"

He stood back and his eyes met those of his body-guards. He gestured first to Gestas and then to Origen.

"Take them away," he commanded.

Gestas was weeping in fear and muttering, "Mercy, mercy," as the one guard dragged him away.

Origen was led away behind the thief. At the door of the office he paused. He did not turn around, but he spoke to Fr. Ryan.

"Have faith. You were right. This is Purgatory."

Satan reached over and slammed the door.

7.

"Did you hear that, Ryan? He called me an old snake. How ridiculous! This is what passes among the faithful as a revelation."

The Prince of Darkness put a hand on Ryan's shoulder.

"Men, not angels, wrote those words. Men. And do you know what inspired them? Fear, Ryan. Plain, old-fashioned fear. Not faith. Now let's see what sort of student you are. What are men afraid of, Ryan? Tell me."

Ryan found it hard to concentrate. The Devil's hand was kneading his shoulder. Origen's parting words were still fresh in his mind. What do men fear? he wondered. What besides everything?

Then it occurred to him that Satan was looking for one answer and only one.

"Freedom?" Ryan asked.

"You seem unsure."

Ryan looked into the cold blue eyes; they were as blue as an empty sky.

"Freedom."

Satan nodded. He walked to the door, opened it, and then turned back to Ryan.

"It is also customary to stand when the Devil *leaves* a room."

Ryan stood.

"Freedom, Jesuit. Think about it. Take a day off. Make a retreat. There'll be plenty of time to process the forms.

"I'll call you sometime, J.J. Until then, remember: no escape. The Egyptian heretic's dream *is* his torment. I can think of none worse. So, beware. It is better to be selfish and despondent than generous and hopeful. Beware, Ryan, lest I devour you as well."

And the Devil departed, leaving the office door open.

Ryan went walking among the rocks in the hills overlooking the city. For the first time, he noticed that the heat was becoming unbearable.

He sat down on a patch of dirt and propped his feet on a small boulder. The heat from the rock came searing right through his shoes.

Now he knew that he was doomed. Hope was simply a necessary stage on the cycle of despair. He was in the Inferno. Reaching for Paradise was the necessary prelude to his fall. To give up hope . . . This was just a taunt. It was impossible to do. Despair depends on hope, and despair is all. Over and over he reached for mercy. Always he was left empty-handed.

Yet even in the black center of hopelessness, in that flattest moment in the very pit of defeat, Ryan thought he saw a pinhole of light. He had seen that same light in Origen's eyes. Origen had said . . .

But Satan had said . . .

Fr. Ryan saw the light but knew it was only the beginning of a deeper torment. A theological pimp . . .

And yet . . .

And yet . . .

Another wave of misery swept over him. A tear formed in his left eye. He felt his phantom heart breaking. Another tear formed in his right eye and rolled down his cheek. What good was freedom, he wept, without mercy?

Then suddenly, Fr. John J. Ryan, S.J., heard hissing, and in terror he leapt away from the Serpent he knew had come to swallow him.

But when he peered between his trembling fingers, he saw nothing. Nothing at all. Nothing but his tears dancing into steam on a hot rock in Hell.

THE EX-KHAN

Robert L. Asprin

My first day in Hell was the worst. I mean, I hadn't thought it would be a picnic, but my wildest imagining still left me unprepared for the reality of my after-life existence.

Actually, I hadn't expected to find myself here at all. On the rare occasions during my former life that my thoughts had drifted toward death, my logical twentieth-century mind had calmly concluded that when I died, that would be the end of things as far as I was concerned. No angels with harps, no devils with pitchforks. Just . . . nothing. Pull the plug. End game.

If I had allowed myself to seriously consider an afterlife, I probably would have figured that I'd end up with the good guys. While I had always kidded around a lot about what a perverted, wicked person I was, most of it was just hooey. Villains are more interesting people than heroes, as a rule, and neither I nor my cronies wanted to be thought of as the "goody two-shoes" type, so we made a big deal of our coarse humor and imagined coups, both business and social. Underneath it all, though, we really thought we were good people. Evil people were killers or rapists or child molesters or something. Heck, I had never even gotten a traffic ticket, just a couple parking fines. My few attempts at sowing wild oats were pleasant and amicably terminated by mutual consent. Surely little things like that couldn't count against you in the grand scales of life.

So what was I doing in Hell?

This question was foremost in my mind upon my arrival in my new home. The horrible Welcome Woman was no help at all, continually insisting that "Everybody feels the same way when they first arrive," and "It will all come clear to you after a while," and generally being a pain in the butt without providing one whit of information in response to my questions. I finally grew frustrated with my unrewarded efforts, and while she was prattling on about the politics of Hell (which did not interest me any more than earthly politics had), wandered off to try to find the answer on my own.

My first impression of Hell was that it was surprisingly ordinary . . . well, sort of. No devils, no pitchforks, no pools of molten lava with tortured souls shrieking in agony. There were, however, a fair number of people moving purposefully about in an amazing array of costumes. It reminded me a bit of the time I took a guided tour of a West Coast movie studio . . . so much so it took me a while to realize that these weren't actors in costume, but individuals wearing what to them were normal clothes from their native eras of history. Aside from the strange wardrobes and the mottled red sky, there was little to distinguish the panorama of Hell from any busy business section or college campus. I didn't know whether to be relieved or disappointed.

The feeling of familiarity continued when I tried to stop people to ask questions. Just like the streets of home, my efforts were rebuffed with comments of "No time now," and "Ask someone else." All in all, the people here were a rather self-centered lot, each caught up in his or her own affairs and not really caring about the problems of a stranger. Of course, that's what I was doing myself . . . expecting everyone to drop everything until my curiosity was satisfied. This gave me food for thought. Was it a sin to be self-centered? If so, then Hell must be a bigger place than I imagined. Even the most saintly people I knew back in the '80s still kept an eye out for the old Number One.

I was still pondering this hypothesis when I noticed him for the first time. If he hadn't been outside the mainstream of normal foot traffic in a small park, and sitting, which placed him well below eye level, I would have seen him at once. Though unimposing physically, he still would have stood out in the crowd.

While most of the people I had seen or tried to talk to were civilians of one sort or another, this one was a warrior. What's more, his armor and weapons marked him as being from the Far East, while most of the crowd seemed to be of Western European origins.

Intrigued, I drifted closer for a better look.

The man raised his head as I approached and regarded me with eyes as hard and dark as obsidian. His face was round and weathered brown, with expression lines as deep as if they had been carved into wood with a chisel. His manner was neither hostile nor friendly, but rather held the detached watchfulness of a reptile contemplating whether I were small enough to eat. I was briefly reminded of an old photograph of Geronimo I had once seen.

I halted my advance and smiled in what I hoped was a friendly and, above all, harmless way. After a moment, he gave a silent grunt and returned his attention to his work.

My distress at not knowing why I had been condemned to Hell was upstaged by my fascination with the man and the chore he was addressing. His weapons were laid out before him on a blanket and he was checking them with the unhurried certainty of one who has performed the same task hundreds, if not thousands of times. With deft precision he checked the edge of sword and knife, then began working his way through his quiver of arrows one by one, checking each for straightness, like a hustler checking a pool cue. Finally, I could contain my curiosity no longer.

"You're a Mongol, aren't you?"

That earned me a longer look.

I wondered briefly if he understood English, but then I noted that his carriage had shifted slightly. While still appearing relaxed, the man was now poised and ready to move fast, and his eyes were warier and more analytical than they had been a few moments before. He understood me all right, and for some reason, my words had raised his guard.

"What makes you ask that?"

His voice was a resonant bass with a bit of a flat accent I couldn't identify.

"Your weapons," I answered with a casual shrug. "Your armor is Chinese, but your weapons are those of the Great Horde. Double-recurve laminated bow, the hooked sword, a thrusting lance . . . that's standard gear for a Mongol horseman, isn't it? The arrows are a dead giveaway. As far as I know, the Mongols were the only ones to use two different caliber arrows: light for flight, or heavier for close, armor-piercing work."

His head dipped slightly in the briefest of nods.

"You are knowledgeable in our ways," he said. "I am not familiar with your manner of dress. Are all men of your era so well versed on the weapons of their enemies?"

"No. Military history just happens to be a hobby of mine . . . and we don't consider Mongols to be our enemies. No offense, but your descendants are no longer the world power they were in your time."

His eyes were distant for a few heartbeats, then his face split in a sudden grin, showing surprisingly white teeth. "So they tell me. Still, one can always hope for a rebirth of the old times, can't one?"

I returned his smile, but shook my head.

"Not much chance of that happening, I'm afraid. Everything today is firearms and missiles. Masses of men and machines are settling today's wars, not the skill of the individual warrior."

"It was much the same in our day," the Mongol shrugged carelessly. "Large numbers of troops won the day for the Horde often enough."

"Really?" I frowned. "I was under the impression that more often than not you were outnumbered. The Mongols I studied relied more on tactics based on psychological warfare and incredible mobility to take advantage of the myth of vast mobs of horsemen."

The dark eyes studied me again, all hint of laughter gone.

"Once more you are correct," the man acknowledged. "I would know the name of the man who is not easily deceived in this land of deceptions."

It took me a moment to realize what he meant.

"Who, me? My name is Will Hawker."

The man nodded, then turned his attention to his weapons once more, picking up his sword to test its edge again.

It seemed that he felt our conversation was at an end. I, however, was eager to prolong the discussion and cast about desperately for something to say.

"Does your sword have a name?"

That at least earned me another glance.

"Does your right thumb have a name?"

I had been expecting a yes-or-no answer, so his question caught me off guard.

"My . . . No. It doesn't."

"Neither does my sword. My weapons are to me as your thumb is to you . . . a part of my body. They require no more thought to use than does your thumb. The custom of naming a weapon as if it were an independent being has always been a puzzle to me."

His level, matter-of-fact tone made me feel chastised to a point where I felt it necessary to defend my question.

"I always felt it was a way of expressing respect for one's weapons. The people I knew who named their weapons usually claimed to love a named weapon with the same passion they did a brother or a lover."

"That is what I've been told," the Mongol said with a shrug. "I have simply never agreed with it. To me a weapon is a tool to be used, not loved. If one becomes too emotionally attached to a weapon . . ."

He broke off suddenly, his attention captured by something nearby in the park.

I followed his gaze, and saw a bush that moved . . . first with a tentative tremor, then flipping back along with a portion of the ground it was rooted in to reveal a dark hole beneath. Before I could speak, a small figure in dark, loose-fitting pajamas popped out carrying a rifle. He scanned the park and the passers-by on the street, his eyes pausing briefly on me, then moving on to my companion. His head dipped in a brief nod of acknowledgement or recognition, then he turned and gestured at someone in the hole.

Four more men, dressed and armed like their point man, emerged from the hole. The last two had their weapons slung and were carrying a sixth man on a litter between them. The borne man was still, though whether dead or unconscious I couldn't tell. The point man replaced the bush to hide the hole once more, and the band moved off silently in single file, carrying their fallen comrade with them.

"Those look like Viet Cong!" I exclaimed, finding my voice at last.

"That's right," the Mongol said calmly, turning his attention to his weapons once more. "Some of them have been included in our honored ranks here in Hell. You'll get used to seeing them. Hell is riddled with their tunnels and spider holes, so there's no telling where they'll pop up next."

He seemed unimpressed by their unexpected intrusion into our area, so I decided to try to match his manner and return to our conversation. "Tell me, we've been discussing weapons here. Why is it that you still have sword, lance, and bow when they have more modern weapons? Those are AR-15s they were carrying, weren't they?"

"I am used to these weapons," he said. "Besides, you would be surprised at how well these old tools work against more modern devices. The sword is still one of the best close-combat weapons ever devised, if one has the time to train with it . . . and I've had lots of time."

"I notice the Cong didn't seem particularly anxious to fight with you."

The Mongol's lips twisted into a flat smile. "There is an unspoken truce between us. While they respect my weapons, sometimes a name is more powerful than the keenest sword. They know me . . . or at least their ancestors did."

Something in his voice sent a chill down my spine, though I couldn't put a finger on it.

"Speaking of names," I said as casually as I could, "I've shared mine with you, but you haven't yet told me yours."

He seemed to hesitate for a moment before answering.

"I am called Temujin by some."

The name struck me like a blow. As I said earlier, military history is a hobby of mine. While that name might be unknown to many of my age and era, it was more than familiar to me. The person I was talking to was none other than . . .

"Genghis Khan."

I was almost unaware of saying the name aloud, my awestruck words matching my thoughts. I would have been glad for the opportunity to chat with any member of the Mongol hordes, but it had never occurred to me that I would ever have the chance to talk to the Great Khan himself! Maybe Hell wouldn't be such a bad place after all.

"You know the name . . . and the title," the man said in a flat tone that was as much an accusation as a statement. "I would know your thoughts regarding your discovery."

I realized with a start that his sword was now between us, held in a loose guard position. I had seen experienced fencers in similar stances so I was not fooled by the apparent casualness of his position.

The Mongol could attack me without even a split-second delay to prepare . . . only his sword was real and there was more at stake here than tournament points! Taking care not to move my hands, I groped for the proper words.

"Um, amazement . . . curiosity, admiration . . ."

"No anger?" the Mongol interrupted. "No desire to attack me or at least raise an alarm?"

"Why should I want to do that?"

The Khan's lips flattened into a humorless grin.

"Forgive me if I'm wrong, but you seem to be of European stock. My people were the scourge of your ancestors, and as their leader, I am one of your greatest folk villains. You would not be the first in these lands who felt it meet to attempt to make Hell a little less pleasant for an old enemy."

"I can't speak for the others here," I said, raising my hands to shoulder height, palms forward, "but you have nothing to fear from me. Even if I could attack you successfully, which I doubt, I wouldn't. You see, I've never really thought of you as a villain. While it is true that you and your troops were ferocious and brutal, your culture and era required a certain amount of viciousness for survival. What's more, even in my era it was difficult to distinguish how much of the documented brutality of the Mongol hordes was accurate, and how much was exaggeration on the part of either your enemies' chroniclers or your own propaganda machine. No, I have been more fascinated by the more admirable side of your reported personality."

"And exactly what is it about me that you feel is admirable?" he pressed.

"Well, first of all, there's the basic success story that would be the envy of any businessman of my time: a boy without family or village in his early teens being actively hunted by his enemies, and in less than three decades building an empire that ruled over a third of the known world. Your abilities as a military leader and tactician are acknowledged by even your staunchest critics, but most of them choose to overlook your other contributions. You not only united the tribes into a massive army, the horde, but you also gave them a written language and a governing set of laws on the Yassa. Your arrow-riders formed a communications network far ahead of its time . . . in fact, it lasted longer and performed better than the Pony Express of a much later period. As far as I have been able to discover, you were the one who introduced the concept of paper money to the world, and you insisted on religious tolerance to a degree that makes the European and Middle East indulgence in holy wars look like ignorant barbarism. No, I have no difficulty admiring you, and I am frankly grateful for the chance to speak with you in person."

Apparently my sincerity was convincing, for the Khan sheathed his sword with a dry laugh.

"It is comforting to know that my efforts have not gone totally unnoticed in your lands," he said, "but beware, Will Hawker. Beware of being as blind with your admiration as others are with their hate and fear. While some of the things I did may have had a beneficial long-term effect on mankind, many of them were instituted from motives as base and greedy as the worst in history."

"Could you give me an example?" I said. "I have often wished I could learn the motives and thoughts behind some of your policies . . . good or bad."

"Well . . . you mentioned our Mongolian scrip— paper money, I think you called it. That was nothing more than bloodless, systematized looting. When we were occupying a new area, we would insist that taxes and tributes be paid in gold, jewels, or other valuables. For our own debts, we would pay with paper notes. The trick was that when it was time to collect taxes again, we would not accept our own paper in return, but instead insisted on another round of valuables. Within a few years, all the hard wealth, such as gold, was in our coffers and all the people had to exchange was paper."

I found myself smiling. "Actually, your concept has been followed with frightening accuracy. In my era, all nations have their citizens exchanging paper while the government holds the actual wealth—be it in gold, silver, or crown jewels. I just never thought of it as organized looting before."

The Khan joined me in my laughter.

"So I've been told. If nothing else, I fear that particular contribution of mine to civilization has guaranteed me a place in your Hell."

A random thought brought my laughter to a slow halt.

"That raises an interesting point," I said. "What are you doing in Hell?"

Though he also stopped laughing, the Khan's eyes still smiled at me with mischievous humor.

"You have to ask? Me? The bloodiest butcher of history? If anyone, surely I've earned a place here."

"No, I meant . . . well, Hell is primarily a Christian concept. How is it that you have been drawn to an afterlife outside your own religion?"

That earned me a shrug. "There have been several theories posed by the various philosophers here to explain my presence. Some feel that the religious tolerance of mine you referred to earned me a place in the eyes of the Christian God, and subsequently resulted in my assignment here. Others feel that my presence is actually a stage prop for the Europeans here . . . that their Hell would not be complete without their arch-enemy lurking in the background. The presence of the Viet Cong here seems to support their theory. Then again, it may be that part of my own afterlife punishment is to exist surrounded by Europeans rather than my own countrymen."

"But what do you think?"

The amusement vanished from the Mongol's manner, and he turned his attention once more to his weapons. "I think that it is pointless to think of such things. I am here. Why I am here is unimportant. The time to plan and ponder a battle is before the conflict is joined, not while actively engaged with the enemy. Then hindsight is a dangerous indulgence, for it draws your concentration away from the task at hand. One must condition oneself to reject such thoughts in favor of studying the terrain and the changing face of the battle in progress. I do not care why I am here. I am, however, very interested in the nature of my punishment and how best to endure it."

For a few moments, I watched him examine the tools of his trade.

"That reminds me of a question I meant to ask when I saw the Cong," I said at last. "You speak of battle. Is there fighting here? War? Can people die in Hell?"

"My words were figurative," he grunted. "In my mind, life itself, or afterlife, is a battle . . . a constant confrontation of opposition in an effort to exert one's own will on others. To answer your question, however, yes, people can die in Hell. I have experienced it myself. As I said earlier, not all the people here share your admiration of me or my kind. The revival process is unpleasant enough that I do not wish to repeat the experience any more than is absolutely necessary. In regard to war and fighting . . ."

He paused and looked around us with the tight-lipped, humorless grin I had noticed before.

". . . There are people here. Anywhere there are people there will be war and fighting . . . sometime, on some level. As a student of military history, I'm surprised you didn't know that."

"Is this the punishment you spoke of, then?" I said after a few minutes' thought. "Are you paying for a lifelong series of battles with eternal battle in the afterlife?"

The hard, dark eyes fixed on me again.

"You know very little of Hell, Will Hawker."

With those words he began to gather his weapons, securing them one by one upon his body. It occurred to me that I had somehow offended the Khan with my last question.

"You're right. I don't know about Hell. That shouldn't be surprising, as I've just arrived today. What you said earlier about not wasting time wondering why you're here . . . I didn't even know that. Since I got here I've been doing nothing but bothering people about why I'm here. I didn't know the protocol or customs, so if I insulted you somehow by asking about your punishment, it was unintentional. You mentioned it yourself earlier is all. I thought it was all right to discuss it."

The man's movements slowed, then ceased completely.

"You owe me no apology, Will Hawker," he said with a sigh, his eyes never leaving the ground. "It is simply that my true punishment is distasteful enough to me that I do not like to dwell upon it, much less discuss it. If anything, our talk has provided me with momentary divergence from my thoughts. For that I owe you thanks, and will answer your questions."

He raised his gaze to meet my own.

"I did fight my entire life, but because of that, battle would not be a punishment to me . . . simply a continuation of my normal existence. No, my punishment in far more subtle than that. You have correctly perceived that I am preparing for battle. Look around you and tell me what you see . . . or more important, what you don't see."

Puzzled, I swept my eyes around in a full circle.

"I . . . I'm afraid I don't understand."

"What you don't see," the Khan supplied, "is followers. I have no army, no horde. Unlike any previous life, any battle I encounter here I must fight alone."

It took a moment for the irony of the Khan's situation to sink in. One of the greatest leaders the world has known—a ruler of nations, commander of troops numbering in the hundreds of thousands—reduced to single combat with nothing to organize other than his personal weapons.

"I'm sorry," I said, and meant it. "It must be very difficult for you."

The Khan was on his feet in an angry surge.

"Do not pity me, Will Hawker," he hissed. "Hate me, fear me, for those reactions I am accustomed to dealing with. But spare me your sympathy. In my entire life I never imposed my burdens or sorrows on another, and I will not have that happen now. I have been stripped of everything I worked to build. Leave me my pride."

Snatching up his bow, he turned to leave.

"Wait!" I called. "Take me with you!"

He faced me again, the dark eyes studying me intently.

"I will be your army . . . or aide. I'm not much, but it will double your force."

"It may not be wise to interfere with the fate planned for me," the Khan said carefully. "Perhaps you should wait until you know more of Hell before making such a rash commitment."

Now it was my turn to laugh.

"To follow Genghis Khan into battle would be the dream of a lifetime for me. I'd face the Devil himself for the chance."

"You may not be speaking figuratively," the Mongol warned. "But come, walk beside me and tell me of yourself. It is clear you have a warrior's interest and heart. What is your background?".

A small chill flitted across my heart.

"Well, as I told you, I've studied military history. I'm familiar with the writings of Clausewitz, Sun Tsu, Hart . . ."

The Khan waved his hand impatiently.

"No. I mean, what is your firsthand experience."

"I . . . um . . . studied the martial arts for over twenty years—you know, karate and kung-fu. I did a little fencing and riflery, but never had a chance to get into archery . . ."

I stopped talking, for the Khan had halted in his steps and was studying me carefully.

"Am I not making myself clear, Will Hawker?" he said. "I am not asking about your studies. I wish to know what your actual combat experience is."

I licked my lips, unable to meet his gaze.

"None," I admitted. "My country had only one war while I was of age to serve, against the Viet Cong we saw earlier. When I tried to volunteer for combat duty, I was rejected. Medically unfit for active service, they said."

"And so you studied war as a hobby."

"That's right. I had always wanted to be a soldier. Not getting into the army was one of the biggest disappointments of my life. It made me feel I had somehow failed as a man, so I kept up my studies as best I could on my own."

"You had friends? You would talk to them of strategy and battle plans?"

"That's right."

"And whenever possible, you would talk to other noncombatants—children and women—explaining to them the mind of a soldier and his necessary role in society?"

"Well, sometimes. Most of them didn't want to listen, but I did what I could."

In the silence that followed, I sneaked a glance at the Khan. He was staring at the horizon, his face expressionless. Finally, he heaved a great sigh.

"You may not fight beside me, Will Hawker. Better that I fight alone."

"But I'm fit enough to fight. Those doctors only . . ."

"I didn't say that you *can* not. I said that you *may* not. I do not wish you for a follower."

"But . . . I . . . Why . . ."

Words failed me in my confusion. The Khan shook his head minutely and turned to face me.

"I told you before, all I have left is my pride, and I guard it jealously. It will not allow me to accept a follower such as you. Still, your offer of loyalty was both generous and sincere, so courtesy demands that I at least try to explain my position to you."

He paused for a moment and his gaze drifted into distant focus as he organized his thoughts.

"I mentioned earlier that I tried not to waste time wondering why I was here in Hell, but the most disciplined minds wander, and I have formed a theory as to the reason for my punishment. My fatal weakness is not that for killing and bloodshed, but rather of vanity. You see, I liked being Khan. Liked it far too much for the good of my followers or the world. When I was elected Khan of the united tribes, the Horde, I perceived that we were too strong to be attacked. Whatever defense I organized would eventually stagnate from disuse, until the tribes fell to bickering among themselves from boredom. Then the Horde would dissolve, taking with it my position and title. To avoid this, I instituted an expansionist policy and put the Horde on the attack. We were constantly pushing our borders outward, which guaranteed the Horde would be fighting, and I kept them fighting, and therefore united in purpose, until my death. Vanity made me a warmonger, so here I am paying the price that I never accounted for during my life."

His eyes focused on me again.

"But I got something for it. It is my guess that you are in Hell because you got nothing for your war efforts. War is a terrible thing, Will Hawker. It is not a game or a hobby, but a horrible means to an end. Wars are fought for land or wealth, or as in my case, a title and power. Noncombatant warriors such as you and your friends cling to romantic ideas of honor and ideals that any combat soldier loses in his first encounter. You never fight the wars yourself, so you have no idea of what is involved. Still, you encourage others to war, or even worse, argue to make battle an acceptable part of life. Blind ignorance makes you a warmonger, and ignorance is uncontrollable because, unlike greed, it can never be satisfied. I may be condemned by history for my part in war, and justly so . . . but you, Will Hawker, and all your friends, are a hundred times worse than I and my

kind, and I will not sully my name and banner by
having you stand beside me in battle."

With a final curt nod, he left me standing there as
he stomped away to his unnamed battle alone.

Watching him go, I had pause to consider the
bitter irony of Hell. The legendary leader of men
was now forced to fight alone, while I, who yearned
for battle all my life, would be denied the chance
even in afterlife. It occurred to me that, unlike the
Khan, my afterlife was going to be simply an exten-
sion of my previous life, for I had succeeded in
building and living in Hell even before I died.

Bowing my head, I wept.

THE CONSCIENCE OF THE KING

C.J. Cherryh and Nancy Asire

Marie smiled as she walked down the hallway—morning in Napoleon's house was orderly, if nothing else. There were certain habits he refused to break even now that she had moved in with him.

Breakfast at eight o'clock was one of them. They took turns at fixing it, and this morning she was the one headed toward the kitchen.

She came to a halt at the edge of the dining room, a strange chill running down her spine. Though she could not say how she knew it, someone was in the kitchen. The obvious question of *who* immediately succeeded itself by *how*. She glanced back toward the bedroom: Napoleon was still in the bathtub—she could hear him singing. The security system (obtained by Attila from unknown sources and highly reliable) had not been breached. She drew a deep breath, considered rousting Napoleon from his bath, scotched that idea as unfair (the plumbing having been fixed only yesterday), and cautiously walked through the dining room toward the kitchen door.

There was a faint light shining out of the semi-darkness of the kitchen. She shivered suddenly, bit down on her lower lip, and edged along the wall until she stood next to the door.

"Marie."

She muffled her gasp behind a raised hand. The voice was deep, melodious, and full of such peace that her heart quivered.

"Don't be afraid," the voice said. "Come on, Marie."

With a last glance to the rear of the house where Napoleon luxuriated in his hot bath, Marie slowly walked into the kitchen.

And nearly fell to her knees before her visitor.

The angel hovered only inches above the floor, his great white wings furled behind his shoulders. A face only mad artists could have painted, eyes only poets could have described, turned her way.

Marie backed up until she felt the reassuring solid-ity of the wall behind her shoulders. She tried to speak, but her voice failed her.

"Your time is up, Marie," the angel said, his eyes shining with an inner light. "You've served your time in Hell. You're a Temp no longer."

Her heart gave an absurd beat. Free? Was she truly free? Could it possibly be that she had suffered her last pass through the soul-cleansing that would allow her into the highest level of Purgatory, only steps away from the eternal bliss of Heaven?

"Yes, Marie." The angel's voice was even quieter now, filled with the same love and warmth. "You're free."

She found her voice at last. "But what of—Napoleon?"

The angel's eyes took on a different color (if such a term could be applied to them). "I have no jurisdiction over him, Marie. That comes from One higher than I."

Marie squeezed her eyes closed, trying to shut off the vision before her. It was no help: she saw the angel's compassionate face as clearly as if her eyes were open.

"But . . ."

"I understand," the angel said, a faint smile touching his perfect features. "You wish more time to say your farewells. Such is granted to you. Three days from now, at this very hour, I'll come to you again and lead you forth from Hell."

"I . . . what I mean is—"

"Be strong, Marie," admonished the angel, his eyes again changing color, becoming light on the sea at morning. "This is your last torment. Heaven waits beyond."

And with that, the angel was gone, leaving only wonder in his going.

Marie stood backed up against the wall, her hands shaking. Her eyes misted over with unshed tears and she angrily blinked them away. Her very existence turned inside out: everything she had learned to accept in her temporary stay in Hell was rendered invalid.

And yet she was free to go.

But without Napoleon?

A quiet sob shook her. She blindly felt her way to the kitchen table, fumbled for a chair and sat down. Memory flooded over her.

The license bureau, Napoleon in the chair across from her asking her to come live with him. She heard herself saying it would make things harder, for they would only be separated when it hurt the most.

And it hurt. It hurt like hell.

A soft step behind her, a tender hand on her shoulder.

"Marie. What's the matter?"

She blinked her tears away and looked up into Napoleon's face.

"What are you doing?" he asked, reaching behind to flip on the overhead light. "*Dieu!* You're crying. What—"

She motioned him silent and watched in rapt fascination as he took the chair at her side. Could she live for the rest of eternity without such small sights?

He reached out and held her hand, his grey-blue eyes serious in the lamplight. "All right, Marie. Take it slow. What happened?"

"Napoleon," she said at last, his very name on her lips of some comfort. "This isn't going to be easy, so listen carefully." She swallowed heavily. "I'm a fraud, Napoleon. I'm not even supposed to *be* here. I didn't end up in Hell when I died—I was sent to Purgatory for my sins. And when I didn't repent of the greatest of them, I was temporarily sent to Hell. Here, I was to be cured of that sin, to be taken back to Purgatory after."

His face had gone slightly pale, but his eyes never wavered. "And that sin, Marie?"

She tried to smile. "My love for you."

"*Dieu en ciel!* You've been punished for *that?*"

"It *was* adultery."

"Oh, bullshit! If I'd had a wife who was really a wife, I suppose it would have been. But Josephine . . ."

She placed her other hand on top of his. "We don't make the rules—we can only play by them. So,

I was to wait here in Hell until I was told I was free to go."

His hand tightened. "And I suppose that was just now."

She nodded.

"With a chance for Heaven waiting?"

She nodded again. "It was an angel, Napoleon."

"In my kitchen? With all the dirty dishes in the sink?"

"And dried peanut butter on the table."

"That was Wellington—Mr. Priss except when it comes to sandwiches." He ran a hand through his hair. "You know, Marie, all this time I've thought you were a plant, a spy, someone used to gain control over me. I didn't know whose. It could have been the Management, the Dissidents—any number of powers here in Hell. And I've never been able to tell you half of what's going on because . . ." His voice faltered.

"Because you couldn't trust me," she finished. "I know, Napoleon. And I don't hold it against you. In your position, I would have done nothing else."

His glance locked with hers. "When are you going?"

She looked away, stared at the clock above the sink, the shadows thrown on the wall—anything but him. The angel had said she was free, but was she? Could she deny her love for the man who sat at her side? "The last torment," the angel had said. Small word to describe the situation.

"The angel said three days from now, this same hour." She looked back to him. "I was given time to say my farewells."

His voice was steady. "Go, Marie. This is your chance for eternal happiness. I want nothing more than for you to be happy."

"But would I be?" She heard her own question as if it had been asked by another. "I wonder," she said slowly, "what they would do if I said no."

"Said no?" he echoed, his eyebrows lifted in genuine surprise. "How could you—?"

"I love you," she murmured. "I *died* loving you. How could I live again and not do the same?"

That shook him. She saw his shoulders stiffen beneath his blue workshirt.

"You'd deny yourself Heaven for me?"

She drew a deep breath. Never to see him again, never to hear his voice, feel his touch. Eternally. Was Heaven worth that?

"I think I might."

"*O bon dieu!*" He let loose of her hand, rose, and walked over to the sink, stood silent for a long while, his hands gripping the edge of the countertop. His voice was muffled. "Think about it, Marie. This is *eternity* we're talking about—not months, not years. If I understand, you haven't been here all that long. You've only seen the very surface of Hell. There are regions far lower than this, fouler than anything you could imagine. Wellington and I are—well, for New Dead, we're left alone most of the time because of our past service in the army and because we don't rock the boat. Our true torment is to know that, as much as we plan and scheme, we'll likely never escape. Pain and death down here are *very* real. That you would choose Hell—"

"Mouse did," she said, standing and walking to his side. "You told me that yourself."

"Mouse is different!" he growled. "Mouse is—well . . . Mouse is Mouse!"

"Why can't there be two of us who've chosen to be here?"

He remained silent. She reached out and touched his cheek.

"Napoleon . . . can't you accept the fact that I love you as much as I do?"

His eyes were shadowed when he turned to her. "I suppose I can. What I find hard to believe is that I'm worth it."

She moved closer and slipped her arms around him. "You are. Wherever you are, that's where I want to be."

"Marie. Don't make up your mind now. Please. You have three days. Promise me that you'll think about it first."

"All right. I promise."

He kissed her softly. "Then for the next three days, let's live as if you've made your decision to go." He smiled slightly. "And when the angel comes back, have him fix the dishwasher, will you? I'm tired of the sink being full."

As days went in Hell, it was not one of the good ones. Sycophants flitted up and down the halls of Augustus' villa like gulls before a storm, carrying this, bringing that, delivering messages in small, quavering voices . . . Augustus had said, Sargon had reported, no, there was no news of Caesar's missing son, none, sorry, sorry, sorry. . . .

As weeks went in Hell, it had already been a bad one, and the black vintage phone in Julius Caesar's sometime office had already borne a considerable traffic of calls—from Scaevola, in the field; from Mouse, at the armory; and from Kleopatra, whose banal chatter delivered information from Machiavelli that could damn them all to a deeper, bleaker Hell.

"You must not compromise yourself," Augustus said—Octavianus Augustus, *pater patriae*, First

Citizen and *tribunus plebis in perpetuum*. He paced, that was the state Augustus was in, and Julius watched the thin figure with the toga flapping about him as Augustus went the course past his desk from the bookshelf to the windows, from the windows to the bookshelf, back again to the windows, beyond which the Hall of Injustice towered up to meet the clouds of Hell, and just out of view of which the Pentagram itself squatted in obdurate hostility, in the hands of Rameses II, the genius of Kadesh, who had lost Egypt Asia Minor; and Rameses' conniving ally, Mithradates the butcher.

Julius rested his head against the heels of his hands. "Compromise myself. *Di immortales*, if I had Mithradates in my reach—"

"You would lose yourself and destroy us. No, *Cai Iuli*. Let Caesarion go. Let him be."

Julius fixed his nephew/adopted son with a dark and ominous stare, which recalled very thoroughly who had murdered Caesarion in life, and who had most reason to dread any rapprochement between himself and his disaffected son. That Augustus did not flinch indicated the depth of his disturbance in the matter.

"You're on thin ice," Julius said, *"son."*

Augustus looked like a thirty-year-old—ears that stuck out, a dusting of freckles, an angularity of nose and jaw which looked younger still, and an Adam's apple that jutted and worked when he was distressed. He had died an old man and he had not lost those years, inside, no more than had Julius, who looked a vital thirty-odd—black of hair, trim and hard in 20th century military khaki, and at the moment with his sleeves rolled up and ink stains on his fingers.

"I know," Augustus said. "But for love of you, *father*, I will say it: you are rarely a fool."

"Are you calling me a fool?"

"I am," said Augustus the First Citizen, "saying that no one profits by this preoccupation of yours except our enemies. If the boy wanted to be found, he would be found. What has this searching gained us? We've turned over every verminous rock in New Hell, we've disturbed situations far better let rest, we've jeopardized alliances and called in debts we had far rather leave for more profitable ventures, cards which we can only play once. And for what? For a boy who wants to kill you?"

"And you, of course."

"*Pro di,* you're not listening—"

The phone rang. "I'm listening. I'm just not pleasing you." Julius picked up the receiver. "*Caesar adsum, quid est?*"

"*This Julius?*" the American voice said.

"What in hell are you doing on this line?"

"*I have my ways,*" Welch said. "*Let me give it to you short and sweet. Alex is back. Got himself Moved, the hard way, and the Devil didn't do it, you got that? That damn Maccabee is back with Guevara, and Alex just sort of dropped in. You following me, Caesar?*"

"I'm following you." There was a knot in his gut that few things could put there. "How dependable is this?"

"*Hundred percent. You want him? Or do we take him?*"

"You want him Moved, *edepol,* why doesn't Administration twitch a finger?"

There was a moment's delay on the other end. It was close to Treason, what he had said, and Augustus had gone pale behind his freckles.

"*You don't ask.*" Welch's low voice came back. "*Julie baby, you just call this a favor—if you don't*" *want him going through Reassignments. You want him, you sit on him."*

"Have I got clearance on this?"

Welch hung up. Julius drew several deep breaths, dropped the phone into its cradle, and looked at Augustus. "Send Publius down to the Armory. Tell them this line's gone unsecure. Have them trace that tap."

"What in hell was it?"

"Alexander."

"On the telephone?"

"In the Dissident camp. Somebody Moved him. He's in there with Judah Maccabee. Welch says the Devil had nothing to do with it. The Dissidents have got themselves a first-rate general." He pushed back in the chair. Alexander: his own second incarnation, as Achilles was the first. "If it wasn't the Devil pulled those strings—one can surmise who would."

"Mithradates?"

Julius folded his arms and balanced the chair back on its springs, rocking gently. "Step one: Mithradates ousts Hadrian and bureaucratic bunglers put Rameses into the number one slot in the Pentagram. Step two: Mithradates insinuates himself and his subordinates right into the special operations division. Step three: Mithradates funnels money and mercs right up to the top of the Dissidents the Pentagram's supposed to be fighting . . . *infiltrate and subvert*, he tells his imperial asininity, and Rameses finds it in a book somewhere and swallows the whole thing. Step four: he aims Brutus at me, divides my sons, confounds my family, and lures me off on that damnable mess at Troy."

"*That* was Mithradates? Gods above, why did you do it?"

"Because he had the right bait. Alexander. Only

he may not have counted on Achilles. I don't think he did count on Achilles. Hell has rules the Devil himself can't subvert. Put me and Alexander together and Achilles *had* to show up. Resonances."

"Gods, you're reaching at straws."

"I don't think so."

"Well, what if it was *Achilles* was Mithradates' cat's-paw? And Alexander the happenstance?"

Julius frowned. "Possible. I don't discount that. I haven't discounted anything. Step five: Achilles shows up, completing the triad. Step six: Mithradates' agents push Caesarion into defecting to the Dissidents. Step seven: Mithradates tweaks Hell's computers and drops Alexander of Macedon into command of the Dissidents, giving them a general, and *I* get an unofficial call from an Administration agent telling me to solve it. Dammit, Mithradates wants me to take the field. He wants me in the field against my own avatar. He wants me back under Pentagram direction and damn him, he wants me where he can get a clear shot at me."

Augustus' face had lost all its schoolboy charm. It was the First Citizen who stood there thinking and thinking, and gnawing a hole in his lip. "If you're right."

"I had rather believe in causality than to think Mithradates is that damn lucky. Or that the Devil himself is moving."

"There is always that chance, uncle." Augustus bit a hangnail and walked to the windows, where the Hall towered distantly into the roiling red clouds and disappeared. "You can't discount that." He turned his back on the windows, grim-faced. "By gods, they're playing you, can't you see that? You're absolutely right that you're in jeopardy, be it Mithradates, be it a stray finger on those damnable computers in Administration. And you *are* a fool if you walk into this, on my word, uncle, a *fool*, and reprehensible. The Family has its rights and its claim on you, first and foremost. I need not remind you of that."

Julius glared at him. "Family rights meant nothing, of course, when you had Caesarion killed."

Augustus opened his mouth, probably to say that he did not consider a half Egyptian as family; and shut it, perhaps recalling that Kleopatra was the Egyptian half in question, for whose death he was also responsible, and who fit within the *familia*. As did Brutus, for similarly tangled reasons.

"That is not the question," was what Augustus did say. "Your safety is."

"I'll see to that."

"The Family, *Iuli*. Dammit, your enemies want you compromised. They want to link you to the Dissidents, by your son, by Alexander, they *want* you to take Alexander to yourself—"

"Then it's about time we taught the Dissidents the legions are still in business. The Tenth and the Twelfth ought to do it."

"—or they want to send Alexander the Trip, where Reassignments can get at him and bend him any way they will. Dammit, I wish you'd tell me what you're up to!"

Julius flicked through the Rolodex, and picked up the phone, dialing a number on the far side of the Park. "Poker, nephew."

"That line's not secure!"

"Damn, so it isn't. Hello? Napoleon, old friend?"

The Iron Duke was mooching again.

Napoleon frowned slightly as his neighbor hovered around the microwave. Wellington had such a good nose, he could smell lunch before it was fixed.

"Lord, Wellington," he said, setting an extra plate on the kitchen table, "don't you have your *own* home?"

"Why, of course." Wellington straightened, the gold braid of his red uniform catching the light. "But it's so much nicer here."

"Huhn. Why don't you go over and beg something from Louis XVI? He's more your type."

Wellington lifted an eyebrow. "Look . . . if you don't want me, I—"

"Stay," Marie said, shutting the refrigerator door. She set a bottle of chilled wine on the table. "We probably couldn't eat it all anyway."

Wellington shot a smug look in Napoleon's direction.

"You're a pest, Wellington," Napoleon said, trying without much success to remain peeved.

"Possibly. But I'm such a harmless sort."

Napoleon threw up his hands in defeat.

The telephone rang, and since he sat closest, he got up to answer it.

"Napoleon, old friend." The voice on the other end was immediately recognizable. "How about a game of poker?"

The world seemed to tilt sideways for an instant. Napoleon's stomach tightened. "What's the limit?" he asked, casually enough, glancing sidelong at Wellington, whose head had jerked up at the question.

"None."

None. The code word for "you're taking the field immediately, if not sooner." Napoleon briefly shut his eyes. "Where?"

"The club, as usual. And bring Wellington. He plays a mean hand."

"We'll be there."

"Good. See you."

The line went dead. Napoleon stared at the phone in his hand, then hung up. He turned to Wellington.

"You catch all that?"

Wellington's dark eyes were wary. "I'm afraid so."

Marie drew a deep breath. "Who—"

"Caesar," Napoleon replied. "Calling in favors."

"You're going somewhere?"

"Yes." His heart trembled a moment. Going somewhere was putting it mildly—he had no idea for what or for how long.

Marie took a step forward, then stopped. "Napoleon—"

He waved her silent. *O God! I can't tell her anything. And I can't let Wellington know what she is—a Temp. And if I'm not back before the three days she was given are up, I could miss her going, if that's what she chooses. And then she'd be gone— eternally.*

Wellington cleared his throat. "Napoleon, let's move it, eh?"

"Hold on, Wellington," Napoleon walked to Marie's side and met her troubled gaze. "Stay here, Marie. Don't go out. You could be in danger while I'm gone. And trust the Romans—*Caesar's* Romans. No others."

She sighed quietly, her eyes shining with tears. "Come back to me soon, Napoleon. That's all that counts."

The bar at the country club was open, if mostly vacant at noon— a clutch of tennis buffs with their mineral water, Walter Scott scribbling away in his usual spot next the window . . . Napoleon surveyed his glass bleakly and sat staring at a knot in the polished wood of their table, murmuring an occasional: *"Oui," "Non,"* or *"Vraiment?"* to Wellington's running monologue.

"I mean, really."

"Oui."

". . . don't you think?"

"Oui."

". . . haven't heard a demned word, have you?"

"Non." Something about the latter seemed awry, and he looked up confusedly at Wellington's under-the-brows frown.

"Well, really. I'd worry, too. I *do* worry." It was not Romans Wellington had been talking about. Or the business at hand. That was the only thing Napoleon could vouch for. Wellington was careful. But he read the frown and the look, and knew the undertone and the accusation. "Bloody business. Bloody foolish business, I say." It was as far as Wellington could go, apart from the martyred, righteous look, and Napoleon flinched from the stare, his mind drifting aside to the thoughts that had occupied him.

Marie, Marie, Marie.

"Oui," he murmured in rhythm to Wellington's "foolish business," and stared at the spot all the same.

". . . something the matter?" Wellington asked. "I mean, outside the evident?"

"Non."

"Well, you're giving a damned good imitation of it."

Napoleon looked up at Wellington's long face, at frustration and, yes, friendship, and a concern which shot all too painfully into sensitive areas. Damn, Wellington could see it. His wits were wandering—when, when, when would he be through with this business, how soon get back to Marie?

And what if it's more than the night, what if it takes me out of here, what if it's halfway across Hell and no way to get back in those three days?

What must she think?

If I call her, if I tell her I love her—

But that would put pressure on her to stay. I can't, can't do it by guilt—

But if I don't come back in time, what can she think, what can she do?

Leave with hurt feelings, for all eternity—is that what I want for her?

Or might she go on waiting past her time, and lose Heaven, all my fault, my fault—would she not regret that, forever?

I should have told her more than I did. I should have told her—

". . . woolgathering," Wellington concluded. "I've watched you for—"

"Excuse me." Napoleon pushed the chair back. "I've got to make a phone call."

"More mysteries? If—" Wellington quirked a brow along the line of a sudden glance doorward. "Ah."

Napoleon's heart sank. He subsided back into his chair at the sight of Goebbels, who walked in and sat down with his newspaper.

"Don't stare," Wellington hissed. "For God's sake, Napoleon."

"*Mon dieu*," he echoed, and looked desperately toward the alcove with the phones, and back to the door as a flash of khaki caught his eye. Wellington's hand reached toward him on the table top.

"Napoleon."

He sat dead still as the Roman drifted up to the table. He looked up at the battle ribbons, the SPQR, the lean, spare face with the scar and the black eye-patch. Horatius Cocles, who stiffly nodded his head.

"*Imperator*," Horatius said, and to Wellington he offered his hand. "General." He clasped Wellington's hand English-style, not wrist-to-wrist. "Caesar sends his regrets. An emergency. He asked me to apologize."

Perhaps it's called off, Napoleon thought in a sudden flood of relief, but there was a sudden stiffness about Wellington's face.

"Too bad," Wellington said. "Really too bad. Do you want to sit in, sir? Make a third?"

"Sorry. I never was good at that game. I'd disappoint you. With regrets, general, *Imperator*."

Horatius walked away. There was a rattle of newspaper at Goebbels lifted it an inch. Horatius walked over beside that table, and took the one next to it. The newspaper stayed erect.

Wellington nudged Napoleon under the table. Napoleon rose, hesitated a moment. One quick dash to the phone—But the Roman had Goebbels off his balance. Wellington was moving.

"Demned shame," Wellington said, laying a hand on Napoleon's shoulder as he steered him for the door. "Never *can* make his appointments, can he? I don't understand why we go on setting up these affairs—"

They made it out the door into the foyer. Wellington's hand pushed. Napoleon walked for the main doors and out onto the sidewalk and the parking lot, remembering to scan left and right and forward— *Wake up, man. Mind on your business, or you may not get back to Marie—*

Wellington went briskly toward the car they had left. Napoleon walked along beside.

Goebbels. That ferret is onto it. Pray Julius is. If someone is ahead of him, my God, they could be waiting out here, they could have a bomb in the car. God knows what they could have done.

I may never see her again. We're gone, and there's no way to call, and what shall I do?

"Barbarians!" Wellington hissed. "*Damn* it, Napoleon!"

Someone had turned a Coke cup upside down on the hood of Wellington's white Eldorado. Trickles of brown, sticky liquid made a star pattern from beneath it.

"Hell's own sense of humor," Napoleon said as Wellington plucked the cup from the mess and tried to scoop the melting ice with it. "Oh, let it go, Wellington, *merde*, who cares?"

"I bloody care! This is the country club, for God's sake! What's the neighborhood coming to? Vandals and riffraff!"

"The Romans didn't stop it," Napoleon said suddenly. "The Romans ought to have stopped it. Where's their surveillance gone?"

Wellington stopped brushing at the ice. He stood there with the cup in his left hand and something clenched in the right, a message, Napoleon was sure now, which had passed in that handshake. Wellington cast a hasty glance at what he held, a small yellow card. Then he flung the cup down, and unlocked the door on his side, thin-lipped.

"Wait," Napoleon said. "The car could have been tampered with."

"Not bloody likely," Wellington said. He jerked the door open, flung himself inside, and unlocked Napoleon's by remote.

Napoleon got in gingerly, and took the card Wellington handed across to him.

GOOD FOR ONE CAR WASH, it said. And gave an address.

Wellington turned the corner, still fuming all these blocks later. Napoleon sighed quietly, listening to the Iron Duke complain.

"—and they didn't have to trash my car, you know. Uncalled for! The club could get a shoddy reputation if anyone saw—"

"Oh, for God's sake, Wellington. You're getting your car washed for free. And you were complaining about it being dirty only yesterday."

"Still—"

"Where is this place again?" Napoleon asked, holding the card up to read it. "It shouldn't be far."

"I suppose we'll be told where we're to rendezvous."

"Huhn. Another damned scavenger hunt. There it is—the next street."

Wellington slowed and turned into the car wash. No one was ahead of them. Wellington rolled down the window and handed the card to a waiting attendant. But instead of giving another code word, or even brief directions, the man waved them forward.

"This is odd," Napoleon murmured, as Wellington drove into the car wash. It was the sort that had brush rollers, the car being pulled along on a cogged affair beneath. "Why didn't he—"

Two men stepped out of the shadows and jerked the front doors open. For a brief moment, Napoleon stared into a lean, hard, Roman face.

"Apologies, sir," the fellow said. "Strip to the waist and put these on."

"Strip to the what?" Wellington had gotten out of the car, and even in the semi-darkness, his face was decidedly red.

Napoleon jumped out of the slowly moving car and snatched at the proffered clothing. "Strip, Wellington."

"I'm jolly well—"

"Shut up." Napoleon handed his work shirt to the waiting Roman and slipped into one that had been tie-dyed, drawing a fringed, leather vest over it. "Hurry."

Wellington's muttering was lost in the rushing water. The Roman handed Napoleon three last items: several strings of love beads, a frizzy wig that looked like it had been left plugged into a light socket all night, and a pair of dark glasses.

"Dammit, Caesar," Napoleon growled under his breath. "Friendship can only go so far."

He glanced up and, despite his mood, hastily smothered a laugh. Wellington was tugging a long blond wig onto his head, slipping a multi-colored headband over it. The shirt Wellington had on would have glowed in the dark.

A noise to the rear. Napoleon turned: coming right behind Wellington's car was a peacemobile straight out of 1968. Even inside the car wash he could make out the psychedelic paint job, the peace sign painted over the VW insignia on front, and the word "LOVE" scrawled across the side he faced. Things began to fall into place.

One of the side doors opened and two men jumped out of the VW bus. Napoleon stared. If he didn't look closely, he would have sworn he was seeing himself and Wellington. Avoiding brushes, spray and such on the way, the two look-alikes ran ahead to where Wellington's car was just about to leave the car wash. At the last possible moment, they jerked open the doors, clambered inside, and disappeared out into the afternoon.

"Shit."

"Is that all you can say, Napoleon?" Wellington huffed. "What the devil are we doing dressed up as some refugees from a love-in?"

"Hurry, sirs," one of the remaining Romans urged, gesturing at the peacemobile, which was gaining on the exit. "You'll be taken to your drop point. Your car will be driven home."

Wellington grumbled something better left unheard. Napoleon pushed him forward until they were next to the cracked door. When the buffers had finished, the door swung open. Napoleon shoved Wellington inside and jumped in after, closing the door behind.

The peacemobile was full of grim-faced Roman hippies and a near arsenal of automatic weapons.

Napoleon met Wellington's eyes. "It's going to be a long night," he said.

The road degenerated into a series of ruts in the center of which grass and brush hit the VW's bumper and raked the undercarriage. Napoleon hung on in grim silence, and saved himself from the seat in front of him with an upflung hand as the driver threw on the brakes.

A dark metal van had turned up in the road, parked and dead in the afternoon light.

"Ecce," the driver said, and no one moved, till an armored Roman got up out of the grass, an apparition in the drylands glare, and banged the hood cheerfully with his javelin.

The driver and his partner opened their doors, one of the men in the back opened the loading door, and Napoleon climbed down after him, into knee-high grass, in the face of a dozen grinning Romans.

"Vae, quidnam habemus?" one asked. *"Circus?"*

"Picti," another suggested, and the lot of them guffawed.

"Damn your impertinence!" Wellington exploded, and jerked off the wig and the headband. "The Emperor of France and the Duke of Wellington, to see whatever officer commands this demned lunacy!"

"Constate vos," the driver snarled, and there was silence and sober faces. He pulled off his own wig

and waved with it toward the van. "If you please, sirs."

Napoleon pulled off the frizz and hauled off a handful of the damned beads, and trod disconsolately behind Wellington's ramrod stiff and psychedelic figure—which still wore the white trousers and spit and polish boots of a British officer—up to the opening side door of the van.

There was relative dark inside. There were green phosphor screens and a handful of dim figures that moved inside like a vision of nether hells. One came to brief light in the doorway and withdrew into a shadow to let them inside.

The door grated and banged shut. The lights came on bright and Napoleon stared at the Roman who stood looking them slowly up and down.

Mouse.

Napoleon's face went hot. He stood under that dour, slow scrutiny of the least demonstrative man in Hell, and saw the least suspicious tightening of the corners of Mouse's mouth, the slightest lifting of an eyebrow; and strangled on his breath.

"Mon dieu, monsieur le souris, j'espère que vous ayez quelque chose á faire au délà de cette comedie en noir—"

"I assure you." Mouse's voice was unperturbed. He folded his hands behind him and walked to a let-down counter, on which charts lay in profusion, and at which he gestured. "Gentlemen. This is the matter at hand."

Napoleon stared at the maps spread below their hands and looked up at the Roman from his side of the table. "Alexander?" he asked with a sinking heart. "Kidnap Alexander? The Great?"

"Exactly," Mouse said. "Lately arrived in command of the Dissidents—*not*, however, in his best form. This is a desperate and difficult man, gentlemen. Never mind the source of our intelligence. He is at a loss. He is drifting from cause to cause, among strangers. Presently he has a friend among the Dissidents, one Judah Maccabee—"

Wellington sat down on the edge of the counter behind him.

"Easiest," Mouse said calmly, "if you take them both."

"My God!" Wellington exploded. "With what?"

"Your wits, gentlemen. Caesar has great faith in your resourcefulness. These are maps of the area—"

"Find someone else," Napoleon said. *"Non.* No. *J'y refus."*

Mouse turned a chill, inquiring eye on him, and then on Wellington. "Your friend chooses to remain in camp. And you, sir?"

"I *choose*," Napoleon said with difficulty, "to go *home*—now, tonight!"

"Our operations are not to be compromised, sir. What you refuse to do is between yourself and Caesar. I cannot compel you. Neither will I permit a man to leave this operation."

Napoleon sat down on the opposite counter and passed his hands over his face, staring at the maps. "Conditions? Objectives? Forces?"

"I say," Wellington objected.

"Do as you wish, Wellington," Napoleon said, running his eye over the river and the marsh which made an oxbow about the Dissident camp. "Damn, camped next to a bog? *Alexander?"*

"He did not choose the site," Mouse said. "That was Guevara, who is still in camp. Caesar proposes this: the Tenth and the Twelfth to engage the enemy's interest on the only dry ground approach to the camp, merely to keep Alexander's attention focused on that hazard."

"He'll bloody well come down your throats," Wellington said.

"Engage interest. There will be operations. Reconnaissance and movement, nothing near enough to rouse Alexander out of his den. While you—with a handful of special troops—will take this approach—" Mouse's lean forefinger traced the oxbow.

"He'll pitch his tent in the center of the camp," Napoleon murmured. It felt like a dream. So much studying of Caesar's wars; and Alexander's. He knew the man, never having met him. He knew his habits. He knew his preferences. "How *many* troops do you propose to move with us?"

"Special forces. American SEALS, to be precise. Four of them. And four of the DGSE."

"*French?*"

Mouse lifted his brows. "We have our connections. Four SEALS, with equipment of their choosing—adequate to create considerable noise on one side of the camp, considerable damage within it, and enable a small special forces group under your command—we reckon four sufficient—to gain the objective and get out again. We want him *alive*, sir. No Trips. The same with Maccabee, if possible."

Three days, Napoleon thought with a sinking heart. *Three days.*

And aloud: "I have conditions."

"Whatever helps the mission."

"I want my house watched. I want Marie kept safe."

"That we are doing."

"I want it doubly watched! I want—" He drew a shaking breath. "I want to send a message to her."

"No communications. My orders, sir. We cannot afford—"

"Tell her I love her, dammit!"

For a moment Mouse looked at him in genuine startlement. Then the mask was back. "That would not seem to compromise us," Mouse said dryly.

"The hell," Napoleon muttered, and flinched from Wellington's astonished stare, settling his eyes on the maps—the damned, twisting, and treacherous waterways. "Eight men. Rafts. With explosives. Magnesium flares."

"That you will have."

"And how do we get *out* of this?" Wellington asked. "Paddle?"

"We can manage an evacuation within thirty minutes once you have your prisoners on the river."

"Helicopters," Wellington groaned. "Demned racketing things draw fire!"

"Helicopters," Napoleon said. "I don't intend to spend days in a swamp sitting on *those* two."

"You have it," Mouse said.

"There will be other things," Napoleon said. "And one more man I insist on."

Mouse lifted a brow. "Who?"

Attila stood next to the grill in his backyard, swatting at flies, gnats, and an occasional B-52-sized mosquito, and eyed the hamburgers, which looked about ready to turn. His yard was filled with five or six especially nasty rug-rats, all between the ages of 3 and 7. Rug-rats? More like linoleum lizards, curtain-crawlers . . . even better, house apes.

He scowled at the pint-sized horde, knowing them for what they were: *his* children. That made them even nastier than the ordinary sort. He glanced over his shoulder and cringed inwardly. Ildilco, his last wife, who had wakened in their marriage bed to find him dead, was headed his way, a particularly venomous look on her pretty face. How anyone that attractive could be so shrewish was beyond his comprehension. Ereka, his chief wife, had just left off complaining about how long it was taking to get dinner on the table. Faced now with Ildilco, Attila was seriously contemplating escape.

"Husband," she said, stopping beside the grill and sniffing primly at the burgers. "Some rude person wants to talk to you on the phone."

"Rude?"

She sniffed again, only this time not at the food. "He wouldn't give me his name."

Hope flared. "I'll go settle it," Attila said, handing Ildilco the long-handled fork. "Watch the burgers. They're nearly done."

"But—"

He turned, trotted across the backyard and into the house before she could think of anything else to yell at him about.

The phone lay waiting on the kitchen counter. He picked it up, listened a brief moment for revealing background noises, then answered.

"Armory, Attila," said a familiar voice. "Bring your Hun outfit. Now."

The line went dead. Attila stared at the wall for a moment, placed the receiver back in the cradle, then grinned widely.

"By the Sky! My prayers are answered!"

He glanced around the house, thought briefly of telling his wives he was being called to duty, then discarded the idea. He would never get away with *both* of them yelling at him. He grinned again, grabbed up the car keys from a hook on the cabinet, and dashed back to his bedroom. Snatching up his clothes, weapons, and helmet, he ran through the house and out the front door.

*   *   *

The Zodiac had been loaded and bobbed waiting at the edge of the River Cocytus, just shy of where it flowed into the Styx. Beyond waited the deeps of the swamp. Napoleon turned from the final preparations his men were making, caught Wellington's eye, and nodded back up to somewhat higher land.

"Where the devil is Attila?" Wellington complained. "That barbarian probably doesn't know the value of time."

"You're maligning him. If Caesar uses him and trusts him the way I think he does, he's all right by me."

"Still—"

Napoleon caught Wellington's arm, turned and pointed. A battered pickup truck was rattling its way toward them down the narrow road. The light was bad enough that Napoleon could not tell who was driving, but he had his suspicions.

The truck wheezed to a halt and the door opened. Out popped Attila, dressed in blue jeans, a western-style shirt, and a straw cowboy hat (complete with feathers enough on its front to fly). The King of the Huns grinned at them, ran around to the rear of the truck, and grabbed under a pile of tarp. When he turned back, he was carrying a bundle of clothing, his helmet, bow, arrows, and spears.

"Nice seeing you again," he said, trotting up to Napoleon's side. "And you, too, Wellington."

Napoleon glanced at his watch. "Let's move it. We're losing time we don't have."

He headed back down to the edge of the river, Wellington and Attila in tow. The SEALS and DGSE men were already aboard. Napoleon slipped into the Zodiac, waited for Wellington and Attila to join him, then motioned forward. One of the SEALS pushed off from shore, started the engine, and the Zodiac began to move upstream through already clogged waters as Attila removed his cowboy hat and started to undress in the rather cramped quarters.

"What's the plan?" Attila asked.

"What were you told?"

"Not much." Attila had his leather breeches on now. "Just that I was to bring my Hunnish clothes."

Napoleon frowned. "This is what we're up against." He moved back slightly and began to draw with his fingertip on the bottom of the Zodiac. "We're moving against the Dissident camp. It's surrounded on three sides by passable river bleeding off into swamp." He glanced up. "Che is out of commission. Alexander has assumed command."

Attila's right eyebrow raised. "As in, The Great?"

"You've got it. And I might as well let you know at the top what we have to do. We're to kidnap him, get him out of camp. We're also to take Alexander's friend, Maccabee, if he gets in the way."

"Oh, shit."

"That sums it up. We have four SEALS with us, four DGSE men, weapons enough, and two extra rubber rafts."

"Huhn." Attila had pulled on his vest and was sitting back on his heels, staring at the invisible map Napoleon had drawn. "And for this I left my back-yard barbecue?"

"For God's sake," Wellington inserted, "you're always complaining enough about the wives. You'd think you'd be happy to—"

"I am. I *am*. So now what?"

"Here's the timeframe," Napoleon said, trying to drive all thoughts of Marie and her impending decision from his mind. "We've got a day of traveling ahead of us. By dawn of the second day, we're going to have to be at the drop point. From there, the SEALS will divide: two of them, the alpha-team SEALS, will head on around the river—" his finger traced around in a circular pattern "—to about 0200 on this circle, if you think of it as a clock. The other two SEALS will head off to the west, to take up a position at around 0700. There's a landing where the rebels receive their supplies at 0600. The beta-team SEALS will have to move slowly so they can get by that in the night."

"Uh . . . Napoleon?" Attila shifted his weight slightly. "What are *you* going to be doing?"

"Wellington and I will come into camp at 0500 position on the evening of the third day, along with the men from the *Sécurité*. We'll all be disguised as medics. *We're* the ones who will make the snatch. By then, the alpha-team SEALS will be in position for diversionary tactics, which will include a lot of sound and light. The beta-team will be waiting for us with the only radio link we'll have. When they see the alpha-team's pyrotechnics, they'll radio for air support to haul us out."

"Why am I getting a bad feeling about this?" Attila muttered. "Could it be because I haven't heard my name mentioned yet?"

Napoleon put a comradely arm around Attila's shoulders. "That's because we saved the best for last. Attila, *mon vieux* . . . have we got a job for *you!*"

Something disgusting welled up through the sand and changed its mind again, sinking back with a noxious exhalation. "Gad," Wellington said, edging back onto the safety of the Zodiac and rubbing his nose. Cocytus fought them, every inch and every turn of its clogged course. Reeds grew profusely on the margins. Unwholesome scum floated on the water. Dying willows and cypress dragged disconsolate branches and gathered the aforesaid scum in sheets and rumples on the surface, and thrust desperate roots and knees every which way to stay upright.

On one of these shores of twisted trees they had pulled the Zodiac to land—if land it could be called, Napoleon thought in disgust, extracting a sodden foot from the hole he had stepped in immediately off the raft. Mosquitoes declared feast and gnats swarmed them in suicidal battalions.

And constantly the fight to stay on schedule—*schedule*, Mouse had insisted, in Hell. They dared not use the field phone until they were ready for pickup, and that time, to Napoleon, looked as remote as the Paradise which rose in sullen splendor on this second morning of their journey.

Second day, Napoleon thought between panic and despair, *second* day. And tried not to think on it at all. *Attention à tes affaires, mon vieux*.

Second morning, and precisely out there where he had declared to be, leading the Tenth and Twelfth legions on the ever-popular pretext of maneuvers, Mouse—Decius Mus—had by now advanced within what Mouse judged an interesting distance from Alexander's camp, and parked, to reconnoiter, and presumably to occupy the attention of the Dissidents without drawing an attack.

And from now on, each step of the operation, each movement of each of their separate forces, went their own way by the clock, by the chronometers each man of them had, in case of calamity to the group leaders.

The four Americans—incredibly young, all of them, fresh-faced and earnest and God help them, volunteers, were doing everything with sure, quick movements, had their two rafts inflated and loaded. Foster was their alpha-point team leader, Jenks the beta-point, quiet, shy men with a tendency to yes-sir and no-sir to the point of obsession, and no one else spoke much— *"Bonjour,"* was the limit of Foster's French, and even Wellington had trouble with his American accent. "All done, general, sir," was what Napoleon made his comment out to be, after thinking about what Wellington had answered with a: "Go and good luck."

By that time Foster and his partner, and Jenks and his, had their small rafts well out onto the water, half-lost in opposite directions in the curtains of willow, and Wellington had slogged his way onto higher ground with Attila, beside the pile the DGSE men had made of their equipment—LeFlore, Anbec, Mirabeau, Barré, their names were wiry, competent men who towered like the Americans and muttered to each other in a French full of *hamburger* and *Coca-cola* and obscenities less religious and more scatological than the men of the *Armée*, but Napoleon absorbed the sound of it as curiously soothing, a reminiscence of power, of security in command—

And flinched from it, as from some sink that threatened him. *Marie,* he thought, twisting the knife deliberately. *Marie.* Like an incantation.

"Damn!" He went up to the knee in water, extricated himself from the clinging mud with a disgusted heave, and slogged his way to where Wellington stood fanning the mosquitoes away with a loop of willow-wand, and Attila squatted in his leathers and fox-fur helmet, his spears across his knees and a stolid tolerance for the bugs.

"Malaria," Wellington said. "Damned malaria, that's what we can look forward to."

Attila spat. "Healthy man, healthy bugs. They *like* you, hey?"

Napoleon looked back as the *Sécurité* men, having sent the Zodiac to the bottom of the marsh, slogged up the bank behind him. He looked at his watch again, reflex action, and at the little sky that was visible between the willows. Half an hour behind schedule now, and the swamp did not promise easy going. From now on the chronos were life itself. "Come on," he said, frowning. "Up. For God's sake, move."

Marie paced up and down the living room, pausing now and again to look out the front window. Nothing. No sign of Napoleon returning. There had been no phone calls, no attempts at delivering a message. Only the arrival, in Wellington's white Eldorado, of four heavily armed Romans sent across the park from Caesar to keep her safe. And *they* had been told nothing more than to protect her. Even now three of them sat in the closed garage playing cards, while the fourth—a quiet, shy fellow—had moved a chair up in front of the TV to watch some awful 1950s science fiction movie.

She sighed deeply, sat down in a chair by the front window, and buried her face in her hands. Tomorrow morning, the angel would return. Tomorrow morning, her decision would have to be made— whether she was leaving Hell or staying.

"O God," she breathed, but as usual, there was no warm feeling to follow the prayer. Not here. Not in Hell.

An eternity of bliss and happiness awaited her. She glanced up from her hands and out the window. Here? Here was Hell. There was no denying that. What Napoleon had said about there being deeper

Hells than this one rang frighteningly true. Having not been condemned to Hell at death, she was certain she had no idea what it was like to arrive as one of the damned.

She shuddered. She had seen enough, heard enough, during her stint at the License Bureau to know that New Hell sat at the very apex of the Infernal Regions. Dark stories filled her memory—things she had heard, about what happened to people. And death was never certain. There was always the Undertaker—his foul breath, his jokes, the whole lot of it. Could she willingly condemn herself to an eternity of this?

But there was Napoleon. When she had first seen him in the License Bureau, Marie had thought herself transported to Heaven. She loved him more than he possibly knew. To be separated from him for eternity would—

The doorbell rang.

Marie froze. The Roman came to instant alert, snatched up his automatic rifle, and carefully went out into the entry hall. Edging up to the door, he peered out through the window. Marie glanced outside: pulled up in the driveway was a slightly grungy van, across the sides of which in large red letters was written "Stygian Plumbing, Inc."

The Roman obviously either knew the caller, or had received some signal. He lowered his rifle, stepped back from the door, and opened it. A smallish woman clad in a brown work jump suit, carrying a toolbox in one hand, sauntered in.

"You may go, legionary," the woman said coolly, motioning toward the garage. "We'll call if we need you."

The Roman saluted briefly and walked quickly off toward the kitchen and the garage beyond.

"What's going on?"' Marie asked. "I didn't put in a call for—"

"I know." The tiny woman hauled off her cap, revealing hair nearly as blond as Marie's own. Something jogged Marie's mind and she nearly recognized her caller. "I'm Kleopatra," the woman said, with a small smile. "From Caesar across the Park."

Marie's heart gave a lurch. Napoleon? Could anything have happened to—

"Caesar sent me to you with a message," Kleopatra said, setting the toolbox down. "Napoleon wanted you to know that he loves you."

"That he—" Marie swallowed heavily. "Was that all? Nothing else?"

"That was all."

"O God." Marie turned away, her eyes brimming with tears. He obviously could send no more than that simple message. Where he was, what he was doing, was to remain a mystery to her. She dabbed at her eyes and turned to face Kleopatra again. "You don't know what he is doing, do you?"'

Kleopatra's face softened. "Only that he's doing Caesar a very profound favor." The Queen of Egypt cocked her head slightly. "You're upset . . . more upset than I think you should be. Do you want to talk about it?"

Marie's heart screamed yes, but her mind counseled caution. She *had* to talk about it with someone, but she dared not reveal her Temporary status. How could she—?

"Yes." She drew a deep breath. "I'd like to very much, Majesty. If you'd be willing to listen."

Kleopatra looked around for somewhere to sit, opted for the end of the couch, and patted the cushion at her side. "Tell me, then."

"It sounds so simple," Marie said, taking her place,

her mind frantically searching for ways to tell her story *without* telling it. "I'm working at the License Bureau. I have a chance for a big promotion, but it means moving to one of the branch offices. I was told that I'd probably never be able to see Napoleon again."

"Ha! The big promotion with a torment attached! How clever of someone." Kleopatra met Marie's eyes. "Which is more important to you?"

Marie bowed her head. "Right now, I'm not sure. It's a *big* promotion. My life would be changed drastically. For the better, you see."

The diminutive Queen of Egypt was silent for a moment. "If I were Hatshepsut, which, thank the gods, I am not, I would counsel you to go for the promotion, to be tied down to no man—especially if your life will be better without him. But I'm not." Dazzling white teeth showed in her smile. "I'm me, Kleopatra, Egypt. And I *died* for love."

Marie stared off through the window, her eyes again clouding with tears. "So I'm right back where I started then, Majesty."

Kleopatra reached out a hand and patted Marie's shoulder. "Hell is full of tortures like this for you New Dead. Thank all gods I died long ago. I can tell you nothing else, Marie, save to go with your heart. What you really long for the most will well up from deep inside it. If that means turning down the promotion and leaving yourself open to further torments, so be it." She pursed her lips and smiled again. "But I really *should* let Hatshepsut talk to you. I'm a terrible influence."

Marie hardly heard her. She stared now at the floor, her indecision even greater than before Kleopatra's arrival. Napoleon. Heaven. Which would she choose? And tomorrow her decision would have to be made.

The camp sweltered toward noon, and Alexander stood watching the supply carts making their way up from the landing, up a rutted and difficult track from the Cocytus shore, where it afforded the camp a source of supply and malaria. He would not have chosen this. He would not have chosen this ragtag of the desperate, the disaffected, the feckless, and the hard-bitten core of the rebellion with which Fate had gifted him; they had chosen him, and he had, perhaps, especially then, been vulnerable.

Now he had full cognizance of his situation, and was appalled at Guevara, who had abdicated command, not even to sulk in his tent, but to languish in it—he was appalled at the filth Guevara had permitted, the insubordination, the mingling of camp followers and troops in a haphazard, as-it-had-grown, arrangement of tents and shanties and brush huts. Pigs and chickens were in some of these shanties, jealously guarded against the theft that was rampant. Whores of both sexes plied their trade from dawn till dawn and doubled as bootleggers, selling a brew four times cut with the water they had gotten from Cocytus and only sometimes boiled. It cut down on drunkenness only somewhat. Beer and whiskey flowed more readily than the polluted water, and brawls were ordinary—the Germans with the Poles, the Spanish with the English and the Thai with the Cambodians, as well as the personal quarrels ordinary to men at a dead end.

But worst were the newcomers, who made their camp toward the north of the oxbow bend, men who came in separately and tended together, who went through the motions of weapons drill under the

officers in charge of those units and passed right by
training in the basics—men who *knew* weapons of all
sorts, men who had a king of tight-lipped and manic
concern for their gear on one hand and a damnable
surly way of dealing with general orders on the other.

Hundreds of them, who had mercenary written all
over them. With officers who looked much the same.
"Have you paid these men?" Alexander had asked
Guevara. "Have you hired them?"

"No," Guevara had said, from the bed where he
had retired, a weary shell of a man, unshaven and
overcome by the day's heat, "no. They came."

Assyrian officers. Egyptians, two or three of them
setting up unauthorized command structures. "Have
you authorized them to keep their own munitions?"
Alexander had asked Guevara then; and:

"Qué?" Guevara had said, lifting his head a second
time from the sweaty, skewed bedding, on which food
stains showed. "Munitions?"

Alexander had left that stinking tent with a per-
turbed mind, and cast an uneasy eye toward that
quarter of the camp, the *only* quarter which was not
a sink.

He had walked through it then—alone—to let them
know that he would. He had marked those places
where he knew that equipment was stored, and he
saw equipment there which was better than anything
in the rest of the camp.

"Lord King," a messenger had said, accosting him.
"Col. Kadashman-enlil would speak to you in his
tent."

He had fixed that man with a cold stare, "In *mine*,
if the colonel has anything to say. Tell him that."

No one had troubled him on that walk. In two
days the colonel had not found it convenient to come
to him.

"That man is the key," he had mused to Judah Maccabee in the night, in the dying of the lamp. "Him I must remove."

"Had you gone to him," Judah had said, "you would have played into his hands. Do not make such gestures! Listen to me: there are men enough in this camp who can walk in there and solve this problem, only Guevara has let them fall apart, and some of them have joined the Assyrians. Give me five days. I will find you these men, and we will go and bring you Kadashman-enlil. *Then* we will have the men who have the weapons. Show yourself the King. *That* is what will win these men."

"Yes," he had said. In that moment there had seemed hope, the whole situation possessing a single knot, like that at Gordion, all of which was bound in retreat from this camp which sat surrounded on three sides by marsh and river, on the fourth by low hills, a position which the guerrilla Che Guevara had conceived of as a fortified retreat—

—and then encumbered his camp with whores and chickens and poets, and all sorts of dependents which Guevara might perhaps have discounted when it came to moving on.

But he, Alexander, was a Great King. He had inherited the camp, and the command, and while he would not risk his soldiers for a handful of whores, neither would he deliver over the poets and the wives and the wounded and the fevered, who were also a part of this ragtag. In point of fact, this army was bogged down, mired in a trap of Guevara's making, with Kadashman-enlil on one side in possession of the armament, with the feckless and the fools and the farmer-folk on this side, and Kadashman-enlil was the source of both men and weapons which might turn a withdrawal from this hellhole into some sort of orderly, defended retreat.

Presently Alexander was counting carts and donkeys and anything else that could bear a load, and Judah and Altos the angel and twenty-seven other reliable agents were out taking census, row to row, tent to tent. And being lied to by the suspicious and the greedy. *How many women are in this tent?—I have a sister, Lord King, very clean—Whose cart is that?—Oh, Francisco's cart, Lord King, I only borrowed it—Where does Francisco live?—Oh, with his brother Enrique, Lord King, sometimes with his cousin, though, I forget his last name. . . .*

"That is *your* cart, Miguel Torres. You are responsible for it and you will account to me for it; and if Francisco wants to claim it, Francisco will come to *my* tent and I will change the record. When we move, Miguel Torres, I personally will expect this cart to carry eight persons, and I personally will look for you in the line. Do you hear?"

"Yes, yes, Lord King." There was genuine fervency in that answer, terror in the eyes which looked at him and wondered if he, like Guevara, had gone mad.

He waved the carter on, and sighted on the man with the push-cart down the row.

"Alexander!"

He turned, seeing Judah running toward him, weaving in and out of the line which came up from the landing. He readied a humorous question, whether Judah had found some treasure trove of carts and crates, and it died in his heart as he saw Judah's expression.

"What?" he said, and yielded as Judah drew him out of the roadway, over next to a stack of rotting baskets.

"The Romans," Judah said. "Word from the boat-man—there are Romans on the plain."

"Where? How close?"

"A hundred miles." Judah gasped after breath. "Maybe less by now. The boatman has no idea how many. He saw the dust. He saw the standards flash." Another breath. "Alexander. They're going to cut us off. Bottle us up in here."

"Julius," Alexander said. His heart had turned to lead. "Julius has done this."

"I told you you could not trust them."

"My other soul, he calls himself. My heir, to all I built. My erstwhile ally. *Damn him!*"

"The word will spread—it is spreading now, all over camp. Too many heard—"

"We proceed," Alexander said. "We proceed with more haste, that is all. We prepare this camp to move. To defend itself."

"If we go out on that plain they will have us!"

"How many will die in the swamp? How many of these can move?"

"Then take those who can! That is the only logic. Take the one in ten and the one in a hundred, and withdraw through the marsh! What is anything worth, if there is no revolution, no army? We will fight them from the hills. Put Kadashman's men on the heights, leave the camp followers and the wounded behind *his* defense, and you and I and a picked force—"

"Of how many men, Judah? With what weapons?"

"With what we have!"

"And will Kadashman-enlil stand there?" He shook his head. "*That* is the one will melt away into the swamp. Go shoot me that man, Judah. Find a man who can walk into the quarter, and shoot me that man."

"Alexander—"

"One for the many. How many times have we said—we fought different wars. I want that man dead. Within the hour. Say it was at my order. Say there are Romans at the gate. And do not you do it, Judah! I will not risk you."

"There is a man I know," Judah said heavily.

The shot rang out over the camp surprisingly faint, a single report, and a fusillade after. Alexander, sitting in his tent with his census-takers, froze in mid-motion, and then completed his mark.

He looked up then, at the eyes of the Angel of God, at the being who was, whatever he was, named Just Al. In that moment he saw the light fade in the angel's eyes as if a cloud had gone over; and for some reason a terrible guilt closed about his heart, like a fist preventing him from breathing.

"A man is dead," the angel said, his whole aspect seeming to fade. The tablet fell from his hands to the table, and Altos rose distractedly and went toward the door.

Judah had gotten to his feet, standing there with a stricken look on his face.

From out in the camp came the sound of shouting.

"I had better see to it," Alexander said then, calmly enough.

Judah caught up his rifle from the door as others thrust back from the table. "Take a gun," Judah said.

"I am their King," Alexander said. "Do I need weapons, when I am in the right?"

Attila came staggering out of the swamp, mud and clinging slime dirtying his breeches to above the knees. He scanned the scene before him—the squalor of the Dissident camp, the seeming uncoordination of everyone who moved in it.

With a scowl, he sat down where he stood, pulled off his boots, and turned them upside down. Slime, water, and loose sand trickled from them. Three large, black leeches had attached themselves to his ankles. He growled a curse to the demon-gods, reached inside his hip pouch, and pulled out a plastic-wrapped packet of salt. Opening it, he poured the salt over the munching leeches, and grinned wolfishly as he watched them shrivel up into agonized balls.

"Hey, you!"

The rough voice intruded on Attila's death-watch. He glanced up, schooling his face to a faint stupidity. Two rough-looking fellows, decked out in camouflage uniforms that probably had not been washed in the last six months, stood before him.

Attila looked down again, pulled one boot on, and reached for the other.

"I said, Hey You!" one man snarled, shoving Attila in the side with his foot. "What the hell are you doing here?"

Gritting his teeth in controlled rage, Attila drew on his other boot. He scrambled to his feet, his weapons in one hand.

"I come to rebels," he said, thickening his Hunnish accent. "I defect. Want fight against Devil, yes? Must see your leader."

"Filthy mother," the Dissident growled to his companion. "Why can't we ever attract anything better?"

His companion scratched a sweat-darkened armpit. "They fight like devils themselves," he offered. "Let him go. Can't you see he's a lackwit?"

"All right, savage," the first man said, hooking a thumb over his shoulder. "Commander's tent's that way." He grinned nastily. "And it'll be a cold day in this swamp before *you* get in to see him."

Attila bowed his head several times, muttering comments about the Dissidents' parentage in such tones that they would consider what he said to be humble thanks. Bowing again, he scuttled off toward the center of camp.

Everywhere he looked he saw filth, disorganization, a total lack of control. If Che had been replaced by Alexander, it had been recently: the Macedonian would never tolerate such conditions among men he led.

He passed tents, shanties, and make-shift huts. Angry, listless eyes followed his progress, and he made sure his hand was always close to his sword. *Damned fools would as soon knife me as look at me!*

The closer he got to the center of camp, the neater the tents and huts were. Marginally neater. Here, he supposed, was where the officers (if one could call them that) would be housed. But here, also, was a pitch of activity lacking in the camp below. Here, men hurried about there business as if something of importance had happened. He scowled again, kept his face schooled to dullness, and walked on.

Alexander's tent was exactly where Napoleon had figured it to be—the center of camp. Attila paused a moment, allowed his mouth to gape open, and counted the guards around it. There were only two he could see, and though they appeared wary enough, they seemed as dispirited as the other rebels he had encountered. He shrugged, set his spears over his shoulder, and walked up to the door of the tent.

"Hold it, you!" snapped one of the men, lowering his rifle so that it was aimed at Attila's heart. "Where the hell do you think you're going?"

"To see your leader," Attila replied in clear, colloquial English.

The second man sniggered.

"And what if he doesn't want to be disturbed, scumbag? You just crawled out of the swamp, from the looks of your clothes. The commander doesn't see the likes of you."

"I think he'll see me when he knows who I am."

"Oh? And *who* might you be?"

"Tell him Attila's here. Attila the Hun."

That made both men start. Attila allowed a little killing smile to touch his lips, set his spears upright, and stood leaning on them with apparent unconcern.

"Huhn." The first guard seemed undecided, then drew back the tent flap. "Commander? There's a man out here who claims he's Attila the Hun. Wants to talk with you."

For a long moment, nothing happened. Then a tall, dark bearded man stepped out of the tent. *Maccabee*, Attila thought.

"So you want to see Alexander?" Maccabee said, his keen eyes focused on Attila's face.

Attila nodded. "Now. It's urgent."

Maccabee folded his arms across his broad chest. "I'll be the judge of that. What do you have to say?"

"That's between me and Alexander. And if you love him, I suggest that you let me see him."

Maccabee's face reddened. "Don't you be telling me what—"

"Judah." The voice came from inside the tent, cultured but profoundly weary. "Let the man in, for gods' sakes."

Judah Maccabee muttered something into his beard, stepped back and, holding the tent flap aside, gestured Attila into the tent.

Surrounded on the floor by a rough-looking pack

of what appeared to be Egyptians and Assyrians, Alexander sat in a camp chair at the far side of the tent. Blond hair gleaming in the light, he lifted his beautiful face. Shadows of old bruises lay there, and shadows of another sort filled the blue eyes.

"Attila?" he said. "King of the Huns?"

"Yes, Great King," Attila said, nodding slightly. "I greet you as king to king, as one who has heard of your mightiness in battle."

Alexander rose from his chair out of respect for another king, the Assyrians and Egyptians standing with him. He chewed on his lower lip for a moment. "Judah. Get Attila a chair."

"But—"

"Get it," Alexander said in a strained but patient voice. "And—" waving to the assembled warriors, "—take these men outside."

"Great King," one protested. "We can't leave now! There are too many questions we haven't answered . . ."

Alexander's face hardened. "I am your king," he said. "You will come at my command and go at my command. Now, go!"

There was a brief muttering among them.

"Very well, Lord King," one said. "But we'll await your notice outside your tent."

"Whatever you will. Judah?"

The tall Israelite lifted the tent flap and motioned for the warriors to step outside. With one last, hard look at Attila, he followed.

For a long moment Alexander stared at Attila, then some of the shadows left his eyes. "You must have wanted to see me very badly to have braved that swamp."

Attila laughed shortly. "The leeches, the scum,

the—" He shrugged. "I don't need to tell you about it from the look on *your* face."

Maccabee returned with a chair and Attila took it gratefully. Coming through that swamp had been no easy thing, even for one such as he who was inured to the harsher sides of nature.

"All right, Attila." Alexander had sat down at precisely the same time as Attila. "What is it you want to tell me?"

Attila made a small movement to the side with his eyes in Maccabee's direction.

"Judah? Believe me, Attila, you can say anything you like in front of him. He has guestright in my house."

"Great King," Attila began, gathering his knowledge of the two men in the tent with him. "I respect the trust you place in Maccabee, but some of what I have to say will be—ah, disconcerting to him. He won't be able to listen with an unprejudiced mind."

Alexander sat very still for a moment, then seemed to relax. "Judah. Wait outside."

"Alex, I don't—"

"Judah. Keep an eye on those warriors." A meaningful look passed between the two men. "I *need* you to do that, Judah."

Maccabee shot a narrow-eyed look in Attila's direction and walked out of the tent. "I'll be outside, then, Alex. *Right* outside."

Attila waited a sufficient length of time for Maccabee to take up a listening position. "Great King," he said, meeting Alexander's clear blue eyes. "I come from Caesar."

Alexander settled back in his chair and regarded this man, this leather-clad successor of the horse-riding Scythians, with his black hair and narrow eyes

and the ready, white-edged grin, and he drew a
deep breath of his own, with more power in his
hands than had been there an hour ago. Col. Kadashman-enlil had indeed died with a bullet in his brain,
and the Egyptian corporal who had done the deed
had died with fifty-odd bullets in his hide, after
which nervous reaction the mercenaries, perceiving
Order had come down with an iron hand and a
ruthlessly efficient stroke, reassessed their loyalties.

Favors, was the coin they traded in. Money and
gear at the lower levels, money and string-pulling at
the highest ones. "You have your choice," he had
said to the mercenaries. "A dead dog or a leader who
can get you out of this pit—and I *can*. Kadashman-
enlil made a mistake. He affronted a man who would
have set him in high position, misjudging *me*, gentlemen, despite my offer to let him cover his mistake.
Now there are Romans out there—*that* is the position Guevara and Kadashman-enlil had led you into,
and I suggest, gentlemen, that you are most fortu-
nate to be in my hands, who know the Roman high
command and all their tricks. Caesar is famous for
his traps and his ambushes, and if any of you think to
run, you may think on what Romans *do* with rebels.
Shall I tell you? Or shall I tell you instead that I do
not throw away the men who follow me? Shall I
remind you that I made the men who followed me
satraps and lords in Persia and Asia and Hellas and
Egypt—you men of the East,—my heirs, do they not
name your cities Alexandria, Iskander, Kandahar,
do they not still fly the red banner of my Macedonians,
dance the dances of Hellas, find my face graven in
images from the gates of the sea to the circuit of the
earth—am I not Alexander, *king*, in the days of your
fathers and your descendants? Are you less men than
followed me to Empire?"

As rhetoric went, he thought, Aristotle would have called it un-geometric. But it brought the mercenary officers to his tent. It kept the rifles quiet, and created that uneasy alliance which bided fiercely outside his tent.

And now came this—this king of the Huns.

"What have you to offer me?" Alexander said with a wide breath. There was in him that sense of power which he had not felt since his youth. It was Bucephalus' gift. It was the personal force that had raised armies and quelled mutinies even with speeches half-coherent from wounds and exhaustion, and driven men to do for him things which would daunt men of ordinary purpose; the power was back in his soul and in his voice and in his countenance, and if this king of the Huns had come to him with offers from Caesar in this hour, then Caesar was not thoroughly confident of the outcome or Caesar had ulterior motives in this maneuvering. It remained to discover which.

"No matter of *offering*." Attila leaned his elbows on the table which divided them, and made a throwaway gesture about them with his right hand. "Caesar respects you. Always has. The whole world respects you. Look, you're in a damn mess in this camp. What kind of place is this for Alexander to die—hah?"

Alexander laughed softly. He gave the Hun a grin of utmost good humor—which, an hour ago, would have come hard. Now no victory seemed impossible. "You, a king—what kind of an answer should I give that?"

"He's your friend."

"Ah. Yes. My friend."

"Haii—yaa, now, now, that's exactly the thing they want." Attila shifted his eyes toward the door, and back again, leaning forward and lowering his voice.

"He *is* your friend. They're putting him in position, you see that? I don't have to say who. Enemies of his and yours—they want this. Nobody gains anything from this mess the way they gain, and Caesar's too smart to let them pull this off. He's out there marching up and down and up and down and in the meanwhile—" Attila's voice faded into a cough that became a spasm. "Damn, damn, I hiked that whole riverside, I don't trust any of these damn amateurs, stick a man just on sight, no asking what his business is. Three days of mud and those damn leeches—" He gave a shudder.

"Meanwhile—"

"Sorry." Attila looked about him, fixed his stare at the left wall of the tent where a table held a pitcher. "You mind? By the Sky, I need a drink!"

"Judah," Alexander said. In protocol, he could not get up, he had no servant he trusted, and a cup of wine was something he could stand himself, at the moment, at this damnable lapse in the Hun's story, which he was certain was for effect.

Judah cast a last and forbidding look outside, and went and brought the wine to them, with a forbidding look his way. *Be careful*, that said, and Alexander gave him back a warning of his own: *Do not interfere. I can handle this.*

He took up the cup Judah poured. Attila hoisted the other and drained it without taking a breath. He exhaled fumes and a sigh.

"Ahhh. By the Sky! I needed that."

Three more of those, Hun, and you will be on your face.

"Caesar," Alexander reminded him, and filled Attila's cup.

Attila's eyes shifted toward Judah's retreating back. Then he leaned forward again, over his arms. "Caesar offers a deal. He'll march up and down a while. We just make a mistake, huh? What you got to do is know when."

"And do what?"

"Hell, you just slip out of this trap." Attila reached into his shirt and pulled out a much-battered and soaked paper, and spread it on the table. "Here you are, right? Here's his positions. You just get this mess loaded up and go right down this track tomorrow night."

Alexander leaned back and laughed. "You must think I'm a fool."

Attila laughed, showing white teeth. "You must think I'm one, to walk in here and tell a lie, Great King. I got wives and kids to think of." He belched and laughed. "Caesar's got something to lose, too. Doesn't want to go up against you. And he's got these orders. So he's got to make a show. You got to do the same. Thing that'll save this, you and he got the same repu-tation."

Alexander drew in his breath. *The same, indeed.*

"He's taking a bigger risk," Attila said. "He's got to let you get away."

"Who said I should run? Let him do the running!" It was all more tangled than seemed on the surface. He felt the weight of the day on him, good humor evaporated, and he felt short of breath. He took a drink of the wine to cool his throat, and another, to steady him. "I'm not about to follow a route he mapped."

"Hey." Attila took a drink, and frowned, looking into his cup. He poured more for them both, then cracked something he found on his arm. "Feh. Look, you don't want to fight him, he doesn't want to fight you. You know another way out of here, you take it, he won't object."

We're not ready. Father Zeus, if it were only the truth— Alexander took another gulp, and finished off the cup.

Attila grinned at him. "You see? Just a little agreement. And I walk out of here and you walk out, that's all, and Hell doesn't get a damn thing. What've you got out there? Damn mess Guevara left you. Credit to you if you can get these poor sods out of here alive. Caesar doesn't want any of his boys on the Undertaker's table. He sure as hell doesn't want you there. All you got to do is a favor."

The cup was full again. He took the gift, not remembering when or who had filled it. The tent seemed warm and close, but the track of logic was easy to follow.

"An agreement between you two. He can't be in the open about it—hell, he can't touch the Dissidents with a pole. But you can. He works on the inside of Administration, you work on the outside. Who can stop you two then, heh?"

"Did he say this?"

"Hell, we got a problem with this damn pitcher. It's empty."

"Judah."

A shadow drifted over out of the light. "Alexander." Judah reached for the cup, and Alexander knew the hidden meaning, the unspoken reproach. He held onto it and fixed Judah with a steady eye.

Not here, and not now, Judah. Fill the pitcher.

"Your father," Judah said pointedly, as no other man in Hell would dare. Philip of Macedon, Philip the drunk, Philip the sot.

"Damn you, fill the pitcher."

Judah's mouth was a hard line. He took the pitcher up, filled it from the skin hanging from the corner-pole, and brought it back again. "I'll call you one of the *servants*," he said in a low voice, and Attila took it and filled his cup and Alexander's.

"Do that," Alexander said; and deliberately drank a healthy swallow.

"The officers are asking," Judah began.

"Then find an answer for them!" He had not meant to lose his temper. He took a breath and a drink. "I'm talking to this man."

"Listen," Attila said, "you ask me questions." He filled his cup again and topped off Alexander's. "We got no hurry. I know Caesar's not going anywhere. You think I want to be a martyr. You ask me wh-whatever you like."

"Alexander."

"Zeus blast you, Judah, take care of business!" His temper had the better of him. He drank to steady himself, and looked at the Hun, who grinned good-naturedly at him.

"Man sounds like my number-one wife."

"He worries too much." Alexander sipped at his wine and leaned back. There was one advantage to being an alcoholic. He could drink any ordinary man under the table and stay cold sober enough to handle questions. Or draw another man out, especially as reckless and flamboyant a drinker as this leather-wearing barbarian. "Tell me exactly what Julius said."

Under the sufficient cover of darkness, Napoleon motioned the DGSE men forward. They had sunk the Zodiac an endless way back in the swamp and had hiked here, tripping over roots, getting caught by tangled branches, and stepping on things in the slimy water they were glad they they could not see.

"God!" Wellington swore under his breath as he crawled up onto dry land. "If I never see another swamp for the rest of eternity, it will be too soon."

Two of the DGSE men growled something un-heard; the one closest to Wellington breathed a heart-felt *certainment*.

Napoleon glanced at his watch. The glowing num-bers told the tale—on time, but barely so. He shrugged off his backpack, snapped it open, and took out dry clothing.

"*Vite! Vite!*" he murmured to the men from the *Sécurité*; and to Wellington: "Hurry, Wellington. We haven't got time to sit here and bitch."

"That's easy for *you* to say," Wellington grumbled, taking his uniform out of the backpack. "You didn't slip into that damned sinkhole!"

"Huhn." Napoleon dropped his muddy, scum-covered clothing in the reeds at the edge of the water. Mosquitoes, sensing exposed flesh, swarmed around him in a cloud. After a few half-hearted swats at them, he slipped into his pants. *No leeches so far, thank the Lord for that.*

Three of the DGSE men were nearly dressed by now, but the fourth was tugging at something disgust-ing that had attached itself to his foot. With a grunt of mingled pain and horror, he tore it off and slung it, overhanded, far out into the swamp.

Napoleon slipped on the Red Cross armband and felt around for his helmet. Twentieth century uni-forms had their advantages, simplicity being one. He ran his fingertips over the front of the helmet: the Red Cross emblem was affixed there, too.

"Stretchers?" he asked Wellington over his shoulder.

"*Ici. Voilà,*" replied one of the DGSE men, indi-cating the two rolled-up stretchers at his side. Though he understood English, he avoided speaking it when-ever he could.

"*C'est bon. Allez! Vite!*" Napoleon rose and turned to Wellington. "Now all we have to do is walk into

camp as if we belonged there. And disguised as
medics, we should be ignored. There are enough
sick and wounded here."

"Huhn." Wellington caught up, then put his hands
to the small of his back and tried to stretch. "Aaagh!
I think I pulled a muscle or something."

Napoleon paused a moment. An idea! He hissed a
halt to the DGSE men. "Wellington. Get on that
stretcher over there. I'll get on this one. Cover yourself up with the blanket, all the way over your head.
And for God's sake, hide your helmet."

After a hasty consultation with the four men from
Sécurité, Napoleon and Wellington entered the rebel
camp, covered with blankets and moaning as if they
had come down with malaria, which, Napoleon admitted to himself, might possibly be true.

The camp was poorly lit, either because there was
little fuel to be had, or because Alexander did not
want to give away his position. As Napoleon bumped
along on his stretcher, watching from under his blanket, he judged it was probably both. All the better
for their plans. It was a stroke of luck that made him
paranoid, however; Hell being Hell, dues time would
certainly follow.

There were few people about—another piece of
luck that made Napoleon nervous. Those who were
stirring watched them pass with only a brief flash of
interest. The four DGSE men kept silent, their red
crosses giving them right of way as they went.

"Hey, you, *medics!*" A Korean officer ambled over,
hand on pistol.

Tossing momentarily as if in the throes of fever,
Napoleon glanced quickly to the other side. No one
was around, and they had stopped in front of an aisle
between two tents.

"Set down," the officer said, gesturing to the ground. "What unit, these men? What disease?"

Wellington moaned softly.

Napoleon winced as the DGSE men who carried him set the stretcher right at the officer's feet. The man bent over and lifted the blanket back.

Napoleon smashed his hand up under the officer's jaw. The Korean went over and sprawled as Napoleon rolled off the stretcher and picked up his helmet. *"Ici,"* Napoleon hissed at his bearers, and dragged at the Korean.

The two DGSE men grinned, a hint of genuine respect in their eyes. Quickly they dumped the Korean to the stretcher and covered him; Napoleon stood up with his medic-emblemed helmet on, and dusted off his trousers.

"En avant," he said. The procession began again, with five medics, and the same number of bodies on stretchers. Napoleon memorized each twist and turn they made, and paid sharp attention as one tent loomed up ahead, larger and surrounded by more space than was necessary. It could be none other than Alexander's, on that scale.

And Napoleon's heart sank: their luck was indeed paying them back. Five Old Dead warriors stood outside that tent, fully armed, arguing with a tall, black-bearded man Napoleon took for Maccabee.

Oh, dammit! dammit! Attila, if ever you got a man drunker than a skunk, let's hope it's tonight!

The four men of the *Sécurité* carried the two stretchers past the command tent at a very respectful distance, jogged right at the next opportunity, and headed into deeper shadows between a makeshift shed and an empty tent.

Not one head at the command tent had turned as

they walked by. Evidently the spectacle of blanket-covered stretchers was not an uncommon one.

In the darkness now, the *Sécurité* men lowered the stretchers to the ground and attended the unconscious Korean with ropes and a gag—no Trips was the rule of this operation, no messengers sped to Reassignment if they could help it.

Wellington groaned beneath his blanket and Napoleon pulled it back to disclose a long-nosed and miserable face.

"God, Wellington." Napoleon hunkered down and adjusted the helmet. "Trip's over. You can cut the moaning and groaning. We can't do anything but wait. It's up to Attila and the SEALS now."

Wellington sat up on his stretcher and threw the blanket off. "Why do you think I'm moaning?" he asked.

"—long time," Attila said. "Long time I had that horse." He snuffled a little and wiped his nose on his sleeve, not far distant as he leaned on the table top. "Fourteen years. Bes' damn polo pony—went down under me. Bes' damn horse. Bay, three white feet, fast—damn, he was special—"

"I know." Alexander wept freely, tears running on his face. He leaned against the table, mirror image to the King of the Huns. "They only come once, horses like that—"

"This bay stud I got now—oh, damn, he looks like 'im, but down here, you know, you can't breed, I could do something with his lines, but damn nothing you can do—"

It was dark outside. They had lit the lamp. Attila felt his wits fuzzing amid the melancholy they had achieved. Outside, the Assyrians and the Hittites were back, bitching with Maccabee about a Cuban officer. Damn, damn, and damn.

He poured another cup of wine, steering the stream of liquid from the table to the inside of the cup. It was very hard to lift the pitcher. It was harder to keep his eyes open. He poured Alexander another, reckoning, in the dim fortress of his mind, that things had gone terrifyingly sour and anaesthesia might be called for.

"Always kept one of that line," he said. "Always—"

Something exploded in the distance. Alexander's head came up from its slow inclination to the table.

"What's that?"

The walls of the tent glowed gold as if an unprecedented sun had risen in Hell.

"Damn!" Alexander cried, and overset the chair and the table on his way to the door as explosions chained one on the next, and one light succeeded the other. "Judah!"

Attila staggered for the tent pole as Alexander rushed out into the unnatural dawn and shouted orders at Maccabee and the Assyrians and the Hittites and whatever officers were in range. Everything buzzed in Attila's ears like a hive of bees, and he risked his balance and grabbed after his bundle of weapons which reposed beside his chair.

Stop him, he thought, got to stop him—

Unfortunately the floor moved as the cup had, and he spilled his arrows, but he had his sword in one hand and two of his spears in the other.

And ran face on into Judah Maccabee, who was bound back inside, who targeted him with a furious look and a swipe of his sword.

"Eyyyyyy—aaaaaaa!" Attila yelled, skipping back with one step and round-housing a parry and a windmill attack with sword and bundled spears. He had lost track of the door and Alexander, till a sword whisshed by his ear and he windmilled and chinged that off in the other direction, swinging a desperate follow-through after Maccabee, who, being sober, had the advantage of knowing which foot was on the floor.

The medic team scrambled down the aisle, over the ropes, around the corner, into a bedlam of fleeing chickens and running soldiers and shouting women. "This way, this way—" Napoleon yelled, waving an arm as the long-legged moderns of the DGSE passed him by.

Steel rang in the command tent, rang and grated and rang: *Hyyyyyyaaaa!* roared out of the dark, the tent wall bellied out and jerked, and a blond Old Dead with a rifle reeled out into the magnesium glare above the tents.

Straight into the whuff! of a dart gun, which staggered him—he stood there like a shaken god, wide-legged, with a bit of black fluff on his chiton, and tried to bring the rifle up, but the legs went, and he went down. *"C'est lui!"* Barré shouted, and fired through the open door of the tent.

Napoleon skidded up behind Barré and Anbec, and saw the dark-headed Maccabee swaying like a tree under the axe, a dark bit of something in the middle of his back, and first his sword clanked down beside a dazed and battered Hun, and then the man followed, whump, right on top of Attila.

"Shit!" Attila yelled, flailing to free himself.

And from outside, Wellington's voice: *"Stretcher-bearers!"*

More flares burst overhead, and the ground shook to a chain of explosions.

"Vite!" Mirabeau yelled. He and Wellington had

one blanket-covered form of a stretcher outbound, running like hell.

Barré and Anbec exited the tent with the other, at a hard jog behind Wellington and Mirabeau.

"Attila!" Napoleon yelled, and grabbed the Hun by the arm as LeFlore propelled him out the door of the tent, rifle in one arm. Attila clutched his sword in one hand, two spears in the other, and refused to drop either handful as Napoleon and LeFlore hauled him along.

"*Merde!*" LeFlore gasped at last, grabbed the failing Hun in a fireman's carry, and ran with him, spears and sword and all.

That left one short and desperate medic bringing up the rear, jogging along with looks over his shoulder and glances ahead of them as they headed their jagged course through the aisles, freeing one startled pig and a chicken in the process.

It was the river ahead. It was safety if they could make it: beta-point. The pickup. *Marie, Marie, Marie.* Napoleon kept up the litany as he ran, expecting a bullet to come smashing into him at any moment. Perhaps it was fate that put him hindmost. Perhaps it was fate had shoved him back into the glare of fire and the popping of rifles and the ambitions he had renounced. If not Marie, then what worth the little house by the park—what worth was a life she had touched and left again?

Wellington and Mirabeau disappeared of a sudden, in the blink of an eye dropping out of sight among trees lit by distant magnesium glare. There was a scream, a splash.

The stretcher with Maccabee went out of sight with more deliberation, Barré and Anbec picking their way down the bank. LeFlore gave up and slid down in a cursing tangle with Attila, and Napoleon sat down and slid after, a long skid down to where a Georgia accent said:

" 'Damn, sorry about that."

They had the overloaded raft scarcely out onto the water when the chopper came beating in, a heartbeat, a sound of life out of the dark.

It set down to wait for them on the far side of Cocytus. There was no way to get two dart-drugged men and a drunken Hun up a swaying ladder.

The chopper swallowed them one and all and rose up with a crazed tilt, over a landscape in which other copters were inbound: "What's that?" Wellington asked, in the dark and wind-blown bay. "Who in hell is that coming in?"

"Strike force, sir," Jenks the SEAL said. "Signal called them in, too."

"Damn him!" Napoleon cried. "*Damn* him!"

"No choice," Wellington shouted over the wind and the beat of the engines. "No damned choice, had he?"

Napoleon sat staring out of the rear of the supply truck at the other vehicles following. The convoy of two empty personnel carriers and three supply vans rattled down the road that led back to New Hell meeting other, heavier-laden convoys going out in this first glimmer of dawn.

Two Roman legionaries, both of whom were heavily armed, drove the supply van. Surrounded by protection before and behind, Napoleon felt more secure than he had for days.

"Damn mud! Damned slimy, filthy mud!" Wellington brushed at the caked filth covering his uniform. "Gad! I *never* thought we'd get out of there!"

Napoleon was barely able to hear the Iron Duke's words over the rattle of assorted empty steel drums, ammo boxes, and large wooden pallets. He sat leaning up against a pile of flat tires, the canvas siding and roof of the truck snapping in the wind.

"Of course *you* didn't take a dive into the swamp," Wellington complained, staring at Napoleon's uniform (only slightly less soiled than his own).

Napoleon frowned, rested his head against the tires, then gave that up: they bounced so that he would end up with a splitting headache. He grunted something Wellington might take as condolences and stared over the Iron Duke's head at the flapping canvas side.

They had gone through a perfunctory debriefing in the field, and though he had asked time and again, no one could (or would) give him news of Marie.

Out here, who would know? And if they do know something, they might not be telling. O God . . . She's gone. I know she's gone by now.

"—you're not listening to a thing I've said, are you?"

Wellington's voice, pitched to carry over the echoing noise, intruded on Napoleon's dark thoughts.

"Sorry. Wool-gathering."

"I'd say." Wellington scratched at a host of mosquito bites that ran down the side of his neck. "Blasted bugs! Or is it insects?"

"Save your entomological comments for later, will you? The way you carry on, you might have been the only one bitten."

"Huhn." Wellington lifted one arm and sniffed. "God, Napoleon. I can't stand my own smell any longer. I've *got* to take a bath."

"What?"

"Napoleon? What is bloody wrong with you?"

"Nothing."

Wellington returned to picking the mud off his

uniform. "Caesar really owes us for *this* one, doesn't he?"

"I suppose he does, though I think he owes Attila more."

"That's a frigging understatement! I wonder how long it'll take for him to dry out?"

"Who knows?"

Wellington gave up trying to talk and subsided into silence.

With a sudden squeal of brakes, the convoy drew to a halt. Napoleon sat up straighter, shared a questioning look with Wellington. Brief words in Latin were exchanged between the driver and someone standing outside. Boots crunched on pavement as the fellow walked away.

"Check point," Wellington judged. "We're nearly there."

His words were prophecy. The convoy heaved itself through an opened gate into the armory parking lot, lumbered past depleted rows of trucks and other military vehicles in a bleak, cheerless morning, and into the cavernous garage. With a last rattle of exhaust pipes, the trucks came to a halt.

Napoleon rubbed the back of his neck, stretched, and tried to stand. Wellington tottered across from him.

"Damn! My rump's going to be sore for days," Wellington groused.

"Huhn." Napoleon clambered over the tailgate, and slowly let himself down to the concrete floor. Wellington followed.

"Sirs." A Roman voice came from behind, audible even over the roar of engines, the rattle of unpacking, slamming of doors, and shouts of the legionaries.

Napoleon turned, blinking in the miasma of exhaust fumes. A hawk-faced officer stood there, his uniform identifying him as tribune.

"Tribune Aemilius Paulus," he introduced himself. "Word from Caesar, sirs. Until things quiet down, he respectfully requests you stay here in the armory. For your protection, you see."

"*Dieu!*" Napoleon's heart froze. "That's unacceptable! I've *got* to go home!"

The tribune's face never altered. "Sorry, sir. Orders."

"*Tribune!*" someone hailed. "*Adsis, sivis.*"

The tribune turned, glanced across the garage. "A moment, please," he said, starting off. "A minor problem. I'll be back myself or send another to show you to your quarters."

"Now wait just a damned minute—"

The Roman was gone. Napoleon looked down at his muddy boots. "Oh damn! Damn!"

"Egads, Napoleon!" Wellington reached out and touched Napoleon's shoulder. "It's my car!"

Napoleon looked up: it *was* Wellington's white Eldorado, parked on the other side of the trucks.

"Our way home," Wellington said, "*when* we can leave."

"Orders or no orders," Napoleon half-shouted over the noise. "I'm going to—"

"Napoleon!"

His heart froze. It was Marie's voice—but it couldn't be. He must be imagining it in all the noise. He glanced around and saw nothing but busy legionaries.

"Oh, I say." Wellington touched Napoleon's shoulder. "*There* she is."

There were metal bars on the windows. There were guards: one could hear them walking, but the only thing that came through the door was food,

delivered three times daily through a slot so devised
that there was no contact with the outside world, no
view of a human hand, no answer of a human voice.

Judah called out to these faceless guards and cursed
them.

Alexander merely accepted the food, and walked
the thirty-pace confines of their prison, and slept,
at increasingly irregular intervals, measured by the
rising and setting of Paradise beyond the bars.

He could see the open land. There were mead-
ows, trees, a small woods. Such kept him sane.

Of the fact of their captivity he said nothing at all
to Judah. Who had done this he knew, and would
not say the name.

Once, perhaps a trick of the eyes, he thought he
saw a horse running in the meadow, a black horse.
"Judah, look—" he said then.

But Judah avowed he saw nothing.

LEARNING CURVE

David Drake

"Watch out!" called the slaving captain as Statius, his contact in this *God*-forsaken place, stepped close to a display of dried fish for sale on the mud-bank bazaar.

Statius glanced down, then hopped to avoid the fish that flipped up from the grass mat and snapped jaws that would have taken the poet's finger off had he been an instant slower.

The creature flopped stiffly back among its fellows. Its eye had sunken in and its fins were crinkled by the drying blast of Paradise. The fish was dead beyond question.

But then, everything in Hell was dead.

Statius's face worked, half a grimace and half a smile, intended to suggest that it was nothing, that he wouldn't have minded being maimed for all the rest of eternity. "Captain Conneau," he said, extending his hand to the other man. "You're earlier than I had expected."

Conneau glanced over his shoulder to be sure that his two guards had his dugout canoe and its cargo under control. The coffle of slaves—nine men and a boy—was dragging the sloping prow higher onto the mud without complaint or need for the hippopotamus-hide whips coiled in the guards' right hands. Reassured, the slaver grasped the hand of the Roman poet and said, "You've found the buyer, then? Everything is as it should be?"

Statius's English was flawless—better than Conneau's, though the slaver had been an American citizen in life—but he still gestured assent by lifting his eyebrows instead of nodding. "Yes," he said, "yes, he's a man named Richard Halliburton who posed as an adventurer in life. Finally, he tried to do something truly dangerous—more dangerous than he guessed: sail a junk across the Pacific in typhoon season. When it went down, he huddled in his bed with his Chinese cabin boy."

Conneau chuckled and nudged the Roman with an elbow. "Ah," he said, "you landsmen can't appreciate the charms of a cabin boy the way an old sailor like me can. But what matters to us is what he's doing now."

"Which is providing consignments of slaves," the poet said grimly, "to stock the larder of an Ethiope king."

He looked at the slaves, who had paused, waiting dumbly for orders now that the dugout was fully aground. "The merchandise is as I directed, then?"

"All prime," Conneau agreed, turning to survey his cargo. In a louder voice he called, "Well, secure them, then. Do you expect to trot them through the streets like a flock of sheep?"

"They seem as docile as sheep," Statius murmured as the guards began lashing the slaves' hands to the hoop of rattan each wore at his waist. The guards carried slung muskets as well as their whips, but the slaves had been so thoroughly broken to the necessity of obedience that the guns were only a burden.

"Let them get loose with a chance to dodge down a twisty alley," replied the slaver with a cynical smile, "or let them get a hint of what they're being bought *for*. Then tell me they're too docile for tied hands and a neck cord."

"Still . . ." said the poet, softly enough that he was almost speaking to himself.

The plump, doe-eyed boy whom Statius had particularly requested to be included in the coffle did not wear a hoop like the adults. Nonetheless, the long leather cord was knotted around his neck as well as theirs so that the coffle formed a living restraint on the urge any of its members had to flee.

"It's hard to imagine what any of those men could have done in life," Statius continued in the same quiet voice, "which would have brought them—here."

"Well, what of you, then, Roman?" Conneau asked, with curiosity as well as a gregarious man's instinct to make conversation. "You wouldn't hurt a fly yourself, would you? And you were even a Christian."

"We'd best be moving on," said the poet, glancing either toward the sullen red orb of Paradise—or away from his companion and the need to answer the question. "You'll need good light for your examination of the premises."

"Suleiman," Conneau called to one of his black guards, "you stay with the boat till we return. Ala-Ninfa, follow the coffle. My friend and I will lead."

The slaver smiled at Statius; then, bowing, gestured the Roman forward grandiosely.

Statius lifted his forehead again in agreement and began to pick a way for them through the dismal clutter of the river bank bazaar. Figures huddled beside assortments of trinkets, garments . . . foodstuffs already rotted beyond conceivable edibility. There did not appear to be any buyers. Some of the would-be sales folk, in caftans and dresses whose colors were subtly displeasing, tried to shade themselves with mats of grass held upright by poles.

Others squatted uncovered, blankly aware that while they could change the appearance of discomfort, they could do nothing about the dull agony that stemmed from their separation from Paradise, glimpsed or unseen.

Upright piles of things that resembled gray-white tombstones straggled across the dry mud, each slab crossed and recrossed by a twist of rope that had chafed into its edges. "What are these?" the poet asked as they walked down a corridor formed by the waist-high piles. He rubbed a forefinger along a slab, then touched the powder to his tongue and made a face. "Gypsum?"

"Salt," Conneau replied. He pointed to a camel nearby from which a blue-robed man was unlashing similar slabs while his partner held the beast's head. "Brought by caravan from dry lakes in the desert. They'll raft it down the river from here."

"Salt?" Statius repeated doubtfully. "Then it's certainly lost its savor."

There was a loud scream, bloodcurdling even in this place. The camel had managed to close its teeth over the face of the man trying to hold it still. As the wide-eyed slaves and their conductors watched, the beast stepped on the man's foot and began stretching its serpentine neck. The screaming continued even after the victim's flesh gave way so that bone glinted in the ruddy light.

The camel chewed in a sideways, rotary motion, oblivious of the other man who beat and cursed it in an attempt to drive it off the fellow its weight pinioned. As the beast bent its red-slobbering jaws for another bite, its eye winked at Statius with an inner light.

The Roman shuddered and began to walk faster than the tethered coffle could comfortably follow.

Conneau put a gently restraining hand on his companion's arm and said, "Well, one thing in the favor of this Halliburton. He's not making the same mistakes he did in life."

Statius took a breath deep enough to swallow the sob that had threatened to escape him. Conneau was obviously trying to change the subject, and the off-hand kindness of the attempt warmed the Roman. "Well," he said with his voice under control, "in a way. But there's a parallel, don't you think? Between selling lies as truth and selling the—material from which a black cannibal constructs false wisdom?"

"Now, be charitable, my good friend," the slaver said cheerfully. "Wisdom that *may* be false."

Statius turned and gestured imperiously toward the camel, still half laden, whose long, ugly jaws were now working to strip the meat from his driver's spindly thighs. "What sort of wisdom does a man find *here* by his own efforts? What sort of wisdom *brings* a man here?"

"Yes, well," said Conneau, fluffing the unbuttoned vest he wore over a white shirt. The action was habitual. Though it stirred the air, that could not cool him here. "Here where we are, you mean."

Statius grimaced, then walked on with measured steps.

The city hunched on the river bank instead of rising above it. Its houses were of bricks molded from the yellow-gray mud of the flats below, a bilious color which hinted that it had long ago been a living thing.

The streets were so crooked that the buildings seemed almost to have been tossed down at random, but the pavements were surprisingly broad. Instead of crowding one another, the houses crouched in lonely misery, windowless and turned inward to courtyards as barren and empty as the mud walls which surrounded them.

They met a goat with a withered hind leg, picking its way along with its head low. It ignored them. Besides the goat, there appeared to be nothing putatively alive in the city.

"No, I wouldn't have hurt a fly," said Statius, loudly enough to be heard but without turning to his companion to indicate he was resuming the earlier conversation. "I was one of the most popular men in the court of Domitian. The emperor liked me, *everybody* liked me, and I never hurt anyone."

One of the slaves in the coffle behind the white men began a wordless song. His voice was as clear as an organ pipe. Three of his fellows joined him momentarily—

—before the desert wind, a dust-laden whisper until then, rose and began to keen a mocking dirge. The men fell silent.

"I didn't think there was harm in praising the emperor," Statius said in a voice made thin by the grit that coated the inside of his mouth, his teeth, and his tongue. "Everyone I knew praised Domitian, except for a few mad Stoics who risked their lives, families—everything."

The wind chuckled.

"I suppose," the poet added softly, "that everyone I used to know is here. Except the Stoics. Everyone who refused to stand up to a tyrant."

"Cheer up, then," the slaving captain said. He linked arms companionably with the poet. "That's all over now."

"I didn't sleep very well," said Statius, his eyes on the mud street and mud buildings but seeing neither of them. "It bothered my wife the way I'd toss and turn. When I was alive."

Conneau nodded toward Paradise, which lowered past the sagging mud spire of a mosque. "Maybe they sleep soundly up there, my friend. And maybe one day we'll know."

"I didn't promise that!" snapped the poet, stopping to lock eyes with Conneau to emphasize his words. Behind them, the coffle straggled to a halt.

The slaver shrugged. "What would a promise here be worth anyway?" he said agreeably. "But . . . I used to say when a disagreeable necessity intruded—in my former business, you see—'Well, I must light a candle to the Devil.' "

"And now you're here," remarked Statius.

"Indeed," said Conneau. "So perhaps we'll light a candle to God, seeing that the other looks to have been a mistake."

The laughing wind flapped Conneau's vest against him. He felt as if he were standing in front of the open door of a blast furnace.

Statius guided them through the sprawling maze with the talent for intricate detail which had always marked his poetry. As they approached their destination, the Roman looked over his white companion with a more critical eye than other concerns had permitted him before. He glanced away, lips pursed, and then looked back to say, "You're armed, I see. As if you were ready to repeat your life."

The slaver flushed. "I have to, don't I? That's what you want me to pretend to be, what I was."

"They're not loaded, then?" Statius asked gently.

"Yes, they're damned loaded," Conneau retorted, sliding one of the brace of big single-shot pistols an inch higher in the belt, where he carried them unholstered. The weapon was at half cock, so that the copper priming cap was fully visible against the nipple blackened by earlier discharges. "That doesn't mean I'm going to use them, does it? I tell you, I've learned from my . . . from my life."

"I hope I have also," said the poet in a conciliatory tone, embarrassed now that he had broached a subject which was none of his business. A soul's salvation was a matter for that soul alone. . . .

"Look," said the slaver, also abashed because of the anger with which he had greeted a well-meant warning. "It's not as though they were plasma guns or the like. I'm—afraid of what we're doing, of the consequences if we fail, or even if we succeed. Having these—" he stroked the smooth walnut grip of the pistol and let his fingertip rest on the brass buttcap "—makes me better able to perform my duties."

"I shouldn't have spoken," said Statius, and neither man was certain whether or not that statement was true.

There was nothing unusual about the house in which Halliburton lived to gather the human merchandise which he sent on to his black master in Pompeii, though the courtyard adjoining the two-story building was rather more expansive than many of its neighbors. The gate was wooden. At one time it had been decorated with brass appliqué, but verdigris had stripped away everything except leprous hints of where the nails had been.

Statius hammered on the panel with the heel of his hand, rattling the gate against the crossbar which secured it within.

An eye appeared at a triangular hole in the wood, then the gate swung open.

The doorman was as black as any of the slaves in Conneau's coffle and his face bore the cross-hatches of tribal scarring, but he wore the red fez that marked him as a claimant of Islam. Lice peeped from beneath the cap's rim.

"Bouba," said Statius, "tell your master that we have brought the merchandise as arranged."

Besides a revolver and what appeared to be a European-pattern saber on separate shoulder belts, the doorman carried a cattle-horn trumpet almost thirty inches long. He stepped back into the courtyard and put the instrument to his lips. The mouthpiece was offset, like that of a flute.

As the two whites preceded the coffle through the gate, Bouba blew a signal that sounded like the despairing blat of an animal being disemboweled.

The courtyard stank, even in a state of existence whose normal atmosphere ranged from sulphurous to solid. A hundred or so slaves were chained at close quarters across the rear half of the open area. Ragged matting provided a partial shield against the blaze of Paradise, but there had been no attempt to clean the area in days, perhaps longer.

"What's this?" said Conneau, so shocked that he forgot he was playing a part—and therefore played it to perfection. "By the good God!"

Ignoring his own coffle and the servitors in rich, filthy clothing who sprang from the house in response to the horn signal, Conneau strode over to the ranked slaves. Each slave—females as well as males—had one leg riveted into an iron shackle. The remaining cuff of the shackle encircled not another human but a heavy chain laid the length of the courtyard.

Some slaves looked up as Conneau approached; most were too apathetic even to do that.

Swearing under his breath in three languages, the slaving captain bent to examine the post to which one end of the chain was padlocked. A servitor in a caftan of stained silk brocade ran up to him, gabbling a mixture of greeting and concern. Conneau brushed the fellow aside, then grimaced, straightened, and kicked the post with disdain.

It quivered, and the line of shackles chimed against the chain in faint discord.

Slaves could be added or removed easily from either end, because the cuffs slipped loosely over the heavy links. The arrangement gave the slaves as little room to move as so many pearls on a string, and their wretched condition made it obvious that they were never released for exercise as they would have been every evening on one of Conneau's vessels.

Flies furred the ankles of slaves where the cuffs had worn festering sores. One female lay on her back with a fly crawling across her eyeball. Her chest rose and fell raggedly with her breathing, but she did not have enough energy to blink.

"Who's in charge of this?" Conneau demanded, prodding the servitor with a finger. The startled man skipped back, silenced by the visitor's attention. "This is disgraceful!"

"Mister Halliburton will see us now, captain," Statius called from the doorway into the house where he had been talking to another servitor. A rope beside the door led upward to an iron alarm bell in a cupola above the second story, ready to summon the whole district in event of a slave mutiny.

Though from the look of these shackled skeletons, mutiny was as improbable as Christ sweeping them all off to Paradise.

"Perhaps . . ." Conneau muttered, but he was unwilling to complete the sentence even in his own mind.

The room to which the visitors were conducted down a short hallway had a high ceiling and would have been cool—if moderate temperatures were possible in the damnable place. The walls were bare brick, hung with dimly glimpsed paraphernalia: photographs whose corners had twisted across their faces; what would be a musical instrument if it were restrung; and moldering fetishes which had perhaps been worshipped by the slaves in the courtyard.

Much good it had done *them*.

Light seeped through a brick lattice near the roof. For a moment, the visitors could see only the face and hands of the man on the room's huge divan. Then he moved, and the maroon pattern of his robes became distinguishable from the dark blue drapes of the couch.

Two young boys, black and nude, stood at the ends of the divan. In a desultory fashion they waved ostrich-feather sweeps which did little to move the air and nothing to cool it.

"Mister Halliburton," said Statius. "My agent is here with the consignment of merchandise which I promised you."

"Well, he's too late then, isn't he?" Halliburton said with a petulant flick of his hand. He wore a beard in an apparent—and unsuccessful—attempt to hide the open sores around his mouth and chin. "I already have enough to ship to Pompeii tomorrow. Come back in a month and perhaps I'll see you."

"Get *them* to Pompeii?" retorted the slaver harshly. "Pfft! Half of them will survive, if you're lucky—a third or less if you botch the business the way you have out there."

"And who do you think you are to teach me my business?" Halliburton demanded, sitting upright on the divan. He was short—at most, the height of his visitors, neither of whom was tall. Perhaps that was why he sprawled to greet them, letting his loose garment suggest a more impressive figure.

The slaver bowed deeply, a gesture containing more of arrogance than obeisance. "Captain Theophilus Conneau, sir, at your service. I've shipped as many slaves from the Guinea coast as any man who ever lived."

Halliburton, taken aback by his visitor's boastful certainty, said, "Well, captain, these folk aren't for work. They're food, and it scarcely matters whether they're dancing or—" he swirled a hand in the direction of the courtyard "—like that, when they go beneath the knife."

Conneau's nose wrinkled, but before he spat out his opinion of a white man who slaved for a black cannibal, Statius edged him back with a firm though polite hand.

"What my agent means, Mister Halliburton," the Roman said in a voice whose false ebullience had been polished in the court of a madman who equated silence with sullen disapproval, "is that the prime merchandise we offer you will assure that your master will receive the full measure he expects. Not only will they be appreciated for their own tender juiciness, but also these healthy bucks will be of service ministering to their feebler brothers and sisters on the journey."

Halliburton scowled. "They're just to be rafted down-river to the sea and transshipped there," he muttered. "I don't see what problem there could be in that."

"Come and see the merchandise, sir," said Conneau, with pride but no longer a blustering sneer in his voice. "Prime, as my colleague says, and well able to aid your boatman on the mudbanks which will otherwise double the time of your journey—and your losses."

"Fagh," grunted Halliburton. "I don't—"

"Our alternative, of course," Statius said, "would be to deal directly with your—" He was too frightened to complete his sentence—so frightened that his eyes could pass no images to a mind already packed with imagined scenes of him confronting a huge black monarch.

The threat was so effective that Halliburton didn't realize how much it terrified Statius as well. He struggled from the divan and shouted, "Do that and you'll join them, I warn you! He appointed *me* his agent, and he won't go back on that!"

"Oh, we're all honorable men here, aren't we?" said Conneau. The slaver hooked his thumbs in his belt, behind his pistols, and flared his elbows. "My colleague has far too much respect for you, Mister Halliburton, to go over your head in that fashion. But if you won't even examine our merchandise. . . ."

"I'll see your niggers," said Halliburton as he stamped down the hallway. "And I'll see you damned!"

It didn't occur to any of those present to laugh.

Conneau's slaves were in line near the gate, either looking at their iron-laden fellows or looking anxiously in any other direction. Their guard, Ala-Ninfa, had uncoiled his whip and was ostentatiously popping it in the air while several of the servitors looked on.

"These don't look any great prize to me," said Halliburton as he skipped forward, clutching a handful of his robe so that he would not trip over the hem. In better light, it was clear that someone had vomited on the garment.

"The adults are all Mandingos," said Statius. He touched Conneau to keep him from angrily stating the obvious—that Halliburton was not really examining the coffle. "Very tractable, ideal stock. The boy chances to be a Dahoman. . . ."

Halliburton had reached the end of the line and the plump boy who waited there with fearful eyes and a hide tether around his neck. The two, man and boy, looked at each other. Halliburton reached out and touched the bare, black shoulder, then let his fingertips trail streaks in the oily sweat down the boy's chest.

"An amusing thing about his name," Statius continued. "Not an uncommon one, of course. His name is Calandola."

"I'll take the boy," said Halliburton in a husky, detached tone. He and the boy stared at one another like a rabbit and a snake . . . but Conneau, watching in amazement, would have feared to guess which of them filled the victim's role.

"I'm sorry," Statius said, with nothing in his tone to suggest the statement was true. "He's part of the coffle."

"Then I'll take them, damn you!" Halliburton shouted as he spun around. "Cut him loose," he added to Ala-Ninfa.

Statius signed the guard not to move. "We'll turn

the coffle over to you," he said, "after you've given us a draft on your supplier in Pompeii."

He smiled, wishing that he were not terrified but delighted that he was able to carry out the plan despite fear. "Sulla's merchandise for ours, with—a ten percent bonus over the usual exchange because of the quality of these . . . men."

If they didn't bargain like businessmen, then Halliburton might wonder what their real business was. That would be disastrous.

"All *right*," Halliburton grunted, tripping on the garment whose length he had forgotten in his haste back to the door. "You'll have it. You'll have it now."

Everyone standing in the fetid courtyard watched him until he disappeared inside. Conneau leaned toward his companion and whispered, "Why did you tell him the boy's name was Calandola? It's Janken."

Statius shrugged. "A slave's name is the name its master gives it," he said.

He looked again at the slaves, his gaze lingering longest on the boy. He went on, "I regret what we have to put them through, you know."

Conneau was trying to judge from the angle of Paradise how long it would be before they could return to this courtyard in darkness. "Needs must when the good Lord drives," he said abstractedly.

It seemed forever. In a manner of speaking, it probably was.

"How do you find anything in this?" muttered Conneau. The night was so dark that Statius's white toga was scarcely more visible ahead of him than were the gleaming black skins of Suleiman and Ala-Ninfa behind.

The Roman fluttered a hand, irritated at having his concentration broken. He paused, then strode around

a corner that Conneau had not glimpsed until that
moment.

The rafts and boatmen they had hired would, God
willing, be waiting at the riverside when they were
needed. There was no one in this place who could be
trusted to help before then. Now that he had seen
Halliburton's stock, Conneau was worried that they
would need help badly.

It wasn't just what they were doing: it was that
they needed to accomplish it swiftly and silently. If
Halliburton's alarm bell began to ring, hundreds of
nearby residents would descend on them with swords
and long muskets. Whatever else that meant, it meant
he and his companion had failed damnably.

"Here we are," whispered Statius.

The certainty amazed Conneau, but when Statius
tapped on the half-glimpsed gate with one finger,
Bouba opened it as arranged.

"Pay me," the doorkeeper demanded hoarsely as
Conneau started past him.

"*Silence*," Statius whispered back, pressing the
packet he held into Bouba's hand. It was not money,
but rather the currency for which men sell their lives
and their very souls: white powder in a glassine
packet.

"We need our lights," said Conneau, certain of
what he had suspected all along. He could not see the
ranked slaves, not even as a mass against the courtyard wall. The operation could have either darkness
or silence, now, and showing a light was the lesser
risk.

Without waiting for the Roman to mumble his
assent, Conneau pulled a punk stick from its gourd
carrier and blew it hot enough to ignite the wick of
his kerosene lantern. A flashlight would have been
easier—if it worked.

Nothing worked very well in Hell. Some technologies worked better than others in some regions . . . but it was damned hard to tell what the boundaries were, or if there were boundaries at all. For now, all that mattered was that the clinging yellow light of the lantern was sufficient to the task.

Bouba had run off down a dark street with his payment. Conneau had intended to co-opt the doorkeeper to help in getting the slaves to the river, but it was too late now to worry about it.

Statius walked swiftly down the chained line of slaves, repeating, "Be as silent as you can. We're here to lead you to safety." His paces flowed with the complex rhythm of his words.

Despite the warning, shackles clinked all along the chain. The slaves who were not too weak or apathetic to move were sitting up to see what was going on. A few began to moan in terror, knowing what lay at the end of the journey they expected.

Ala-Ninfa and Suleiman stood at the headpost of the chain, one with a blacksmith's saw in his hand, the other with his double-barreled musket.

"Well, get to—" growled Conneau more loudly than he had intended.

He stepped close to the guards. In a lower but no less harsh voice, he said, "No, give me that," and snatched the saw away. "You two help Statius. Make sure they all know to carry the shackle, not to drag it, till we get clear. And *shut* those niggers up if you have to knock them on the head!"

The guards bolted down the line with such alacrity that Conneau repented his words. A calm explanation would be enough to quiet the moaning slaves, and, if the good God willed, a calm explanation was what the black guards would offer them.

If not, well—he had made a mistake in haste and

anger, and such mistakes were no doubt among the lesser reasons for his damnation.

Conneau set his lantern on the ground and began sawing at the hasp of the padlock. He risked one glance behind him, toward the house. Its windows were dark and the door was still closed, but the look of his hunched shadow thrown against the wall's cracked covering (mud slurry, in lieu of plaster) was hellishly unpleasant. He bent to the job.

The first nine slaves on this end of the chain were the adults from the coffle Conneau had just delivered. They had been told Statius's plan and their duties in carrying it out, but Conneau had doubts as he met their eyes.

The slaves were terrified. They had not resisted while Conneau brought them down the river and marched them here, but the bite of their iron cuffs had driven from their minds any thoughts but those of immediate escape. Unlike the others, weakened by longer confinement, these men were as physically able to rush for the gate as they were mentally prepared to do so.

Conneau paused, though the sound of a saw at the other post continued like a petulant echo of his. He touched the grip of one of his pistols, shifting so that the lantern threw highlights from the buttcap across the staring eyes.

"When I release the chain," the slaving captain said in a voice that made up in menace what it lacked in volume, "you all will obey your instructions. I will pistol the first man who bolts—and the second."

Several of the men began to shiver, but the tension went out of muscles which until then had been springs wound to hurl them into flight.

The steel teeth of Conneau's saw seemed at first to be wearing faster than the verdigrised bronze hasp of the lock. He stifled a curse behind clenched teeth and put his back into the strokes, averting his face from what he feared was the utter failure of tools, a normal thing in this place. The slaves cowered back from the furious grimace they were sure was meant for them instead of just pointed in their direction.

The hasp clinked apart just as lack of friction convinced Conneau that his saw was no longer cutting at all.

Conneau rose to his feet. The abrupt motion made him dizzy and threatened to collapse his legs at the knees, cramped while he worked.

"All right," he muttered to the nearest black. The man's hands reached to unhook the chain from the opened hasp and snatched themselves back as swiftly as the tongue of a snake. "Go ahead, you know what to do."

Conneau strode to the gate, leaving the lantern where he had set it. His first step wobbled slightly, but he was steady again by the time he reached the panel and leaned his back against it.

It would have been useful to have someone responsible at the chain. A number of the slaves were clanking shackles over the links with as much noise in Conneau's hypersensitive ears as that of the blacksmith who had forged the chain. There was still no sign of alarm from the house. Thick walls and the chance that all those within slept the sleep of the damned were as much protection as he could hope for.

Conneau might have prayed, but he didn't have Statius's assurance that God heard prayers from this place.

There was movement in the light of Statius's lantern at the farther post. The slaves confined there were less able to act than those of the recent coffle, but the Roman and the two guards were sliding the shackles off the chain by brute force when the folk were too weak or confused to free themselves.

Limping, half-blind with fear and fly-eggs on their eyeballs, freed slaves drifted toward the gate. Here and there a slave unable to walk was supported by another pair in only marginally better condition. Conneau cursed under his breath. They'd need the Devil's own luck to reach the shore by dawn.

If Halliburton gave the alarm within the hour, the straggling column would be lost as utterly as if there had been no release, and it was inconceivable to Conneau that the noise in the courtyard had not aroused the house already.

Perhaps it had, but none of the servitors were willing to disturb their master. Statius's planning was looking increasingly expert as well as increasingly intricate.

Suleiman pushed through the cringing slaves with Statius following in his wake.

"He'll start them off," said the Roman, with a nod toward the hulking guard. "Your coffle and Ala-Ninfa are freeing the rest, and we need to clear the courtyard."

We need more than that, Conneau thought, but he said aloud as he stepped back from the gate, "You won't have any problem reaching the head of the column before he gets lost, I'm sure."

Statius grimaced agreement and returned to supervise the freeing of the last slaves.

The freed slaves shuffled out behind Suleiman faster than Conneau would have guessed. Most of them even remembered to carry the loose end of their shackles. That made walking easier as well as less noisy. The number who had to be helped by their stumbling fellows shocked Conneau deeply, and he

knew that the worst off would lie near the chain until
the healthy men of the recent coffle could carry them
out by main force.

He had never denied to himself the humanity of
those in whom he trafficked. Nor did he deny now
that what he found most shocking about the condition of these staggering men and women was the
horrible waste of a valuable commodity. How *could*
Halliburton be such a fool?

Though the answer was as obvious as the question:
because he was a damned fool.

Conneau was so absorbed with patting the freed
slaves forward and placing shackles in the hands of
those who dragged them—sometimes it worked, sometimes the iron clanked back to the ground as soon as
Conneau released it—that he did not notice Statius
until the Roman whispered from beside him, "They're
all loose now. I think your men are enough to handle
those who must be carried."

"No matter what we do," said Conneau, watching
the gray faces and empty eyes of the freed slaves,
"we'll lose ten percent of them. Probably twenty."

"I know that," agreed the Roman.

"We can try to heal their sores and feed them back
to health," Conneau continued in a soft, wondering
voice like that of a child watching a butterfly as it
spreads wings still damp from the cocoon. "They'll
still be back in a place like this or worse as soon as
we turn them loose."

"I know that."

"And some other poor souls will fill this nigger
king's pot if these don't," Conneau said, no longer
able to avoid frustrated anger. "What good have we
done? Why are we bothering?"

"As much good as we can do for these," Statius
said, making a gesture that was almost a caress of the

woman who filed past at that moment, crooning to herself. "And as much as we can do in this place to redress the sins that brought us here."

"It can't be enough, Roman," Conneau whispered.

"Probably not," Statius agreed. "But that isn't in our hands either."

He patted at his toga, trying to settle it and conceal some of the stains it had received from the puling men and women he had labored to save. "Has the boy come out?" he asked.

"Not yet," said Conneau. Then he added, in a flat voice, "He understood the situation, so he's probably unable to come. Maybe he doesn't even want to come. We can check back for him when we've got the others safe."

"I must go get him," Statius said. He drew himself upright, but he could not prevent his lower lip from trembling with fear.

"You'll spoil it all!" Conneau snarled, gripping Statius's shoulder as the poet started toward the door of the house.

"I've got to face—" Statius said.

"Halliburton isn't Halliburton's master!" Conneau interrupted. "Come on. We have a job to do."

The Roman's visage settled again into an expression of composure and dignity. He shrugged free of Conneau's grip and said, "Our job, my friend, is to face our demons. Halliburton now. Perhaps his master later—as God wills."

He stepped in the direction of the door, which had already started to open.

The boy, Janken/Calandola, slipped out like a puff of wind. His plump face was set and no longer childish.

Statius ran to him and swept him up with a muted cry.

There was reason to be thankful indeed, thought

Conneau sourly. Not only was the boy safe, surely a plus, but also, his appearance had prevented the Roman from quixotically dooming them all, slaves and slave-stealers alike.

The captain waved Ala-Ninfa through the gate with a lantern in one hand and a comatose woman draped over the other shoulder. The courtyard was empty at last save for the three of them—the two whites and the boy.

"Let's *go*," Conneau called through clenched teeth.

The others turned, still clutching one another in desperate affirmation. The door beyond them opened again.

Halliburton stood in the doorway, his face yellower than the lantern light could account for alone. He was naked. The glinting thing in his left hand was not a weapon but a gin bottle, emptied to within a few swigs of the bottom.

"Calandola," he wheezed. His eyes locked into focus.

The boy screamed and bolted for the gate. Halliburton reached for the bell-pull.

"*Don't*, Halliburton!" Conneau cried.

"*Don't*, Conneau!" Statius cried as he saw that the captain had leveled one of his pistols at Halliburton.

Halliburton's hand closed on the bell rope, and Conneau shot him.

The pistol's single barrel was long enough to dull the muzzle blast, but the pair of ounce balls with which the gun was loaded made it recoil into Conneau's face. The shock was more blinding than the red powder flash had been.

Halliburton reeled backward, the balls marking his chest like a pair of supernumerary nipples a finger's length apart. When he fell, he fell on his face with his hand locked in a death grip on the bell rope.

An axle squealed in the cupola. The alarm bell spun over the top in response to the dying pull. It did not ring, because the clapper was rusted to the body of the bell.

"Come quickly," Statius murmured to Conneau, unable to see for blood and tears. The whites stumbled from the courtyard together like another pair of crippled slaves.

"I wouldn't have had to shoot him," Conneau said. "The alarm wouldn't ring." His hand was clamped to the pressure cuts on his eyebrow and cheekbone. He cherished the pain, because he could pretend it was his punishment.

His only punishment.

"We can't control what happens," said Statius quietly. "Only what we do."

Conneau stopped and gripped his companion with both hands. "It was more important to make sure the slaves got away, wasn't it?" he demanded. "Than that I—than that I shot a man again?"

"I hope so, my friend," the Roman said.

Then, with the bitter humor he had never dared express during life, he added, "But I'm God damned if I know."

SEA OF STIFFS

Janet Morris

The Undertaker's Table was home base to Nichols—Slab A. The Mortuary was his wardroom, his supply depot, and his officer's club all rolled into one, a place where "floating poker game" was a literal description because the other players were sycophants—disembodied voices, translucent wisps of servile shades, brown-nosers without noses looking for brownie points in a game Nichols didn't want to contemplate.

Nichols wasn't anything like the sycophants he'd just taken to the cleaners at five-card stud while he played his real game of waiting. Nichols was two hundred pounds of all-American crew-cut brawn, as graceful as Fort Bragg could make a man. Nichols was ex-101st with a Screaming Eagle on his tanned biceps. Nichols was ex-Team 6, ex-Joint Special Operations Command, and ex post facto, since America

had proved that it could field enough bang for its
bucks to shock the whole world halfway back to the
Stone Age.

But Nichols didn't mind any of that—not even
being dead. He didn't miss life because afterlife, for
him, wasn't a whole hell of a lot different. But he did
mind screwing up.

He minded screwing up intensely. He minded it
with every fiber of his oft-reconstituted flesh. Since
he'd been seconded from the Pentagram to the Devil's Children, Satan's personal Agency, he'd had an
impeccable performance record.

And now this. A screw-up of the first order. What
the fuck had happened? Where was Enkidu, the
ape-man Nichols had dispatched to the Undertaker?
Nichols had staked out the Mortuary since he'd come
in from the field, and verified that Enkidu hadn't
shown up at Slab A like he should have.

Nichols had personally shot the hairy proto-man
with a special round filched for him by a grinning
sycophant—a round designed to mark the target for
Express and Holding. He'd had orders to bring this
Enkidu back to New Hell for Reassignment.

The orders hadn't said how. The operation had
gotten complicated. And when Welch, Nichol's com-
manding officer, had given the word, Nichols had shot
Enkidu square in the back. Sent the hairy man back
to Slab A the hard way. Or tried to.

But Enkidu had never made it back. Welch said it
was a glitch somewhere in Records, or in Reassignments itself. But Welch was up to his ears in New
Business—drug interdictions, the intelligence and pre-
planning thereof. And in Old Business—the Dissidents, the ass-kicking thereof.

All of which put Nichols in a state of nearly perpetual R&R: until Welch was ready to move out, Nichols didn't have squat to do.

So he'd come back here to squat in the Mortuary and see if he could turn up some lead on the misplaced person, Enkidu. After far too long, Nichols didn't have a clue. He'd beaten the sycophants out of everything they had that he could possibly use for the rest of eternity, and his mood was beginning to blacken.

Nichols needed to be told what to do, and currently, he was on his own recognizance. Welch didn't need him right now, and yet would need him later: that made things worse. Nichols *had* to have an interim goal, and finding this Enkidu, eradicating the black mark on his record, seemed like a good one.

Until Enkidu showed or Welch called, Nichols was going to sit right where he was, playing cards with the sycophants, getting his necessaries out of the vending machines in the staff lounge.

Or so he thought until the shift changed, and a sycophant flitted around his head.

He almost swatted it. The instinct to do so was nearly overwhelming. And he was frustrated, inactive, ready for a little bug-squashing. The sycophants always reminded him of giant mosquitos when they got this close—it was the noise they made.

And mosquitos can be deadly enemies. But Nichols kept his hands on his cards with an effort that made the eagle's beak on his arm jitter.

"Yeah, go ahead," he said through clenched teeth, and forced himself not to flinch as the thing brushed its ectoplasmic self against his ear to whisper in it. Nichols's sycophants were devoted, useful—his own platoon of eager buck privates. They always brought him what he needed, sometimes even when he didn't know what it was he needed.

This one whispered: "The angel, he's in the Mortuary looking for Enkidu. Looking for Enkidu, too, hoo hoo. Looking for Enkidu, too, hoo hoo, as Gilgamesh used to do. Ask about Marilyn, too, do. Achoo!"

"Get away from me! Don't you know better than to goddamn sneeze on somebody!" Nichols exploded into action, all the self-control that kept him from fending off the creature gone in a rush of animal panic. He was up against the wall before he knew it, his machine pistol out and ready to strafe the air. But that was what it was—just air.

He couldn't shoot the sycophants, like he couldn't shoot his way out of Hell. Easy, easy. Nichols, backed against the wall stiff-legged, broke into a sweat as he used all the discipline at his command to squeeze shut the crack that had opened in his equilibrium.

It wasn't nothin'; it wasn't shit. Hell wasn't any worse than the Green Line or Saigon or Peshawar or the Golan Heights or the fucking District. No, it wasn't. And these sycophants were like any other bunch of indigs—they helped him out, lots.

He kept talking to himself, pushing the horror away, closing the chinks in the mind-armor he'd so carefully crafted for himself. Mind-armor was like body-armor: you wore it—no matter how heavy it was, no matter the debits—because you couldn't get through without it.

Because underneath it was soft, weak, human frailty; was flesh and blood and fear and disgust and repentance and the awful certainty that God has forsaken you. You don't go to Hell for no reason.

Some of 'em thought they were here by mistake, but Nichols knew better. He was here because of all those confirmed kills on his *other* record—the earthly one—and because God didn't bless America, right or wrong. Freedom, evidently, wasn't worth all it was cracked up to be worth. Fighting for it didn't give you carte blanche. Killing in the name of God and Country was still killing, and somebody should have checked with God before they sent all those boys out to kill and be killed in His name.

But nobody had, and Nichols had shot and bombed and napalmed his way in here. He rubbed his eyes with the back of one hand and slowly holstered his pistol while the sycophants, packed so tightly in the middle of the air that they looked like a swirl of opaque mist, chittered nervously to one another and made soothing noises at him.

"It's okay, guys," he said harshly. "I'm just jumpy, a little strung." And he slid down the wall on weak knees, then brought those knees up, balanced his elbows on them, and hung his head.

Easy, man. Don't make no never mind how you feel about it. And it didn't: he was here for the foreseeable, along with countless hornswaggled freedom fighters and crusaders and zealots and self-proclaimed patriots and damnfool kids who'd been taught that military service was the way to become a man.

Sometimes Nichols wondered if he could get transferred to a haunt platoon: become a ghost, so he could try to let some of the guys still living know what they were buying into.

But the haunts he'd heard about never managed to get their messages across; and, like the sycophants, they were a lower form of . . . 'life.'

Slowly, his breathing shallow, the soldier laboriously reconstructed the armor that kept him sane. You didn't want to go crazy here—it was just too long a hitch. You made yourself useful, you did the best you could.

Maybe, someday, if he did well enough and was useful enough, he'd get a shot at some of the bastards who put him here: at MacArthur, at Churchill, at Kennedy, at the rest of the modern lords of blood who'd put so many grunts in Hell.

Yeah, someday. Meanwhile, it wasn't really any different from what he'd done in the World—not really. He looked past the huddled sycophants with slitted eyes, and then the words whispered by the sycophant with the message finally penetrated his damaged psyche.

"Fuckin' A, *where?* Take me to him!" And Nichols shot upright, all malaise forgotten, now that he had a target of opportunity: the angel! Altos! Here, in the Mortuary! Looking for Enkidu!

Nichols was up and running, down the granite hall with its shivery fluorescents, past the empty gurneys and the elevators, the cabinets of stainless steel, toward the huge vaulted chamber, before he began having second thoughts about confronting God's representative.

Welch had had some sort of run-in with Altos, and had been real shaken for a while after. But Welch was a thinker; Nichols was more of a doer. The angel couldn't *do* anything to you. He could only make you think about things better left unthought. And, too, Welch had been pretty vulnerable, having a rough time then, Nichols remembered, slowing his pace in the hall as he reached the corbeled arch and the double doors beyond which was a sea of stiffs.

Nichols would welcome a rough time right now—anything to break the monotony.

Blocking with his elbows, he bashed through the double swinging doors. They slammed back against the wall and the noise reverberated like gunfire.

The angel looked up and stared at him. Altos was

square in the middle of the white-and-red-sheeted sea.

The macabre tableau stopped Nichols in his tracks, or else the angel's stare did. There was the angel, with no wings, but some sort of flickery suggestion of wing potential rising above and behind his back, like blue neon at low power. The face was like something from a church. The hands were folded into the sleeves.

You've seen him before, Nichols reminded himself. And he had, at a distance. He'd seen that stare turned on Welch and seen how Welch had reacted.

Now he knew why. The angel's eyes broadcast palpable hope, then dismay, then pity. Nichols just knew that when Altos looked at him, the angel could read Nichols's sins from his flesh, and that was why the final expression in those pinwheel eyes was despair.

"Shit, hotshot, I hear we're lookin' for the same guy," said Nichols, strolling through the corpses waist-high on their gurneys with less aplomb than he felt.

The angel seemed to glide toward Nichols. "I have been, for quite some time." His voice was too beautiful for a man's voice, and yet there was nothing feminine about it. "Your people, your comrade Welch—what you have done to Enkidu is an unspeakable evil." The angel, two corpses away, stopped.

"Well, it's Hell, ain't it? That's what we're supposed to do, right? I don't come around rating your record." Nichols put his hands on his hips. "I've got orders pertaining to Enkidu, official-like. Do you?"

"And do you have orders regarding your own wizened soul? There's always hope, my son."

"*Cut the crap!* You think I don't know where I am? You want to dispense hope and salvation, get up there on the fifty-odd battlefields—in the World—where maybe it'll do some good. Don't come down here slumming, trying to make like there's no collusion between your boss and mine! Some goes there, some comes here," Nichols shrugged. He wasn't Welch; he wasn't going to let this piece of walking regret skew him. "You got *no business here!*" Nichols tried to keep his voice down, but it roared among the stone arches. "It's too little, too late, for every damned soul of us!"

The angel looked away. It couldn't meet his eyes. It shuffled its feet and they scraped loudly on the stone floor. It seemed to grow somewhat smaller.

Nichols pressed his advantage, bearing down on the angel, pushing corpses on wheeled gurneys out of his way. "Now, if you've got anything to do with the disappearance of this Enkidu, I want to know about it. Now!"

The angel's shoulders slumped, and Nichols remembered something he'd heard Welch say in passing: the angel couldn't lie.

Altos raised his beautiful head and it hurt Nichols to look upon that countenance. But pain was something the soldier understood. He held his ground and locked his stare on his target.

"The hairy man, Enkidu," said Altos in a voice so full of regret that it made Nichols's shoulder muscles knot, "has been intercepted, Reassigned to a deeper Hell by a hostile faction in the Pentagram—a faction that wants your Agency discredited."

"Mithridates and that lot?"

The angel nodded miserably and started to back away.

Nichols bore down on him, pushing another gurney from between them, wondering if he dared grab the angel by the collar of his robe. "Then how come you're here, looking for him—waiting for him just like I am?"

"Perhaps he has not yet gone. Maybe he will die there, in Thebes, and be returned here quickly." The angel's eyes raised again. This time, they were pleading for mercy. "This is a terrible thing to mix in, poor soul. Go away. What you have done to Enkidu is more than—"

"I didn't do shit to Enkidu but get him out of a rough situation the quick and dirty way. I've been hanging out here, waiting for Enkidu, same as you. And what's this about Marilyn, anyhow? What's she got to do with this?" One thing Nichols could do was remember crucial data such as the whispering syco-phant's hint, and use it.

The angel shuddered as if he'd been struck, and Nichols, who'd been reaching out toward Altos's robe, grabbed the rails of a handy gurney instead. "Tell me," he grated.

"Marilyn . . . meddled with the record-keeping system, for personal reasons. The Pentagram faction you named took advantage of this, and Enkidu is now in a hell where a *false god* reigns." A tear issued from the angel's eye and rolled down his cheek, to fall upon a sheet-covered corpse.

The corpse stirred.

Nichols muttered, "Shit," watching the corpse, and took a backward step. "So Marilyn's in this? That's too bad."

"But she is *not*, I tell you."

"Right, and you don't lie. What do you want with the ape-man?"

Altos was retreating, also; the corpse upon which the tear had fallen was beginning to groan. "Enkidu is . . . primal. He can renew my strength, which was depleted by the Dissidents' struggle. When you see your Welch, tell him for me that I am disappointed, for the Dissidents' sake and his own."

"You bet, I'll tell him," said Nichols, sidling toward the swinging doors as fast as he could, now. The last thing he wanted was to be there when the corpse that was beginning to thrash got its sheet off. The angel had preempted a proper resurrection with his careless tear, and even the emissary of God didn't want to stay around to watch the results. "But I'm telling you, I expect you to send word to us immediately if you find Enkidu before we do—to withhold that data will be the same as lying," Nichols called out as he felt the doors at his back, just before he bolted through them.

Running down the halls, he wasn't sure *where* he was running to—but he knew to whom: Nichols had to find Welch and tell him what he'd learned, and what he'd done.

He was hoping fervently, as he hit the elevator's up button, that Welch wanted to be found right now. Otherwise, Nichols was on his own with crucial intelligence he wasn't prepared to handle. Because when Welch went to ground, not God or the Devil could flush him out.

"Yo, Welch!" the interloper stage-whispered, and Nichols, in a tight black t-shirt, sneakers and jeans, hunkered down beside Welch, who was waiting in the bushes.

"Hello, Nichols," said Welch laconically, as if they'd run into each other in one of New Hell's bars rather than on the grounds of Caesar's villa. "How'd you find me?"

Nichols wriggled in among the asphodel and eucalyptus, until his back was against the low wall. "Achilles," he replied, his voice even softer because Caesar kept perimeter guards and Welch had no business here but monkey business.

Welch squinted once more across the formal gardens to the shed where Caesar's prisoners were, then turned his back on his surveillance target and slid down against the fieldstone wall, next to Nichols. Suddenly he was overcome with an intense desire for a cigarette. He reached out and flicked the pack that Nichols carried in the turned-up sleeve of his t-shirt.

There was no reason they couldn't smoke. It wasn't dark, just hellishly dusky—red and purple and blood brown, an ominous twilight that had lasted, by the sweep on Welch's Rolex, for over four hours now.

Nichols raised an eyebrow, but got out his lighter and lit two cigarettes, palms shielding the open flame. When he handed one to Welch, the junior officer said, "Whaddya get on your Enki when you leave it out all night?"

With a shudder of resignation, Welch sighed, "I don't know. What?"

"Enki-dew."

"Cute. What brings you here? I'm just looking." He jerked his head slightly to indicate the gardening shed beyond the wall at his back.

"I bet," said Nichols wolfishly. "New business or old?"

"Old," Welch admitted. "Alexander's locked up in that shed. With Maccabee. I'm trying to decide whether to leave them for Caesar to look after."

"Better than having Alexander leading the Dissidents. Caesar may not be treating him like we would, but it beats us having to go after him."

"Alexander deserves better than a permanent bed in some Roman dungeon," said Welch uneasily. Nichols had this way of hitting a nerve every time, while seeming to do it accidentally. Welch had worked behind the scenes to prompt Caesar to remove Alexander as interim leader of the Dissidents precisely because, in Welch's own terms, he owed Alexander for favors done on past sorties. He'd exceeded his authority doing as much as he had, and he ought to let things lie.

But he didn't want to. The Macedonian was special, and not just because Welch's major in school had been Classical Greece. Alexander inspired loyalty. Welch wanted to get the Macedonian the hell out of Caesar's clutches and he couldn't say why—he couldn't justify it in terms Authority or Agency would condone or understand. Couldn't, because those terms had more to do with Welch and the way he did his job than any master plan devised by the Dulles brothers for the Devil's Children.

Welch brought to his tasks the peculiar combination of ruthlessness, duplicity, and absolute integrity that made a good intelligence officer. No matter what he was asked to do, he always did the best he could—for the abstract joy of perfect performance, for precision's sake, for the ideal result, and for the sake of the people working under him. He did his best even when less was indicated or desired.

When they wanted something different, up there in Admin, they tasked somebody else. Hell might be the venue, but the standards Welch strove to meet were his own.

So he'd been sitting here, trying to make up his mind whether to go in there and get Alexander out, trying to make up a reason that would satisfy Authority without laying Caesar open to any charges or reprisals.

Maybe there wasn't one. "You didn't answer me, Nick. What brings you out of Admin?"

"I told you I was waiting for Enkidu." Nichols's voice took on a defensive tone. "Well, I didn't find him."

"That's okay, stuff screws up." Welch dragged on his cigarette, enjoying the perk. The Devil's Children got cigarettes and good booze; they got to eat and shit and, occasionally, to get their ashes hauled successfully. It was a lot to risk. You didn't want to lose perks like that. No Child wanted to get busted to civilian. Maybe Nichols just needed some reassurance.

But it wasn't that simple.

Nichols said, "Sir, I gotta lay this out for you," in his Reporting voice, quick and clipped.

"Shoot," said Welch, and slid down on his spine in the grass, staring into shadows among distant trees, beyond which was the villa itself, its stables, its garages, and servants' quarters. Caesar had lots to lose, too, and powerful enemies. Maybe Welch had *better* let things lie here.

"I was in the Mortuary, and one of the sycophants tells me Altos the angel is in the Mortuary, too, and to ask him about Enkidu and Marilyn."

"Hold on, Nichols. You're going too fast. And Marilyn's off limits, you know that."

There was only one Marilyn, and that Marilyn had the closest thing to diplomatic immunity you could come by in Hell.

"I'm layin' it out the way I got it, like you'd want me to if you were thinkin'—sir."

"Okay, Nichols, okay." Welch leaned his head back against the stone wall and rolled it until he was eye-to-eye with Nichols. "You've got my full attention."

Five minutes later, having heard the entire story, Welch ticked off points on his fingers: "First, forget Marilyn. Not our problem. Not yet. Second, we're going to break Alexander out—we can use him for this. Third, are you sure Altos said 'Thebes'?"

"Yep."

"Shit. There was—is—more than one, you know . . ." But Nichols didn't know, or didn't care. Welch's aide de camp did know, however, that Welch was about to move and his relief was palpable.

"Just tell me one thing," Nichols asked as both men got to their feet, crouched low, and began making a list of what they'd need to free the Macedonian.

"What's that?" said Welch absently, weighing the difficulties at hand—whether to confront Caesar and ask politely in order to avoid ill will and casualties, or to try an unattributable raid for secrecy's sake.

"How come we need the Macedonian for this?"

"Well, Alexander has experience with more than one Thebes. And you said that Altos mentioned a 'false god.' You fight fire with fire, right? If we're going up against a self-proclaimed deity, we ought to have our own 'Living God' with us when we try it, I think."

"Going to burn Achilles' butt somethin' fierce—he don't like Alexander none."

"We're not in Hell to make Achilles' life easy." Welch stood straight now, decided.

Nichols followed suit: "What's next?"

"You go to Requisitions with that list. I'm going to see Caesar. If you don't hear from me before you've got the B team armed and ready, go in and get Alexander and Maccabee, then meet me at the Mortuary."

"Yessir. Hey, Welch?"

Welch had already turned to go. He looked back and said softly, "Yes, Nichols."

"What about Tanya? She's not on this personnel roster."

"Gee, I must have forgotten," said Welch dryly. "I'll talk to her myself, okay? Go on, now. We're on the clock." Welch pointed to his wrist, where the stopwatch function of his Rolex was engaged.

"Yessir. And sir—thanks."

"No sweat, Nichols. I'd rather go looking for Enkidu now than later."

The two men parted and Welch, heading up the garden path toward Caesar's villa, was smiling, now that his adc couldn't see him. Sometimes you had to let a man know that he was valued, even in Hell. And sometimes you had to pin some ears back, even when those ears were Julius Caesar's.

And when all that was done, what remained was just the hard part: Welch couldn't go traipsing off into a deeper hell looking for Enkidu on his own when he was supposed to be busting drug traffickers.

Not without getting tasked for it, he couldn't. Which was where Tanya Burke was going to come in.

Alexander had languished in the cell too long with only Judah Maccabee for company. He was seeing things.

First it had been Bucephalus: he would see his horse's black mane and tail, the white flash on the finely shaped head. He would hear the hoofbeats he knew so well and his heart would leap.

But Judah always said there was nothing there. Out the one tiny window, Judah never saw Bucephalus. And it became a wedge between them, a wedge driving deeper and deeper into their comradeship. Maccabee was the only other human Alexander ever saw, in his confinement, and Judah looked back at him askance.

Food came and dirty dishes went through a slit in the cell door. The guards never spoke; they might well not have tongues to speak with. This was a horrid, haunted place and the only other inhabitant of it clearly thought that Alexander was losing his hold on reality.

They had fought with words, and it had come to blows. Or it had come to Maccabee holding Alexander's wrists while he struggled vainly against the larger man. But Maccabee could not hold Alexander's anger, any more than could the Macedonian once it was loosed.

He'd come to the point of scheming to brain Maccabee with one of the metal dinner plates while the Israelite slept. He'd actually planned to kill his cellmate so that he could be alone with his hallucinations of Bucephalus. It had gotten that bad before Alexander had taken himself in hand.

Then came days of speechless sulking, and the horrible weight of estrangement, like a thick fog in the cell between them. The right words were impossible to find, let alone to say.

Maccabee's big round eyes kept accusing Alexander of misjudgments, and yet Maccabee had been with the Dissidents before Alexander had gone among them; before they'd been captured by Caesar and brought here.

Now they'd spent so long in silence that the first spoken word between them surely would become like an arrow shot in deadly night, striking one or the other of them down from nowhere, without warning, without reason.

The quarrel was now an entity on its own and neither man could overcome its strength; it was a curse, and Alexander couldn't break its spell.

In the morning, Bucephalus would come racing through the meadow, tail flagged, nostrils open to the wind, and freedom was a ghost who rode him.

In all his time in Hell, Alexander had never felt its burden so. He had killed men for lack of faith in him—rivals and plotters and Clitus the Black once when he was drunk. But he had never felt from them such danger for his own soul as Maccabee's simple headshakes threatened.

It had been too long like this. They could never make it right between them. They might have been here for centuries; they might have forgotten the very mechanics of speech. And if they had, this was just as well, for Alexander could not ask forgiveness and Maccabee, a Jew, could not give it.

This man whom he'd chosen out of all Hell's teeming damned to love could not bring himself to love Alexander in return—not sufficiently to have faith in the vision of Bucephalus.

So when Alexander looked out the window and saw the demons stalking through the grass, he didn't mention it.

What was the use? These demons were of the same stuff as Bucephalus, obviously—figments of the dusk as Bucephalus was of the dawn.

There were few enough dawns and dusks in Hell that Alexander thought to merely wait it out. The demons would never reach his prison, for Bucephalus never did.

He lay his bearded chin on the windowsill, his hands laced beneath it, and watched the demons come.

They were black and horrible of face, with great bulging eyes and trunks like elephants where their noses should have been. The eyes were soulless and blank, and there was no hair upon their heads. Their backs were humped and bowed, and out of them grew antennae like those of insects. And into those misshapen backs their trunks were curled.

The tramp of their feet was muffled, like Bucephalus's

hoofbeats, and Alexander watched until they were so close that he could see the weapons in their hands.

Weapons of the New Dead—Uzi slingshots, automatic rifles with low-light scopes, plasma guns with glowing coils. If they didn't veritably fly—if they didn't move across the ground in giant steps thrice those a man could take; if from their humped and awful backs steam did not issue when they flew— then Alexander would have taken them for men.

But they were demons—silent demons—and they did not disappear. They came on and on, sneaking through the grass, and then Alexander couldn't see them anymore.

He sat back, his throat as dry as the march to Siwah, his heart pounding as if he had seen a Sibyl.

They had disappeared, like Bucephalus. They had disappeared like what they were—hallucinations. Maccabee was right; Alexander needed help.

Tears flooded his eyes, and then mortification overcame him. The loss of one's wits was the thing most to be feared here. Pride goeth much quicker and cheaper.

He turned a tear-streaked face to Maccabee, without shame, and blurted, "Judah, I'm sorry. My anger overcame me. Please forgive me," and held out his arms.

Before Maccabee could do more than open his own arms in response, a clamor began and a roaring.

There was heat and then flame, smoke and screaming. There were men running and Maccabee, grabbing him and bodily lifting him from the ground, saying into his ear, "Fire! Fire, Alexander! Under here, quick!"

Maccabee threw a blanket over him, and then Judah's own body landed atop Alexander's.

Pinned, in a close and awful tent of wool, with

straw under him that would be his funeral pyre, Alexander could think only of Hephaestion. Of the pyre at Babylon, of the gilded ship's prow and all the gifts thrown upon his friend's bier. And how none of it made any difference. No matter what you do, once a friend is dead and gone, the hole in your heart remains forever.

The worst part of Hell, for Alexander, was that he never found those pieces of him that were missing, those absent friends. And now, about to die once more and be revived, he knew not where or how or with whom, he struggled and writhed to turn over, to grab Maccabee around the waist, despite the other's weight upon him and the blanket over him, to clutch Maccabee with his arms and yell above the din: "We will not be separated. I will not lose you! I I will not lose you like I lost Bucephalus, Judah! I will not!"

And the strength of spirit that made Alexander what he was kept those arms locked around the Israelite long after smoke had overcome them and driven consciousness away.

When Nichols's team finally broke through the last door into the holding cell with fireaxes, they found the two men thus—locked together, the blanket in between—and had to carry them outside in that death-grip embrace before they could separate them.

And then, while some men held them and others forced oxygen masks upon their faces, Nichols had to try to explain to the two ancients about jetpacks, and get them off Caesar's grounds before someone came to put out the fire.

". . . so Caesar stonewalled me, sitting in that fancy-assed office of his like he'd earned it, until the fire broke out. Then, since he wouldn't admit he had

Alexander in the first place, he couldn't do anything but let me go with some lame story about a 'domestic emergency' when Machiavelli came in with the news." Welch shrugged irritably, his eyes on the highball glass he was turning in his hands. Then he glanced up at Tanya and added, "But I'm dead sure Machiavelli's mixed up with Mithridates' faction—part of the Pentagram's network of traitors." Only his voice and his stare, so far, said, *And I need your help with this*.

Tanya Burke let out a long, slow breath and, when Welch didn't continue to debrief, asked: "But can you prove it? Everybody knows about the vendetta between you and Machiavelli. Everybody." Welch had come to her apartment, in the thick of New Hell and the dead of dusk, his eyes full of shadows and his body radiating tension like a live wire. She could almost see the sparks coming out of him—sparks that might set her shabby furniture smoldering and her life ablaze, leaving only gutted wreckage when he'd gone.

"No, I can't prove it," Welch retorted. "I don't even want to try. I want to get off this drug-running duty, though. It's Machiavelli's doing, too, I'm willing to bet—strings he's pulled to get me out of his way."

He paused for her comment but she didn't add one. Welch always made her want to do unprofessional things like strip him and stroke him and comfort him. He was her own private *deformation professionelle*. He was trouble and he was in trouble—and smart enough to know it. Staging a raid on Caesar's villa wasn't smart. Machiavelli wasn't without resources. The Pentagram's spies were everywhere and the Devil's Children weren't without their weak points. Lately, Welch seemed to be one of them.

They stared at each other until it hurt. Stared in the light of the floor lamp with its fringed, red-silk shade; stared across the Bauhaus coffee table, from opposite ends of creation. If you could fall in love in Hell, then Tanya Burke was in love with the man sitting opposite her.

It was a secret she had to keep, even from him. She couldn't afford the vulnerability; she couldn't handle the pain. She'd seen what love had done to Che Guevara, what it did to men like Alexander. Love was one of the Devil's most potent weapons, and the operatives of His Satanic Majesty's Secret Service couldn't afford to stand in the line of fire.

She couldn't. She just couldn't. But as the pause lengthened and Welch's glance cut like glass, she found herself saying, "What do you want me to do? You can't prove any of this."

"I know that. If I could prove we had a problem, we wouldn't have a problem, would we?" Snappish, tired, disappointed in her reaction, Welch got to his feet and began to pace back and forth across the flowers-of-evil linoleum.

Tanya rose too, and stood in his path. He had to go around her, back away, or hold his ground. He did none of those. He put his arms around her and pressed her head to his shoulder. Into her hair he said, "You're back on line. Get me tasked to find Enkidu and bring him back. For Nichols's sake, for the hell of it, because we can't let things start to slip. That's all I want."

"Bring him back from where?" she demanded of his collarbone, inhaling the salt of his sweat and wanting to press herself against him but just standing there, every inch of her on fire, and trembling like a skittish mare.

"Thebes. Nichols said the angel told him Thebes."

She stiffened and craned her neck to look at him, the heat she felt changing to cold so fast every hair on her body stood on end. "Thebes? The angel? Are we in collusion with the Other Side? It'll never fly. I'll never get it past Authority."

Lame excuses, and he knew it. Tanya had been bumped up to a desk in Admin; tasking was part of her job now. But Thebes was a deep Hell, an Old Dead bastion, not amenable to manipulation, nearly inaccessible by normal means, and probably impossible to get out of, except via the Undertaker's Table. It was the last thing Tanya wanted to do for Welch.

"Tanya, I wouldn't be asking if there was any other way."

"Fuck Enkidu," she suggested. "You're playing into the Pentagram's hands. If they do want to discredit Agency, we've got to be careful. Play by the book. You going off on a personal—"

"The ability of my people to function effectively," he said softly, running one spread hand along her spine, "isn't a personal concern—it's business. I need those orders cut."

"Shit, Welch, don't do this," she said, and she meant his hands and what they were doing to her as much as she did his request. If he wasn't touching her that way, she might have been able to get angry at him over what he was asking her to risk.

But as it was, she only managed to mutter, "All right, all right, but you're going to have to take me with you," before she forgot all about business, and strategy, and tactics. Welch was offering her the rarest coin in Hell in exchange for a little harmless treachery—lovemaking that didn't lead to frustration.

She'd been with him once before and she wasn't even afraid they wouldn't make it; one thing you had

to know about Welch was that he got the job done,
no matter what it took.

As their clothes dropped to the floor, she was
wondering why the Pentagram hadn't remembered
that.

The Mortuary looked like a damned convention
center by the time Nichols got back with three Cokes
and a black coffee for Welch, into which he'd already
poured a dollop of Old Number 7 from his hip flask.

Among the sea of stiffs, the principles were faced
off: Tanya Burke and Welch versus Alexander and
Maccabee—New Dead versus Old Dead, and the
outcome wasn't in doubt.

"Look, Alexander," Welch was saying patiently, "I
don't see that you've got a better choice. Do this for
us, and you'll be on the right side of Agency—we'll
be able to help you, make life easier for—"

"As you did the Dissidents?" Maccabee interrupted,
big arms crossed over his chest.

Nichols bulled his way through the waist-high sea
of red-and-white-sheeted corpses, bumping gurneys
with his hips. "Here's your Coke, Mac." And, whispered: "C'mon, be cool. Don't blow this for everybody."

"Will you promise," Alexander stipulated, "to re-
unite me with Bucephalus?"

"Buceph—? Oh yeah, the horse. Sure thing. If
he's in any accessible Hell, we'll find him for you.
Won't we, Tanya?"

Tanya Burke was pale as the sheeted bodies around
her. Her reluctance to go on record verbally was
obvious as she answered reticently, "Certainly, King
Alexander, we'll do our best."

"*Great* King," snapped the short Macedonian, taking the Coke can from Nichols like Nichols wasn't

anything more than a servant. "Or, 'my Lord,' will
do."

"Right," Tanya said and rolled her eyes at Welch,
who touched her arm.

This was a screwy place for a meeting, among the
stiffs waiting for resurrection. It gave Nichols the
creeps. When he'd threaded his way through the
waist-high surf of unmoving bodies without spilling
the drinks he carried, and given Tanya her Coke and
the coffee to Welch, he said, "Come on, guys, let's
get this show on the road."

"Everything's ready?"

"If you've got the tasking orders, I've got the
rest." Achilles and the heavy equipment were already in the freight elevator, ready to go on signal.
That signal was the entrance into the Reassignments
elevator of Welch's party, the insertion of a destination punch card into a slot on the floor selector.

Tanya Burke held out the credit card-sized tasking
order and Nichols took it, wondering what it had cost
her. There were black circles under her eyes and her
hair was ratted, dull. Nothin' was free, not this sort
of thing. For Nichols's money, getting out of New
Hell before Caesar's people started playing tit-for-tat
was a real good idea.

But then, Welch always had good ideas. Nichols
cast a furtive look at the two O.D.s, so unapprecia-
tive of the Children's efforts on their behalf, and said
in a raspy voice, "Y'know, we don't really need these
two, boss. Leave 'em, let 'em end up back in another
Roman hospitality suite. They're just gonna be a
problem, what with that Living God in Thebes to
deal with. He ain't gonna want to meet another God,
not when he's claiming to be the Sole God."

Alexander stiffened, and the left corner of Welch's
mouth twitched appreciatively. The two Old Dead

started muttering to each other and then came toward them, pushing aside the gurneys.

"We shall accompany you," said Alexander, in a voice that reverberated off the corbeled vault. "To this unexplored and darkly ignorant land."

Welch didn't respond immediately. His eyes were fixed on a dark corner, and Nichols glanced that way just in time to catch a shadowy movement, then looked at his superior.

Welch said, sotto voice, "Take them to the elevator. I'll be right along." And, louder: "That's great, gentlemen. I assure you that Agency will be very appreciative. If you'll just follow Agent Nichols, I'll join you at the debarkation area."

"No," Tanya Burke whispered. Whatever was in that corner, she'd seen it, too. "Or I'm staying with you."

"Terrific." Welch's voice had a cutting edge. "Why don't we all stay, forget this after everything we've risked to—"

Nichols took Tanya's arm. "You heard the man."

She shook it off. "Not in front of the O.D.s. Please, Welch, come now."

Alexander and Maccabee were watching with uncomprehending eyes.

Welch whispered in Tanya's ear, and when he was done, she turned on her heel and, with a smile at Alexander, led the way: "Come with me, gentlemen, if you please."

When the swinging doors had closed behind Tanya and the Old Dead pair, Nichols tapped the computer card against an open palm. "They're not goin' anywhere without this."

"They might not be going anywhere, period." Welch's eyes were still fixed on the corner, and Nichols peered again in that direction.

And blinked. And said, "Oh shit," and took a dozen quick steps toward Welch. At Welch's side, he said, "You want to go, sir, I'll handle this best I can."

"I don't think it's you he wants, friend," said Welch as the Devil coalesced out of shadow.

You didn't have a face-to-face with the Devil. It just didn't happen. Nichols had never laid eyes on Him once, during his whole tour.

And there was no doubt that this was Satan himself. The eyes materialized first: cat's eyes—huge yellow, slitted eyes with fiery depths. The teeth were bigger than a Siberian polar bear's. The skin was . . .

Nichols blinked and looked at his feet. The urge to get down on his knees and cover his head was almost unendurable. He felt Welch's hand on his shoulder, heard the other man's voice say, "Why don't you go make sure they find the elevator, Nichols. If I'm not there in ten minutes, start without me."

Nichols wanted to say he'd stay. He wanted to put himself between Welch and the danger, but the danger was the Devil and the Devil was the ultimate Authority. What the hell had Welch done? Had any of them done?

Nichols never remembered stumbling out into the hall and down it to the elevator. He was absorbed in an internal inventory of demons he'd blown to smithereens and dragons he'd deep-sixed and nightmares that maybe were as real as daymares in a Hell which suddenly didn't want to make logical, human sense to a man who needed order like he needed oxygen.

Nichols had never come so close to wetting his pants on innumerable Trips as he did on that outwardly uneventful walk to the Reassignments elevator.

When he got there, his face was sheened with sweat and he leaned against the cinderblock, breathing hard. Tanya Burke, inside with the Old Dead, her finger on the "Hold" button, was too well-trained to say anything, but he saw her eyes go wide.

"Ten minutes," Nichols said, casually checking his watch. He didn't have any more comfort than that to give her. Or himself. He was shaking with suppressed emotion, and some of it was anger.

It might be Hell, the work might be crushing, the penalties for failure inexorable, failure itself a given, but you didn't pull the rug out from under a formed-up team ready to take the field in your behalf. You just didn't.

If it had been any representative of Authority but Him, Nichols would have shot the shit out of whoever it was.

Now, all he could do was wait. And sweat. And wish there was something he could do to help Welch. But then, when you got right down to it, there wasn't anything you could do to help anybody, not even yourself—not in Hell. In Hell, you just went through the motions.

The Devil was about fifteen feet high and he raised a claw at Welch, pointing.

Welch steeled himself for a blast of pain, for dissolution, for whatever was to come. He'd pushed things, exercised too much unilateral authority, tried to do too much. . . . He should have known it was going to come to this.

He realized he had his eyes closed and he opened them. Then he realized his head hadn't exploded, he hadn't been changed into a pillar of salt, his guts weren't dribbling out of his stomach onto the floor.

The Devil was sitting on his haunches, his wings half-spread, sort of fanning himself with them. He had a pointed tail and it was lashing among the gurneys. Every time it hit one, a corpse tumbled off.

Some lost their sheets and stared upward; some landed askew; some were so stiff they stacked like cordwood. Pretty soon, there were more of them than the room ought to be able to hold. There were grinning mouths and staring eyes and holes where chests should be. There were blackened limbs and yellow bruises and swollen throats. There were maggots everywhere.

Welch realized he hadn't moved, that he was frozen in panic, and that he ought to get out of the way because the Devil's long, lashing tail was sweeping increasingly near. He took a step backward, then another.

And a voice like thunder said, *"Hold!"*

He stopped stock still and listened to his heart try to beat its way out of his chest. Whatever he'd done this time, the punishment was going to be something more than missing the trip to Thebes. He'd never made enough waves to rouse Leviathan; he'd never gotten this close to the Ultimate Evil.

The smell of sulphur was thick and noxious, and he began to cough. His eyes were smarting. The corpses kept falling to the floor, their number rising, like some awful tide.

He wanted to run but the impulse was ludicrous. He was going to pass out any minute, probably join the sea of stiffs rising around him. Then . . . what? He didn't have any regrets. He'd done the best he could in a bad situation, like he always did.

And he knew, somehow, from the way the pupils of the eyes regarding him widened and narrowed, that that was part of the problem.

He thought, *I'm just human, doing the best I can. Or I was* . . . Welch, who had met his own standards

even in Hell, couldn't bring himself to recant anything, if that was what the Devil wanted.

He considered the repercussions of breaking Alexander out of prison. Was that the problem? Had he
actually managed to do something . . . good? If so,
he couldn't say he was sorry. He was fighting for
Satan's Order, in behalf of Agency, and that didn't
include letting Caesar's bunch or the Pentagram bunch
or anybody aid and abet the Dissidents.

He raised his head and stood squarely, his eyes
tearing, fighting to keep them open. There wasn't
any good and bad except in relation to performance,
as far as Welch was concerned. Even in Hell, you
were supposed to do your job as best you could.

The eyes on Him—the huge, glowing, yellow eyes
with the palpitating pupils which slitted, and then
widened into full rounds like black moons—blinked.

The Devil said, *"Behold!"*

His clawed finger pointed to a gurney on which a
corpse sat up and pawed away its red sheet. The face
under it was broad and hairy, the chest revealed
hairier still, and even broader. The hairy man looked
slowly around and uttered a wordless growl of animal
distress. Then it brought up its legs and crouched on
its gurney, knuckles brushing the ground, teeth bared.
The smell of excrement wafted.

Welch started to put up his hands. *Enkidu*, he
wanted to say. *Sorry, wrong objective,* he wanted to
apologize. But he couldn't get control of his tongue.
He just stared at the hairy man until the thunderous
voice pealed again:

"Go to a deeper Hell, damned soul," the Devil
said to Welch. *"Your punishment awaits."* And as
those words thundered, reechoing so that Welch's
eardrums threatened to burst, the hairy man let out
a scream of his own and began to burn.

Enkidu combusted in place, as if his every hair had caught on fire. He contorted as he flamed. The flames were first red and yellow, then green and blue and white, with a dark thing crumbling in their midst.

Welch closed his eyes to the stench and the flame.

When he opened them this time, no trace of Enkidu was left—not an ash or an ember. The gurney he'd burned on was nowhere in sight. There were no corpses on the floor, not one overturned gurney, no sheet out of place.

Everywhere was just the calm sea of neatly sheeted stiffs, exactly as it had been before.

Welch blinked and turned slowly, gazing around at the Mortuary in its deserted austerity. When finally he'd turned to face the double doors, he broke and ran.

He slammed through the doors and outside, the corridor was normal—just dirty white tile and white-painted cinderblock. At the end of it was the elevator where Tanya, Nichols, and the Old Dead waited.

It took every ounce of his self-control to walk at a measured pace down that corridor. But he needed the time to think.

When he got there, Nichols was smiling in relief. "Everything okay, sir?"

"Close enough," said Welch, and stepped into the Reassignments elevator beside Tanya. What was he going to say to them—that he'd just gotten fired? He wasn't sure he had. That this was a disciplinary posting? Any posting, in Hell, was that. That they should, for their own safety, stay here, stay away from him?

Welch had a feeling the Devil wouldn't like it if he said that. He leaned back as the elevator door closed on New Hell. The wall against his back felt solid; the vibrations coming through it were of downward motion. He could handle that—going down to a deeper Hell was still going somewhere.

Tanya's breast brushed against his arm and he could hear the Old Dead chattering in Greek. He could hear his own breathing. He could feel the warmth of the woman next to him.

Whatever the Devil threw at him, he was going to do his best. Sometimes, in Hell, you told yourself you didn't have anything left to lose. Welch knew better. He could feel and touch and move and think; he could make personal judgments and bend the rules enough to matter. He could make mistakes. He'd just made one, judging from what he'd seen amid that sea of stiffs. Warning received and understood.

But that was what life—and afterlife—was about: trying and failing, losing and winning, being appreciated and misunderstood. For all of those, you had to *be*.

Once Welch had thought his biggest enemy was time; now he knew time was his greatest asset.

Tanya whispered, under the chatter of the Old Dead, "You look awful. What happened back there?"

"Devil chewed my ass out about this mission."

"But we're still going?" Nichols butted in.

"What do you think, soldier?" Welch retorted with a grin, grateful to be able to think at all.

"It had to happen," Tanya said, flicking a glance at the Great King of Macedon and Judah Maccabee. "Had to, the way we've been pushing it. Bending the rules."

"Yeah, I know," said Welch, still with a rueful grin, and accepted the flask of Old Number 7 that Nichols held out like salvation.

*   *   *

After the elevator doors had closed and the Devil shuffled out of the Mortuary with drooping wings, the angel slid out from under his sheet.

Altos sat up on the gurney, rubbed his eyes, and, humming, began to float along in Satan's wake. Never coming close enough to be noticed, he shadowed the Devil down the long hall as the Prince of Darkness looked in upon his minions and took stock of his work.

Yet three times the Devil stopped and looked over his winged shoulder, his great slitted eyes glowing. Through the Hall of Records they proceeded thus, and up into Reassignments itself, where the damned labored to make Hell hellish.

There was no use, no sense, in forcing a confrontation with Satan, Altos knew. What should he do, stick out his tongue at the farthest-fallen of all angels and gloat because the incident with the Devil's Children had gone Heaven's way?

The Devil before him was shaken, ruminative, perhaps distressed. Hell must be Hell for Satan, too. Losing faith in His Private Agency was more than an accident. It was part of the Devil's rehabilitation.

The Devil had put his trust in Evil and that trust was beginning to weaken. The implication that Welch had been suborned by Good, since Alexander's escape had not been tasked, was not lost on Satan.

And if the Devil couldn't trust his Children, then who could he trust?

Altos, drifting down the hallways of New Hell's Admin complex, felt a thrilling tide of hope oversweep him as Satan, ahead, around the corner, bawled loudly for Michael, his familiar, to attend him.

Marilyn had taught the Devil something about love, and the Devil's very Children had taught him about honor, The Dissidents continued, even without Alexander, to teach him about the human spirit.

Satan had a mandate, surely, but the angel had his orders, too: Hell might run, but it would never run well. For Satan to be saved, even by the end of eternity, the lessons must continue.

Hope must be everywhere, even here. Fully levitating and filled with a revivified strength of purpose, Altos floated back the way he had come—back toward the Reassignments elevator and the deeper Hells waiting beyond.

Somewhere down there was Enkidu, the hairy man, with whom Altos wanted to sit and talk. For both their sakes.

Here is an excerpt from Heroing *by Dafydd ab Hugh, coming in October 1987 as part of the new SIGN OF THE DRAGON fantasy line from Baen Books:*

Hesitantly, Jiana crawled into the crack.

"It's okay, guys," she called back, "but it's a bit cramped. Toldo next—wait! —Dida, then Toldo. I want . . . the priest in back." She felt a twinge of guilt. What she really wanted was the boy where she could reach out and touch his hand when needed.

Dida whimpered something. Jiana turned back in surprise.

"What's wrong?"

"Oh, love . . . are we really going—into *there?*"

"Dida, it's the only way. Are you a mouse? Come on, warrior!" He pressed his lips together and crawled toward her hand. When she touched him, she felt him trembling.

"Don't fear. I came through here, remember?"

The tunnel smelled as fresh as flowers after the stench of sewage. Jiana could breathe again without gagging.

The ceiling of the passage sank and sank, until she was almost afraid it would narrow to a wedge and block them off. But she remembered her harrowing crawl from the prison, her heart pounding with fear, feeling the hot, fetid breath of *something* on her neck, and she knew the passage was passable. At last, they were scraping along with their bellies on the floor and their backs against the splintery ceiling. Jiana wondered how Toldo Mondo was managing with his prodigious girth.

Suddenly, she knew something was wrong. She crawled on a few more yards, then stopped. Dida was no longer behind her. She heard a faint cry from behind her.

"Jiana, help me—please help me . . ."

"Lady Jiana," called out Toldo, "I think you had better come back here. The boy . . . seems to have a problem." Jiana felt a chill in her stomach; Toldo sounded much too professionally casual.

"What's wrong?" She turned slowly around on her stomach, and inched her way back to where the two had stopped. She stretched out her hand and took Dida's; it was clammy and shaking. With her fingers she felt his pulse, and it was pounding wildly.

"I can't do it," he whispered miserably. "I can't do it—I just can't do it—all that weight—I can't breathe! —I can't . . ."

"What? Oh, for Tooqa's sake! What next?"

As if in answer to her blasphemy, the ground began to shake and roll. Again she heard the scraping, grinding noise, only this time much closer. Dida continued to whimper.

"Oh gods, oh gods, oh please, let me out, oh please, take it away . . ."

"Too close," she whispered, trying to peer through the pitch blackness.

"Oh my lord," gasped Toldo Mondo, "don't you hear it?"

Again the ground shook, and this time the scraping was closer yet, and accompanied by a slimy sucking sound.

For a moment all were silent; even Dida stopped his whimpering. Then Jiana and Toldo began to babble simultaneously.

"I'm sorry," she cried, "I'm sorry, o Ineffable One, o Nameless Scaly One, o You Who Shall Not Be Named! I never meant—"

Toldo chanted something over and over in another language; it sounded like a penance. The fearful noise suddenly became much louder.

"Toldo! It's coming this way! Oh lordy, what'll we do? Crawl, damn you, crawl, crawl! And push the kid along—I'll grab his front and drag!"

"You fool! It's here! Don't you hear it? Am I the only one who hears it?!"

"Shut up and push, you fat tub of goat cheese!"

In a frenzy, they began to squirm away from the sound, dragging Dida, and Jiana discovered that the tiny crawlway was as wide as a king's hall, though the ceiling was but a foot and a half off the floor. Dida was no help. He was in shock, as if he'd been stabbed in a battle. He could only move his arms and legs in a feeble attempt at locomotion, praying to be "let out."

After a few moments, Jiana realized she was hopelessly lost. Had they kept going straight from the hole by the river, they would have found the next door. But they were moving to the right, and she did not know how far they had gone in the pitch black. In fact, she was not even sure which way they were currently pointing; the horrible noises had seemed to change direction, and they had concentrated on keeping them to their rear.

"Oh gods, I've done it now," she moaned; "we won't ever get out of here!" A sob from Dida caught at her heart, and she cursed herself for speaking aloud.

"We shall make it," retorted Toldo Mondo. "There must be *something* in this direction, if we go far enough!"

Soon, Jiana herself began to feel the oppression of millions of tons of rock pressing down on her. She had terrifying visions of being buried alive in the blackness by a sudden cave-in caused by the movements of whatever was behind them. With every beat of her heart it got closer, and the shaking grew worse. She could clearly hear a sound like a baby sucking on its fist.

"Jiana, go!" cried Toldo in a panic. "Crawl, go—faster, woman! It's here, it's—Jiana, I CAN SMELL IT!"

"How does it squeeze along, when even we barely fit?" she wondered aloud. *You're babbling, Ji . . . stop it!*

She surged and lunged forward, not letting go of Dida, though he was like a wet sack of cornmeal. And then, there was a rocky wall in front of her. There was nowhere left to crawl.

Coming in October 1987 * 65344-X * 352 pp. * $3.50

To order any Baen Book by mail, send the cover price plus 75 cents for first-class postage and handling to: Baen Books, Dept. B, 260 Fifth Avenue, New York, N.Y. 10001. And ask for our free catalog of all Baen Books science fiction and fantasy titles!

Here is an excerpt from Mary Brown's new novel The Unlikely Ones, *coming in November 1987 from Baen Books Fantasy—SIGN OF THE DRAGON:*

MARY BROWN

After breakfast the next morning—a helping of what looked like gruel but tasted of butter and nuts and honey and raspberries and milk—the magician led us outside into a morning sparkling with raindrops and clean as river-washed linen, but strangely the grass was dry when we seated ourselves in a semicircle in front of his throne. Hoowi, the owl, was again perched on his shoulder, eyes shut, and he took up Pisky's bowl into his lap. Although the birds sang, their songs were courtesy-muted, for the Ancient's voice was softer this morning as though he were tired, and indeed his first words confirmed this.

'I have been awake most of the night, my friends, pondering your problems. That is why I have convened this meeting. We agreed yesterday that you had all been called together for a special mission, a quest to find the dragon. You need him, but he also needs you.' He paused, and glanced at each one of us in turn. 'But perhaps last night you thought this would be easy. Find the Black Mountains, seek out the dragon's lair, return the jewels, ask for a drop of blood and a blast of fire and Hey Presto! your problems are all solved.

'But it is not as easy at that, my friends. Of your actual meeting with the dragon, if indeed you reach him, I will say nothing, for that is still in the realms of conjecture. What I can say is this: in order to reach the dragon you have a long and terrible journey ahead of you, one that will tax you all to the utmost, and may even find one or other of you tempted to give up, to leave the others and return; if that happens then you are all doomed, for I must impress upon you that as the seven you are now you have a chance, but even were there one less your chances of survival would be halved. There is no easy way to your dragon, understand that before you start. I can give you a map, signs to follow, but these will only be indications, at best. What perils and dangers you may meet upon the way I cannot tell you: all I know is that the success of your venture depends upon you staying together, and that you must all agree to go, or none.

'I can see by your expressions that you have no real idea of what I mean when I say "perils and dangers": believe me, your imaginations cannot encompass the terrors you might have to face—'

'But if we do stay together?' I interrupted.

'Then you have a better chance: that is all I can say. It is up to you.' He was serious, and for the first time I felt a qualm, a hesitation, and glancing at my friends I saw mirrored the same doubts.

'And if we don't go at all—if we decide to go back to—to wherever we came from?' I persisted.

'Then you will be crippled, all of you, in one way or another, for the rest of your lives.'

'Then there is no choice,' said Conn. 'And so the sooner we all set off the better,' and he half-rose to his feet.

'Wait!' thundered the magician, and Conn subsided, flushing. 'That's better, I have not finished.'

'Sit down, shurrup, be a good boy and listen to granpa,' muttered Corby sarcastically, but The Ancient affected not to hear.

'There is another thing,' said he. 'If you succeed

in your quest and find the dragon, and if he takes back the jewels, and if he yields a drop of blood and a blast of fire, if, I say . . . then what happens afterwards?'

The question was rhetorical, but Moglet did not understand this.

'I can catch mice again,' she said brightly, happily.

But he was gentle with her. 'Yes, kitten, you will be able to catch mice, and grow up properly to have kittens of your own—but at what cost? You may not realize it but your life, and the life of the others, has been in suspension while you have worn the jewels, but once you lose your diamond then time will catch up with you. You will be subject to your other eight lives and no longer immune, as you others have been also, to the diseases of mortality.

'Also, don't forget, your lives have been so closely woven together that you talk a language of your own making, you work together, live, eat, sleep, think together. Once the spell is broken you, cat, will want to catch birds, eat fish and kill toads; you, crow, will kill toads too, and try for kittens and fish; toad here will be frightened of you all, save the fish; and the fish will have none but enemies among you.

'And do not think that you either, Thing-as-they-call-you, will be immune from this; you may not have their killer instinct but, like them, you will forget how to talk their language and will gradually grow away from them, until even you cross your fingers when a toad crosses your path, shoo away crows and net fish for supper—'

'You are wrong!' I said, almost crying. 'I shall always want them, and never hurt them! We shall always be together!'

'But will they want you,' asked The Ancient quietly, 'once they have their freedom and identity returned to them? If not, why is it that only dog, horse, cattle, goat and sheep have been domesticated and even these revert to the wild, given the chance? Do you not think that there must be some reason why humans and wild animals dwell apart? Is it perhaps that they value their freedom, their individuality, more than man's circumscribed domesticity? Is it not that they prefer the hazards of the wild, and only live with man when they are caught, then tamed and chained by food and warmth?'

'I shall never desert Thing!' declared Moglet stoutly. 'I shan't care whether she has food and fire or not, my place is with her!'

'Of course . . . Indubitably . . . What would I do without her . . .' came from the others, and I turned to the magician.

'You see? They don't believe we shall change!'

'Not now,' said The Ancient heavily. 'Not now. But there will come a time . . . So, you are all determined to go?'

'Just a moment,' said Conn. 'You have told Thingmajig and her friends just what might be in store for them if we find the dragon: what of me and Snowy here? What unexpected changes in personality have you in store for us?' He was angry, sarcastic.

'You,' said the Ancient, 'you and my friend here, the White One, might just do the impossible: impossible, that is, for such a dedicated knight as yourself. . .'

'And what's that?'

'You might change your minds . . .'

'About what, pray?' And I saw Snow shake his head.'

'What Life is all about . . .'

432 pp. • 65361-X • $3.95

To order any Baen Book by mail, send the cover price plus 75 cents for first-class postage and handling to: Baen Books, Dept. B, 260 Fifth Avenue, New York, N.Y. 10001